THE NIGHT
SHE
VANISHED

BOOKS BY WENDY DRANFIELD

The Birthday Party

DETECTIVE MADISON HARPER SERIES

Shadow Falls

Cry for Help

Little Girl Taken

Gone to Her Grave

Catch Her Death

THE NIGHT SHE VANISHED

WENDY DRANFIELD

Bookouture

Published by Bookouture in 2023

An imprint of Storyfire Ltd.
Carmelite House
50 Victoria Embankment
London EC4Y 0DZ

www.bookouture.com

ISBN: 978-1-83790-236-1
eBook ISBN: 978-1-83790-235-4

For my husband; for everything.

PROLOGUE
SUMMER 2008

Several thoughts go through Lori Peterson's head as she lies dying. She didn't see it coming. She trusted the wrong people. She should have been more careful. More suspicious. But even though she can feel her life draining away, she doesn't really believe she's going to die. She has things to do: assignments due, chores outstanding, books due back at the library. And she had promised to teach her little brother how to ride his bike. The thought of sweet, sometimes annoying, five-year-old Tommy being upset that she will never come home makes her heart ache. He won't understand. He might think she didn't care about him. He'll have to endure growing up as the boy with the dead sister.

Lori tries to swallow but her mouth is dry. She clears her throat and attempts to force positive thoughts. Someone will find her before it's too late. They have to. People don't die at fifteen. It wouldn't be fair. Although Alice Shepherd from school died when she was fourteen. She was hit by a truck while out on her bike delivering newspapers. Rumor has it her head exploded like a watermelon as the truck's front tire ran over it. A tree was planted in the field behind the school as some kind of memorial. Everyone cried as they watched the principal plant it. Even the girls who had ruthlessly bullied Alice since third grade. They had sat in the cafeteria fake crying and basking in everyone's attention. It had made Lori sick. Will they do the same for her?

Pain suddenly breaks through her thoughts. A searing-hot stab tears through her head. With a wince, she's jolted back to reality. Lying on her back, she's completely alone in a park in the Midwestern town that she and her best friend had always planned to escape from once they were old enough. Stars twinkle in the night sky overhead. The day was hot and clear, and the night is set to remain warm. If she can hold on long enough, maybe someone will find her early tomorrow morning.

An all-consuming feeling of dread sets in. She's kidding herself. It could be hours before she's discovered and by then she would have bled to death. It's up to Lori to save herself. She tries wiggling her feet. They both cramp at the sudden movement and she gasps in pain. She has no choice but to ride out the cramps. At least she can feel her feet. That should be a good sign. It means they would probably hold her weight if she's able to get up.

Next, she tries moving her hands. She has no feeling in her fingers but her arms lift off the ground slightly at the elbow. Her head doesn't. It's heavy and painful and, when she tries lifting it, something in her neck cracks, sending another jolt of pain through her entire spine. She screams, startling two huge flies into the air. Were they drinking her blood? Laying eggs in her wounds? Are they going to start feasting on her before she even starts decomposing? She pushes the thought away as terror grips her.

Liquid, warm and wet, runs into her left eye. The blood mixed with sweat stings, blurring her vision. She gives up on moving, and her body begins to tremble all over. It's clear there's no way out of here without help.

A laugh—harsh, mocking and close—sends shivers through her entire body. It sounds evil. Like death coming for her. She squeezes her eyes shut. She doesn't want to see who it belongs to. She wants to sleep. To wake in her bed tomorrow morning to sunlight streaming through her drapes like this morning. To Tommy bursting in uninvited and insisting she play hide-and-go-seek with him.

A tear leaks from her eye and runs down the side of her face with the blood. There's no escaping her death. And once she's found she'll be on the news. Reporters and police will flock to the park and photograph her body. She cringes at the thought of men staring at her like this, with her skirt raised up over her waist from the position she collapsed in. They'll see her underwear. If she could only move enough to cover herself, but she doesn't have the energy.

Some people will probably think she deserved what happened to her. That she did something to put herself in this position. She's seen how her parents react to watching similar news on TV.

Why did she go out dressed like that?

No female should be out alone at that time of night.

She was drinking, what did she expect?

Lori's teacher says people tell themselves these things in order to feel better about crime rates in their town. Blaming the victim instead of the perpetrator allows them to believe it couldn't possibly happen to *them* because they aren't as stupid as the victims were. What's so infuriating for Lori is that her parents come to those conclusions even before listening to the facts of the case. It's always the girl's fault. Even though they have a daughter themselves.

Had a daughter. They won't have one by morning. Maybe that will force them to reconsider their opinions when they watch *her* murder played out on the news. Another tear falls. Lori knows her story will be nothing more than a brief shock to the locals before they become immersed in their daily routines. She'll be quickly forgotten. Just like Alice Shepherd. No one talks about her anymore. The tree they planted is dying from the heat. No one even waters it.

A blade of long grass tickles Lori's ankle. It doesn't drown out the pain in her head, but it's something she can focus on as she waits for the life to drain out of her.

ONE

SUMMER 2022

Nicole Rivers sips her soda and leans back in the old plastic patio chair in her backyard. When she turns her face to the sun, she can feel the warm rays burning through the sticky layer of sunblock on her skin. It's the first time this summer that her day off work has coincided with a nice day. With her bare feet resting in a children's paddling pool filled with tepid water, this feels like the closest she'll get to a vacation this year, and probably next year too, unless a miracle happens. The hum of a lawnmower can be heard a few doors down, along with her neighbor, Patty, giggling as she plays with her toddler.

A bumblebee hovers in front of Nicole, attracted by her floral perfume. She watches it buzz over to the nearest sunflower. All that's missing to make this day perfect is a cocktail and a swimming pool. Not that her small yard could accommodate the latter. She sighs. Days like this can fool you into believing that all is right in the world. That bad things don't happen to good people.

The screen door slams shut behind her as her husband, Lucas, appears. "Have you taken your vitamins today?" He has the packet in his hand ready.

Lifting her glasses, she looks up at him with a smile. "Of course."

He leans down and plants a kiss on her forehead before gently stroking her belly. "I can't wait until you get a bump."

Nicole isn't pregnant, but they're both hoping it's just a matter of time. They've been trying for around seven months and had hoped it might have happened by now. Her doctor wants to send her for tests, but she isn't ready to learn she might have fertility issues, and besides, she can't afford the tests right now. So she's trying not to overthink it and let it happen naturally, because many women have warned her stressing over it can add to the problem. Besides, seven months isn't that long.

Lucas has already started decorating the spare room in anticipation, although progress has slowed recently. Their five-year wedding anniversary is coming up, and if she gets pregnant soon, she'll be thirty by the time the baby arrives. She just wishes they were financially stable so they could afford to lease a larger house in preparation.

Her cell phone buzzes on the grass beside her chair. Lucas holds her soda while she leans over to retrieve it. The landline number burning urgently across the screen isn't stored in her contacts. It doesn't need to be. She'll remember this number for as long as she lives. Her parents have never moved house and have never changed their ways. They still live in the same old farmhouse in the same Midwestern town that she grew up in. Her stomach fills with dread.

"Aren't you going to answer it?"

Nicole looks up at her husband. "It's my parents."

He raises his eyebrows. "Oh."

He's right to be surprised. She hasn't spoken to them in any meaningful way since she left home at seventeen. They have her number for emergencies only. Hesitantly, she presses accept. "Hello?"

"Nicole, it's me." Her mother's tone is cold and Nicole's

reminded of just how much Debbie Chambers prefers her husband to her eldest daughter.

A cloud obscures the sun, making her shiver. She absently swats a large fly but it immediately returns, buzzing around her head. Lucas makes her jump when he claps his hands over it right in front of her face and then grins as the buzzing stops. It makes her feel sick to think the fly is squashed against his skin.

"Nicole?" says her mother. "Are you there?"

Nicole braces herself for what's to come. "What's wrong?"

A heavy sigh. "Your sister's disappeared. She hasn't been seen or heard from in a week, so we thought it was time to let you know."

A shudder runs through Nicole's body. When she left home twelve years ago, she reluctantly left behind her only sibling. Aimee was only six at the time; Nicole was almost eighteen. Her parents made it difficult to keep in touch with her, so their relationship is nonexistent, but she remains hopeful that once Aimee is out of their grasp, they can reunite and become close. There's nothing more she would love than a sister to confide in. A family member in her life. An aunt to her future baby. But now Aimee's gone missing, that might not be possible.

A familiar sensation of dread creeps over her. "What did he do?" she whispers.

Her father comes on the line. "Nicole? Now don't go making a big deal out of this." Ron Chambers sounds like he's talking her down from committing a crime, maybe something small like stealing a pack of cigarettes from the grocery store. Being the sheriff of Oates County, his tone can be condescending. "I'm trying to keep a lid on it because the last thing I need is a bunch of reporters springing up and spreading fake news. They'll scare the locals with talk of serial killers and the like."

She closes her eyes against his voice. Hearing him again after all these years causes flashbacks to the summer her best friend disappeared. Smart, vivacious Lori Peterson was never found. Her body likely dismembered and dumped somewhere so dark and remote that her spirit will never be allowed to rest in peace. Just an ominous pool of blood on a patch of flattened grass was left behind, indicating probable homicide.

Barely audible, Nicole says to her father, "What have you done?"

"You can stop that crazy talk right away, young lady," he replies sternly. "Just come home. Your room is made up, ready for you both."

He ends the call and Nicole lowers her cell phone into her lap. Her hands are trembling as she thinks about what her sister's disappearance means. This feels all too familiar. The moment she's feared ever since she fled her childhood has finally arrived.

"What's the matter?" asks Lucas, crouching beside her, dead fly cupped in one hand.

She looks into her husband's concerned brown eyes and swallows. "It's happening again."

TWO

The glare from the hot midday sun makes Nicole wince. Her stomach flips with dread as the bus she's traveling on passes the large weathered sign welcoming her and her fellow passengers to the town of Henderson, or as she and her friend Lori used to call it, Enderson. End of the road for anyone who wants an interesting life.

Nicole hasn't returned home once since she left, unlike Lucas who visits his mother once or twice a year. She's a little annoyed he couldn't join her but he has a conference to attend for work. Sure, it's a conference about insurance, but he gets to spend five all-inclusive days in a nice hotel *and* he took the car, so Nicole's had to travel by bus. Her car gave up the ghost a couple of months ago and it could be some time before she has the means to get it repaired.

She stares out of the window as they pass her old childhood haunts like a physical trip through her memories. A faded *For Sale* sign hangs outside the movie theater where she had her first awkward and unromantic kiss. They pass the elementary school where she first met Lori, years before the unthinkable happened. The playground where she got drunk for the first time has been modernized, with better facilities for children and their parents. She averts her eyes to avoid seeing the stone memorial erected in the aftermath of Lori's disappearance.

As a teenager she had always felt out of place here. Like she'd been born to the wrong parents, in the wrong town. It didn't help that she once watched a TV show about two families that each took the wrong baby home from the hospital by mistake. They didn't notice for almost a year. Nicole had tried to convince herself that that's what had happened to her. She wanted someone to pluck her from obscurity and take her to where she was actually meant to live. The townspeople of Henderson seemed so small-minded to her, determined to live here forever in their quiet, predictable lives. Few people had any dreams of moving somewhere with better job prospects or a more modern way of life. Even from a young age Nicole knew she wouldn't be here forever. Then, once Lori vanished, she feared she might not get out alive.

The passengers seated in front of her, an attractive young couple, laugh at something they're streaming on a cell phone. Nicole glances around at the other people on board. No one is paying attention to the fact these two women are holding hands, and that one has her head resting on the other's shoulder, sharing a set of earphones. Maybe they haven't noticed yet. She hopes they never do, because the couple seem happy, and she wouldn't want the locals to ruin it for them.

The bus pulls into the station and everyone makes moves to get off. Nicole didn't bring much with her, unless you count emotional baggage. Her one suitcase is filled with light summer clothes and underwear, a pair of sneakers, two books, her vitamins and some toiletries, as well as her purse. She gets off the bus and waits in line for the driver to retrieve it from the luggage hold. Her oversized sunglasses hide her face from anyone who might recognize her. She may have been gone awhile but locals never forget. Not when your father is the beloved sheriff and your mother a nurse-midwife who has helped deliver a lot of the town's babies.

The entire community has a fondness for her parents, which is why Nicole had to get out when she did. Because these people didn't grow up in her parents' home. They didn't see what happened behind closed doors. They don't know what she knows. And they wouldn't believe her if she told them.

It's been two days since her mother's phone call telling her that Aimee is missing. Text messages Nicole sent afterward, asking for more details about the disappearance, have gone unanswered, except for one to say they will discuss it once she gets home. That doesn't surprise her. Ron and Debbie Chambers have always been secretive. With lives like theirs they have to be.

Nicole had half-expected Aimee to turn up safe and sound in the time it took her to find cover for her job at the animal shelter. Nicole works in the office, supporting the manager, and helps to feed the cats and walk the dogs when needed. Having no vacation time saved, her boss agreed she can take some unpaid leave while her sister is missing. That will hurt financially, but Aimee comes first so Nicole didn't hesitate.

As she waits for her luggage next to the bus, she looks around. Some things have changed. The station has been updated with new seating, and a large roof has been installed to keep the sunshine and rain off passengers while they wait. Apart from that the stores around the station are more or less the same: coffee shops, a strip mall, some independent gift stores, clothes stores and a couple of fast-food joints. The tall ancient trees that used to line Main Street are gone, replaced with faded floral displays that are struggling against the oppressive July heat. There appears to be a good mix of younger and older residents milling around. Certainly more young adults than when Nicole lived here. She can't help wondering why they stay and where they work.

A police cruiser slowly approaches the station, so Nicole slips farther behind the bus to hide from its view. The driver pulls over in front of one of the coffee shops and Nicole watches as a young deputy gets out. She can't see his face but it doesn't matter. It's not her father. She didn't expect that he would go out of his way to collect her, but that's okay. She's glad he didn't. She needs time to acclimate before she comes face to face with him.

"Nicole Rivers!" shouts the bus driver. He's holding her suitcase. She winces. Although her maiden name is Chambers, the deputy has spun around at hearing her married name being called aloud. Her father must have alerted his team that she was coming home. The deputy spots her. He raises his hand from across the street and a smile breaks out on his face.

Nicole's mouth drops open as she recognizes him. "Well, I'll be damned," she mutters.

Deputy Kurt Butler carefully crosses the road and approaches her, stopping just short of pulling her in for a hug. Instead, he removes his sunglasses and rests his hands on his hips. "My God, it's been forever. Your dad said you were on your way home. How are you?"

She breaks into a smile herself. "I'm good. But, Kurt? Why the heck are you wearing that uniform?"

He laughs. "Your dad never told you I work for him?"

Her smile fades. "I haven't spoken to him in years until recently." Kurt's father was a cop, probably still is for all she knows, so the uniform kind of makes sense. But in high school he always swore he would rather flip burgers all his life than follow in his father's footsteps.

"This yours?" The bus driver is getting impatient.

"Right, sorry. Thanks." She takes the suitcase from him and

says to Kurt, "So you've been sent to make sure I get home before I can change my mind?"

He grins. "Still suspicious of everyone, I see." He takes her suitcase and leads her to the cruiser. "You can sit in the back with cuffs on if you want the full experience, or you can ride up front with me."

She opens the front passenger door and gets in. It's oppressive inside.

Kurt slams the trunk closed before slipping into the driver's seat. "The A/C's out of gas, so open your window and make like a dog. I'll drive as fast as I can." He pulls away and they leave the downtown area.

It's not long before they pass huge cornfields and vast, flat farmlands. Mechanical harvesters noisily work the land and the smell of freshly cut hay hits her, bringing back a flood of good memories this time: her and Lori sunbathing atop giant haystacks instead of doing their homework, while their younger siblings, Aimee and Tommy, try to climb up and reach them. This part of town hasn't changed at all. She would bet the same old families occupy these farms. She catches a glimpse of the Marshes' property. It looks rundown and lifeless. "Did Mr. and Mrs. Marsh move away?"

Kurt glances over. "They died. Edna first, then Jim. If you listen to the rumors, they let the farm go to ruin so their kids wouldn't get any decent inheritance."

She raises her eyebrows. "Family feud?"

"Right. The kids are auctioning everything off tomorrow. You should go," he jokes. "Grab yourself a bargain."

She scoffs. "Families. Who needs 'em, right?"

He doesn't reply.

Only a slight breeze passes through the car's windows as they drive toward her childhood home. She quickly becomes sweaty and wishes she had some bottled water. Her mouth is dry at the thought of seeing her parents. If Aimee weren't missing, there's no chance she would be here right now. There's no way she'd risk staying one night in that house. But Aimee lives with them, so the house could hold vital clues about her disappearance.

While her parents are at work, Nicole intends to investigate. That's if they let her spend a minute alone there. If they're truly worried for Aimee's safety, her mother might have taken time off work. That would mean Nicole's every move would be watched. She tries to distract herself from the thought by reminding herself that she's an adult now and she can leave whenever she likes.

She looks at Kurt. He's still handsome with his thick black hair and deep blue eyes. She wonders who he ended up with after she left town, but she doesn't want to pry. "I always hated that brown uniform, but to tell you the truth, it looks better on you than it ever did on my dad and his buddies."

He glances at her. "Oh yeah?"

She nods.

"Thanks. I work out. Maybe that's the difference. No offence to your dad or anything." He winks.

Nicole smiles. Kurt was a close friend when she was in high school. He was dating Lori. She was dating Lucas. The four of them spent most of their spare time together. She had no idea then that she would go on to marry Lucas, and that Lori would never have an opportunity to marry. If she had known Lori would vanish, Nicole would have left town long before she did, and she would have taken Lori with her.

"What's happened to Aimee, Kurt?" she asks. "Mom said she's been missing for a week. That's all I know. I can't find any reports online about her disappearance, no newspaper articles. So what's going on?"

His expression turns serious. "I have no clue where your sister is. We don't have much to go on so far." He hesitates. "I'll let your dad fill you in. I don't think he'd want me stepping on his toes."

She frowns. It sounds like Kurt's been given instructions on how to deal with her. Which means her father's controlling the narrative, as usual. Her chest tightens as she realizes this is going to be exactly like last time.

THREE

Nicole tenses as they creep up the long, straight driveway to the wooden farmhouse beyond. It always reminds her of the house from *The Waltons* TV show, just a little smaller. This farm was left to her mother by Nicole's grandparents when they died. Debbie and Ron Chambers have never farmed, so the barns and outbuildings have been sitting empty for decades. They considered selling the property before Aimee came along in 2004, but there was little interest in a farm where the land had been allowed to spoil. The house was always kept nice, and she and Aimee loved growing up with lots of outside space, but it needs a family larger than theirs to bring this place back to life. Especially now Aimee's turned eighteen and will be thinking of moving on soon. If she hasn't already.

Nicole swallows. She's trying to think of her sister's disappearance as something Aimee had a choice in; that she chose to leave town of her own accord and make a fresh start somewhere well away from their parents. But her instinct tells her otherwise.

"To tell you the truth, I'm surprised you're staying here," says Kurt when he turns off the engine and notices her hesitancy to get out of the cruiser. "What with everything that went down back then. I thought I'd never see you in town again, never mind at your parents' place."

She lowers her eyes. "We have unfinished business. And now with Aimee missing..."

He leans in and gently asks, "Want me to go in with you? Maybe it'd go easier with a third party present."

She would love that, but it would be unfair on him. Her father is Kurt's boss. Kurt shouldn't get mixed up in their drama as it could have serious repercussions for his job. "No, that's okay. Thanks for the ride. I appreciate it." She opens the door and steps out. The temperature is slightly cooler than inside the vehicle.

Kurt retrieves her suitcase from the trunk. "Let me give you my number in case you want to go for a drink while you're in town." He hands her his card. It includes his cell number on it. "I thought maybe you'd want to reminisce about Lori."

She takes it from him and looks up at his face, sensing he's the one who wants to reminisce. His eyes give away the unresolved feelings he has. He misses Lori too. It's the unanswered questions that do it. When someone vanishes, it messes with your mind. It plays cruel tricks on you. You try to bargain with a God you're not even sure you believe in.

If Lori comes home today, I'll never do anything bad again in my life.

If Lori comes home today, I'll start going to church not just every Sunday but as a volunteer too.

And so on.

Kurt gets into the cruiser and she turns to watch him drive away. She closes her eyes, wishing Lucas had been able to make the trip with her. Her husband is planning to join her once his conference is over, if she's still here by then. He tried persuading her to stay in a hotel as he's concerned for her well-being. Nicole had declined. She can't find her sister from a hotel room. Not when whatever happened to her probably occurred on this property.

She hears the creak of a door opening behind her and forces herself to turn around.

A slim woman stares back at her. Her mom has aged. For a woman of fifty-three she shouldn't look so exhausted. Her long hair, once brown with curls that bounced—like Nicole's—is now faded and sprinkled with gray. Her curls are frizzy and neglected. She's wearing an old plaid shirt that's several sizes too big for her, over blue jeans. Debbie's arms are crossed and her face is unsmiling. She reserves her smiles for the babies she delivers. Babies born to other people. After a critical glance up and down Nicole's figure—a little fuller since the last time they saw each other—Debbie asks, "Are you hungry?"

Nicole feels sick but thinks she could eat something. Some people cope with stress by drinking too much, or using drugs. Nicole finds comfort in food. Besides, it's lunchtime and the journey was long. And the truth is, she wants her mom to feed her. To care for her. It's lonely living without parents. With no extended relatives to speak of, the Chambers family consists of just the four of them, and she's been away for twelve years now. It would be great to be part of the family again. But she wants a mother who wants the best for her. She wants parents who don't keep secrets. Who don't try to control her in order to protect the family name. And parents who aren't a serious risk to her life.

Knowing she won't get any of that here, she blinks back tears and picks up her suitcase. "Thanks. That would be nice."

Debbie disappears inside and Nicole follows. It's cooler indoors. The two large oak trees that sit on either side of the house offer good shade and there are plenty of ceiling fans moving the air around. In the spacious hallway several smells reach her, bringing flashbacks with them: breakfast at the large wooden table in the kitchen, her father smoking cigars in front of the TV on his rare days off, and studying in her bedroom with Lori while candles burn. Lucas and Kurt were never allowed in her bedroom. They had to stay in full view of her parents when they were over, so the four of them preferred to spend time at Lucas's place instead. His mom was alone and she liked the company. She let them get away with whatever they wanted while she would sit watching the soaps on TV with her favorite companion: a bottle of Jack Daniel's hidden under a dishcloth in an attempt at discretion.

Now, Sindy Rivers is Nicole's mother-in-law and their relationship is almost nonexistent. Sindy tolerates her, but Nicole can't shake the feeling she was hoping for someone else as a daughter-in-law. And that's despite the fact that Sindy and her own mother used to be friends once, when Nicole and Lucas were younger. Once their mothers stopped hanging out with each other, Sindy didn't seem keen on the idea of her son being with Nicole. So when Lucas comes home to visit his mom, Nicole doesn't join him. It's just easier all round that way.

She leaves her suitcase at the bottom of the stairs and hesitantly walks along the hallway, stopping at a collection of framed color photographs on the sideboard. She spots a photo of herself when she was a teenager, but she doesn't recognize the surroundings. A closer inspection reveals it's actually Aimee in the photograph, not her. Her breath catches. Her little sister is pretty with her long curly hair, dyed blonde. She's taller and slimmer than Nicole ever was, and she finds herself wondering whether she was a cheerleader. Nicole wasn't athletic or popular enough for that. It feels strange that this girl she's looking at is her sister. She could be a stranger given the amount of time that has passed since they last saw each other.

Putting the framed photo back, she prepares herself before entering the bright kitchen. It's exactly as it was when she left home, with just a new microwave on the counter. Its newness makes it stand out from the older appliances. Her mother is buttering bread with her back to Nicole, but she says, "Take a seat. How have you been keeping?"

Nicole does as she's told. "We're both good. Working all the time. You?"

"Same as always. Busy at the hospital."

With the pleasantries over, a silence engulfs them. Nicole's never been good in awkward situations. When her mother doesn't attempt to break it, she asks, "Where's Dad?"

"He'll be here soon enough." The way her mother says it makes it sound more like a threat than a fact. Debbie turns with a plate stacked high with buttered bread in her hand. She brings it over to the table and places it next to the salad items. Ham and cheese sit in the center of the table. "Help yourself." From the fridge she retrieves a large bottle of Diet Coke. "I bought it especially. And I know you'll only drink it cold."

Nicole looks up at her in surprise. That was a nice gesture. Her parents don't drink soda. Maybe there's some hope for their relationship. "Thanks. I appreciate it." Hope swells in her chest. "You should have some. It's more refreshing than water in weather like this."

Debbie pours her a glass. "Maybe later." She walks away and busies herself with some dirty dishes.

"Aren't you going to sit down?" asks Nicole, disappointed.

"When your father gets here."

Nicole reminds herself not to expect miracles. Things have started better than she could have hoped, and that's something. She places a wedge of cheese into a slice of bread. She can tell everything was made locally as the dairy items taste amazing compared to the cheap imitations she buys from the grocery store at home. When her mother still won't make eye contact with her, Nicole stands and approaches her at the counter. "Mom? What's happened to Aimee? Please tell me. I'm worried about her. You must be too if you reached out to me."

Debbie drops the dishcloth into the sink and with a bitterness in her tone says, "Your sister's eight months pregnant."

Nicole's mouth drops open. She takes a step back. "What?" A stab of undeniable jealousy runs through her. How can her little sister be pregnant before her? How come she got pregnant so easily? Nicole shakes her head. That doesn't matter. What matters is that Aimee's only eighteen years old, so it's unlikely this was planned, which brings Nicole out in goosebumps as she considers the alternative. "Was she assaulted?"

Her mother scoffs. "Trust you to assume the worst."

Regret washes over Nicole. She should have come back for Aimee before now. She might have been able to stop any of this from happening. "Why didn't anyone tell me before now?"

"Because you're not a part of this family anymore. You're a stranger to her."

"Sure, because of you and Dad! I wanted to be in Aimee's life but you wouldn't let me. You refused to pass my letters on to her."

Debbie spins around to face her. "You're the one who ran out of here like a bat out of hell when Aimee was still small. That was a decision *you* made."

"And for good reason! Are you forgetting that part?" Nicole tries hard to hold back the tears in her eyes. She hates feeling this way. As if *she's* the cause of all their problems. There's so much unwarranted resentment in her mother's face.

"For God's sake, Nicole," says her father behind her. She didn't hear him come in. "You've been here five minutes and already you're upsetting your mother?"

She swings around to look at him. His brown uniform strains at the gut, but he carries his extra weight well on account of his height. With his six-foot-two frame, he fills the doorway. His voice is deep and booming, making her want to shy away from it. He's lost a little more hair since she last saw him, but overall, he looks the same. She briefly wonders how she looks to them.

"Come on," he says wearily as he grabs a slice of bread and cheese before turning away from them. "I don't have much time."

Nicole and Debbie follow him out to the porch where the sweet scent of honeysuckle fills the air. Ron wolfs down his food as he and Debbie take a seat on a cushioned wicker couch. Nicole chooses the old porch swing. As she sits, she feels a small splinter of wood puncture the back of her thigh. Her hands are trembling slightly, so she sits on them. She's afraid of her father. Of both of her parents. It's not easy to sit here with them after all this time, but she wants to keep things amicable. She's here for one reason only and that's what she has to focus on. "I'm not here to cause trouble," says. "I just want to find Aimee."

Ron takes a deep breath. "So do we. So here's what we know: Aimee is eight months pregnant and the identity of the baby's father is unknown. She won't talk about it. She's about to give birth to our grandchild and she's gone missing. That's about it."

That won't be all he knows. He's just choosing not to tell Nicole everything. "Did she take anything with her; her purse, cell phone or any clothes?"

Debbie says, "Her purse and phone aren't here. Her phone isn't working. It won't take calls or go to voicemail, so your father thinks the battery has been disconnected or the phone's been destroyed."

That makes Nicole nervous. Maybe Aimee didn't want to be located by their parents. Or maybe someone else destroyed it.

"As for clothes or a suitcase," says her mother, "it's difficult to tell because we never really went in her room until she went missing. I don't think she even owned a suitcase."

"Has her bank card been used since she vanished?" asks Nicole.

"No."

"Does she have a boyfriend?"

Ron scoffs. "You think she'd tell us if she did? We have no idea."

Nicole tries to keep her breathing even as she closely studies his face for signs of deception. Because despite everyone trying to convince her otherwise at the time, Nicole still strongly suspects it was her father who killed her best friend when they were just fifteen years old. And that her mother helped him cover it up. Which means that, now they've coaxed Nicole back here, she could be in danger too.

FOUR

A welcome breeze ruffles Nicole's hair. The sun reflecting off the windshield of her father's vehicle is causing a headache behind her eyes. As her father lights up a cigar, she asks, "So when and where was Aimee last seen? And what have you done to find her? I mean, it can't be too difficult to find a heavily pregnant woman."

Ron sighs, as if her questions are trying his patience. The smoke he exhales reaches her, sparking off more unwanted memories. "Should I lawyer up?" he says with a smirk. "Because it's starting to feel like we're being formally questioned."

Maybe he's trying to be lighthearted, but she senses he's mocking her. "You have to remember, you guys called me here. You can't expect me not to ask questions about my sister's disappearance."

"I'm just messing with you, Nicole. You need to lighten up." He sighs. "Aimee was due to attend her graduation ceremony a week ago. That morning I'd already left for work before she got up, so I didn't see her at all, but your mom spoke to her."

Debbie nods. "I made us both breakfast, but she didn't eat much. She picked at a plate of scrambled eggs, maybe ate a bite of toast. I put it down to the baby making her feel nauseous. She looked about ready to pop any day, except it's her first, so it's more likely to be late."

"Do we know whether it's a boy or a girl?" Nicole asks.

"No," says Debbie. "Aimee wants it to be a surprise but, in all honesty, I think she's just in denial, not wanting to face facts just yet. That's not to say she doesn't want the baby, but she's reluctant to talk about it."

That's unusual. Nicole would be talking about it nonstop if it were *her* who was pregnant. Don't most new moms itch for that first trimester to be over so they can share the good news and plan for the baby's arrival with their friends and family? A thought slips into Nicole's head. "Are you planning on helping to deliver the baby?"

"No. She's chosen someone else to do that." And Debbie's not happy about it, judging by the look on her face. "Although if she doesn't come home soon, she might be delivering it all alone in the woods."

Nicole frowns. That's a strange comment. Why would Aimee deliver it in the woods? A shudder runs through her. Has her mother just slipped up?

"I left for work at eight and I haven't seen her since," continues Debbie. "No one has as far as we can tell. She's always been secretive, same as you, and not even her closest friends have a clue what she's up to. They said she'd been a little aloof in the weeks leading up to her disappearance, probably nesting for the arrival."

Nicole really hopes her mother wasn't the last person to see Aimee alive. Because that could mean her sister was harmed in this house by her parents and now they're covering it up. If that's the case, Aimee could never be found. Like Lori. "Were there any signs of a struggle in the house? Forced entry?"

Her parents shake their heads in unison.

"What was her mental state at the time? Was she excited about being pregnant?"

Debbie sighs. "It's difficult to know. She's always been up and down. But then, everyone seems to have something wrong with them these days. In our day we just got on with things, didn't we?" She looks to her husband who nods.

Nicole's disappointed, but not surprised, by her mother's attitude to mental health. "What have you done to look for her?" she asks. "Traced her cell phone, spoken to the neighbors, watched CCTV?"

Ron laughs. "You've been watching too many crime documentaries. And bad ones at that."

A rage runs through her then. He's not taking any of this seriously. "I don't consider Aimee's disappearance to be funny, so how come you do?"

The smile vanishes from his face and he leans forward. "Now you listen to me, young lady. You will show your mother and me some respect while you're in town. I'm the sheriff here, and if you think I haven't done everything humanly possible to locate my daughter, you'd be wrong. And I don't need to be schooled by someone who chose to be estranged from her own sister." He stands.

In an effort to hide how intimidating she finds him, Nicole asks, "So when's the press conference? I'd like to be there."

Her mother's expression is guarded. She remains silent.

"There is no press conference," says Ron. "My entire office is searching for her and that'll be a lot easier without a bunch of reporters getting in the way and having our family name dragged through the mud in the meantime. You want the press and media looking into us, Nicole? Digging up the past?"

She lowers her eyes.

"Listen, everyone who needs to know about Aimee knows," he says. "The citizens of Henderson are our friends and they want to see her home safe. When she's found, it will be by one of us, not by a roving reporter who's looking to cash in on a family tragedy."

That doesn't sit well with Nicole, but there's not a lot she can do about it. Except maybe leak the news to a reporter. That would have to be a last resort because they would undoubtedly look into what happened in the summer of 2008 and link it to her family. It would be hard not to, considering the sexual assault allegation that was made against her father back then. He may have silenced the alleged victim and buried her statement, but he can't silence rumors. Rumors stick. Especially in a town like this.

Nicole knows she might have to risk opening that can of worms if Aimee isn't found soon, especially as she's pregnant. There's a baby to consider. Her own precious niece or nephew. "What do you think has happened to her?" she asks.

"If you ask me, it's obvious," says Ron, with his hands on his hips. "She's realized she made a mistake getting pregnant so young and now she's running away from her responsibilities. She's embarrassed."

"If you believe that, then why call me home?"

Her mother speaks up. "We thought that if word reached her that you were home, she might come back to see you and we can put this whole sorry episode behind us. After you left, she never stopped asking about you. She put you on a pedestal as if you were some kind of saint. It was only when she became a teenager that she realized you didn't care about her."

Nicole gasps. "I wrote to her every month at first."

"Sure, and I helped her reply to every single letter. Then your letters became few and far between and she assumed you'd forgotten about her, so we stopped passing them on. They were upsetting her. I figured if you really cared about your sister, you would come and visit her once in a while. Take her out for the day. But you never did."

"I had a lot to deal with back then," says Nicole. "You know that. Our relationship had broken down beyond repair." Blinking away tears, she looks at both of her parents as she speaks. "We couldn't stand to be around each other. That didn't mean I didn't want a relationship with Aimee. I thought you would make that clear to her. You're meant to protect her from all the drama. That's your job." A single tear breaks free.

"Oh boy. Here come the waterworks." Her father stubs out his cigar. "I need to get back to work. And you need to let me find your sister." He turns to leave.

Nicole wipes her eyes as shame burns her cheeks. They're making her feel bad for getting upset. And they're rewriting history when it comes to her feelings for Aimee. It leaves her feeling frustrated. Quietly, she says, "I'd like to know how you think you can find Aimee when you never found Lori."

Ron stops in his tracks before turning around, his jaw tight. "I should've guessed you'd bring that up, but I hoped you would've matured by now. If you've still got a bee in your bonnet about what happened to your friend, then you might as well leave right now. I did everything I could to find Lori Peterson but sometimes things don't work out how you'd like. Just like our relationship with you."

Nicole looks away. She doesn't think he did everything he could for Lori at all. Because she suspects he knows exactly where Lori is and he's hoping no one will ever find her.

"I don't think you understand that everything is good in our lives except for our relationship with you, Nicole," he says. "We have good friends, a nice home and great jobs. But you bring us nothing but trouble. And now Aimee's following in your footsteps." He shakes his head. "Sometimes I wish we never bothered having kids."

She closes her eyes as he walks to his cruiser. She feels her mother brush past her to enter the house. Both ignore her tears and she realizes then that being estranged from her parents is better than this painful alternative.

FIVE

SUMMER 2008

The bright sunlight peeping between her drapes wakes Lori earlier than she would like. Normally she's woken by Tommy standing beside her bed in his pajamas and begging her to play with him. She stretches her arms and yawns before a feeling of dread weighs heavy on her. Something horrible happened yesterday. She'd argued with Nicole.

Sitting up in bed, she grabs her phone off the nightstand. No messages await her attention. She flops back against her pillow and lowers the phone. Their argument had been vicious. No one knows how to hurt you more than your best friend does. Lori's not proud of the things she'd screamed at Nicole. She accused her of flirting with Kurt. She suspects they're interested in each other. She saw Kurt pretending a bug had fallen down Nicole's top and offering to scoop it out with a stupid grin on his face. Nicole appeared to love the attention. Lucas hadn't been around at the time and neither of them noticed she was paying them any attention.

Lori had been overwhelmed with jealousy, so she'd stormed over there and screamed at her friend. Kurt disappeared after calling them both immature. That had hurt more than anything, but he'd made it up to her later by taking her to the movies, just the two of them for a change. She's still annoyed with him but she had expected more of Nicole. Friends don't flirt with each other's boyfriends. It's like a golden rule of sisterhood or something. Or at least, it should be. She takes a deep breath, which makes her cough. Her chest is heavy after smoking pot last night.

Both she and Nicole hate smoking pot, so half the time they just pretend to inhale. They haven't been doing it long. It's something Kurt introduced them to. Lucas can take it or leave it. He prefers alcohol. With school over for the summer they've been getting bored. It's getting more and more difficult to find ways to pass the time. Henderson isn't the liveliest town. Sometimes sitting in the park with a couple of joints and a six-pack of beer is the only thing there is to do.

Her bedroom door bursts open and Tommy runs in. His pajamas are wrinkled and he has serious bed hair. "Play with me!" he begs.

She rolls her eyes with a smile. "It's not even seven yet."

"I don't care! I'm going to hide. Come find me, okay?"

She pulls the sheet back and swings her legs out of bed. "Okay. I'll count to a thousand. You go hide."

He shakes his head. "No. Not a thousand. You did that last time and never looked for me."

She bites her lip in an attempt not to laugh. He had fallen asleep in their parents' closet while he waited. She was getting dressed and then got distracted, completely forgetting that he was hiding. "Okay, okay. I'll count to ten. Now run!"

He screams in delight and makes off out the door. She hears him run downstairs with just socks on his feet and winces in case he slides on the wooden treads and breaks his neck. Their mom must be downstairs preparing breakfast because there's a lot of noise coming from the kitchen. Lori hears the newsreader on TV. Her parents are obsessed with the news channel, even when nothing's happening. Lori listens as her mom scolds Tommy for running in the house. Which means he's hiding in the kitchen.

She smiles as she pulls on some clean underwear, a T-shirt and a denim skirt, and slips her feet into a pair of battered sneakers. She needs to find Tommy before she forgets about him again. Before she can leave the room her phone pings with a new text message. She grabs it and reads the screen.

I'm sorry. Do you hate me?

Lori smiles at her friend's apology.

No!! I blame the pot. Where does Kurt get that stuff?

Nicole's reply is immediate.

He probably grows it himself knowing him.
*   Meet at 2 at Lucas's house?*

Lori replies.

OK.

She takes a deep breath. Everything is right again. Petty jealousy is forgiven just like that. Because there isn't anyone else at school who Lori would want to be friends with, so you have to pick your battles.

"Ten!" she yells. "Ready or not, here I come!"

SIX

SUMMER 2022

Nicole takes Kurt up on his offer to go for a drink that evening, because her mother showed no signs of leaving the house to go to work. Instead, she had been quietly sitting alone on the rear porch all afternoon, staring out over the cornfields beyond their land while a stunning sunset formed.

Nicole had wanted to approach her, to speak to her openly and ask what was really going on, but they're just not close enough. Her mother picked a side years ago, and it wasn't Nicole's. It's unlikely there's any prospect of her changing her mind after all these years. Debbie Chambers is loyal to her husband. Maybe because she has to be, or else she'll be implicated in whatever happened back then. And whatever's happening now. It's more than disappointing for Nicole. It's heartbreaking.

Not wanting to dwell on it, she had to get away from the house. Her old room is comfortable enough, although mostly filled with water-damaged boxes from the attic. As a result, a musty aroma hangs in the air, making it unpleasant to spend too long in there. She had intended to get straight to work searching Aimee's room, but as that wasn't possible with her mother home, she called Kurt before arranging for a cab to take her downtown.

Nicole enters Mackey's Saloon just before eight o'clock. She looks around. She's only been inside once before, but not for drinks. Being the daughter of the local sheriff means she never got to experience using a fake ID to score liquor, not in Henderson anyway. Everyone knew who she was and how old she really was. Kurt had the same experience growing up, what with his dad being the chief deputy.

She spots Kurt over at the pool table with a couple of guys. He's wearing jeans with a blue T-shirt and looks younger out of uniform. She can see a couple of tattoos poking out from under his right sleeve and a hint of one around the neck area, above his chest. When they were younger, he always said he'd get a full sleeve of ink, but Nicole would bet his job makes that impossible. Her father hates visible tattoos on his deputies.

Once Kurt notices her, he leaves the guys behind and smiles as he approaches. "Hi." He leads her to the bar. "What'll it be?"

"Diet Coke, heavy on the ice."

Kurt raises his eyebrows. "You don't want a beer?"

"No, maybe later. I'm not much of a drinker."

He nods. "I'd love a real drink but I can't have one in case I'm called into work."

"You're off duty, aren't you?" she asks.

"Right. But with your sister being missing and all..." He doesn't finish the thought.

The female bartender leans in to Nicole, lifting her glasses up. "Well look what the wind blew in!" A smile spreads across her weathered face. "How are you? Still with that cute boyfriend of yours?"

Nicole reddens. "Hi, Lorraine. Sure, we've been married almost five years now."

"That's good to hear. So many high school sweethearts break up. Got any kids?"

Nicole's always thought it's a strange question to ask someone you're not close with. It's really none of their business. Or maybe it's just a sensitive subject for her. "Not yet."

"Well, keep trying. After all, trying's the fun part." Lorraine winks at her as if it's an original comment.

The older woman doesn't ask her if she's in town to help find Aimee. It makes her wonder whether her father was honest when he said all the locals are aware that Aimee's missing.

When they have their drinks, Nicole leads Kurt to a small table in a dark corner, away from prying eyes. The table is clean, with a lit candle in a bourbon glass in the center. She looks around the bar. It isn't filled with the usual suspects she would expect from a place like this. Instead, young couples and groups of friends sit together, enjoying animated discussions. It isn't smoky or run-down inside like it used to be. It feels like somewhere she and Lucas would go for their rare date nights.

"How's Lucas?" asks Kurt. "I spotted him here last year, visiting his mom, but I didn't get a chance to speak to him."

"He's good. He's at a conference right now, but he might make it in a few days depending on whether I'm still in town."

Kurt nods. "And the showdown with your parents? It must've been strange after not seeing them for so long. I can't imagine not being in touch with my dad for any length of time."

She sips her Coke and crunches on some ice. "It was predictable. They think I'm going to cause trouble."

"Are you?" he says, a smile playing at his lips.

"Only if finding my sister causes trouble." She sighs. "My folks said she's pregnant. Are there any rumors about who the baby's father is?"

"Not that I've heard." He sips his alcohol-free beer. "The last time I saw her she was standing outside the ice cream parlor on Main Street having a heated discussion with someone on her phone. That was two days before she vanished."

Nicole leans in. "Did you hear what she was saying?"

He shakes his head. "I was driving by in the cruiser. I stopped for a second to see if she needed any help, but she turned her back on me."

After considering it, Nicole asks, "Do you know if she was in any trouble? Or what kind of crowd she hangs out with?"

"She isn't the kind of kid who gets into trouble, but it's concerning that I've seen her with Tommy a lot lately."

She frowns. "Who's Tommy?"

"Tommy Peterson. Lori's little brother."

Nicole hasn't thought about Tommy in years. He was a cute kid who always wanted to go wherever she and Lori went. Sometimes they'd take him with them, and bring Aimee too since she was just a year younger than him. Those two kids loved each other and would hold hands as they walked. It was adorable. A pang of grief washes over her. She misses that time. Those kids.

"He's nineteen now and working as a mechanic," says Kurt. "I'm pretty sure he has the hots for your sister. Probably always did."

She swallows. "Have they ever dated?"

"I wouldn't know." He takes another sip of his drink. "Why? You think he might be the baby's father?"

"I guess it's possible. I should pay him a visit."

"Your dad already has. I think he hates Tommy."

Surprised, she says, "Why?"

"He doesn't want him to drag your sister down, I guess. Tommy's been in trouble a bunch of times. He's got a serious drug problem from what I've heard. Rumor has it he sells drugs to high school kids."

Her heart sinks. "Little Tommy on drugs? Think it's because of what happened to Lori?"

Kurt picks at the sticker on his bottle. "Probably. It sure changed me. I'd go as far to say it changed the course of my life.

And Tommy was just a kid when it happened. That's got to screw someone up."

She rests a hand on his. He's clearly still hurting. "Has it screwed you up?"

He tries to laugh it off. "You tell me. Do I appear normal to you?"

She squeezes his hand. "There's no such thing as normal. And thank God, right? I like my friends to be interesting." She smiles before leaning back in her seat.

"You ever think about Lori?" he asks. "Even after all these years? I know you suffered badly at the time, so I wasn't sure whether it's something you try not to think about in order to move forward."

She tries not to think of Lori too often because it makes her sad, but flashbacks of that night still haunt her. "Sure. I wonder what she'd be doing now. Whether she would've gone to college, and whether you two would be married with a bunch of kids by now."

"I doubt it." Kurt's expression turns serious. "It's like Lorraine said: you and Lucas are the exception when it comes to high school sweethearts marrying." After a second's hesitation he adds, "I had a lot of nightmares after she disappeared."

"You did?"

He nods. "Once the patch of blood was confirmed as belonging to her it became real. But we didn't know enough, did we? About what had happened to her. So my mind filled in the blanks while I tried to sleep. It was months before I got a dreamless night. It almost sent me crazy." He swallows. "I still miss her. Remember her laugh?"

Nicole smiles. "It used to drive me insane! But what I'd give to hear it now." She sips her drink thoughtfully. "Is there anyone special in your life?" Nudging his arm playfully, she says, "I don't see any wedding ring on your finger, which means you must be Henderson's most eligible bachelor with a line of women at your door."

He reddens. "Nah. I'm too picky, I guess. Most people I meet are wearing handcuffs."

She rolls her eyes. "Oh please. Don't feed me that old line. You haven't let what happened to Lori put you off getting close with anyone else, have you? Because that would just be so tragic that I'd be forced to set you up with someone."

He looks at her with a serious expression, like he's weighing up whether to confide in her. Then he glances around to see if anyone's listening in. No one is even looking at them over here in the corner by themselves. He swallows, and his nervousness becomes apparent. "There might be someone."

She leans in to hear him. "You don't need to tell me if it makes you uncomfortable. Just tell me to mind my own business."

He takes a deep breath. "I met them online originally, and we've only met twice in person." He hesitates, before adding, "I like him."

Nicole's taken by complete surprise. She had no idea. With a smile she says, "And here's me thinking I knew everything there was to know about Kurt Butler."

He smiles, but there's trepidation there. Maybe some angst. "It's kind of new to me too. Well, not really. I mean I'm almost thirty, so you'd think I would know for sure by now, but all my previous relationships or flings have been with women." He glances around again. Keeping his voice low he says, "And I *am* attracted to women. I was ready to propose to my ex before I caught her cheating. But there's always been this other attraction too." He takes another deep breath before laughing nervously. "Man, you don't know how good it is to talk about it. There's no one else I can tell."

She understands. He's trapped by other people's expectations: his father's and the town's. "I think it's great that you're exploring it. Is he hot? Show me a photo."

Kurt reddens. "No, not here. He's attractive to me. But it's more than that. There's chemistry. And he lives two hundred miles away, so when I visited him, I could be someone else. Or I guess I mean I could be myself."

She wonders what will happen if this guy ever wants to visit Kurt's hometown.

"I don't know," he says, trying to downplay it. "Maybe nothing will come of it. He hasn't called for a while, so it's probably already over before it started. It's been a welcome distraction from work though."

"Romance always is," she says. "I envy you in a way."

He turns to her. "Really?"

"Sure. The newness of it all. The butterflies in your stomach. The 'will he call me tonight' phase. Being married means things get a little stale. Lucas and I will go out for dinner occasionally and find ourselves with nothing to say because we live together, so we already know everything that happened that week." She smiles. "It can get awkward."

"I guess that's why people have kids," he quips.

She laughs. Not wanting to pry any further into his love life, she changes the subject. "Do you know what my dad learned from talking to Tommy?"

"Not really. Ron doesn't tell me anything. In his eyes I'm only useful for the call-outs he and his buddies don't want to attend. My dad's retired now but he and Ron are still pretty close, so I can ask him if you like?"

"Thanks. I'd like to know exactly what's being done to find her." She sips her drink again. "How come your dad's retired already?"

Kurt hesitates. "Cancer's got ahold of him. I moved back in so I can be around to help care for him, but I don't know how long he might have left."

Nicole knows Kurt's mom passed away years ago and he has no siblings, which means the burden falls to him. "I'm sorry to hear that." She means it, despite the fact she never liked Chief Deputy Brian Butler. He was always condescending toward her and acted like she was something he scraped off his shoe, even though she was the daughter of his closest friend. It used to annoy her that he had no respect for her whatsoever, but that was true of most of her father's co-workers. They all acted like they ran the town, and their word was gospel. They were a special breed, and one best avoided. Which is why she was so surprised to see Kurt in the uniform. He's nothing like any of them.

"I've never heard of your sister going missing before now," says Kurt. "She's not one of those kids who does it as a cry for help."

Which is why Nicole's convinced she hasn't left town of her own free will. "Something bad must've happened. I'm worried someone's harmed her." Her eyes well up. "We need to find her, Kurt. Before she gives birth. I can't bear the thought of her and the baby being unsafe."

He places a hand on hers. "I'll speak to my dad. Don't worry, we'll find her."

It's comforting to think she at least has his help. But she can't shake the nagging feeling they might already be too late.

SEVEN

The next morning, after a night of tossing and turning, Kurt races to the Marshes' farm. He doesn't bother with the cruiser's lights or siren. They're unnecessary. Even though the discovery is gruesome, this isn't an emergency. It's a cold case. Just which one remains to be seen.

The call-out from dispatch came at 7.46 a.m. He checks the time and sees it's taken him just six minutes to get here. All he knows so far is that bones have been discovered on the property on the same day that the land, the mechanical equipment and the vehicles are scheduled for auction. The house, deemed uninhabitable, is due to be demolished in a few days.

A large rusting sign greets Kurt as he turns on to the property.
Trespassers = target practice

Crawling along the dusty driveway toward the house, he spots Sheriff Chambers already here. He's standing alone next to his vehicle, looking up at the weathered farmhouse with his hands on his hips, aviators clutched in one hand. Kurt gets out of his cruiser and joins him. "Bones?"

Ron doesn't turn to greet him.

Kurt's always felt a certain amount of resentment from the sheriff, but he doesn't know why. He suspects it's because he was friends with Nicole, and the guy clearly has issues with his daughter. It feels as if Ron doesn't trust him. Kurt suspects he would never have even been considered for a job as sheriff's deputy if his own father hadn't been friends with Ron. But now his dad's had to retire, he wouldn't be surprised if the sheriff is planning on finding an excuse to let him go.

Eventually, Ron says, "There are bones in the silo. Looks like they've been there a while." His voice is off.

Kurt looks at the steel cylinder to the right of the house. It's clear it hasn't been used for years, just like the rest of the equipment on this property. The steel is rusting, with overgrown plants creeping upward, their tendrils slowly claiming it for themselves. Abandoned bird nests are visible among the branches and Kurt would bet the inside of the silo is full of less appealing creatures, scurrying about in the dark.

The Marshes used to run this place as a cattle farm but, after a dispute with their kids, they sold their cows and let the rest go to ruin. Both their kids refused to take over and run the farm, to keep it going for years to come. They wanted different careers, and not in Henderson. So Jim and Edna took mighty offence and decided they didn't want the kids inheriting anything of worth, but they also didn't want to sell up and move, so they let the place deteriorate around them, just as they were doing inside the property until they both succumbed to old age. First Edna then, three years later, Jim. Some people carry a grudge to their grave. Now it's only worth scrap prices, along with a price for the land.

The auction arranged by the offspring will need to be canceled. This place needs to be protected in order to secure any potential evidence.

"You remember Bobby Howell?" asks Ron, finally glancing

at him. "You would have been in the grade below him in high school."

Kurt nods. Everyone remembers Bobby Howell. "Sure. He shot himself with his dad's handgun when he was eighteen."

"Right. Do you know why he did it?"

There were rumors, of course, but Kurt was just a kid, so he didn't have access to the truth. "Not really."

Ron nods to the house. "He used to help Jim out on the farm. Lived down the road with his parents at the time. When he turned eighteen, Bobby alleged that Jim Marsh had raped him when he was just fourteen years old. Here in this house. Jim would've been sixty-eight when it happened."

Kurt rubs his forehead. "Was Marsh arrested for it?"

"Sure. But there wasn't any evidence. I had to let the son of a bitch go." He's quiet for a second, before adding, "Bobby shot himself an hour later. Right after my phone call."

The day is heating up already, and Kurt wishes he was anywhere but here. A fly keeps hitting his neck, attracted to the sunblock. He bats it away. "You think the bones in the silo belong to another of Jim's victims?"

"I guess we'll find out."

Kurt should be springing into action, collecting potential evidence and securing the scene. But a creeping sense of dread has ahold of him and he's frozen to the spot, same as Ron. Lori Peterson's face flashes before him. Laughing at something he said. Leaning in for a kiss. Out of the four of them, Lori was the only one who suffered from teenage acne. Her face would erupt into large, pus-filled boils that took weeks to dry up. She'd spend hours sunbathing after someone told her UV rays could help clear it up. All that did was burn her skin, making it flaky as well as angry.

Lori wasn't an obvious choice to go missing. With her straight black hair that was always tied back and a boyish figure, she hadn't yet grown into herself, although there's no doubt she would've flourished eventually. If the perpetrator's motive was sexual, Kurt would have thought one of the cheerleaders from high school would have been a better target. Just like Nicole, Lori was studious and shy, and rarely seen without either her little brother tagging along, or with Kurt or Nicole by her side. So, for her to be caught alone like she was, it always struck him as strange.

Kurt carries a good amount of guilt about that night. Guilt that he wasn't with her. That he didn't protect his girlfriend.

He clears his throat. "I really hope it's not Lori."

Ron glances at him before turning to face him. He slips his aviators on and in a strained voice says, "It's probably better that she's found, so we can bring some peace to her family after all these years. But do me a favor. Don't speculate around anyone else: the press... Nicole. I don't need that headache until we know for sure."

Kurt meets his gaze. Nicole will assume the same as him the minute she finds out about this, and Ron knows it.

"Why don't you stay out of the way while the coroner retrieves the remains?" says Ron. "If it is your old girlfriend in there, you won't want to remember her that way, and besides, I need you to record the property. Film every single item in there in the hope of finding something relevant. Let's expose Jim Marsh for the sick son of a bitch he really was."

It might be masked as a suggestion but Kurt knows it's an order. The rumbling of a car engine behind makes them turn in unison. Deputy Gareth Hayes has arrived. Gareth is in his forties and by his own admission has a thing for fast food and what he considers loose women. He spends his spare time at the only nearby strip club, over in King County. He has three ex-wives and an undisclosed number of children. Kurt can't stand the guy.

They watch as he gets out of the car. "Morning," says

Gareth, chewing tobacco. "Julie told me to get over here. Who called it in, the son?"

"No," says Ron. "Brad and Bernadette aren't in town. They're using an auctioneer to sell off the items because they never want to see the place again. I'm about to call Brad to let him know what we've found."

"Who can blame them, right?" says Gareth. "I bet it's a shit-show inside that house since Jim's body lay undiscovered for so long. So who called it in?"

Ron takes a deep breath. "Scrapyard Steve did a deal for the silos a couple of days ago and he was here early to take them apart. He started by making a hole in the side of this one." He points to the smaller of the two. "Wanted to check the condition of the interior. When he shined his flashlight through the hole, he came face to face with bones."

Gareth whistles.

"Yep. Thought they were animal bones at first, but then he saw a skull. The coroner's on his way."

Kurt's heard enough. From Ron's car he retrieves one of the team's digital cameras, hits record and heads up the creaky porch steps to the front door. It's surrounded by thick cobwebs and some mean-looking spiders. Kurt's never been inside the property before. The first thing to greet him is the stifling heat mixed with the unmistakable aroma of decomposition. It's offensive to his nostrils. He knows from experience that he'll need a long shower to get it off him later and his uniform will need the hottest wash possible.

It's clear no windows have been opened for months, and with no blinds or drapes on any of them, the property has been collecting hot sunshine. Although Jim's remains were removed a while ago, the smell has had time to seep into everything: wooden floorboards, soft furnishings and anything else that's absorbent, no matter how far away it was from the body. The only way to truly get rid of it would be to demolish the house.

Kurt tries not to breathe in too deep as he progresses farther into the house. The next thing he notices is the flies. Hundreds of dead flies cover the floors beneath the windows, thwarted in their attempt to escape once Jim's body was removed.

"The date is July 16, 2022," he says for the benefit of the recording. "I'm walking through the property formerly owned by Jim and Edna Marsh. The current owners are Brad Marsh and Bernadette Levers, the couple's adult children. The time is..." He checks his watch. "Eight sixteen a.m." Slowly, and careful to avoid the dead flies, he takes one step at a time as he records the living room through the lens, focusing on the furniture first, followed by the belongings.

In the living room, two well-used armchairs sit side by side, their covers worn bare on the arms. A brown oval of grease stains each headrest. On the coffee table in front of them sits an array of items: a dirty mug with mold growing inside, used tissues, a TV remote with fading buttons and a cigarette lighter. All signs of a life interrupted. Mixed among everything is what looks like mouse droppings, but Kurt knows is more likely fly larvae.

It looks as though the couple's children made little attempt at cleaning up after their father's body was discovered in here. Normally in these circumstances the family would hire a specialist clean team to remove as much of the biowaste as possible. The wooden floor shows the stains from where Jim's body was found decomposing on top of a rug that's since been dumped out back. Kurt didn't attend the scene but he saw photographs taken by the deputy who responded to the call-out. They had turned his stomach and, sometimes, when he's trying to eat dinner, images of the remains will flash up, causing him to lose his appetite. The old farmer had been here for weeks in the midsummer heat before the mailman raised the alarm.

Kurt moves on, toward the couple's bedroom. The hallway has crates of unopened soda and dog food running along its

length. As far as he knows, they never owned a dog. The
bedroom is stacked full of clutter—boxes and random belongings—signaling they became hoarders toward the end. Old
newspapers bundled up, trash that belongs in the kitchen
garbage, children's toys still in their boxes, and masses of deliv-
eries from places like Amazon and eBay sit unopened. He
suspects the dilapidated barns outside will also be full of crap.
Brad and Bernadette could probably make some money if they
retrieved all this stuff and sold it online or at a yard sale, but he
can understand why it wasn't even worth considering. No one
should have to set foot inside this house when it's in this condition, least of all the guy's kids.

Still viewing everything through the camera's lens, Kurt
turns around to film the vanity behind him. He jumps in
surprise when he sees a baby lying in the open bottom drawer.
His heart skips a beat. "Holy crap!"

He lowers the camera for a closer look. It's just a doll. She's
lifelike and she's been tucked up as if she's about to take a nap.
It's creepy. "These guys were something else," he mutters. He
briefly wonders whether they spent their remaining money on
all this crap not just so their kids wouldn't see a penny of it, but
so they'd also have a big mess to sort out after their parents were
gone.

He moves on to the bathroom, which is filthy. Brown stains
cover almost every surface and there are more dead flies on the
windowsill. A pistol sits among toothpaste on the sink. The
coroner concluded Jim most likely died of a heart attack, but
maybe he considered killing himself after Edna died. Living
alone in this house for the three years after she passed must
have been difficult.

In the bathtub Kurt finds a stack of old pornographic magazines and his heart sinks. He considers checking the covers to
see what kind of porn Jim Marsh was buying.

Kurt thinks of the kid who made the allegations against him,

Bobby Howell. Then he gets an image of Lori's face again. He turns away from the magazines. No. Someone else can do that. He peers out of the bathroom window and watches as Ron walks the coroner to the silo outside. He closes his eyes and mutters a silent prayer in the hope that it's not Lori in there.

EIGHT

Nicole is up, showered and dressed by 8 a.m. She slept surprisingly well thanks to the lack of street noise and having no neighbors nearby revving their engines at the crack of dawn. Some people just love to make everyone else suffer when they have to get up early for work. She had one missed call overnight, from Lucas, so as she sits on her bed rubbing anti-frizz serum into her damp hair with one hand, she returns his call with the other.

He answers almost right away. "Hey, you. How's it going?"

"Where do I start?" She takes a deep breath before bringing him up to date with everything that's happened so far. When she mentions Aimee is pregnant, he goes silent before releasing a long sigh.

"Jeez. *Pregnant?*"

"I know. It's shocking that no one told me before now."

Another long silence. Then he asks, "Who's the father?"

"No one knows," she says.

"That's not good. How do you feel about being an aunt before you're a mother?"

She shakes her head. "I don't know. I'm happy for her, if it's what she wants. But I have a bad feeling about it."

He agrees. "I know she's an adult now, but she's at the age where she should be out partying at college, or getting her first real job. Having a baby this young will limit her options. Hey, maybe that's why she disappeared? She might have hurt herself because she's feeling overwhelmed."

Nicole could really do without those kinds of theories right now. "I don't even want to consider that." She sighs. "Being here is like being a helpless teenager again. My parents haven't changed at all."

"I'm sorry," he says. "I wish I could be there for moral support."

"How's your conference going?"

"Well." He takes a deep breath. "The training is dry to say the least, but the food is amazing, and my hotel room has every TV channel I could ever want."

She groans. "Can we switch places please?"

"I would if I could. And I wish you and your parents could get along. This disconnect has gone on too long already."

She doesn't reply. Lucas always had a good relationship with her parents and doesn't enjoy being caught in the middle.

"Why don't you stay in a hotel like I suggested?" he asks. "Forget about the cost. It's worth it to avoid more stress."

She's starting to think it might be a good idea. But not just yet. "I need to search Aimee's room. There's got to be something in there that could give me an insight into what was going on in her life and what her state of mind was before she vanished."

"You don't think your dad would've removed anything like that already? I mean, if you genuinely believe he could be responsible, it's likely he'd cover his tracks again."

Lucas is aware she's always suspected her father was involved in Lori's disappearance. He never went along with her theory, but he's never declared her foolish for believing it either. With a mother like his, he knows better than anyone that families are complicated. "Maybe." She sighs. "I just need to feel like I'm doing something, you know?"

"Sure, I get it. Listen, I've got to go. The first session begins in thirty minutes and I haven't hit the breakfast buffet yet."

She shakes her head with a smile. "You're going to gain so much weight."

They say their goodbyes and she braces herself for leaving her room. As she passes her parents' bedroom on the way to the kitchen, she hears her mother crying. It stops her in her tracks. She lowers her eyes and listens to the gut-wrenching sobs. It brings tears to her own eyes to hear her mother in so much pain. Her heart skips a beat as she considers whether the worst has happened. Maybe Aimee has been found dead. "Mom?" She knocks on the bedroom door. "What's happened?"

The crying stops and Debbie makes no attempt to open the door.

"Is it Aimee?" she presses. "Has she been found?"

The bedroom door finally opens. Her mother's expression is guarded. She's tried to dry her eyes but they're still red. "No. I'm just hormonal, that's all. Stop making a big deal out of everything, would you?"

Nicole follows her to the kitchen. It feels like her mother's keeping something from her. "Cut the crap, Mom. What's going on?"

Debbie spins around. "My daughter's missing! Isn't that enough?"

Of course it is, but Nicole wants to point out that she has another daughter who's returned home after a long absence. She has an opportunity to bond with *her*. She tries not to be selfish. "What can I do? There must be something? I could make an updated missing person poster? We could spend the day going door to door handing it out and questioning people."

Debbie turns away from her. "It wouldn't do any good."

Frustrated, she says, "Then what would? Tell me, Mom. I want to help!"

Quietly, her mother says, "I don't think you should be here. It's too hard. I've got enough on my plate."

Tears spring to Nicole's eyes. Her mother's words are like a slap to the face and she doesn't know what else to do. She goes back to her room to collect her purse and her sunglasses. She exits the house and steps into the already warm day. The sun is relentless. So far, she's resisted the temptation to hire a rental car because of the cost, but the ten-minute walk to the bus stop makes her reconsider. She's sweating by the time she arrives downtown. The stores are busy already, with customers lining up for breakfast in coffee shops as well as the town's diner.

As she steps off the bus and onto the sidewalk, she pays attention to the noticeboards and lampposts she passes. They are all bare, with no missing person posters for Aimee. The town's largest noticeboard sits outside the huge grocery store. No posters there either. She checks under the flyers for dog-sitting services, hairstylists, aerobics classes and so on. Nothing. And none for Lori either. That's less surprising considering Lori vanished fourteen years ago, but it's still disappointing. She's been forgotten. Doesn't anybody care?

Nicole feels anger building in her chest.

Lori's mother and father must be devastated that their daughter's disappearance is nothing more than a blot on the town's history. They had struggled to cope in the immediate aftermath. Nicole had found it difficult to watch them on TV, pleading for their daughter's safe return. They refused to believe the blood found on the grass at the park—eventually confirmed as Lori's—meant she was dead. *She was just injured and disorientated*, they had argued. *There was still hope.*

Theresa Peterson had begged Nicole to give her some nugget of information about Lori's last movements in the hope of sparking a new lead. But Ron had made it clear Nicole needed to stay away from Theresa and Antony, as well as from Tommy. He said he didn't want her to feel pressured into making anything up in a bid to be helpful. He'd seen it a million times before, he'd explained. Witnesses who become less reliable over time because they want to help the investigation. They fool themselves into believing they must know something and, low and behold, new memories pop up. Untrustworthy memories that do nothing but harm the investigation.

In the weeks and months that followed, Nicole missed being around Lori's parents and brother. Missed going to their house. She didn't just lose Lori that night, she lost her other family. That's what your best friend's parents and siblings are when you're a teenager. They're your second family. And sometimes you prefer them to your own.

She pulls her phone out of her pocket and texts Kurt.

Do Lori's parents still live on Cedar Ave? I'd like to visit them.

She heads inside the grocery store to buy a bottle of water and something for breakfast while she waits for his response. She hasn't eaten yet. It's refreshingly cool inside. When she turns into the bread aisle she almost bumps into a woman. "Sorry," she says automatically.

"Watch where you're go—" The woman stops as a look of recognition sweeps over her. "It's you."

It takes a second for Nicole to recognize her. Mia Phillips used to have bleached blonde hair and a body to die for. Now she's returned to her mousy brown roots and, like Nicole, she's a little heavier than her high school days. Unlike Nicole, she has two toddlers trailing along beside her. The boys look like twins but only because they're in matching clothes. "Hi. How are you?" she asks.

Mia gives her a thorough survey from head to foot before frowning. "I think the question is, how are *you* these days?"

Nicole fixes a smile on her face. "I'm good. Still with Lucas."

Mia's expression changes. "That's a long time."

"Right. What about you?" Nicole nods to the boys. "Who's the lucky guy who gets to call these two cuties his sons?"

Mia glances at them before saying, "I suspect neither of us has time to get into *that* conversation." She looks around before lowering her voice. "I hear Aimee's disappeared. It's a damn shame. When was the last time you spoke to her? Did you keep in touch over the years? Because as far as I know, she didn't talk about you ever."

That's disappointing to hear. Not wanting to admit she hasn't spoken to Aimee in years, Nicole says, "Not recently. What about you? Do you know anything?"

The former cheerleader shakes her head. "I mean, not really. I've heard rumors of course, but I doubt you'd be interested in those."

"Are you kidding? Rumors always have some shred of truth to them in my experience."

Mia frowns. "I'm surprised you of all people would say that."

She must be referring to the time surrounding Lori's disappearance. Lori's parents weren't the only ones who struggled to cope in the aftermath. Nicole experienced a sharp decline in her mental health. She was the talk of the school apparently. Some say the talk of the town. Luckily, she was too out of it to notice what people were saying and Lucas protected her from the worst of it. Her relationship with her parents nosedived at that time, just when she needed them the most. "What have you heard?"

Mia's distracted. "Corey, stop slapping your brother." He

isn't slapping him; he's repeatedly shoving his head against a metal display case. The boys run off, out of sight, and their mother makes no moves to follow them. "My niece is in the grade below Aimee, so she tells me what her friends are saying. Now, Aimee's pretty and she's pregnant, right? So of course there are rumors about who the baby's daddy is. From Tommy Peterson to the male teachers and everyone in between. But I don't know. I think we'll be surprised when the truth comes out. Unless the truth got her killed precisely so that no one would ever know who he was."

Nicole's taken aback by this woman's bluntness, but on the other hand it's refreshing to have a straightforward conversation with someone at last. "Does your niece know what Aimee's relationship was like with my parents?"

Confused by the question, Mia says, "How's that relevant?" She waves the thought away. "I don't know about that. Anyway, I need to be somewhere. Say hi to your folks for me." She looks around for her boys. Before she leaves, she says, "You caught up with Kurt Butler yet?"

Nicole nods. "A little."

Mia grins. "Of course you have." And with that she walks away, out of sight.

Nicole buys a sandwich and a bottled water and finds a seat in the shade outside the store. As she eats, she checks her phone and sees a reply from Kurt.

That's not a good idea. Especially today.

She wonders why today's a bad day to visit Lori's parents.

Why?

She manages to drink half the bottled water and take another bite of her sandwich before he replies.

Because I think we've found Lori's remains.

Nicole chokes on her mouthful. She spits it onto the grass as a shudder runs through her entire body. She struggles to take a breath as she rereads his message. "Oh my God."

NINE

Nicole begs Kurt to tell her where he is. Where Lori's remains have been found. But he won't. He says he can't. That, because of his position, he must be discreet and, besides, nothing has been confirmed yet. She had ended the call feeling let down by him. She understands his position, but this is *Lori*. This is the most devastating thing to happen to both her and Kurt. They share that pain, so why can't he share what he knows?

She's drained of energy as she sits on the bus heading back to her parents' house. Not wanting to break down in public, she didn't know where else to go, and she thought her mother might know more about the situation from her dad. As the bus heads away from downtown it crosses Nicole's mind that if it *is* Lori's remains that have been found, and it was her father who killed her, he could become desperate to cover his tracks. His job and freedom are at stake and she's willing to bet he'd do anything to keep both. Maybe that includes silencing *her*.

She rubs her temples, trying to ignore the way her lungs are constricting, making her breath shallow. She can't have an anxiety attack. Not here. She wishes Lucas was here right now. He was affected by Lori's disappearance too. He wasn't as close to her as she and Kurt were—they had nothing in common—but he comforted Nicole afterward. She pulls out her phone and sends him a text, not knowing when he'll get a chance to read it.

Kurt says they've found human remains that might be Lori's. Will take time to confirm.

The bus feels airless as it rumbles past farmland. She stares out of the window without noticing anything. Her eyes are seeing her best friend instead. Her head fills with questions. Where was Lori all these years? Who put her there? What would even be left of her after all this time? Her skin crawls at the thought of it all. The last day of Lori's life was almost perfect. They had spent the whole afternoon being lazy. Sunbathing in Lucas's backyard before a trip to the library. After that is when things took a downward turn.

Nicole's brought back to the present when she spots three police cruisers parked on Jim Marsh's land. "No way." The bus passes by too fast. She stands, collects her things and heads to the front of the vehicle. "Can I get out here?"

The driver rolls her eyes in the rearview mirror. "Sorry. You'll have to wait for the next stop. If you get hit by something after I let you off early, it'll be me who suffers."

Nicole's not sure about that logic, but they're not far from the next stop so she doesn't argue. The minute the door opens, she jumps out and turns back the way the bus came. She has a five-minute walk along an overgrown verge, and the closer she gets to Jim Marsh's farm, the more questions she has. Kurt said the farm equipment was up for auction today. Someone must have been digging around the Marshes' belongings and found something. But what would Lori be doing here? This isn't anywhere near where Nicole parted from her the night she vanished.

When she arrives at the end of the driveway, fear stops her

from going any farther. From here she can tell that the three police vehicles are empty and a coroner's van is parked behind them. Movement makes her eyes shift to the right of the house. The sun reflects off something behind the silo before it disappears. Nerves make her stomach ache. She needs to find Kurt.

Keeping out of view, she walks along the dusty driveway, passing a tireless, rusting tractor as she heads toward the house. She shoots Kurt a text message.

I'm outside.

She notices that Lucas hasn't responded to her earlier message yet. She puts her phone on silent in case he calls, because she doesn't want her father to know she's here. Not yet.

It takes just seconds for Kurt to emerge from the house. "How did you know where we were?" he asks, clearly irritated.

"I spotted the cars as I went by on the bus."

"Your dad will never believe that. He'll think I told you. I could get fired." Kurt's face is pale and drawn.

A sudden gust of wind makes her aware of a terrible smell emanating from him. She can't put her finger on what it is, but it must be a flavor of what's inside that property. She takes a step back and wonders how he can bring himself to go in there. "I'm sorry," she says. "I just need to know what's going on."

He sighs and moves her behind his car. "There are human remains in the silo. Bones and a skull. They've likely been there years. The coroner will need to run checks before he can identify who they belong to."

She feels like she might vomit. It must be Lori. For a moment she's lost for words as she stares at the ground. "Are there any other missing people it could be?"

Kurt bats away a wasp. "I don't know yet. Certainly no one recent. Whoever's in there was likely a victim of Jim Marsh." He looks at her. "Listen, this is strictly between us, but there were some allegations made against Marsh years ago that would make him the most likely suspect."

She swallows. There were allegations made against her father too. But Kurt doesn't know about that. She looks at the silo. It's got to be twenty-five or thirty feet high, but it has an attached ladder running up the side of it. Only a fit person could carry a dead body up there. But Lori barely weighed anything. And Nicole knows her father wasn't always out of shape.

Voices come to them. Nicole watches as her father and a man she doesn't recognize emerge from behind the silo. "That's Gerry Smith, the coroner," says Kurt.

Gerry is tanned, with thick brown hair, probably in his mid-late thirties. He's wearing gray pants and a pale-blue shirt, open at the throat. His hands are gloved and Nicole would bet they're sweating under the latex. When her father spots her he shakes his head. "You shouldn't be here, Nicole." He glances at Kurt. "And you shouldn't have told her."

"He didn't," Nicole says. The sun is so bright she has to shield her eyes from it as she asks, "Is it Lori in there?"

Gerry speaks up. "We won't know that for some time, so it's best not to speculate. You wouldn't want to upset her parents for nothing now, would you?" His tone is patronizing.

She notices her father is also wearing latex gloves. He's holding an evidence bag but keeping it out of her view. Her mouth goes dry. In a small voice, she asks, "What's in there?"

Gerry and her father share a look. Kurt reaches for her hand. His is warm and clammy as it tightly grips hers. "What've you found, Sheriff?" he asks.

Ron glances at their entwined hands and manages to keep his feelings to himself. He takes a deep breath as he takes a minute to consider whether or not he should tell them. He turns to Gerry. "It would be the fastest way to give us an informal identification. A starting point."

"True," says Gerry. "I'd still have to run my other checks though, to be certain."

Nicole sways with dizziness. She worries she might pass out. "Please, Dad. You know what she meant to me."

He stares at her with curiosity in his eyes. Like he's trying to weigh whether she's acting. He knows she suspected him of Lori's murder back then. Is he wondering whether she saw him dispose of Lori's body? Whether she's testing his response?

With some reluctance, he holds the bag out for them to see. Nicole's eyes slowly lower to the contents. She gasps. The silver earrings she bought Lori for her birthday sit alongside the cheap necklace Kurt once gave her. They're covered in brown dirt. At least, she hopes it's dirt. Tears come fast and heavy. Kurt pulls her to him and she sobs into his chest, trying to ignore the awful smell on his shirt. He strokes the back of her head as he holds her up with his other arm, squeezing her tight.

"I'm sorry for your loss," says Gerry.

Her father remains silent. After a few seconds, she hears them both walk away.

With obvious emotion in his voice, Kurt whispers into her ear. "She can be laid to rest now, Nicole. So can our pasts."

TEN

SUMMER 2008

Lori looks over at Nicole, who is glistening on the old weathered sun lounger next to the inflatable swimming pool designed for kids. Apparently, Nicole's heard from somewhere that if you cover yourself with cooking oil, you get a better tan. And with the summer dance coming up, she wants to look good. It didn't sound like a great idea to Lori, especially because her acne is flaring up right now on her face and her back, so she's tanning without the oil. She figures she's greasy enough. She's also a little more self-conscious of her body than Nicole is, so she's not wearing a bikini.

Lucas appears from his house with Kurt behind him. They've just taken away the leftovers from the barbecue. Lucas can work a grill and, as a result, Lori ate more than she intended to. She pulls in her stomach and tries to lean in a way that makes her look slimmer.

"Here you go." Lucas hands both her and Nicole glasses filled to the top with iced water. The afternoon sun is so hot that the ice has already started melting.

"Thanks." Lori holds the cool liquid in her mouth for as

long as possible. Nicole does the same before leaning over and spraying some on her. Lori screws up her face. "Eww, gross!"

Nicole laughs. "You said you were too hot!"

"So what are we doing tonight?" Kurt asks.

He's topless, wearing just a pair of shorts. His feet are bare on the unkempt lawn. Lucas is just as naked. Of the two of them, Lori's more attracted to Kurt. She still can't believe he's her boyfriend and she can't shake the feeling she's a consolation prize for Kurt. That he had to date her because Lucas wanted to be with Nicole and the boys had come as a pair ever since they met in high school. But if Kurt's faking his affection for her, he's good at it. That doesn't mean they never argue. Not one for drama, Kurt tends to disappear when she's upset, but maybe that's due to his age. He still has some maturing to do.

"We have football practice for the charity event, remember?" says Lucas.

"Oh man." Kurt clearly doesn't want to go, which isn't a surprise as he doesn't enjoy playing football. "In this heat?"

"It'll be cooler by tonight."

The sound of something shattering makes them turn their attention to the house. Lucas rolls his eyes and none of them dare say anything. He's sensitive about his mom's drinking problem. Lori glances at Nicole and they exchange a discreet look.

Eventually Sindy Rivers appears in the doorway. She rarely ever looks or acts drunk, apart from mumbling to herself a lot, as if in conversation with someone. Lori's mom says Sindy's a functioning alcoholic. She drinks slowly throughout the day as opposed to bingeing. She manages to work at Talbot's Convenience Store with no problem, so she still has some kind of control over it.

"Lucas, honey?" she says. "I need some help."

He heads over to the house, his expression neutral.

"You girls having fun?" shouts Sindy with a smile.

"Yes, Mrs. Rivers," says Lori.

"Why don't you join us?" suggests Nicole.

Lori's alarmed by the suggestion. That would be weird. She watches for Sindy's reaction. The woman has a pale complexion. Maybe some sunshine would do her good.

"Maybe next time, sweetie. My show's on right now." Sindy disappears inside with Lucas behind her. Lori and the others listen to him sweep up glass in the kitchen. If he's having a conversation with his mother, they don't hear it.

"What happened to Lucas's dad?" asks Kurt. "No one ever told me and I don't want to ask him."

"He skipped town when Lucas was a kid," says Nicole. "Just before his twelfth birthday." She lowers her voice as she adds, "Sindy told me he got another woman pregnant and went to live with her, but she never told Lucas because she didn't want to break his heart. Lucas thinks he went away for work and just never came back."

Lori's shocked that his mom would keep that from him. "You should tell him the truth."

Nicole leans back in the lounger and looks thoughtful. "I've thought about it, but I don't want to upset him."

"He can handle it," says Kurt. "The dude's sixteen years old. He's not some little kid who's pining after his daddy anymore. He's probably already figured it out."

Lucas eventually returns with a beer in his hand and a grin on his face. "My reward."

Lori watches as he sits in the pool. Kurt gets in beside him and starts rolling a joint. If her mother knew she was around drugs and alcohol, she wouldn't be allowed anywhere near her friends. Luckily, Sindy would never tell her. She says all teenagers need their fun because once you turn eighteen, you're thrown out into the world and expected to have your shit together.

"So, if they've got football practice," says Nicole, "what are we doing tonight?" Before Lori can answer Nicole says, "Ooh, I know! If we went to the library this afternoon, we could look for that series you wanted. I need something new to read too."

Lori smiles. "Yeah, let's do that."

With a mocking laugh, Lucas says, "Wow, you girls lead such interesting lives."

"Shut up!" says Nicole, playfully kicking his shoulder. She gets up, her legs lean and shiny. "Can I use your bathroom?"

Lucas nods. "My mom's in the living room."

Nicole self-consciously pulls her denim shorts on over her bikini bottoms and slips her T-shirt over her head. Without putting her sandals on, she walks to the house. Kurt's eyes follow her. He doesn't know Lori is watching him. Lori wishes she wasn't jealous, but she can't help it. No one wants their boyfriend's eyes on another girl.

Kurt turns to Lucas and swings an arm around his neck, pulling him close. Their naked torsos touch as he gets him in a headlock. "That's not all for you, jerk." He pulls the beer from Lucas's hand and downs some.

Not for the first time, Lori wonders who Kurt really is. He doesn't fit in with Lucas's other friends, who are mostly jocks. He's not particularly sporty or studious, and he's dating an unattractive nerd. Every now and then Lori will notice that he seems uncomfortable around people, and she'll get the feeling he's putting on an act. Like around Lucas; he clearly likes his friend but he's not really into football and drinking. He does it to be near Lucas. And with her, he'll patiently listen to her talk about books, TV shows and assignments, but he isn't interested in any of that. She can tell. And he can't really be interested in her. Not when he could have any girl in school, and some of the guys if she thinks about it. It leaves her feeling as if a lot of his behavior is all an act.

She wishes he'd drop his guard and be himself. But then again, she knows all too well that being yourself is easier said than done at their age.

ELEVEN

SUMMER 2022

Kurt drives Nicole to her parents' house. Debbie isn't home when they arrive and Nicole asks him to stay awhile, until she can get her head around what's happened.

Kurt doesn't want to take the smell from the Marshes' farm inside with him, so he changes into the spare uniform he keeps in the trunk of his car and sprays his whole body with deodorant before entering. He finds Nicole in her old bedroom. It's smaller than he imagined. One wall is obscured by storage containers and boxes, and there's a double bed in the center of the room with an old oak nightstand next to it, covered in scratches and water rings.

Nicole is lying on the bed, sobbing. Unable to stand by and watch, he lies next to her and pulls her to him, feeling all the frustration and sadness leak out of her while he stares at the ceiling and tries to make sense of his own reaction to the discovery. He feels numb. Like it's happening to someone else. He suspects there will be no sleep for him tonight, and that's probably a blessing. He could do without a return of the nightmares he once suffered. They're bound to be even worse now he knows where Lori was all this time.

Once Nicole regains her composure, he considers heading back to work. Ron will either be wondering why he's taking so long or glad he's not around. It's difficult to say which. "Jim Marsh might have raped a teenage boy years ago," he says. "So it's highly likely that he killed Lori."

Nicole doesn't reply. The heat radiating from her body feels comforting.

He attempts to lighten the mood. "You know, I always wanted to see inside your bedroom, but Lucas and I weren't allowed. You remember? Your dad would have a fit if he saw me in here, either then or now."

She nods. Still silent.

"Think that's why your dad hates me?" he asks. "Because he knew I wanted to be with you?"

She leans back and looks up at him. Her eye makeup is smudged beyond a quick fix and her beautiful curls cover her forehead. He strokes them out of the way with the hand that isn't pinned underneath her. "What?" she says with a frown.

He feels himself redden. "You were my first real crush. I thought you knew. You must've caught me staring at you a million times."

Her expression is pained. "But what about Lori?"

"I miss her a lot, and we had a good time together back then, but..." He shrugs. "You can't help who you're attracted to."

"Lucas would've punched you if he knew," she jokes.

He smiles sadly. "He would've done a lot worse if he knew that he was my second crush."

Her eyes widen in surprise before she rests her head back on his chest. "It all makes sense now."

"What?" he asks.

"Why you would hang out with a guy who was more immature than you." She looks up at him again. "You said you spotted him here last year. Are you still attracted to him now?"

He laughs. "Probably not. I think when you're a teenager

you're attracted to everyone, you know? Proximity and hormones are a dangerous combination."

They fall into an easy silence. He would lie here all day if he could get away with it. After all, this is where he always wanted to be.

Eventually Nicole asks, "Have you heard from your online guy yet?"

"Yeah. He gave me the brush-off."

"No!" She sits up. "I'm sorry."

He swings his legs off the bed, his back to her. "It's probably for the best. I don't think the good citizens of Henderson could handle a bisexual deputy just yet."

He feels her warm hand on his back as she says, "You'll meet someone better."

His radio crackles into life. Deputy Hayes asks where he is. Kurt replies to say he's on his way back to the crime scene, then stands and turns to face her. "Your dad's probably on his way to break the news to Lori's parents. It wouldn't surprise me if they want to talk to one or both of us once it sinks in. They'll probably want to hear stories about how great she was."

Nicole nods. She's kneeling on the bed. "I'm fine with that. I have plenty of those stories."

Seeing her so vulnerable makes Kurt want to kiss her. Instinctively he leans in, takes her face in his hands and kisses her on the lips.

She pulls away. "Kurt." Her cheeks are flushed. "I'd be lying if I said I wasn't tempted. You're such a warm, kind person..."

"Don't forget sexy," he quips, trying to pretend he's okay with the upcoming rejection.

She offers a sympathetic smile. "I'm married. To your best friend from high school. Nothing can happen between us. I'm sorry if I gave you the wrong impression. It's just that I was upset, and you're probably the only person in this town who I feel safe around."

He's touched. "No, it's my fault. I'm sorry. I just always wanted to do that. It won't happen again." He wonders whether she'll tell her husband. Part of him hopes she does. "I hope Lucas is as faithful to you as you are to him."

She frowns. "Of course he is."

He battles with his conscience for a minute and decides she doesn't need to know Lucas was cheating on her back then.

Nicole gets off the bed and checks her phone. "I told him that remains were found but he hasn't responded yet. He must be in a training session." She looks at Kurt. "Be honest. Do you really believe Jim Marsh killed Lori?"

He's unsure. "I don't know. It makes sense, given the previous allegations."

She appears to wrestle with something before fixing her eyes on his. "What would you say if I told you—in confidence—that someone also made similar allegations about my dad back then?"

Kurt's stunned into silence. *Ron Chambers* accused of sexual assault? "While he was sheriff?"

"Right. A girl from school. Lori told me."

"What? How did she know?"

"I don't know, maybe she heard it through her parents. I don't have any details, except that it never went anywhere. I think my dad silenced the girl somehow, maybe with threats. I mean, he was the sheriff, right? There's no way she could win against him. So it all just went away."

So many questions run through Kurt's head. "Do you know the victim's name?"

She shakes her head. "Lori didn't know. I've tried to find more information over the years, but there's no record of it in any news articles from back then, and there are no other public allegations against him that I've found." She steps forward. "I don't know how it works, but is it possible for you to check the police database?"

He frowns, surprised she'd want to give these allegations any credence. "If I get caught searching for information on your dad, I'll be fired. But also, where are you going with this?"

Nicole walks to the door and pokes her head out, checking the hallway. The house should still be empty as he hasn't heard anyone return, but she closes the door anyway before turning to him. "You can't tell anyone this, but... I've always believed my father killed Lori."

His mouth drops open. "*What?*" Suddenly everything makes sense. Her rapid spiral into depression after Lori's disappearance, when she was pulled out of school and no one set eyes on her for months. There were so many rumors about her, but no one knew for sure what was going on, only Lucas. But he never told anyone. He just retreated into himself and stopped socializing. All Kurt knows is that Lucas was the only person allowed to visit her. Kurt had been angry he couldn't see her. "That's why your relationship with your parents broke down back then and why your father can barely look at you now. You accused him of killing her?"

She nods. "At the Marshes' property you said we could finally lay Lori to rest now she's been found, but that's not true. Her killer needs to answer for what he did."

"But we don't know for sure who that was." Kurt can see the intensity of her convictions on her face. "Nicole, we have no real evidence to prove it was a homicide, let alone who did it."

She's unfazed. "My father has no alibi for that night. He got home in the early hours of the next morning, before anyone knew Lori hadn't made it home. Later he said he was working, but when a reporter asked him for a timeline of his whereabouts he struggled to answer. He eventually said it was confidential."

"Maybe he was on a call-out that he didn't want to talk about. He could've been protecting the people involved."

"But it's not just that," she says. "He used to flirt with Lori. Just subtle things that boys wouldn't notice but that girls are sensitive to. He'd tell her she looked pretty. He'd talk to her mostly out of my earshot. He'd jump at the chance of giving her a ride home. Lori seemed awkward around him. I started noticing all this after she told me about the girl who made the allegations against him, which was close to the time Lori vanished." It all comes flooding out of her as she wipes back tears. "Kurt, I believe he raped her that night and then had to silence her, and I believe my mother knows about it. Maybe even helped him cover it up. I just need evidence. You're the only person who can help with that because you have access to whatever evidence was taken from the crime scene."

Kurt doesn't know what to say. The whole scenario is unthinkable.

Nicole takes a step forward. "You have access to the notes and statements from the investigation. If we find a link between my dad and Lori, we might be able to figure out what's happened to Aimee." Her eyes implore him. "You've got to help me find my sister and get justice for Lori. *Please.*"

Kurt tries to take it all in. Nicole's jumping to massive conclusions, and he's worried she'll start to spiral again. Being back here clearly isn't good for her, and just saying these things aloud is dangerous, especially in the sheriff's own house.

He runs his hands through his hair, unsure what to do for the best.

TWELVE

Nicole's emotionally drained after their conversation. Kurt left to return to the crime scene. Although it was inappropriate for him to kiss her, she felt a longing she hasn't experienced in a while. Maybe because she's only ever been with Lucas. She can't pretend she isn't curious about Kurt, but she would never cheat on her husband. He's been with her through so much darkness. Besides, Kurt is on the rebound from that guy he met online. He's in a strange place right now, exploring his sexuality while being tethered to the past due to this latest discovery and her own return to town. It feels like neither of them will ever be allowed to move on.

Kurt left the house with doubt in his eyes, as well as something else. Concern for her well-being. She's seen that in Lucas's eyes too, whenever she mentions her theory. The problem is that once you've suffered with depression, people don't take you seriously anymore. They think you're being paranoid or unreasonable due to the illness. But she didn't expect that from Kurt.

He was noncommittal about checking into the allegations made against her father and reading up on the investigation into

Lori's disappearance. She doesn't blame him. He could get in a
lot of trouble and she doesn't want him to risk his job. She had
hoped there was a way to do it that would be untraceable, but
his reaction suggests she's on her own when it comes to finding
proof to back up her theory.

Now she's had some time to think, something's bothering
her about the timing of Lori's remains being discovered. What
are the chances of it happening the day after she comes home
for the first time in twelve years? She considers whether her
father is messing with her. If he put Lori in that silo, he could be
showing his hand in order to mess with her mind. To show he's
still in control of everything that happens here. That he's in
control of her too. Did he enjoy watching her reaction to seeing
the earrings from the silo? Is he so messed up that he wanted to
see her in pain?

She tries to control her breathing, in order to steady her
nerves. It's exhausting being back and she's tempted to skip
town forever, without telling anyone. She would do it in a heartbeat if she knew Aimee and the baby were alive and well. But
with no one else seemingly alarmed about Aimee's disappearance, Nicole is all she has. She feels her fingernails digging into
her palms. She doesn't know whether she's capable of helping
her sister. All she can do is try.

As her mother still isn't home and her father could be tied
up at the Marshes' farm all day, she figures now would be a
good time to search Aimee's room. The door has remained shut
since Nicole arrived. She goes to it now. After hesitantly
swinging it open, she steps inside. The drapes are open, spilling
sunlight onto the bed and the oak vanity. A citrus scent washes
over her, from some kind of perfume. It's the opposite to what
Nicole likes in a perfume. It hits her then that this is the room of
a stranger. Nicole didn't know her sister past six years old. The
girl who lives in this room has just become an adult. She's about

to become a mother. She'll be nothing like the child Nicole remembers.

A sense of loss fills her. She missed out on Aimee's teenage years. She would have loved to have been around to impart wisdom about boyfriends and school and everything else Aimee went through during those years. All she can do is hope that she'll get an opportunity to be a part of Aimee's life once she's found.

A book of baby names sits on the nightstand, bringing home the fact that Nicole's going to be an aunt. There will be another member of the Chambers family at last. A sudden sob surprises her and her hand flies to her mouth. She can only pray that her niece or nephew hasn't already been taken from her before she even gets a chance to meet them.

She takes a seat on the bed as she's overwhelmed with the part of her life that she's kept compartmentalized. She has a sister. She has a small family. They should be one tight unit, looking out for each other and sharing family meals, holidays and memories. Instead, they're full of mistrust, deception and hatred. Despite everything, Nicole doesn't hate her parents, but she can sense that they hate her.

She understands why. Her accusation after Lori disappeared could have ruined her father. If it had got out, he would have been investigated. There's no way he would have been reelected as sheriff with that kind of rumor hanging over him. His reputation would have been in tatters and they could have faced financial ruin as a result. But she was only fifteen and impulsive, unable to control her emotions. She had no choice but to tell her parents what she suspected, because when she'd held it in, it had threatened to kill her. She had worried for her sanity and her safety.

So she did tell them. A few days after Lori's disappearance.

From what she can remember through her hazy recollection of

that time, they didn't react how she expected them to. There were no vehement denials or raised voices. Her parents had shared a long, lingering look and then her mother had burst into tears and left the room. Her father had poured himself a drink, probably whiskey, and collapsed into his armchair. Nicole needed more. She needed an angry denial. Instead, he seemed to concentrate on how to minimize the situation. Maybe he thought that if he upset her, she would tell other people. So his only response was something about how Nicole should go to bed before she got too upset.

It was then that her downward spiral began in earnest, because she genuinely believed she was living with a killer. She felt unsafe and confused, all the while grieving for her friend who, according to news reports, must have been brutally murdered in that park, just hours after Nicole angrily left her there alone.

THIRTEEN

Pushing those memories aside, Nicole thumbs through the book of baby names and finds herself wondering whether Aimee settled on a name or two. She finds her own favored baby names among the pages. Names she hasn't even told Lucas she's chosen. Grace for a girl and William, shortened to Billy, for a boy. Two children would be ideal, but she would happily keep going. If she ever gets the opportunity.

At the back of the book is a hidden flyer. Nicole pulls it out and sees it contains information about family planning and reproductive health care. The flyer is folded open at a section about adoption and abortion. Her heart sinks. At some point in her pregnancy, Aimee must have had conflicting emotions about whether or not to keep the baby. It's understandable given her age, but could it also suggest she was raped and desperate to get rid of her attacker's child? Nicole's hands start to shake. If that's the case, Aimee's attacker might also not want the baby around, in order to destroy evidence of what he did. Desperate to keep his identity a secret, he could have realized the best way to do that was to dispose of Aimee before the baby was born.

With it being so close to her delivery date, he was running out of time.

"Please, God, no," she whispers. Nicole takes a deep breath to try to calm her nerves. Her mind always runs away with her when she's anxious. She focuses on reading the section about what to do when you don't feel able to keep the baby. It would have been agonizing to consider abortion as an option. And only Aimee knows whether she regrets not having one. Maybe she left it too late to choose and is now terrified of what's to come. So terrified she didn't feel able to face it. Nicole feels dread rising in her chest. She doesn't want to consider the possibility that Aimee took her own life, but she has to be realistic.

She stuffs the flyer back in the book and puts it on the bed before opening the only drawer in her sister's nightstand. The drawer is filled with tissues, several used lip balms, indigestion tablets and two books. Both romances. Nicole smiles. She and Lori had loved reading too. So much that Nicole used to own a gold necklace with a beautiful book pendant on it, a gift from her parents. Her love of reading has helped her through some tough times and she doesn't know how she would have coped over the years without fictional worlds to escape into. But, unlike Aimee, Nicole never read romances. That was Lori's favorite genre. She flicks through the two books in case there are any hidden notes inside, but there aren't. Just a bookmark.

As she puts them back she finds something else at the back of the drawer. It's gift wrapped in silver paper. She pulls it out and sees the gift wrap has been opened. It contains a pretty hardback notebook with matching pen. A flick through reveals it's unused, but the front cover has two kisses, written as Xs, in the top corner, presumably from the person who bought it for her. The fact they didn't even add their name or a message suggests they don't want their handwriting on it. Because that could identify them should something happen to Aimee.

The thought worries Nicole, but it's difficult to tell whether she's reading too much into a simple gift. For now, she slips the notebook back in the drawer and closes it before looking around the rest of the room. A laptop sits on the dressing table, next to a big pile of academic textbooks. Her parents said Aimee didn't show up for her graduation, but it looks like she was planning to. A smart black maternity dress hangs from the closet door as if it was the next outfit she would wear. She's sorted through her schoolbooks, with some dumped in the small trash can next to the dressing table.

Nicole goes to the laptop and switches it on. Her father should already have checked it for any clues, but wouldn't it still be down at the sheriff's office if that were the case? Isn't this potential evidence? A prompt requests a password. Nicole tries a couple of obvious ones but they don't work. It makes her wonder whether her sister is on social media now. She's never received a friend request from her, but she isn't on social media much herself. She has accounts but doesn't check them very often. Getting friend requests from people she and Lori went to school with was too depressing. She remembers Kurt tried friending her a few years ago, but she had ignored it. She's more of an occasional lurker, only logging in when she wants to know something. She has searched for Aimee on Facebook in the past but didn't find anyone who matched her sister's details. That would be a few years ago now. Every time she's considered it since then she was put off by the guilt that comes with having left her sister behind. What she was most fearful of was Aimee rejecting her online before they had a chance to reunite in person. Before she had a chance to explain why she stayed away all these years.

People don't realize that being estranged from your family is mentally draining. You don't know how to respond when someone asks seemingly innocuous questions like: are you close with your siblings, what do your parents do for a living, are you going home for the holidays? You'd love to go home, but it's not that easy. There is so much you want to say to your parents, but to just turn up out of the blue after years away and try to get them to listen would be an impossible task, and because of that Nicole has always held off. She hasn't felt ready to reopen those old wounds.

She rubs her tired eyes and considers grabbing some coffee for a caffeine boost. A photograph on Aimee's bulletin board stops her in her tracks. The board is full of snapshots of Aimee and her friends over the years. She has an awkward smile in some, probably a result of the braces she's wearing. Then, as Aimee blossoms, her smile becomes vibrant and confident.

The feeling that Nicole's staring at a stranger, rather than her own sister, persists, but the resemblance is clear. The photo Nicole is most drawn to is the one she's also in. It's of the pair of them taken just before Nicole left Henderson. They're sitting on the couch next to each other, sharing a festive blanket over their knees. The drapes are closed and the soft glimmer of the two side lamps and the Christmas tree lights are evident. Nicole leans in to look at herself. She's only seventeen here but she looks exhausted and wary of the photographer. Aimee is six and resting her head on Nicole's arm. They've been snapped while watching TV.

Nicole remembers how she had bought her little sister a cute journal as a Christmas gift that year. It was the last present she ever bought her. It's unlikely Aimee still has it all these years later, but she might have kept it for nostalgic reasons. Nicole thinks of the brand-new notebook she found in the nightstand. Maybe the person who gave it to Aimee knew she likes documenting her day-to-day life. If she was in the habit of journaling, there could be filled notebooks in her room somewhere. They could reveal clues as to her state of mind and her relationship with their parents. They might even name the father of her baby.

At the large dresser, Nicole opens a drawer and comes face to face with a neat stash of baby clothes. It takes her breath away for a minute. The white woolen cardigans, clearly knitted with love, and tiny yellow rompers are lined up. Cute little booties that would fit only a newborn's feet sit ready for action. Nicole's hit with a pang of jealousy that she isn't pregnant herself. She wants a drawer filled with baby clothes. And she wants the baby to go with it.

She swallows back the lump in her throat. Pushing her feelings aside, she knows that this preparation suggests Aimee was looking forward to the baby's arrival, not running away from it like her father suggested. She didn't believe that anyway. There's no running away from labor when you're eight months pregnant. It's going to happen one way or another, whether you're embarrassed about it or not. But the abortion flyer suggests Aimee *did* consider other options at one point. Maybe she felt pressured by someone to keep the baby. Maybe they gave her all these baby clothes as a way of emotionally blackmailing her into accepting her fate.

Nicole turns, looking for a crib. There isn't one. Maybe that was the last item to be purchased. Some women are superstitious about buying too much in case it jinxes things. A thought occurs to her. Where are the letters she sent her sister over the years? Wouldn't Aimee have kept them? She has all of Aimee's replies before they stopped coming. The early letters are peppered with childish typos and they don't make too much sense, but they make her smile. Maybe her letters are hidden with Aimee's journal somewhere.

Nicole gets on her hands and knees to look under the bed because she doesn't think any teenage girl would keep her journal anywhere her parents could read it. There's nothing under there but shoeboxes; some empty, some with heels or sneakers inside. She lifts the heavy mattress next, one corner at a time, but there are no journals or diaries under there either.

Disappointment sweeps over her. It looks like Aimee never kept her letters or wrote in a journal. Unless she did, and someone has already taken them.

FOURTEEN

From the Journal of Aimee Chambers

December 25, 2010—Age 6

My name is Aimee. I am 6 years old. You are a gift from my big sister. She says I shud write in you evry night. 2day was the best crizmass ever. I got

2 dolls
choklit
a dress
a toy pony and stuf.

Mommy says I need to go to bed now coz I ate too much shuger. Night.

December 25, 2011—Age 7

Santa didn't bring Nicole back for cristmas. Daddy says what I got was better but it wasn't. I hate dolls. Tommy is sleeping

*in my room like he does evry year. His mommy and daddy are
2 sad 2 have cristmas. I gave him my chocalit.*

December 25, 2016—Age 12

*Christmas sucks. This journal sucks. Parents suck. I want to
run away and find my sister. She's stopped writing and I don't
know why. Tommy says he'll go with me, but I don't want him
to. He never leaves me alone. I don't know why I'm even
writing in this dumb journal.*

FIFTEEN

Nicole jolts awake in her parents' living room. The sun is lowering in the sky, casting shadows across the room. She must have fallen asleep watching the news. Reporters have been showing up at the Marshes' farm all afternoon, and they're rightly speculating that the bones belong to Lori.

She hears a noise behind the couch that makes her jump. She spins around.

Her mother, dressed in blue scrubs, hovers in the doorway having just arrived home from work. "Your dad told me the news," says Debbie with pity on her face. "He says Gerry's taken the remains to the morgue."

Not trusting her emotions, Nicole looks away. "How can you go to work when Aimee's missing?"

Debbie drops her purse and keys on the empty armchair. "What would you have me do? Your dad assures me there are no signs of foul play and he's doing everything he can to find her. I need my job, Nicole. I can't stay off indefinitely. And besides, I've spent most of my time calling around other hospitals to see if anyone matching Aimee's description has been admitted, like I do every day."

Surprised, Nicole says, "And?"

"There was one girl who came in after giving birth behind a dumpster, but it wasn't Aimee. The poor girl hid her whole pregnancy from her family."

Maybe she had to. Nicole mutes the news footage. "Did dad tell you it's definitely Lori in the silo? The earrings I bought her were in there. She was wearing them that night." She blinks back tears. *Lori must have been so lonely in the silo.* She knows it's a ridiculous thought. She was likely dead before she was even dropped inside the steel coffin. But the thought of her lying there all alone for fourteen years is devastating.

Her mother surprises her by taking a seat on the couch and gently touching her knee. "I'm sorry. Lori was a wonderful girl. I really wish this hadn't happened to her. I can't imagine what Theresa and Antony are going through right now." Her voice breaks.

Nicole looks at her mother closely. She's unsure whether to trust her display of grief. "You didn't say anything like this when she went missing. Why now?"

Debbie lowers her eyes. "I guess because it's official now. There was hope before. Hope that maybe she ran away after hurting herself..."

Nicole hopes she can hear how ridiculous that theory was.

"But she was just yards down the road this entire time. Jim Marsh killed her." Debbie leans in to hug Nicole. "If he hadn't done that, we would still have you in our lives. We've all suffered so much." She cries.

Seeing her mother this way triggers many emotions for Nicole. She's desperate to hug her back and forgive her for everything that's happened, but she's uncertain whether this is all an act. In the end, she gives in and hugs her mom. She wants to believe this is real. "I miss you all so much," says Nicole. "I can't even tell you." Her chest rocks with sobs.

Debbie rubs her back. "We miss you too. I know you won't believe it, but we do. Aimee especially."

Nicole pulls away and wipes her eyes with a tissue, unable to speak.

"Aimee's always had a large gaping hole in her life where her big sister should be," says Debbie. "She felt rejected by you and she couldn't understand it. I'm sorry to say it but the truth is, if she chose to run away, it was because of you."

The tender moment is over. Here comes the guilt trip. Not wanting to react, but having to be true to herself, Nicole quietly says, "I don't think she left of her own accord. She has baby clothes in her room. She was set to attend her graduation. I think something terrible has happened to her, Mom."

"You don't know that." Debbie stands, quickly composing herself. The shield is back up. It's unclear whether that's because she's unable to face the possibility her youngest daughter is dead, or because she knows what's happened to Aimee and can't let on. "No one had any reason to hurt her."

"Since when did anyone need a reason to kill?" Nicole realizes this is her best chance of getting her mother to come clean about her father's true nature, while they're alone and listening to each other. If her mother had anything to do with covering up Lori's death, or burying those sexual assault allegations, then Nicole needs to make her see she's protecting the wrong person. She stands before blurting out, "Is Dad the father of Aimee's baby?"

Debbie's reaction is immediate. She takes a step back with a look of disgust on her face. "How dare you come up with something so sordid!"

"Mom, listen to me. I know you're hiding something; I've always known! You're a bad liar, and it's time you picked your daughters over your husband. If you know anything about him that could help us bring Aimee and her baby home, you *have* to tell someone. You can't keep covering for him! You could be part

of your grandchild's life if you choose us over him." Her heart is
hammering against her chest for daring to speak so honestly.
"Please, Mom! Aimee and I need you more than ever right
now."

Her mother's speechless. Eventually she steps forward and
slaps Nicole hard across the face. It stings immediately. "You
need to leave this house for good. After that little outburst I
never want to see you again. You have ten minutes before I tell
your father what you just accused him of, so you better not be
around for that." She storms out of the living room.

Nicole is frozen to the spot, with her hand on her burning
cheek. Her mother has made her choice, and it's clear now that
there will be no changing her mind.

SIXTEEN

It's almost 8 p.m. by the time Nicole's cab drops her downtown. Most of the stores are getting ready to close and anyone she passes is either on their way home or out for dinner or drinks with friends. She enters Mackey's Saloon with her suitcase by her side and orders a beer. She probably shouldn't, given her emotional state, but one drink never hurt anyone. Her stomach rumbles. She considers ordering food too, but doesn't think she can stomach it just yet.

The bar is quiet inside, which is fine by her. She isn't capable of small talk after what's happened. Unfortunately, it doesn't take long before the aging bartender, not Lorraine this time, recognizes her. He's a friend of her father's. Not what she needs right now.

"I hear your dad's had a terrible day," he says. "Out at Jim Marsh's farm."

She pays for the drink and takes a sip of the beer. It's deliciously cool. "Uh-huh."

"I always knew there was something wrong with Jim," he says. "His wife was a prisoner in that house if you ask me. I'm pretty sure that if she had a say in anything, she wouldn't have let the farm deteriorate around them like it did. She probably wanted her kids around her as she died. But Jim held a misguided grudge against Brad and Bernadette, and all because they didn't want to take over the farm and follow in his footsteps." He shakes his head. When Nicole doesn't reply he continues. "I feel for Ron. He takes his job seriously, protecting this community and all. Finding a child's remains out there will weigh heavy on him."

Nicole scoffs.

The old man takes offense at her reaction. "What's that supposed to mean? Have you fallen out with your folks again or something?"

Nicole stares at him. "Listen, I just came here for a quiet drink." She grabs the handle of her suitcase and turns away, but not before the bartender gives his ten cents worth.

"Your folks are good people, young lady. Stop causing them problems."

"Amen to that," says Lorraine, appearing behind the bar. "You and your sister have put them through so much."

Nicole turns back to face them. "And what about what they've put us through?" she spits. The temptation to tell them about the sexual assault allegation against her father is almost overwhelming. *Almost.* Instead, she heads to the table she shared with Kurt last night and takes a seat. She rummages in her purse and pulls out her phone so she can book a hotel for tonight. She has no notifications. She can't understand why Lucas hasn't returned her calls, unless cell service is bad where he is.

"Hi." A woman appears in front of her. She's tall and slim with long red hair, probably in her late thirties. "I'm Jennifer Manvers." She slides a card across the table. It says she's a journalist for the local newspaper.

Nicole eyes her warily. "What do you want?"

"I couldn't help overhearing that you're the daughter of

Sheriff Chambers, and I've been at the Marshes' farm all after-noon. I know a little about the disappearance of Lori Peterson and I'd like to cover it in more detail for the newspaper I work for." She talks fast, probably because she's used to people walking away the minute they learn she's a journalist. "I've also recently learned your sister is considered missing, although no one will confirm it on record. Would you be willing to talk to me?"

Ordinarily, Nicole wouldn't give any journalist information, but things are so bad now that she's considering whether this is the only way to find Aimee. "What do you want to know?"

Jennifer's face lights up. She takes a seat next to Nicole and pulls her phone out of her pocket, to record their conversation.

"Sorry, it has to be off the record," Nicole says. "This is my family we're talking about. I mean, things are already bad between us, but this would take it to a whole new level."

The journalist hides her disappointment. "I understand." She opens her battered leather purse and pulls out a pen and legal pad. "My memory's not great, so do you mind if I take a few notes? You'll still be an anonymous source."

"I guess."

As she's about to grill Nicole, Lorraine approaches them, oozing hostility. "Nope. No press in here. Not if you're talking to the sheriff's daughter."

"Lorraine," says Jennifer. They clearly know each other. "I'm just doing my job. Don't you want Aimee Chambers found? The girl's pregnant for God's sake."

Lorraine rests her hands on her hips. "Of course I do, but I don't see how you two swapping salacious rumors will help that happen. The sheriff is dealing with it. That's all you need to know. We don't need more press turning up in their droves, rehashing the past and drawing baseless comparisons."

Nicole can't believe what she's hearing. Is the whole town covering for her father now? She downs most of her drink before saying to Jennifer, "Come on. We'll go somewhere else. They can't stop us talking to each other."

Jennifer collects her things and follows her to the door.

"Nicole!" shouts Lorraine behind them. "You only get one family in this life. Think about what talking to the press will do to your folks. Aimee will come home when she's good and ready."

Nicole clenches her jaw as she continues out of the bar. She won't be shamed into keeping her father's secrets.

Outside, Jennifer leads her to a red Ford. "We can talk at my place. It's evident you need to be protected from the locals."

Nicole stops in her tracks. "I don't know if I should." She's having second thoughts. "Lorraine will tell my dad I was talking to you. There goes my anonymity."

Slamming the driver's door shut, Jennifer approaches the sidewalk with a sympathetic look. "It was always going to be pretty obvious who spoke to me anyway. So why not make it on the record and screw the lot of them?" She has a wicked glint in her eye. "Do you owe these people anything?"

With a deep breath, Nicole says, "I don't bear any resentment toward them. They've been friends with my parents for years. He's their sheriff. I just..." She doesn't know how to articulate her feelings, and she's exhausted. "I don't know. I just want my sister home."

"Okay, how about this," says Jennifer. "Instead of going into any family drama, just tell me the basic facts around Aimee's disappearance. It will help me get the ball rolling with my article and I can at least get it out there that she's missing, so that more people are looking for her, right?"

Nicole considers it. "That would probably help. We need sightings of her."

"Exactly. And as for the remains found in the silo, I imagine that's a distressing discovery for you and I don't want to upset you further. I know how best friends at that age can mean everything to each other, so I don't want to open old wounds."

Nicole decides to go for it. She gets into Jennifer's car and they remain parked as she reels off what little information she's discovered about Aimee's disappearance so far: the date she was last seen, the nonattendance at graduation, the fact she's almost ready to give birth. Nicole tells the woman she's worried her father isn't taking it seriously and might not be doing enough to find her. How there are no missing person posters up around town and no press conferences being held. She also mentions he didn't appear to take Lori's disappearance seriously either, but after an internal battle, she's careful not to let slip that she thinks her father was involved in that. When it comes down to it, she just can't bring herself to betray him.

Maybe because she's hanging on to the hope that she's been wrong about him all this time. She would love nothing more than to be proven wrong. But for that to happen, she needs to find Aimee alive.

SEVENTEEN

Nicole wakes to someone knocking on the door of her hotel room. She grabs for her phone to check the time. It's only a little after 6 a.m. She swallows but her mouth is dry. Has something happened? No one but Lucas and Jennifer know she's here. She messaged Lucas last night before she fell asleep, and Jennifer gave her a ride here when Nicole told her she needed somewhere to stay.

Pulling her T-shirt low—she had forgotten to pack pajamas—she goes to the door and peers through the spyhole. Her husband's handsome face stares back at her. "Nicole, it's me," he whispers.

She's in a budget hotel on the outskirts of Henderson, only one step up from a highway motel. The room is small and beige, with a dark carpet to hide stains and a bed whose mattress is so lumpy it must be twenty years old. But the shower is hot and she can't hear the neighbors either side of her through the walls.

She unlocks the door and pulls it open with a wide smile. "You don't know how relieved I am to see you."

Lucas enters. He dumps a brown leather duffel bag on the floor and closes the door. "I've missed you too." He pulls her in and leans down to kiss her all over her face. At six feet tall, compared to her five-six, her neck has adapted to the height difference over the years, but when they first got together and would spend all their time making out, she used to get a terrible neckache. She runs her hands through his thick brown hair.

When he pulls away and looks down at her he says, "I'm sorry about Lori. How are you holding up?"

She lowers her eyes and hopes he doesn't notice all the candy wrappers in the trash. "I don't know. I'm distracting myself as best I can."

He gently moves her backward to the bed. "That's something I can definitely help you with."

"Wait!" she says. "How come you're here? What about your conference?"

"I told them my sister-in-law was missing. They understood. After I heard Lori's remains were found, I was worried about you." He kisses her forehead. "I'm sorry. I should've come with you from the beginning."

Relief at having him here washes over her. Lucas has always been able to help her relax. He's levelheaded and he helps her see both sides of an argument. "You're here now. And for that, I love you."

"Oh yeah?" he says with a devilish grin. "Want to show me how much?"

She laughs as they undress. The same thought as usual goes through her head as they fool around. *Maybe this will be the moment we conceive.* But this time she feels guilty for thinking it. What if Aimee and her baby are lying dead in a ditch somewhere and then *she* gets pregnant? She'll never be able to celebrate her child's birthday without remembering what was happening around the time she conceived. They should wait. She should go back on birth control until Aimee's found.

Another thought that plagues her when thinking about having children is about her parents. What if they want to see their grandchild and be a part of their life? Does she have to allow them to visit? Last year she read an article about some grandparents who sued for visitation rights. They won. Even though they both had convictions for various things, and their son was estranged from them, they were allowed to visit their grandchild with a neutral third party present. That had filled her with dread. It almost put her off trying for a baby.

"I love you." Lucas gets her attention.

She realizes she just daydreamed her way through sex. "I love you too."

He kisses her before moving over to his side of the bed and they lie next to each other as their breathing evens out. Nicole updates him on everything that's happened since she arrived in town. Lucas squeezes her hand when she needs it and listens carefully. The only part she leaves out is Kurt's kiss and the revelations about how Kurt had a crush on them both when they were younger. It's not that she thinks Lucas would react badly, but she doesn't want any awkwardness between him and Kurt while he's here. They all need to focus on finding Aimee.

"I've been thinking about who could be the father of Aimee's baby ever since you told me she was pregnant," says Lucas. "My bet would be Tommy Peterson."

It's not impossible, but Nicole can only picture Tommy as Lori's cute little brother. "Did you ever bump into him on your visits to see your mom?"

"Only once. Last year. He was at a fast-food restaurant with Aimee, so I couldn't talk to him."

Lucas stays away from Nicole's family when he visits his mom. He and Nicole don't know if Aimee would even recognize him, considering how young she was when they left town together, but he avoids her parents too. It's just easier. Her parents always liked Lucas, and they must know he returns regularly, but they've never sought him out to ask how she's doing. That was enough to confirm Nicole's suspicions that they didn't care how she was doing. That they didn't miss her or want her back in their lives.

"Kurt says my dad has the same suspicion about Tommy," she says. "Apparently he's already questioned him informally. But is that because he wants to pin her disappearance on someone else? I guess Tommy makes a good suspect. He has a drug problem now, according to Kurt."

"Doesn't surprise me. The poor guy lost his sister then had to grow up in her shadow." Lucas leans on his elbow and looks at her. "You'll never get past this issue with your folks until you know for sure what happened to Lori. I don't want you dragging this around with you for the rest of your life."

"Which is partly why I'm still in town," she says.

"Can't Kurt look into the evidence taken from Lori's crime scene?" he asks. "There must be something that can either clear your dad or point to him being involved?"

She scoffs. "If there was any evidence to suggest he was involved, he would've disposed of it years ago. He has that power, remember? I did ask Kurt to run a check on my dad, to see if those sexual assault allegations were ever made formal. I don't know if he's done it yet. He didn't seem keen, in case it gets him in trouble."

"I'd like to see Kurt again," says Lucas. "We should grab a beer. Catch up. It's been a long time." He pulls one of her curls gently and watches it bounce back into place. "I wonder if he's out of the closet yet."

Nicole's eyes widen. "What?"

"Kurt. He wanted me back then. I could tell."

"You *knew*?" she says, sitting up.

"You didn't?" He laughs. "All that play fighting was a dead giveaway. He never tried anything, but I kind of thought he was into me. I mean how could he not be, right?" He winks.

With a smile she says, "You weren't ever curious or tempted to explore with him?"

"Nah. Not my thing. Besides, I had you to explore with." He kisses her cheek. "He was cool though. He always had access to good pot."

She groans. She has whole chunks of time missing thanks to Kurt's pot. As a result, she hasn't touched the stuff since. "What about Lori? Were you ever attracted to her?"

He shakes his head. "No. Not my type. At least she never knew her boyfriend was gay. She would've taken it personally. She was sensitive like that."

"He's bisexual. Even had a thing for me once apparently."

"What?" Lucas looks surprised. "Did he ever try anything?"

"Of course not. I had no idea. I actually feel sorry for him."

"Why?"

"Because he's waited until now to explore that part of his sexuality," she says. "It can't be easy living somewhere like this where everyone knows him and his father. He doesn't have the freedom to date guys without everyone gossiping about it. He's hidden that side of himself for so long that it probably feels like it's too late to live the life he wants to live."

Lucas scoffs. "There's nothing to stop him from moving away. We did."

"His dad's sick. Brian's had to give up work, so it must be bad."

Lucas doesn't seem annoyed at his former friend for once having the hots for his wife. "My mom loves Kurt," he says. "Whenever I visit, she talks about how he checks in on her occasionally. She always says he'd make a better sheriff than your dad."

Nicole gets a flashback of a conversation she'd forgotten. "That reminds me... Sindy once told me that my dad was an asshole. She's one of the few people in town not under his spell. Did he ever arrest her for anything?"

Lucas's expression turns serious. "Maybe. She didn't tell me if he did, but it wouldn't surprise me if she was caught shoplifting. I've seen her do it myself."

Nicole feels for him. She knows he's embarrassed by his mother. "Let's visit her today. I haven't seen her in twelve years —not in person anyway." She's joined the occasional video call with them, but she hasn't been to Sindy's home since she left Henderson.

He glances at her. "Really? What if she upsets you? She has no filter anymore. Says exactly what she thinks."

Nicole raises her eyebrows. "Did she ever filter her thoughts?"

"No. I guess not." He slips off the bed. "I need a shower."

She hears the hot water splash into life and rests her head back against the pillow. It's a relief to have Lucas around. She needs him to keep her sane.

EIGHTEEN

At 9 a.m. sharp, Kurt pulls up outside the home of Theresa and Antony Peterson. Apparently, Theresa had been too distraught to take in the news after yesterday's discovery, so Sheriff Chambers is paying them another visit to answer any questions they might have. His car is already outside and the front door of the house is ajar. Ron invited Kurt to join him as he thought it would be good for the couple to have a friendly face on hand as he plans to discuss in more detail what they found at the Marshes' farm. Although Kurt sees the Petersons around town occasionally, he hasn't had a proper conversation with them in years.

Kurt exits his vehicle and inhales the morning air to ready himself for what's to come. There isn't a cloud in the sky and it occurs to him today would be a good day to go fishing. To get far away from this house and the grief inside it. Instead, he braces himself as he climbs the porch steps and enters the home without knocking.

He hasn't been inside since Lori vanished, but the house smells how she used to. Maybe it's the laundry detergent they use, or a favorite scented air freshener, he doesn't know, but the familiar smell evokes a lot of memories. He stops in the narrow hallway. His eyes climb the stairs. He used to wait in this exact position for Lori to get ready. She would either be getting changed, collecting her homework, dropping something off or just taking her sweet time while he waited here, bored out of his mind. He smiles at the thought.

He was never allowed upstairs, not even to use the bathroom. He had to use the one downstairs instead. Theresa would always watch him closely in case he tried to follow Lori upstairs, which he never did. She wasn't unfriendly at all, and she did approve of Kurt dating her daughter, but she was suspicious and rightly so. She might have spent way too much time glued to the news channels back then, but she wasn't paranoid. Many young females are hurt by those they trust, so she was just making sure she'd entrusted her daughter to the right boy. And he would bet Theresa has spent every day since Lori's disappearance wishing she'd watched the other men in her life closer than she'd watched him.

Kurt can't tear his eyes away from the bright landing upstairs. He finds himself wondering whether they left Lori's bedroom exactly as it was when she was alive. The thought fills him with dread. He hopes not. He hopes they've been able to move on in some small way.

He hears voices in the kitchen and wanders through to the rear of the house. Theresa and Antony both stare at him as he enters. They're sitting at the small kitchen table with Sheriff Chambers. An empty seat awaits him opposite Antony. The two men's knees almost touch when Kurt sits. "I let myself in. I hope you don't mind."

"That's why we left the door ajar," says Antony. His face is lined with sadness. Theresa's eyes are red. A box of tissues is the only item on the table. The room is as clean as a professional kitchen. Every surface is wiped, there are no utensils on display, no magnets or photographs on the fridge. A potted plant on the windowsill has perfect upright flowers, all facing the right way. He glances at the floor. Not one crumb or dirty streak.

Ron looks at him and the strain in the sheriff's face is evident. "I was just explaining how the remains got to be found."

"Please don't call them that," says Theresa, gripping a tissue to her mouth. "They're what's left of my daughter."

Ron must have explained how the coroner believes the bones match that of someone Lori's age, and about the identifying jewelry found with them. Kurt can't help but see Lori in her mother's face. With her black hair and green eyes Lori resembled her mother more than her father in many ways, but the scarring on Antony's skin shows signs of the teenage acne he once suffered from, just like Lori. Bile stings the back of Kurt's throat. He'd give anything for a glass of water right now. Or a bottle of Scotch.

"My apologies." Ron clears his throat. "Sometimes we forget we're using police talk." He inhales deeply before continuing. "Gerry will provide a full report in due time, which will list the findings of his examination of her rem—" He stops himself. "Of Lori. But I want to brief you first about what he found. The back of your daughter's skull shows a clear depressed fracture, which, in Gerry's opinion, occurred due to some form of blunt force trauma."

Theresa closes her eyes.

"Which means we're almost certain your daughter was murdered. We believe Lori was struck on the head from behind, meaning she may not have seen her attacker coming. The injury would account for the blood found in the park the day after she vanished."

"Couldn't she have fallen and hurt herself?" asks Theresa with hope. "Landed on a rock?"

Ron shakes his head. "If that were the case, we would have found her body there."

Kurt lowers his eyes. It wasn't a stupid question, it's just that Theresa's clutching at straws to make the news more bearable.

Antony rubs her back. "So who did it?" he asks.

"Well," says Ron, "given where she was found it was likely Jim Marsh, but we'll have to scour his property for evidence. The demolition and auction have been canceled in preparation for a full search."

The couple share a look. Kurt knows it's highly likely Jim Marsh was never on their personal suspect list. As far as he knows they weren't friends with the guy. He doesn't remember Lori ever mentioning him.

Ron adds, "Try not to get your hopes up about getting all the answers you need. It's been fourteen years and the man's dead. If he were still alive, I'd be doing my best to secure a confession."

"If he were still alive, I'd kill him myself," says Antony, his jaw tight. "Maybe Brad and Bernadette knew their father was a killer. Maybe I need to go speak to them to get the answers I need."

"Now, now. Let's not start thinking about revenge or confrontation." Ron's using his soothing voice. Kurt hates it. It comes off as patronizing to him. "You can't blame the children for what their father may or may not have done."

"What if it was Brad who did it?" says Theresa, her eyes lighting up. "How old was he in the summer of 2008? Did you ever question him? Come to think of it, did you ever question Jim? Was he ever a suspect?"

Ron's losing control of the conversation. "Brad was forty-five when Lori was killed. He wasn't living here; he'd already moved away by then. And Jim was never a suspect in this case. You have to remember there was no evidence to lead us to any suspects."

Antony sighs heavily. Theresa wipes her eyes before looking at Kurt. "How did you react to Lori being found?"

Kurt swallows as he struggles to find the right words in order to remain professional. When he realizes it's impossible, he says, "I'll be honest with you both, I got a little drunk last night." Ron tenses beside him. "I had to. I thought it would be the only chance I'd have of halting the flashbacks and falling asleep, but of course it didn't work. It just made things worse." He shakes his head. "Yesterday felt unreal. To think that someone in our town was depraved enough to have chosen a silo as her final resting place... It's barbaric. I mean, who in their right mind had the nerve to walk among us, acting normal, after doing something so terrible?"

Ron's eyes are fixed on him, conveying annoyance that he didn't remain controlled, but Lori's parents are nodding. It's clear they appreciate his honesty. There's sympathy in their eyes for him, which is crazy if you think about it.

Theresa says, "We missed you all afterward."

"You did?" says Kurt.

"Sure. Before, there was always someone knocking on the door or calling the house; either you or Nicole. Not so much Lucas. The house already felt empty once Lori vanished." Her voice hitches, so she takes a second to regain her composure. "And then to not have any of you around either, that made it even harder. I had less mouths to feed. I had to stop buying the snacks you all liked."

Kurt lowers his eyes. "I'm sorry. I guess I didn't know how to handle the situation. It never occurred to me that you'd want to see me without Lori. I wish I'd known actually. I could've done with some help myself. My mom..."

She leans over and squeezes his hands. "I know, you don't have a mom, and now your dad has cancer. I'm sorry. And I can tell that you miss Lori. I see it in your eyes."

Ron shifts position in his seat. "How did Tommy handle her disappearance?" he asks.

"Tommy was never the same boy afterward," says Antony.

"At first, he just wouldn't stop asking when she was coming home. I'm ashamed to say we let him stay with friends far more often than we should have. Just for some reprieve from all the questions. It felt like we were lying to him by giving him false hope because we didn't want to tell him she wasn't coming home. You had him every Christmas for the first four years, remember?"

Ron nods.

Kurt didn't know that.

"He's a good boy," says Theresa. "I know you think he's trouble now, Sheriff, but he's not. He works hard and he loves your daughter so much. He's protective of her."

Kurt glances at Ron to see how that goes down because she's talking about Aimee. Ron's expression is guarded.

"Tommy's making your grandchild a crib," she adds. "Did you know that?"

Ron shakes his head. It's clear he doesn't want Tommy mentioned in the same sentence as his missing daughter because he steers the conversation back to Lori. "How did he take yesterday's news?"

"We haven't seen him in a couple of days." Theresa sniffs before wiping her nose. "That's not unusual. He doesn't live with us anymore. He has his own life to lead. When he didn't answer his phone, I had no choice but to text him the news. He replied to say he'd seen it on TV and he'll come to visit us soon. I guess he'll deal with it in his own way."

Tommy's nineteen but she talks about him like he's still a child.

She takes a deep breath as she leans back. "Talking about all this brings back the anxiety and confusion from that time. Our friends and neighbors, they were afraid of our grief. A lot of them stayed away. Maybe they thought whoever took Lori would take their children too. It was very isolating. You know, I didn't appreciate how much pain a person can go through and still be able to function. The pain becomes an internal battle, especially when you're supposed to be at the stage where your boss is asking when you'll return to work, and your doctor is telling you it's time to lay off the strong antidepressants now or you'll become reliant on them." She scoffs. "I'm still on them now, all these years later. Yet I never touched one before she vanished. Never needed them."

A silence falls over them. All three males present know there's nothing that can be said in that moment to make her feel better.

Suddenly she asks, "Where's the rest of my daughter?"

Ron squirms. "Sorry?"

"Well, you said you found some bones and her skull, but what about her hair and teeth? Her finger and toenails? I want to bury all of her together."

Ron clears his throat and glances at Antony as if looking for help, but Lori's father appears to want to know the answer too. Finally, he says, "Theresa, you have to understand, it's been fourteen years. The body... It breaks down."

"But hair is already dead. And teeth wouldn't rot that fast, would they?" she says. "And what about her clothes? Are there any remnants left? I want it all. It all has to be in her casket. As much as possible." Her eyes reveal her mind is clutching at more straws.

Kurt's uncomfortable witnessing this. He wants to discreetly walk away and erase this whole encounter from his memory, but he can't. He sits silently while Ron struggles to come up with a credible answer.

Eventually the sheriff says, "Theresa, I can assure you that whatever we find of your daughter will be made available to your chosen funeral home just as soon as the investigation is over."

It's a diplomatic answer, and Theresa appears to accept it. She pats Ron's hand. "Thank you. I guess I need to put all my energy into organizing a wonderful funeral for her now. At least I get that opportunity." Despite the smile on her face, her voice falters. "So many parents don't."

Kurt chokes up. He leaves his seat and heads outside as fast as possible.

NINETEEN

The morning is already heating up as Lucas and Nicole drive to Lucas's childhood home. They stop on the way for gas, and Nicole goes inside to grab a bottle of water. She spots the local newspaper on a stand by the door and is greeted with a color photograph of Aimee's face staring back at her. It almost fills the whole page and Nicole finds herself wondering how Aimee would feel about being front-page news. If she's vanished of her own accord, it might be enough to bring her back to reality and make her call home.

Nicole grabs a copy of the paper and her eyes race to read the brief article.

Pregnant Woman Missing Feared Abducted

By Jennifer Manvers

Local sheriff's daughter Aimee Chambers, 18, hasn't been seen since the morning she was due to attend her graduation ceremony at Henderson High School on July 7.

Her mother, Debbie Chambers, was the last person to see her. Aimee was eating breakfast at the family home when her mother left the house for work at 8 a.m. Despite there being no signs of a struggle or forced entry at the house, Aimee has not been seen since. She is eight months pregnant with her first child, making it imperative that she is found soon.

Ron and Debbie Chambers have stated the sheriff's office is doing everything it can to locate their daughter. It is understood that no arrests have been made and there is no evidence of foul play. Her bank card hasn't been used since her disappearance and it's believed she's in possession of her cell phone and purse, although her cell phone appears to be disconnected.

Anyone who might have seen Aimee in the time since her disappearance should contact the Oates County Sheriff's Office immediately. All potential sightings will be taken seriously.

It should be noted that the human remains found at the farm belonging to Jim Marsh yesterday are not currently thought to be connected to Aimee's disappearance.

Nicole swallows. Nothing in the article points to her as the source of Jennifer's information, except maybe the part about Debbie being the last person to see Aimee and where that was. Nicole chews her lip but then decides not to care what her parents think. They should be speaking to as many journalists and reporters as possible in order to get Aimee's name and image out there. They should be stopping at nothing to find her.

A tap on her shoulder makes her turn.

Sandra Beaumont, her parents' nearest neighbor, offers a warm smile. She's holding her purse and some canned goods to her chest. "Hey, sweetie. How are you?" With her spare arm Sandra pulls her in for a hug. The older woman is frail now.

"I'm good, Mrs. Beaumont. How are you?"

"Oh, I can't complain. Jack and I still have most of our faculties and we're moving to a small apartment on my daughter's property soon. A granny annex they call it."

Nicole laughs. The warmth radiating from her former neighbor makes her realize she misses the woman. "I bet you'll both be well taken care of. Have you sold the farm then?"

"Sure did. It's time for a younger family to make their mark. I'm ready for retiring my weary bones." Sandra's eyes sweep over Nicole. "You look so well. What are you doing these days?"

"I work at an animal shelter, so I basically get to cuddle furry things all day. I'm married to Lucas. You remember him, right?"

"Sure." Sandra takes a quick glance around before gesturing to the paper. "Any word on Aimee yet? I can't sleep at night for worry about her and that little baby she's carrying." The concern on her face is genuine.

Nicole's reminded that there are some good people in Henderson. People who are pleased when they hear she's doing well. She misses people like this. The kind of people who would do anything for their neighbors. "No word yet. We still don't know what happened. Did my dad's team canvas the area after she vanished?"

"Oh, sure. Jack and I had a visit from Deputies Hayes and Moore," says the older woman. "They checked our entire property to see if she was hiding anywhere. Or maybe if her body had been... you know."

Nicole nods.

When Lucas walks in Sandra gives him a hug. "Lucas Rivers. You always were a big, strong boy, but look at you now!" Lucas has managed to retain his footballer's physique.

He laughs. "Hey, Mrs. B. Glad to see you're keeping well."

"Are you on your way to visit your mother?"

"Sure am."

"Good boy. Send her my regards." Sandra leaves, and Lucas pays for the gas and bottled water. He and Nicole climb into his car and make the short journey to Sindy's house. They have to pass the park and children's playground where Lori was murdered on their way. Nicole closes her eyes at that point and takes a deep breath. She says a silent prayer for her friend. Lucas rests a hand on her thigh.

Sindy doesn't greet them at the house, so Lucas lets himself in. "Hey, Mom. It's just us," he calls.

Nicole tentatively steps into the hallway. The house is dark inside, like always. Sindy keeps a lot of the drapes closed as her eyes are sensitive to sunlight. She follows Lucas into the living room which is warm and stifling. Untidy too. When he moves out of the way, after kissing his mother on the forehead, she sees Sindy. She's sitting in her favorite armchair with the TV remote in one hand. She doesn't mute the volume, but Sindy's face lights up when she looks at Nicole. "Hey, stranger."

Nicole smiles and steps forward to hug her mother-in-law. The older woman is skinny but not exactly frail. She's only fifty-five and still works a physical job at Talbot's Convenience Store stacking shelves and serving customers. But she does have that telltale bag-of-bones look about her that suggests nutrition isn't something she concerns herself with.

Nicole's surprised the convenience store is still open in today's tough economic times. The owner, Gil Talbot, must be in his late eighties by now. He's one of those people who has always looked old. Lucas recently told her how Gil barely turns a profit these days and can only afford to employ two staff: Sindy and some teenage kid who only shows up when he's got nothing better to do. Gil watches the store whenever they can't. The decaying building is slap bang in the middle of two car dealerships and Nicole understands both owners have tried to buy the land from Mr. Talbot. He's always rebuffed any offers to sell. Nicole suspects he's the only person in town willing to employ her mother-in-law in her current state.

"How is it being back?" asks Sindy.

"Weird. I've been pleasantly surprised in some ways, but I wasn't expecting Lori to be found. It's a lot to deal with."

Lucas heads to the kitchen. "I'll make coffee."

"I brought home some of those cakes Nicole likes," his mom shouts after him. "Bring them with you." She winks at Nicole. "They were half off."

Nicole smiles. "Thanks." A headache is forming behind her eyes. Sugar and caffeine might help ease it as she hasn't been drinking her normal amount of coffee since she arrived in town.

"Lucas is a good boy," says Sindy. "The complete opposite of his father. Wayne never helped around the house or showed me any affection. I can't tell you how many times he claimed he was working late when really he was screwing around. That piece of shit was a walking cliché."

Not knowing what to say to that, Nicole changes the subject. "What are you watching?"

Sindy waves a dismissive hand. "I don't know, just some crap. I keep it on for the company more than anything. There's nothing so depressing as a silent, empty house."

Nicole's overridden with guilt for not visiting more often. She'll have to make sure she comes with Lucas from now on. "Is there anything we can do for you while we're here? Mow your lawn, wash the dishes, fix something... take you out somewhere?"

"That's sweet of you to ask, but I have a kid who takes care of the lawn and odd jobs. He reminds me of Lucas at that age. Speaking of which, how's operation pregnancy going? Lucas told me you've been trying." The woman's eyes move to Nicole's stomach. "If you're having problems, it's probably time you saw someone about it. Don't leave it too long."

"It'll happen soon enough."

Nodding, Sindy says, "I'm sure it will. I wish I had more kids. A girl would've been nice, but once Wayne took off I wasn't interested in meeting anyone else. Not after what he did.

It wrecks your trust in people, not to mention your confidence, when you're left high and dry for another woman."

"I can imagine," says Nicole.

Sindy only told Lucas the truth about his dad running off with another woman once he turned eighteen. Until then he was told Wayne Rivers left town for a better job and just never came back.

"How's your mom?" asks Sindy. "She must be going out of her mind with your little sister vanishing like she did."

"I wouldn't know. She doesn't exactly confide in me."

"That's a crying shame. A daughter needs her mother." She coughs. "How about your dad. He still an asshole?"

Nicole laughs in surprise. She should probably be offended, but she's not. "Yeah. I guess."

Sindy peers in the direction of the kitchen before saying, "Lucas will probably tell me to mind my business, but I can't help thinking it's strange how your friend was found the minute you returned home. Wouldn't you agree?"

Nicole's eyes widen. Does Sindy share her thoughts on her father? "That's what I thought, but Lucas says coincidences do happen."

"That they do." Sindy lights up a cigarette. On closer inspection, it's a joint. Nicole had no idea she smoked pot. "I'll blow the smoke away from you, but you can open a window if you want."

Nicole walks to the windows and pulls back the nicotine-stained blind to open the largest of them. The breeze that sweeps through the room is much needed.

"Want some?" says Sindy.

She turns to face her mother-in-law, who is holding the joint out to her. "No, I can't smoke that stuff. It always did strange things to me. I guess I have no tolerance for it."

Lucas enters with a tray of three mugs and a small sugar pot. The coffees already have milk in them and the small fancy cakes are open on the tray, an array of brightly colored fondant. After making some space he places the tray on the wooden coffee table.

"Why don't you like my father?" Nicole asks.

"Honestly?" says Sindy, mulling the question over. "I think he's a sex pest."

"What?" says Lucas, horrified.

"Well, she asked!" says Sindy. "And we're family. I can be honest around you two, can't I?" Nicole nods, so Sindy continues. "Sheriff Ron Chambers..." With a slow shake of the head she says, "I heard rumors he assaulted a fourteen-year-old girl back in the day, and I always wondered if it could've been your friend."

Nicole's heart rate speeds up. It occurs to her that she never considered it could have been Lori. It was Lori who told her about the rumors, but she had made it sound like she was referring to someone else. Could she have been trying to tell Nicole what her father was doing to her? She seriously hopes not.

Lucas rolls his eyes. "Mom, don't start spreading unfounded rumors. Like you pointed out, he's the sheriff. You could get in a lot of trouble."

"I'd like to see him try. I'm allowed to have an opinion, aren't I? Besides, he was an asshole to me after your dad left. Here I was raising a boy on the cusp of puberty all by myself and him and his buddies made a joke of it as if I deserved to be traded in for a younger model. As if Wayne did the right thing."

Before Nicole can apologize for her father's behavior Lucas says, "Stop it, please. We've come to talk about you, not anyone else."

Sindy looks at her son and her expression visibly melts. It's clear she doesn't want to upset him. "Alright, alright. If that's what you want."

Unable to let it drop, Nicole asks, "Who told you about the allegations?"

"Oh God." Lucas rubs his temples and takes a seat on the couch.

Nicole sits next to him. "I'm sorry, but I want to know."

"I don't remember," says Sindy. "Someone was gossiping. But it sounded credible to me. The next thing I know the rumors just stopped in their tracks. It's like the whole town teamed up to bury them. It was the darndest thing. Even so, they can't wipe people's memories." She tilts her head as she meets Nicole's gaze. "Why? Do you have concerns about your father, honey?"

Nicole licks her lips, unsure whether to confide in her mother-in-law. "He never touched me. And I never saw him touch anyone else. But I think he paid a lot of attention to Lori. I just got a feeling from him, after she told me about those same allegations you heard."

"Interesting," says Sindy. "And now your sister's missing."

"Right. Did you see much of Aimee around town before she disappeared?"

"Here and there. Occasionally she'd drop by the store for something. Sometimes with your mom. There didn't appear to be any animosity between them, but that doesn't mean there wasn't any. People are good at hiding their true feelings when they're in public. After all, sometimes you have to, right?" She sucks on her joint. "And of course, Tommy Peterson follows her around like a lovesick puppy. They appear to spend a lot of time together. Sometimes I get the impression poor Aimee just can't shake him off."

Nicole tenses. That doesn't sound good. "I need to speak to Tommy, but my dad might have spooked him."

"Wouldn't surprise me. Tommy makes a good fall guy."

Nicole swallows. He's also a good suspect if it's true that Aimee was growing tired of his company. Maybe he was possessive. Maybe he got her pregnant. She wonders if Aimee was using drugs, same as him. They could be codependent on each other for their next hit, or even just for emotional support.

"I know Tommy was bullied at school after Lori vanished," says Sindy. "I heard he would break down in tears a lot because he missed his sister, so he became an easy target. It's sad really." She takes another puff of her joint. "I hear you're staying at your parents' place. Have you been snooping? I know I sure would if I were you."

"I've checked Aimee's room but didn't find anything," Nicole says. She doesn't mention the flyer she found in Aimee's baby-name book. Abortion is a sensitive subject at the best of times and Nicole doesn't want people to think that just because Aimee once considered abortion and perhaps adoption that she didn't want or love her unborn child and isn't deserving of being found. "And my mom has since asked me to leave, so Lucas and I are staying at a hotel now."

"Maybe you were getting too close to the truth," says Sindy. "Wait a minute. Do you think your dad could be the father of Aimee's baby?"

"Mom!" says Lucas, shocked. "Don't encourage her. You can't just make shit up! This isn't one of your soap operas! This is real people we're talking about."

Nicole looks at her husband. "You know how I feel about this, Lucas."

"Let her do some digging," says Sindy. "There's no harm in it, and let's face it: no one else seems bothered by Aimee's disappearance. It hasn't been on the local news or in the paper. That girl's carrying a baby. You'd think her face would be plastered everywhere until she's found."

"It's in today's paper," says Nicole. "But only because I spoke to a journalist last night."

Lucas glances at her, irritated.

"Well, good," says Sindy, impressed. "That'll get the ball

rolling. If your father's hiding anything, it'll all come out now the press are involved. If the journalist is any good, that is."

Nicole thinks Jennifer Manvers will push for answers. "I think she'll try her best to make some noise."

"I really wish you hadn't gone to the press," says Lucas.

"Oh shush," says Sindy. "She has every right to speak her truth. That's what the kids say these days, isn't it? 'I'm speaking my truth.'" She laughs before leaning forward. "Listen, honey, if there's anything I can do to help—plaster the store with missing person posters, help you search the town, speak to that journalist of yours—you just say the word. We need to get your sister and her baby back alive so they don't end up in a silo somewhere like your little friend."

Nicole feels invigorated by her support. Finally, someone is taking her concerns about her father seriously.

TWENTY

Lucas stays at his mother's house a while longer so they can eat lunch together. Nicole takes the car and drives downtown to the office building where Jennifer Manvers works. She finds a free parking space nearby and is buzzed into the building by a receptionist. Jennifer greets her in the small foyer with concern in her eyes. "Is everything okay?" she asks.

"I want to make and print some missing person posters," says Nicole. "There doesn't appear to be any around town. I thought you might be able to help me? I don't really know where to start."

Jennifer nods. "Of course." She leads Nicole up a wide staircase and through an open-plan office to her desk. The office isn't huge but there are at least ten other staffers concentrating on their computer screens or making calls. Some desks are empty. Phones and computers regularly ring and ping with notifications and calls. "Take a seat."

Nicole drops her purse on the floor and sits in a well-worn office chair. Jennifer's desk is covered in legal pads, stationery and a couple of dirty takeout cups. A stack of old newspapers sits under her desk, leaving little room for her feet. The computers and furniture look dated, and Nicole finds herself wondering how much longer local newspapers like this one can stay in business. "Has anyone called about your article?" she asks.

Jennifer sighs as she sits at her computer. "Just a couple of psychics, but we don't tend to give them any credence. I told them to call the sheriff's office. The article hasn't been out long enough for most people to see it yet." She wakes the computer screen up by shaking the mouse and then locates the photograph of Aimee that she used in her article. "One of your sister's friends gave me this. It was taken earlier this year before her pregnancy started showing. Shall we use it on the poster?"

"Sure."

"Now, I'm not a cop, so I don't have a template to use for this, but I'll google missing person posters. I'm sure I can come up with something similar."

Nicole watches as she gets to work.

"Is there a reward for information?" asks the journalist.

Nicole tries to think. "No, I don't think so. No one has mentioned a reward. Do you think it would help?"

Jennifer points to other missing person posters online. A lot of them have *Reward Offered* as their title banner. "I guess it's a fine line between a reward prompting people to come forward when they wouldn't have otherwise done so, and a reward bringing out the kind of people who would lie for a chance to grab some free cash. Maybe the fact your dad hasn't offered one yet suggests he doesn't want to attract the wrong kind of witnesses."

Nicole has just under two thousand dollars in her savings account. It's for the baby, if one ever materializes. She would offer it as a reward in a heartbeat if she thought it would work. But she's not sure what's for the best because she's not a cop either. She shouldn't have to make these kinds of decisions. She rubs her temples. "Not yet. Maybe we can try that if all else fails."

"I agree. We don't want to ruin the investigation."

Once Jennifer has made a poster template, with the photo of Aimee in place under a red *Missing* banner and a bullet list ready to be filled in, she asks, "How tall is Aimee and what did she weigh before she got pregnant?"

Nicole blinks. "I don't know, sorry."

"That's okay. How tall are you?"

"Five-six. But I saw a full-length photograph of her at home and I'd say she's a couple of inches taller than me. She looked slimmer than me before she got pregnant too."

Jennifer lowers her hands from the keyboard and studies Nicole's face. "When was the last time you saw her?"

Fearful of being judged harshly, Nicole takes a deep breath. "Aimee was six. I was seventeen." Her head pounds harder, making her wish she had some painkillers in her purse.

"I had no idea. I'm sorry. I only moved here a year ago, so I don't have that much background knowledge of the locals yet. Just the ones I've written about." Jennifer's expression softens. "I knew you didn't live in Henderson anymore, but I didn't realize you'd been gone for so long, or not stayed in touch with your family."

"I tried. I used to write to Aimee when I first left." Nicole forces herself to stop talking. She has to be careful what she says around journalists. "Anyway, this isn't about me. What else do you need to know?"

Jennifer reluctantly continues. "Do you know if there are any complications in her pregnancy so far? With your mom being a midwife, I'm wondering whether she told you anything. Because if Aimee's pregnancy or labor could be at high risk of complications due to an underlying health condition, it adds another sense of urgency, making it more likely people will want to help find her fast."

"I'm sorry, I don't know. All I know is that Aimee didn't want our mom to deliver the baby."

With raised eyebrows, Jennifer says, "Do you know why?"

Nicole shakes her head. But *she* wouldn't feel comfortable with her mother being present at such a moment either. It's weird. You're so exposed. And you have to be able to trust the medical team complicity. "My mom told me she regularly calls around other hospitals nearby to see if anyone's turned up in labor who fits Aimee's description."

"Good. That's something. Hopefully she's checking if any abandoned newborns turn up too."

Nicole blinks. "You think Aimee would dump her baby?"

Jennifer chooses her words carefully. "Not necessarily Aimee. But if she was abducted, maybe whoever abducted her doesn't want the baby around. That's if she's even given birth yet. The chances are she hasn't, what with this being her first. I hear the first baby is usually late."

That's what Nicole's mother had said.

"What was Aimee wearing the morning she vanished?"

"I'm sorry, I don't know." Nicole hadn't thought to ask her parents when she was quizzing them. She takes a deep breath and, between them, they manage to fill in enough information to make the poster more useful than not.

"I'll print two hundred copies for now," says Jennifer. "You need to get them on as many lampposts, noticeboards and store windows as possible. The rest you can hand out in person, and maybe go door-to-door in Aimee's neighborhood. I can print more when you need them. And I'll print one on tomorrow's front page if my editor's agreeable."

Nicole's overwhelmed with gratitude. "Thank you so much. I just wish this had been done as soon as she went missing."

"Why do you think it wasn't?"

She shrugs. "My dad said he's doing everything possible and

that the community already knows she's missing, so I guess a poster might not be that useful. But I've got to try."

"Absolutely," says Jennifer. "If people don't keep seeing Aimee's face and hearing her name, they'll forget about her. I wish we knew more about the police investigation. I don't remember a search being carried out. That would've alerted me to her disappearance, so maybe your father did it discreetly, or overnight. Maybe he has a suspect in mind and he's keeping his cards close to his chest." She looks as confused as to why he would do that as Nicole is. "Anyway, I've left a message with his office for a call-back. It's fair to say I have a *lot* of questions for him."

It feels good to know Jennifer has taken this on. She's much better qualified to find answers, and it gives Nicole a chance to focus on doing whatever she can.

Before Nicole can get up and leave, Jennifer asks, "Have you thought of setting up a Facebook page to help spread the word farther than Oates County? Posts from those kinds of pages can go viral fast."

Nicole hadn't thought of that. "That's probably a good idea." Except her parents would hate it. She turns to the computer next to Jennifer's. The desk is empty, the computer switched off. "Can I use this computer? I think it would be easier than trying to do it on my phone."

Jennifer stands and peers over at an office in the corner. "Give me a second."

Feeling warm, Nicole removes her cardigan as she watches the journalist enter the office to talk to an older woman, presumably the newspaper's editor. The editor glances over at Nicole through the glass partition. Eventually the older woman nods in agreement. When Jennifer returns to her desk, she says, "I can't let you use a computer because of data protection, but I can help set up the Facebook page."

Nicole wonders if they're expecting anything from her in

return, such as the inside scoop on the night Lori disappeared. Or maybe she's just paranoid.

Jennifer brings up Facebook on her computer and moves aside so Nicole can log in. The problem is, Nicole hasn't been on Facebook in so long that she can't remember her password. She pulls out her phone and opens the app. She's currently logged out but the email address she uses as her login is visible. It's an old one, and that prompts her memory for the password. She successfully logs in and sees red notifications in the top-right corner. Instinctively she clicks the notification button. Most are friend requests or random DMs from strangers, but her breath catches when she spots a message from *Amy Chambers*. "Oh my God. Aimee messaged me."

Jennifer leans in. "When?"

The date shows June thirtieth, which is two and a half weeks ago. Aimee's first name is spelled differently and Nicole wonders whether that's so that their parents couldn't easily find her online and spy on her account. She clicks on the message.

Can you call me? I know it's been a while, but I need to talk to you urgently. I can't live like this anymore, and I have to see you. Please call me. Mom and Dad were wrong to keep us apart. I have to know for myself if what they're saying is true.

Jennifer leans back after reading it. "She was in turmoil about something."

Nicole's stunned. "She wanted my help and I didn't even know." If she had seen this sooner, she might have been able to stop Aimee from going missing.

"I don't get it though. Why would your parents want to keep you from her? Why did you stay away for so long?"

She looks at Jennifer. There's so much she wants to say but she can't. She shouldn't. Not until she has proof. She leans into the computer and types a reply with shaky hands.

I'm so sorry. I've only just seen your message. If you read this,
call me ASAP. I'm so worried about you and the baby. Don't
do anything stupid. Come and live with me. I don't know
what's going on but we can figure this out together. You don't
have to go home to them. Seriously, call me. I want to help.

She ends her message with her cell number, then rereads
what she's written. It's desperate and random, but she just
wants her sister to know she has someplace safe to go. She hits
send, then logs in to Facebook on her phone so she'll receive
notifications if Aimee replies. She turns the volume up loud in
case Aimee calls. Relief washes over her as she takes a deep
breath. She feels hopeful now that she has some way of commu-
nicating directly with her sister. Assuming Aimee is physically
able to respond.

Jennifer says, "I'm going to scour her Facebook page to try
to build a picture of who her friends are and what she was up to
before I set up the missing person page. Although..." She leans
in to the screen and clicks a few things at random. "It looks like
she's got most of it locked down." She frowns. "I thought her
first name was spelled differently?"

"Me too. No one's mentioned she changed the spelling, so
I'm willing to bet it's just online, so our parents can't snoop."
She hasn't used a real profile picture either. Nicole pulls her
cardigan on and grabs her purse before standing. "Thanks for
your help with these." She grabs the posters from the printer
behind them. "And for offering to set up a page for her. Call me
if you learn anything."

"Sure. You too. Where are you rushing to?"

"I need to speak to someone." Nicole races out of the office
before Jennifer can ask any further questions.

TWENTY-ONE

The drive to Theresa and Antony's house seems to go in slow motion. Nicole glances at the neighborhoods she and Lori used to walk past on their way home from school, including the library where they would read books deemed unsuitable for them. Lori would pick out the juicy bits from the romance novels she enjoyed and they would laugh discreetly at all the different ways a man's appendage was described.

Nicole would compare it to how sex was handled in the horror books she loved to read. They learned a lot about men and relationships—both good and bad—from both genres, but it's fair to say they never once entertained the idea that one of them would be at risk of being hurt by a man in their lives. It seemed so unbelievable that someone they knew could do anything bad to them.

Nicole thinks of Jim Marsh. Is he too obvious a suspect for Lori's murder? Probably. But that doesn't mean he wasn't responsible. She doesn't remember any interactions with him when she lived here. She and Lori knew who he was, but he wasn't a friend of their parents, so they never spoke to him when they'd occasionally bump into him around town. Nicole just remembers seeing him driving around in his pickup, getting supplies. He probably knew who she was, being the sheriff's daughter, but it's doubtful he knew Lori's name.

Memories of Lori's little brother run through her thoughts as she nears their parents' house. Tommy adored his sister. He adored Nicole's sister too, so she can't imagine he would do anything to intentionally hurt Aimee and the baby. She also doesn't think it's too far-fetched to assume that he's the baby's father. Maybe they were in a relationship, or maybe there was one night where they gave in to boredom and familiarity. Nicole hopes he is the father because Lori would have loved that. It would make her and Nicole aunties to the same baby. And besides, if he isn't the father, the alternative could be a lot worse. She doesn't even want to think about that.

She pulls up outside the house. She was intending to try to locate Tommy and quiz him on her sister, but judging by the police cruiser outside, she might be too late. She springs out of the car and rushes to the front door, which is open. When she steps inside, she's greeted with raised voices coming from the living room.

The familiarity of her surroundings stops her in her tracks. Last time she was here Lori was alive. The same paintings hang in the hallway, next to the large round mirror that she and Lori checked themselves in a million times before leaving the house to meet Lucas and Kurt. The carpet hasn't been replaced and is worn in all the same places. Her eyes are drawn up the staircase to the door that sits firmly closed against Lori's childhood. Nicole's breath quickens as she imagines going up there. Opening the door to the past would be too much for her to handle. She goes dizzy at the thought and leans against the wall for support.

"I'm not a drug addict and I didn't do anything!" The frustrated declaration of innocence brings Nicole back to the present.

"Then you won't mind taking a polygraph, will you?" Her father's voice. Nicole's heart sinks.

"He would never hurt Aimee of all people!" Theresa Peterson is backing out of the living room, trying to stop Ron dragging Tommy away. "The only drugs he takes are antidepressants, same as everyone else!"

Nicole wonders if his mother is blind to her son's problem, or whether that's the truth. "Dad?" she says, stepping forward. "What's going on?"

The house falls silent as Theresa turns. The grieving woman's hands fly to her mouth as she stares at Nicole. Nicole swallows. They're both seeing a ghost right now, in each other. Theresa has aged, of course, but she still looks like Lori.

"Nicole?" Lori's mother steps forward and pulls her in for a hug. "Oh my God. It's so good to see you."

Nicole sniffs back tears. Over Theresa's shoulder she sees her father's angry reaction to her showing up here. As the hallway is narrow she can't see Tommy yet. He's still in the living room. "I'm okay," she says. "How are you?"

Theresa pulls away and stares intently. Nicole knows she's trying to reconcile her with the teenager who spent so much time here. She's probably wondering how Lori would have aged in comparison. "I've missed you so much."

Before Nicole can reply, Ron awkwardly clears his throat and says, "It's time to leave." He pulls Tommy into view and Nicole stares at the tall young man, now nineteen years old. He has the same green eyes and black hair as Lori. He doesn't look like someone in the grip of a drug addiction. He's physically fit, and tanned, although maybe a little tired around the eyes. His expression is one of anger and fear, either because he suspects the sheriff is going to frame him for something, or because he's guilty.

"What's going on?" she asks.

"None of your damn business, Nicole," says her father. "You shouldn't be here. Get out of my way."

"He's saying I killed Aimee," says Tommy, shaking his arm free. "I would never hurt your sister."

She's mortified her father would cause this family more pain at a time like this. "Dad, come on! Why are you doing this?"

Ron doesn't listen. He pulls Tommy past her and out of the house into the bright sunshine. When Tommy tries to resist again, Ron threatens to call for backup.

"I don't get it," says Theresa. She's barely holding back tears as she stands on her porch, gripping the rail. "When you were here this morning you didn't say anything about arresting my son. So what's changed in the last four or five hours? I'm supposed to be planning my little girl's funeral and you want to arrest my only other child? You're torturing me!"

Ron doesn't reply. He has one hand clutching Tommy's arm, the other hovering over his weapon.

Tommy stares at his mother. "Mom, do something."

Theresa looks out of her depth and desperate for her son not to get shot while resisting arrest. Eventually she says, "Just go with him. But don't say a word until I find you a lawyer. I'll call your dad home from work. We'll figure this out."

Nicole wants to tell Tommy she believes him, but she doesn't know the facts. Her father could know something she doesn't. There could be evidence linking Tommy to Aimee's disappearance. It wouldn't be the first time love has turned into a deadly infatuation. Maybe Aimee told him she didn't want a romantic relationship and he couldn't handle it. Nicole closes her eyes against the thought because that would mean Aimee and the baby are likely dead.

Her head pounds harder, making her wince. The mention of Tommy being on antidepressants reminds her she hasn't taken hers since she arrived in town. Lucas calls them her "vitamins" because he thinks it sounds more socially acceptable, but she doesn't hide behind social niceties. She doesn't care who knows what she takes in order to get through her day. Now she thinks about it, she hasn't taken any since she received the call from her mother about Aimee's disappearance. That was four days ago. Maybe that's what is causing her headache. She feels a little groggy too, like she could sleep all day. Her prescribed dose isn't exactly low, so it's not surprising her body would start to feel withdrawal effects already.

She watches Tommy as he's pushed backward into the backseat of her father's cruiser. Ron's having problems getting him inside. His eyes wild, Tommy looks like he's going to make a run for it. And that's exactly what he does. She and Theresa gasp as Tommy overpowers her father, shoving him to one side, giving himself room to escape. He's faster than the aging sheriff. Before they know it, he runs between two neighboring houses, disappearing behind the mature trees in their backyard.

Theresa grips Nicole's arm as she notices Ron has his weapon raised. "He's going to shoot my boy!"

Nicole pulls away and runs up to her father. "Don't hurt him! He's afraid, that's all. Think of his mother." She nods toward Theresa, who has her hands to her head, looking in the direction Tommy vanished.

Ron Chambers is clearly not in the mood to be schooled by his daughter. "Stay out of this, Nicole. You're making everything worse with your meddling." He lowers his voice as he adds, "As well as your disgusting accusations about me. Why don't you just get the hell out of town for good?"

Nicole reels back as if slapped.

Ron turns to Theresa. "If your boy's not at my office within the next hour, I'm launching a manhunt. And all bets are off then, Theresa. So make him see sense." He holsters his weapon.

Her father might be professionally embarrassed at being given the slip, but that's no excuse to take it out on other people.

Nicole feels anger rising in her chest. She's not going to let him get away with dismissing her again. As he turns away from them both to get in his car, she says, "I wish you would put as much effort into searching for Aimee as you are in trying to frame Tommy. Maybe then she'd be home by now."

Ron slowly turns to look at her. His cheeks are red, his eyes mean. He could easily lash out right now but of course he won't, not in public. Instead, he says, "You need to stop acting like I'm the bad guy here, Nicole. You're the one running to the press without authorization, making me and your mother look bad. If you want to help the Petersons so badly, how about you tell Theresa what happened the night her daughter vanished?"

Nicole takes a step back. "What?"

"What do you mean?" says Theresa, suddenly joining them. "What happened, Nicole?"

Nicole hears her heartbeat in her head, each beat a painful throb. "I don't know what you're taking about."

Her father eyes her for a full minute. He looks like he's on the verge of saying something else, but instead he turns and slips into his vehicle. As he tears out of there, she hears him radioing dispatch about Tommy's escape.

Theresa spins her around to face her, painfully pinching her upper arms in desperation. "Nicole? What's going on? Who are you protecting?"

She struggles to answer. "I don't know what he's talking about. He's mad at me. He'll say anything." Theresa's eyes bore into her. "Honestly, Mrs. Peterson, I don't know anything about that night. Just that Lori was a little upset when I left her, that's all."

As they stand on the lawn, Theresa looks like she's about to break down. She clutches Nicole's arms tighter. "If there's anything you haven't told me, I want to know. Your father—" She swallows. "He kept you away from us after she vanished. There were things he didn't want you to tell us. I knew it. I could sense he was being odd. I couldn't understand why you stayed away until Antony shared his suspicions with me."

Nicole looks her in the eye. "He had suspicions? About what?"

The older woman hesitates. She looks around before leaning in and saying, "You know more than you let on back then. I know you were pulled out of school for a while, and then left Henderson before you even turned eighteen." She pauses. "I'm not stupid, Nicole. There can only be one reason for that."

Nicole's eyes wince with the throbbing in her head. It feels like she can't get enough air into her lungs. She can't speak. She needs to let Theresa say the words. But the woman won't. So, when Nicole's met with silence and that piercing stare, she whispers, "What reason would that be?"

Disappointment clouds Theresa's eyes. She thought she could get Nicole to confess to what she knows. The woman's expression quickly turns to one of defiance. With her hands now on her hips she says, "Your father killed my daughter, didn't he? That's why he never found her body during the search. He wasn't *looking* for it. He was *hiding* it."

Before Nicole can react, a car comes speeding to a halt by the sidewalk. Someone gets out and approaches them. "What's going on?" says Kurt. He must've heard Ron on the radio.

Nicole hasn't even got the strength to answer him. She can't tear her eyes from Lori's mom. Everything starts to go dark. She feels someone catch her as she collapses.

TWENTY-TWO

From the Journal of Aimee Chambers

September 14, 2019—Age 15

I've joined Facebook but Mom and Dad don't know. Dad would hit the roof. He thinks kids on social media are a target for predators, but I'm 15 and I'm not stupid. I can spot a weirdo a mile away and already have. They're relentless with their disgusting dick pics and "Hey, beautiful" DMs. I've spelled my first name the bland way, as there are hundreds of girls with the same name, making it unlikely Mom or Dad will find me on there. I found my sister's profile. Dad would probably ground me if he knew I was looking for Nicole. I haven't contacted her. Not yet. I'm too scared. She stopped writing to me for a reason and my parents won't tell me why. I can't figure out whether it's because I did something wrong or she's just a heartless bitch.

Her FB page is frustratingly empty. She never posts anything! I don't know anything about her other than what my parents tell me.

Tommy offered to friend her, to see if she's interested in talking to me. But I don't know if I can handle it if she says no.

August 8, 2020—Age 16

Tommy beat up Callum today, despite Callum being bigger than him. Tommy ended up in the hospital with a fractured thumb. He has two black eyes now too. He's jealous. I've told him a million times I only think of him as my brother and he always says he's good with that, but then he beats the shit out of my new boyfriend. WTF?! Well, he's my ex-boyfriend now as Callum broke up with me over it. Urgh! I wish Tommy wasn't a part of my life. I feel suffocated. I just want to leave this place and start fresh someplace where no one knows me. Like Nicole did. I'm starting to understand why she didn't stay in touch with any of us. I just wish she'd taken me with her.

TWENTY-THREE

Nicole sips from a bottle of water, embarrassed that she passed out on Theresa's lawn. "I'm fine, honestly." Her hotel room is too bright and her head is still aching.

"Could you be pregnant?" asks Lucas. He's sitting next to her on the bed with his arm around her. "Is that why you fainted?"

She shakes her head. "No. I'm not pregnant. I fainted because I was too hot, my head was pounding and my dad had just stressed me out."

"How could anyone tell their own daughter to leave town?" he asks, annoyed.

"Your father's under a lot of pressure," says Kurt, sitting at the desk. He'd given her a ride here, where they'd waited together for Lucas to collect his car from Theresa's house. "I heard he's mad about the newspaper article. He thinks it makes him look like he's not really trying to find Aimee."

"Well, is he?" says Nicole. "No one will tell me anything, so how am I supposed to know what he's done?"

Lucas glances at Kurt. "You must know something? What about your dad? Are they still friends?"

Kurt nods. "I'm not a part of that investigation so I don't know any details, but I asked my dad. He said Ron visited him yesterday and they talked about it. Apparently, Ron's waiting for Aimee's cell provider to produce a copy of her call records and to see which tower her phone last pinged from. He and a couple of other deputies have already searched various locations, including the park and playground where Lori's blood was found. They didn't find anything."

Nicole wonders why her father thinks Aimee could have been where Lori was last seen alive.

"At least now we know he's taking it seriously," says Lucas. "Why couldn't he have told Nicole that?"

Kurt doesn't have an answer for them.

"I've made some posters." Nicole retrieves them from her bag and splits the pile into three, handing both men their share. We need to get these up everywhere."

Both Kurt and Lucas stare at Aimee's face on the poster. "She looks like you at eighteen," says Lucas. "Except blonde." He turns to Kurt. "Has Ron interviewed all her friends and co-workers? Did she have a part-time job?"

"I'm sure he would have interviewed her friends," Kurt replies, "but she didn't have a job as far as I know."

Nicole thinks of her parents' house. "Did they check the house for prints? Stranger DNA? Tire tracks?"

Kurt smiles. "You watch a lot of crime shows, don't you?"

She smarts. "I'm a woman. I'd be stupid not to."

His smile fades. "Sure. Sorry. Listen, Ron knows how to run a missing person case. I'm sure he did all that and more. I can't get into the evidence locker at the sheriff's office without him knowing, and I can't go sneaking around the database. That leaves a digital trace and it would only take one thing for the guy to fire me. So I can't look for whatever he's found, I'm sorry. Like I told you before, he keeps me at a distance. I'm not in his inner circle, and I think that's down to my relationship with you."

"You mean friendship," says Lucas. "Not relationship."

Kurt rolls his eyes and stands. "Whatever. I should be out looking for Tommy."

Lucas turns back to Nicole. "I think it's time we left town and went home. Today's proven you're in no fit state to tackle your parents. It's too stressful, especially after everything you already went through with them."

Kurt scoffs. "You make it sound like she's frail or ill. How about treating her like a grown woman?"

Nicole feels Lucas's body tense next to her. He doesn't like being ridiculed. "Why are you even still here?" he asks. "If you're not involved in the investigation into Aimee's disappearance, you have no need to be around my wife. Is it because you're still obsessed with her?"

Shaking his head, Kurt heads to the door. "You're still a grade-A asshole, I see."

"What did you call me?" Lucas springs off the bed, confronting his former friend. They go chest to chest until Nicole gets between them. The missing person posters scatter onto the floor.

"Stop it!" She pushes Lucas backward onto the bed before turning to Kurt. "I think you should leave. Sorry. I appreciate you taking care of me. You turned up at just the right time."

"He's a cop, it's his job," says Lucas. "Don't act like he's a damn hero or something."

The room bristles with tension but Kurt doesn't attempt to leave. He stares at Lucas with a look in his eye that suggests he's ready to do some damage. "Tell me something, *buddy*. Because I'm curious. Are you still cheating on Nicole these days?"

Nicole gasps and turns to look at her husband. His face turns bright red and he looks like a coiled spring, ready to lunge again. "What's he talking about?" she asks.

"While you were being chaste back in high school," says Kurt, "Lucas was screwing Mia Phillips and Sally Ford from the cheer team."

"You son of a bitch!" Lucas jumps up and hits Kurt square in the jaw, barely missing Nicole. She ducks out of the way and lets them go at it, because she's no match for either of them.

She sinks onto the bed as she considers the accusation and her husband's reaction to it. Lucas wouldn't cheat on her. He was the only person she could rely on after Lori vanished. He left their hometown and his mother behind for her. They lived in a tiny, cheap apartment working crappy jobs to make their rent. Lucas could have gone to college if he'd wanted to. He could have kept his old life. He wouldn't give up all that if he didn't love her.

"I knew you couldn't be trusted," says Lucas, pushing Kurt into the door. "You're trying to break us up, so you can get your claws into her. As if she'd ever be interested in a loser like you."

Kurt flings his arm off and spins around, his black hair covering his eyes. "Is that so? Then how come we kissed yesterday?"

It's Lucas's turn to be shocked now. He turns to Nicole, his mouth agape.

Kurt grabs some of the posters off the floor before opening the hotel-room door. He looks back before leaving. "If he lays a finger on you, Nicole, call me." He lets the door slam shut behind him.

Nicole doesn't know what to say. She doesn't even care that Kurt has made it sound like they had some passionate embrace yesterday. She's still trying to get her head around the claim that Lucas cheated on her. With at least two different girls. Mia hadn't said anything when they bumped into each other in the grocery store. But then, why would she? Nicole thinks of Mia's twin boys. Her mind tries to convince her that Lucas could be their father, which is ridiculous given how much time has passed since they were all at school together. But he has regular trips home without her. Supposedly to see his mother. Has he been screwing around on these trips?

She leans forward, clutching her head in her hands. Her stomach feels heavy with dread.

"You didn't?" says Lucas, approaching the bed. "Not with him."

"What?" She looks up, incredulous. "So it's okay to cheat as long as it wasn't with Kurt? Grow up, Lucas. He tried kissing me and I pulled away. That's it. Was he telling the truth about *you*? Because he was pretty specific."

Lucas sits next to her on the end of the bed, his eyes lowered. The silence becomes heavy, leading Nicole to conclude he's trying and failing to come up with a cover story.

"So it's true," she answers for him. Tears spring to her eyes. Her hands tremble with the thought of what this could mean for their marriage. The only person who has ever protected her isn't who she thought he was. "How could you?" she sobs. "And with *them*. Is that your type? Tall, blonde and easy? Because I've never looked anything like a cheerleader. Lori and I..." She tries to calm her breathing. "We were so self-conscious about our looks. We knew we were just average, especially compared to the cheerleaders. We couldn't understand what either of you saw in us. How lucky we were." She wipes away her tears. "And all the time you were screwing the hot girls from school. Which means our whole relationship has been a lie." She stands as another thought occurs to her. "Were you laughing about us behind our backs? Was it all a big joke to you?"

"Nicole, you're being dramatic." He won't look at her as he says, "It was only with Mia and only when you and I first got together. I'm sorry. I was a kid. I followed my hormones." He stands and finally meets her gaze. "I never knew we'd end up married at that point. I fell in love with you the longer we were together. I'm still with you now because I love you." He falters before adding, "I almost told you about it, but you had so much to deal with already. Then, as time went on, it seemed so irrelevant. So high school, you know? And it's never happened again since then."

She tries to wipe her tears away but they just keep coming. She doesn't know what to believe. If he was cheating on her back then, he could still be cheating on her now. How can she ever trust him again? Then a gut-wrenching thought occurs to her. "Did you ever cheat on me with Lori?"

He opens his mouth to respond but her phone rings. Her heart races in case it's Aimee. She grabs it off the nightstand and is disappointed to see it's Jennifer Manvers calling.

Lucas grabs his own phone as well as some of the posters. He heads to the door. "I need some air."

"I think you should just take your things and leave," says Nicole, feeling completely betrayed. "I need some alone time. I'll call you in a few days."

"Seriously? Over something that happened years ago?"

"It doesn't matter when it happened, Lucas! I only just found out! I need time to think things through. You've broken my trust." Her voice cracks. The phone stops ringing in her hand.

He shakes his head in frustration before collecting his clothes and throwing them into his duffel bag. He leaves the posters on the bed and exits the room without looking back.

Nicole briefly wonders whether he intends to catch up to Kurt and finish what they started, but that's not her problem. They can act like morons if they want to. She takes a few minutes to compose herself before calling Jennifer back. "Hi," she says when Jennifer picks up. "Sorry I missed your call."

"Are you okay?" asks Jennifer. "You sound upset."

"I'm fine," she lies.

"Okay, if you're sure. I'm calling because I've just heard Tommy Peterson has resisted arrest and gone on the run. Do you know if that's true?"

"It is." Nicole takes a deep breath. "My dad tried to take him in for questioning but he got away. He was adamant he didn't do anything to Aimee."

"Are you concerned he might come after you?"

She frowns. "No. Why would he do that?"

Jennifer chooses her words carefully. "Well, it's just that, if he's angry with your father, or if he really did hurt Aimee... I'd watch your back if I were you. Just in case. Hold on just a second." Nicole hears voices in the background. She listens as Jennifer says to someone else, "What time?" Then, "Thanks for letting me know." She comes back on the line. "Nicole?"

"Yeah?"

"I just found out your father's holding a press conference tonight at six."

Nicole's eyes widen. That's two hours away. "Do you know if it's because he's found Tommy? Or is it about Aimee?"

"He hasn't released any other details. Just the time and place. He's holding it outside his building and he's only invited local press and media. It's about time, to tell you the truth. He had to do something since Lori's remains were found. And now her brother's on the run, and his elder daughter is missing, it's all one big mess that needs a display of leadership."

Nicole nods. "I just hope it's not more bad news. I don't think I could take it." She was already feeling exhausted and overwhelmed by recent events, but with the added revelation that Lucas—the only person in her life she could trust—cheated on her, she feels as though she could sink under the pressure at any moment. If she were at home now, she'd be making an appointment to speak to her doctor, or a therapist.

"I'm sure your father would give you the heads-up if it was about your sister."

Nicole scoffs. Because Jennifer really has no idea what her father is like.

TWENTY-FOUR

Instead of heading straight back to work, Kurt goes home to check on his father first. Brian Butler used to be a person to reckon with, but since his cancer diagnosis he's become a shell of his former self. The decline is so rapid that Kurt suspects they won't share another Christmas, but since his father won't discuss it with anyone, there's no way of knowing.

Kurt enters the house and heads straight to the kitchen to grab some frozen peas from the ice box to rest against his jaw. A glance in the mirror on the way shows a purple bruise forming, and it feels like one of his teeth might be a little loose. The spot where Lucas hit him hurts like hell and if he wasn't a cop, he'd be tempted to teach the guy a lesson. He takes a chair from the dining table and moves it over to a high shelf that sits above the kitchen units. "Dad?" he calls.

"In here." The response comes from the home office at the back of the house, where they moved his father's bed a couple of weeks ago. Brian couldn't manage the stairs anymore, at least not on his own. Most days he spends his time in the living room or out on the porch watching the neighbors go by. There's usually always someone willing to sit and chat with him on their way past. Other days, more frequent now, he can't muster the energy to get out of bed at all. Kurt knows he's not attending his hospital appointments and there's not a damn thing he can do about it. His father seems hellbent on letting the cancer win, which is distressing for him to watch.

Kurt drops the peas on the kitchen counter and steps onto the chair. He reaches for the clear bag of pills he keeps inside an old vase on the shelf. He takes two out and slips one into his mouth, swallowing it without water. The other goes into his shirt pocket before he replaces the bag and the chair.

Holding the peas to his face he finds his father almost sitting up in bed with this morning's paper in front of him. He's working on the sudoku. The sun is on this side of the house, shining through the large window directly onto his father's aging face. It highlights every line and imperfection. He's only fifty-five, but he looks at least a decade older now that his muscles are wasting away. His hair hasn't grown back from his one and only course of chemo earlier this year, so his dad wears his favorite old baseball cap all day, no matter what the temperature. It's not that he's too proud to admit he's bald apparently. He just doesn't want people to pity him for looking so ill.

"Have you taken your pain relief?" asks Kurt.

"You think I could do a sudoku without them?" says Brian. "What are you doing home at this time anyway? Checking I'm still alive?"

"No," says Kurt. "I needed ice for this." He removes the bag of peas and shows off the bruise.

"Who did that?" Brian's eyes narrow and he looks like he'd be willing to march over to the guy's house and threaten him to try it again, just like when Kurt was a kid.

"Lucas Rivers."

"Son of a bitch. He must be as messed up as his mother to take you on. I hope you gave as good as you got."

"Of course not. We're cops, remember? We have to turn the

other cheek."

Brian's expression softens. "Looks like you turned it right into his fist."

It's moments like this Kurt wishes more than anything that his father wasn't dying. He'll be completely alone once he's gone. Alone in a town full of mistakes and memories. Most of them bad.

"Is Ron's daughter still in town, acting like a reporter?" his dad asks.

"She's still looking for her sister, yeah."

"Hmm. I wouldn't go digging for secrets if I had something to hide. Because you can't control what will come to light." Before Kurt can ask what he means by that, Brian says, "I take it you and Lucas Rivers are still fighting over her affections then?"

Kurt's surprised by the question but he keeps his expression neutral. He drops the peas on a chair and leans against the doorframe, crossing his arms. "What do you mean?"

His father smiles ruefully. "Teenagers think their parents don't see anything. That we're dumb to what's going on. Your little group of four was a prime example of every relationship in town. Probably every relationship in the world."

"Is that a fact?" Taking the bait Kurt asks, "How so?"

Brian rolls his eyes as if it doesn't need spelling out. "You were with Lori, and your buddy Lucas was with Nicole, right? But you wanted to be with Nicole, and Lucas was sleeping around with any girl who'd glance in his direction probably. And why not, if you look like he did and have girls throwing themselves at you, right?"

Kurt doesn't reply.

"And poor Lori Peterson, well, she was overlooked by everyone. She was the girl no one really wanted. As for Nicole, I couldn't figure out if she was happy with Lucas or whether she secretly harbored feelings for you." He chuckles. "I'm not gonna lie. It was entertaining to watch your foursome from the outside." The laughter suddenly leaves his eyes. "Until Lori vanished." He pauses, before adding, "I think it was jealousy that got her killed."

Kurt frowns. "You're not making a lot of sense, Dad." But in some ways he is. He's seen right through all of them. Was it that obvious? When you're young, you think you're being clever, and sneaky. You think no one can tell what you're thinking, or see who you're staring at. Looks like he was wrong. But one thing his father never knew was that Kurt was also lusting after Lucas as well as Nicole. He wonders what he'd say if he knew. "According to the sheriff, Jim Marsh killed Lori. How's that got anything to do with jealousy?"

Brian nods. "Right. Jim Marsh. That's what you're paid to say. Maybe one day I'll tell you the truth." His eyes cloud over, as if recalling something dark.

"Why don't you tell me now? I'm a grown man. I can take it."

His father locks eyes with him. "If you're a grown man and you're interested in full disclosure all of a sudden, then how about you tell me your secret?"

Kurt stands straight and drops his arms. "What are you talking about?"

Eventually, deciding now's not the time for brutal honesty, Brian changes the subject. "I'm just messing with you. Now get back to work. You need to find Tommy Peterson before he does something stupid. If he's the father of Aimee's baby, he needs to be around in order to pay child support. Don't let the asshole take the easy way out."

Kurt stares hard at his father's face. "Jim Marsh's farm has been vandalized overnight. His kids have had to hire security in case it gets torched to the ground and the fire spreads to the barns, or the vehicles they're hoping to sell." Deputy Hayes was supposed to be watching the property but probably fell asleep, knowing him.

There's no sympathy in his father's eyes. "Jim may not have killed your friend, but he raped a boy. That much I believe. And he's gone to his grave without paying for it. So what do we care if his property gets torched?"

"You don't care about Brad and Bernadette?" says Kurt. "And what Lori's bones being found in their father's silo is doing to them?"

"They're grown-ass adults and they're not my problem. Anyway, I'm tired. Thinking of the past does that to me." With that, the conversation is over and Brian's attention returns to the newspaper.

The whole exchange leaves Kurt feeling uneasy. "You're not going to tell me who killed Lori, are you?"

Brian ignores the question. "Fetch me something nice for dinner on your way home tonight, would you? I'm sick of that frozen crap you keep serving. It's no wonder I'm wasting away."

Kurt shakes his head. He knows his father is grateful that he moved back in to take care of him, so he's not offended by the comment about the frozen food. He's frustrated the guy won't tell him what he knows. "Whatever." He slowly turns and walks out of the house, unable to get the conversation off his mind on the journey to the sheriff's office.

He arrives to find a scrum of reporters setting up mics and video cameras outside the main entrance. They barely glance at him as he passes.

Deputy Hayes spots the bruise on his jaw as soon as Kurt walks by the front desk. "What happened? Let me guess, you walked into a door?" Hayes laughs.

Kurt ignores him and carries on to his desk. The office is pretty small with everything more or less open plan apart from three partitioned offices up here and the holding cells downstairs. The front desk is also partitioned off from the main office but they can hear everything that's said from here, which can be irritating when the drunks talk loudly and you're trying to fill in a mountain of paperwork. The building is old and run-down, and in need of some serious repairs. The wooden doorframes have warped over the years, or maybe the walls have shifted, so the internal doors don't close fully, making the building one big fire hazard. Plans are ongoing to move to another building but there never seems to be much urgency about it.

Kurt approaches Julie on dispatch to ask what's going on outside. Her desk is spotless. She has three computer monitors, two landlines, a cell phone, a headset and a cup of herbal tea on her desk. She's a real stickler for neatness and has championed turning this place into a paperless office. Unfortunately, the old timers are past learning new tricks and their desks are messy in comparison. Julie's always threatening to shred everything to teach them a lesson.

"Sheriff Chambers is holding a press conference," she says. "Starting in five minutes."

"Has he found Tommy Peterson already?"

"Don't ask me. I just work here." She slips her headset on as she accepts a call.

Kurt leaves her to it.

Sheriff Chambers emerges from his office. "Where have you been?"

"I had to check on my dad."

Ron's face softens. "How's he holding up today? He was in some pain yesterday. You making sure he has enough meds on hand?"

"Of course. He's fine now."

Ron nods. His eyes travel to the bruise on Kurt's jaw but he doesn't ask what happened. "Stay away from the cameras. And if my eldest daughter turns up, keep her away from them too." He heads out of the building to meet the press.

Kurt's heart beats a little faster as he follows him, unsure what the sheriff is about to announce.

TWENTY-FIVE

Now that Lucas has left town, Nicole has given in and rented a car, figuring she'll be sticking around for some time yet. She drives straight to the sheriff's office. The last time she was here she was about twelve years old. She was placed next to the dispatcher and listened in to calls while she waited for her father to finish work and take her out for dinner. Life was much simpler back then.

As she gets out of the car, she's taken aback by how many people are present. News vans line the road and reporters wait eagerly alongside passersby who have gathered to see what's going on. She recognizes Jennifer Manvers in the crowd.

Jennifer glances at her as she approaches. "Oh, hey." Her expression is awkward, as if she was hoping she wouldn't bump into Nicole. "Are you okay? You look like you've been crying."

Nicole sighs. "Long story. I'm fine though."

Ron appears at the lectern, taking his place in the center of a crowd of microphones. He glances either side of him at the deputies present. "We ready?" They nod. Ron straightens his shirt and takes in the crowd. He spots Nicole.

She wishes she could speak to him privately before he starts as she would appreciate the heads-up before he announces something to the whole town. She could do without any more surprises today.

Her father's gaze soon glosses over her. He clears his throat. "Okay, folks. I have some updates for you and I would appreciate it if you would let me say my piece before you start throwing questions at me." The crowd goes silent. He glances at his watch. "I make it dinnertime already, so I'm sure you'd all appreciate it if I kept this brief, and that's certainly the plan." He takes a deep breath. "There has been a lot of speculation about the discovery at Jim Marsh's farm yesterday. We had to give the coroner time to examine the remains before we commented, which he's since done. And it's with regret that I can confirm that Gerry believes the remains belong to local teenager Lori Peterson, who vanished in 2008."

There is no audible reaction from the crowd, but eyes lower in unison and heads shake in sadness. Lori's disappearance rocked this town at the time, and Nicole knows many locals will be dismayed to have it confirmed that she was killed here that night.

"Gerry believes the cause of death was blunt force trauma to the back of the head, and he believes the manner of death was homicide." Her father takes a sip of water.

The reporters present are frantically trying to capture every word. It's clear they're going to have a lot of questions for him before he tries to disappear back into his office.

Jennifer unexpectedly reaches out and rubs Nicole's back. "You okay?" she whispers.

It's a welcome gesture, but Ron notices it. His eyes narrow. Nicole discreetly nods at Jennifer.

"We haven't discovered anything on the Marshes' property that would specifically point to Jim being the perpetrator," he continues. "But fourteen years have passed, so that's not surprising. There was one allegation of sexual assault against a minor that was made about Jim years ago, but again no evidence was found at the time."

A murmur of disgust ripples through the crowd.

"The allegation, together with the fact that young Lori was found on his property, would make Jim Marsh our number one person of interest if he were still alive. We intend to continue this line of investigation for the foreseeable future, but if anyone has any information about the night Lori Peterson was murdered, please come forward so we can help her family get the justice they deserve."

Nicole feels the sun beating down on her scalp. It's just after six but the sun is still intense. She wishes they were doing this inside, where the A/C could cool her down. A bottle of water would be welcome too. Her mouth is bone dry.

"Sheriff?" A male reporter speaks up. "I have a question."

Ron ignores him. "Now, the next thing I want to talk about is personal to my family, so I would appreciate it if you'd listen closely and only report the facts as I state them. If anyone twists my words in their articles or broadcasts, you can rest assured that I won't be holding any further press conferences about this topic. Have I made myself clear?"

An excited murmur runs through the crowd. He has their undivided attention.

"Most of you will already know this but I haven't spoken publicly about it yet, for personal reasons. My youngest daughter, Aimee, hasn't been seen for ten days now. She's about to have her first child and we're desperate to get her home safe. My deputies and I have done everything in our power to locate her, but so far, we have no evidence or witness testimony to help us. There was no reason for Aimee to disappear. Her mother and I love her dearly and have an excellent relationship with her. We were looking forward—" He stops, before correcting himself. "We *are* looking forward to the arrival of our first grandchild."

Nicole discreetly wipes tears away as she listens to her father talk so lovingly about his other daughter. She can't remember a time when he's said anything like that about her.

"I'm now calling on your help," he continues. "Someone knows where Aimee went, whether that was through her own volition or by force. Someone must have seen her after eight a.m. on July seventh. Please get in touch with me, my office, a deputy or my wife if you have any information at all."

A few seconds pass before he speaks again. "My final piece of news is that we tried to bring a local man in for questioning earlier today, in relation to Aimee's disappearance. He absconded before we could do that." His expression turns deadly as he stares directly into the biggest camera lens present. "It is imperative that *Tommy Peterson* comes in for questioning as a matter of urgency. If you see him, do not approach him yourselves as it's likely he's dangerous. He wasn't armed at the time he fled, but that could've since changed. If you get a sighting of him, call my office. My aim is to have him in custody by midnight tonight, and to immediately question him on the disappearance of my daughter and unborn grandchild."

His words are impactful due to the anger and indignation behind them. He's put on a good show for the cameras. But is that all it is? Nicole doesn't know, but she's glad Aimee's disappearance will finally receive much-needed news coverage. She considers the possibility that her father had nothing to do with Aimee's disappearance. Where would that leave her? Would it mean that Tommy hurt her? That Aimee left because she was unhappy? Or maybe that a stranger abducted her on her way out of the house. But there would be evidence if that were the case.

Nicole's mind races as she tries to figure out what happened. She feels lightheaded being stuck in the middle of the crowd with the sun beating down on her.

"I'll now take questions."

Several reporters throw questions at him, asking what has already been done in the search for Aimee, and why he believes Tommy was involved in her disappearance. His answers are vague, which is frustrating for Nicole, but understandable. He's never trusted the press, even when it wasn't his own daughter missing.

"What was she wearing when she was last seen?" asks a male reporter.

"Red plaid pajamas and white slippers," says Ron. "She hadn't yet gotten dressed."

"What would you say to Aimee if she's listening to this?" asks the same reporter. "If she left town to escape her problems for a while."

"I'd say call your mother, Aimee. End this misery for her." His expression is solemn.

Jennifer whispers into Nicole's ear, "You might want to move away from me."

She looks at the journalist. "Why?"

There's sympathy in Jennifer's eyes. "I need to ask him about something he's not going to like, and I don't want him thinking it came from you."

Nicole tenses. "Oh God. What is it?"

"I'm sorry. I'll explain afterward. Take a step back." Jennifer raises her hand and tries to get Ron's attention. Eventually he nods to her.

Nicole sinks backward, into the row behind. Her heart pounds harder with dread.

"Sheriff Chambers," says Jennifer confidently, "my question is in relation to Lori Peterson's murder. I've recently learned that there were some sexual assault allegations made against you around that same time by a teenage girl, and I wanted to know what was done about those and whether they were made by Lori."

Nicole's mouth drops open and a hush comes over the crowd. Everyone's surprised. Nicole makes eye contact with her father. Instead of looking at Jennifer, he's looking at her, and his expression suggests he could happily kill her right now. He must think she told the woman, but she didn't. Jennifer must have got straight to work on digging up the past as soon as Nicole left her office earlier.

Ron's face flushes with anger as Nicole's hands tremble. Her fingernails painfully dig into the palms of her hands.

Eventually, after a long silence, her father says, "That's preposterous." He turns and strides away, ignoring the follow-up questions thrown at him.

The male and female deputies present glance at one another with raised eyebrows. They're clearly blindsided. It's difficult to know which of them were privy to those allegations back then. Half of them wouldn't have been working at the sheriff's office at the time. And Chief Deputy Butler—Kurt's father—isn't present to give his reaction or to defend his boss. He almost certainly knew about them though.

After the sheriff disappears, the crowd slowly begins to disperse, leaving just the reporters behind to do their summing up to camera before signing off. Jennifer turns to Nicole. "I'm sorry you had to hear that. I was contacted by a source who told me a fourteen-year-old girl made the allegations the year before Lori went missing."

"I know about them already," says Nicole. She can't help but wonder what her father will do now. She's afraid he'll aim his anger toward her. There's a chance Aimee heard about the old allegations too. Maybe she threatened to tell someone and he felt he needed to silence her in order to save his own skin.

"You do? So it's true?"

Nicole's torn about what to do. She still has a sense of loyalty to her father, even after the way he treats her and her own suspicions about him. "I'm sorry. I can't talk about it."

"Sure, I understand," says Jennifer. "But just clear up one thing for me. Was it Lori who made the allegations?"

"I honestly don't know. She's the one who told me about them, but she made it sound like it wasn't about her."

Jennifer nods. "You realize that doesn't mean it wasn't though, right?"

Nicole closes her eyes. She can only pray that it wasn't.

TWENTY-SIX
SUMMER 2008

Lori slips her sunglasses on as the midafternoon sunlight is too bright when it reflects off of car windshields. Having left Lucas and Kurt behind in Sindy's backyard, she and Nicole are on their way to the library. It's near the high school and it's Lori's favorite place in town. It's always cool inside and the librarians are like ghosts—silently going about their business without comment or judgment, leaving her and Nicole to read whatever they want. Besides, who can resist a building filled with books? She can spend hours in here, and she and Nicole sometimes come after school to do their homework before heading home. She doesn't invite the guys because Lucas can't stay quiet. It's just not in him to talk quietly or act mature.

"I'll be over at the horror section," says Nicole, disappearing behind a stack of books. She's recently discovered Stephen King and can't get enough of his early work.

Lori heads to the Young Adult section. She's not a fan of horror and prefers books with romance and high school drama. Besides, her mom checks everything she brings home to make sure it's not too "mature" for a girl of her age. Although Lori's not ashamed to admit a few juicy ones have slipped past her.

The YA section is over near the counter and on her way, she hears Sheriff Chambers talking to Winnie, one of the librarians, about an attempted break-in last night. They seem to think it was just some kids from school messing around. "I've covered the broken pane of glass with a sheet of plywood," says the sheriff, "but you'll want to get someone in today to fix it properly. We wouldn't want anyone stealing all these precious books now, would we?" He winks at her.

With no hint of a smile on her face, Winnie appears unimpressed. "Well, I've told you who I think did it, so the ball is in your court now, Sheriff."

Sheriff Chambers nods, then turns. When he spots Lori, he breaks out into a grin and comes over to say hi. "What a surprise to find you in the library," he teases.

Lori reddens. "Hi." She's awkward around the police, especially the sheriff. She knows things about him that could get him arrested. Except she doesn't trust that his deputies would do it, what with them all being so close. Sheriff Chambers and Kurt's dad are especially close. She can even imagine they would kill for each other. Which is why she hasn't told anyone but Nicole about the sexual assault allegations.

"I can see you've been working on your tan," he says, eyeing her bare legs. "Are you enjoying your summer break, Lori?"

"I guess." She feels herself squirming. "I'm looking forward to school starting up again, to tell you the truth. I like structure to my day."

"Well, that's admirable," he says. "It sounds like you'll make a fine employee one day. Hey, maybe you could come work at my office. How about that?"

She lowers her eyes. "I don't think office work is for me, sorry." She turns around, looking for her friend. "Nicole's here somewhere."

"Oh, she is?" He looks around, suddenly straightening.

"Looking for more twisted tales, I'll bet. I don't know how she can read that stuff. It would give me nightmares."

"Really?" She frowns. "How can you be afraid of horror stories when your job literally involves arresting bad people and turning up at bloody crime scenes? Maybe you're in the wrong job." It comes out blunt and she realizes from the change in his expression that he doesn't appreciate her opinion.

"I'm just messing with you, Lori. I've seen more dead bodies than I care to and I could happily go without seeing another, so you make sure you girls stay safe." He plasters a smile on his face. "Anyway, I should get back to work. I hope to see you at our place for dinner soon, you hear me?"

Reluctantly, she nods.

"Dad?" Nicole appears. She approaches her father with a forced smile and lets him squeeze her shoulders. There's been tension between the pair lately. Ever since Lori told Nicole what she knows.

"Hey, sweetie," he says. "I hope you're being good?"

Nicole rolls her eyes. "I bet you wouldn't ask me that if I were a boy."

He misjudges her comment as a joke and laughs. Lori's always been a little jealous of their relationship. Even though Sheriff Chambers deals with crime all day, he manages to trust his daughter far more than her own parents trust her. They always want to know where she is, who she's with and what she's doing. She swears that's why they make her take Tommy with her everywhere she goes. They think she won't do anything risky if he's with her, plus he can report back if she does.

"Catch you girls later." The sheriff heads for the exit.

Nicole has five heavy hardbacks in her hands, all clearly horror judging from their spines. "I still have four at home, so this is my limit. Want to go back to my house and read?"

Lori glances at the YA section. "I haven't picked any yet."

She feels for her library card in her back pocket and realizes she left her wallet and her phone at Lucas's house. "Oh crap. I've left my things by the sun lounger. I'll have to go back to Lucas's."

"Lori!" exclaims Nicole. "I can't walk all the way back there with these." She motions to the books.

"Why don't you ask your dad for a ride home and I'll meet you there once I've collected my things? You've still got time to catch him."

Nicole eyes the exit, clearly tempted. "You don't mind walking?"

"No, it's fine. You should hurry."

"Okay." Nicole heads to Winnie who scans her books quickly for her and then she rushes out the door. Lori follows, slower, and spots Nicole climbing into her dad's cruiser just in time. She checks the clock on the front of the building: 4 p.m. Lucas and Kurt won't have left for football practice yet.

She starts off in the direction of Lucas's house, sweltering under the full glare of the sun.

TWENTY-SEVEN

SUMMER 2022

Nicole doesn't know what to do with herself. Lucas has returned home, her father thinks she's betrayed him by talking to the press, and her mother doesn't want to be anywhere near her. She finds an empty bench located in the shade just left of the sheriff's office and rests her head in her hands. She can feel herself slipping into a familiar dark place and it worries her. Whenever she suffers with anxiety, she gets shooting pains across her chest, and they just increase her unease. Each breath she takes feels too shallow. Each thought she has makes sense until the next one contradicts it, making her go around in circles.

Maybe she should have left Henderson with Lucas. At least they could have figured out their issue at home together and she'd have one less problem to overwhelm her. Her stomach flips with dread at the thought of what his cheating might mean for their marriage.

Nicole doesn't know if she can stay with him now. She needs details before she can process it, but she doesn't want details. If it was a one-off incident while they were teenagers, she could try to forgive it. But if there were more women over the years, then there's no way. They'll need to separate.

Just the thought of losing her husband makes her want to throw up. To distract herself, she checks her phone. Aimee hasn't replied to her Facebook message. She hasn't even read Nicole's message yet. Aimee's account holds no clues about her life as everything is set to private. Nicole can't even access her friend list. She's tried searching for her on Instagram and Twitter too, but there were too many girls with the same name, especially when spelled the conventional way.

Footsteps approach. She looks up. A girl of about seventeen or eighteen hovers in front of her. She's pale with long brown hair. Instead of wearing shorts or a summer dress she's in jeans and a hoodie. She must be sweltering. "You're Aimee's sister, right?" says the stranger.

"Right. Nicole. Are you a friend of hers?"

The girl nods. "I'm Stacey. Aimee's my closest friend."

Nicole moves across the wooden bench so the girl can sit next to her. Once seated, Stacey fidgets, pulling her sleeves down over her hands. Nicole wonders if she self-harms and that's why she covers up. "When did you last see my sister?" she asks gently.

"A few days before she disappeared," says Stacey. She glances around a lot, as if she's worried someone will see them together.

"Do you know where Aimee might be?"

Stacey shakes her head. "No. God, I wish I did. I miss her."

"Did she seem happy the last time you saw her?"

Stacey scoffs. "Is anyone really happy? I mean, she wasn't as okay as usual, but she wasn't talking about hurting herself or anything like that."

Nicole feels like the girl is being careful with her words. She won't make eye contact. "You obviously know her well. So where do you think she could be?"

There's a long silence, until, "I have no clue. But my first thought was that she'd gone to find you."

"Me?" Hope fills Nicole's heart. "Why? Did she miss me?"

Stacey finally looks directly at her. Her eyes are a deep blue color and her skin is flawless. The kind of complexion she and Lori always strived for at that age. "I think so. She told me she sent you a message on Facebook but you didn't respond. That really upset her. Like, *seriously* upset her."

Nicole looks away, consumed with guilt. "I didn't see it in time. I hate social media, so I rarely use it. My family and I, we've been estranged, and..." She stops herself from going into all the details.

"I know," says the girl. "Aimee told me you left town with your boyfriend. Lucas Rivers, right? I know his mom, Sindy. Only from calling in at the convenience store every now and then."

Nicole nods. "I had good reason to leave. And I didn't leave her behind on purpose. She was only six. I wasn't old enough to take care of her. My parents wouldn't have let me take her anyway. Turns out you can't just rescue your sibling from a shitty household. It's classed as abduction." She scoffs. "I tried to stay in touch, but they stopped passing on my letters."

Sympathy fills Stacey's eyes. "I get it. I'm not judging you, honestly. I have problems with my parents too. They hate me."

Nicole wants to reach out and touch this girl's hand to tell her that her parents are probably just hard on her because they care so much. But she doesn't want to minimize Stacey's feelings, and besides, who is she to say that? Maybe her parents *are* assholes. Just because someone gives birth to you doesn't automatically make them a good person. "I'm sorry you have crap parents too."

Stacey smiles faintly. "Aimee doesn't fight with your parents," she says. "Not that she's mentioned, and I think she would mention it if it was bad."

"No? They have a good relationship?"

"As far as I can tell. She never talks badly about them. But something *has* upset her recently."

Leaning in, Nicole says, "Do you know what?"

"No." Stacey shakes her head. "She was fine one day and then the next she was distant. She'd clearly been crying all night as her eyes were puffy."

"What day was that?"

"I've been trying to remember, but I can't. Sorry. I smoke a lot of pot and I'm pretty sure it's wrecked my short-term memory." She offers an embarrassed smile. "I know I shouldn't, but it's all I've got to get me through the day. Antidepressants don't work on me. Not in the dose the doctor gives me anyway." She laughs nervously. "Shit, I don't know why I'm telling you all this."

Nicole smiles warmly. "I used to smoke pot too but it didn't agree with me. It just made me feel sick and depressed. Pepperoni pizza however... Now that's a whole other level of comfort, and one you can get without seeing a doctor."

Stacey looks at her. "Aimee's going to love you. You remind me of her in some ways. It's not just your curly hair. You have a way of getting through bad things by joking about it. I wish I could do that more. My parents keep telling me I need to lighten up and get a sense of humor."

Nicole's floored for a second. She doesn't know what to say. Being compared to her sister means the world to her. "Tell me about her. What's she into? What does she want to do career-wise? I don't know anything at all."

Stacey lowers her eyes. "She loves athletics. Aimee's good at most sports on account of her height and build and she was offered scholarships for college but she turned them all down."

Nicole's never been athletic, so that's something they don't have in common. "Didn't she want to go to college?"

Stacey shakes her head. "No. She wasn't academic at all.

She couldn't concentrate on subjects like math or science. She found them boring."

"Doesn't everyone though?" says Nicole.

"Sure, but she got bored super easily and she always said that boredom felt painful for her. She couldn't cope with it. She liked keeping busy and preferred art, books and movies to what they teach in school. But your parents wanted her to study 'something serious.'" She sighs. "I think if she could've gone to art school, she might have been more interested, and maybe she will one day, but with the baby and all, she knew she'd be behind everyone else. So she stopped planning beyond the baby's birth."

Perhaps Aimee was descending into a depression from knowing that her life was on hold while her friends would be moving away and starting new chapters without her. "Was she happy about the pregnancy? I'm guessing it wasn't planned."

"No, it wasn't planned," says Stacey. "She was afraid, mostly. Once she got used to the idea she started collecting cute baby clothes and thinking about names, but she's definitely scared about being in labor and having no help with the baby."

"Of course. Who wouldn't be, right?" Nicole glances at a couple of older women approaching their direction on the side-walk. They stare hard at her before whispering something to each other and continuing past, toward the diner. They might have seen the press conference and be gossiping about her father. Or perhaps they're just surprised to see her back in town. "Do you know who the father of Aimee's baby is?"

"No," says Stacey. "But I wish I did. She wouldn't tell anyone. I don't know why. And I'm ashamed to say we argued over it. I couldn't understand why she wouldn't trust me to keep her secret."

"Does the father even know? Because if he does, and he didn't want her to keep it, that could be a motive for her disap-pearance."

"She wouldn't talk about it at all, so I don't know." Stacey's eyes fill with tears. "I don't even want to consider that as a possibility because that could mean she's already dead."

Nicole's disappointed. It can only be a bad sign that her sister didn't even feel able to confide in one of her closest friends about who the father was. "Could it be Tommy Peterson?"

Stacey visibly squirms. "I mean, I guess. But Aimee never dated him."

"Was he obsessed with her? Some people have suggested he was."

It takes some time for the girl to answer. Eventually she says, "All I can say is that I dated Tommy briefly. I ended it when I suspected he was only with me in order to have a legitimate reason to spend time with Aimee." Her lip quivers. She clearly feels used.

Nicole instinctively pulls her in for a hug. "I'm sorry. Men can be assholes." She thinks of Lucas and how he was able to deceive her.

After a few seconds Stacey pulls away and uses her sleeves to wipe her eyes. "Tommy isn't a horrible person. He'd do anything for Aimee. They have this weird connection, probably from being friends since childhood. I don't want to believe he'd hurt her. He knows she doesn't want a relationship and I think he's accepted that. He's just overprotective, like a brother. I put it down to the fact he lost his sister."

"Sure," says Nicole. "That makes sense. I really want to talk to him, but we'll probably never see him again now the police are after him."

A cruiser speeds past them. The siren makes them both jump.

Stacey's phone buzzes. She pulls it out of her pocket and glances at a notification. "It's my mom. I should go."

"Sure. Take my number in case you hear something about Aimee."

They both stand as they swap numbers.

"Thanks for talking to me," says Nicole. "It was nice to meet one of my sister's friends. Hopefully next time we see each other, Aimee will be with us."

Stacey offers a sad smile before walking away. It bothers Nicole. Because it suggests Stacey doesn't believe for one second that Aimee will be coming home alive.

TWENTY-EIGHT

From the Journal of Aimee Chambers

May 25, 2021—Age 17

School sucks. Everyone's desperate for scholarships and college places and I don't even know what I want to do with my life. I have no career aspirations at all. We're only seventeen, how the hell are we meant to know how we want to spend the next fifty years of our lives? And why does it have to be in one single career? I can't do anything longer than a few months because I just don't have that kind of attention span. The thought of working a 9–5 desk job makes me want to blow my brains out.

Dad says I could work for him as a clerk or train as a dispatcher, and Mom suggested I become a nurse, but I don't want to be around them twenty-four-seven. That's not healthy for anyone. I'd rather move away and become who I'm meant to be over time, not be shoehorned into a job I have no interest in just so that I don't look like a deadbeat in the eyes of their friends. I can tell Mom's disappointed I don't want to go to college.

I saw Nicole's husband today. He was at one of the coffee shops downtown. He didn't see me. I was building up the nerve to go over and say hi. I don't even think he'd recognize me after all these years even if he noticed me staring at him. Tommy had to point him out to me a few years ago, when I first learned he returned home every so often to visit his mom. The problem is, I don't know whether he'd talk to me or whether he and Nicole don't want anything to do with me, so I've kept my distance. I figure if Nicole wanted a relationship with me, she'd come to town with him, right? I know she left things in a bad way with Mom and Dad, but wouldn't she try to see me? Wouldn't she friend me on social media? Doesn't she care?

Her silence speaks volumes and I'd be mortified if I reached out to her and she blocked me without responding. It sucks. So Lucas seems to be my best chance at getting answers. Next time I hear he's in town, I'm going to talk to him. It's the only way to stop constantly thinking about it and to find out why they stay away from me.

TWENTY-NINE

A bang outside her hotel room makes Nicole jerk awake. Sitting up, she's confused at first, unable to remember where she is and why she's alone. The room feels alien, and the drapes are closed, although that doesn't stop the sunlight leaking in around the edges. Slowly, everything comes flooding back to her. She remembers last night's press conference. The conversation with Aimee's friend. The allegations about her father finally being made public.

She groans as she rests her head back on the pillow and pulls the light blanket over her face. Dread fills her stomach. Lucas is gone, Aimee's still missing and her parents will be on the warpath. Even so, she almost falls back to sleep. Stress is catching up with her. Maybe she could spend the whole day in bed and let everyone else figure themselves out. It's tempting. She finds herself dozing off until someone else walks by her room, catching her door with their luggage. It sounds like new guests are checking in.

With a frown, she reaches for her cell phone on the night-stand. It was on silent overnight to allow her to catch up on her sleep. Nicole's shocked by what time it is: 2.15 p.m. She's managed to sleep for sixteen hours. No wonder she feels groggy. She drops the phone back on the nightstand. Her mouth is in desperate need of water and she needs the bathroom. But she can't find the motivation to get out of bed. It seems like too much trouble. Pointless even. It's a familiar feeling and it reminds her she needs to get back into the routine of taking her antidepressants in order to stop her downward spiral. She needs the extra help now more than ever.

A familiar pain around her lower stomach grabs her attention. Premenstrual cramps. Her heart sinks. Every month she secretly hopes she'll skip a period, then another, until she can finally say she's pregnant. The disappointment that comes from knowing she has to wait longer makes her teary. Or maybe it's the looming period messing with her emotions. Feeling selfish for even thinking that way when her sister, who *is* pregnant, is in danger, she reaches over and reads the notifications on her phone's screen.

There's still nothing from Aimee. She opens Facebook and checks the message she sent her sister. It's still unread. That's not a good sign. If Aimee had run away, she would probably still check social media. Unless she's ditched everything in a bid to start fresh elsewhere. The thought gives Nicole some hope. Lucas has sent a brief text message.

I miss you. I'm sorry.

It would probably make her feel better if she didn't also have three missed calls from her parents' landline. No voicemail though. Jennifer Manvers has texted to say she hopes Nicole's okay, and there's a missed call from Kurt, followed with a text message.

Where are you? Are you okay?

She drops her phone on the blanket and sighs. Over-whelmed by how many people want something from her, she does nothing but stare at the white ceiling and allow the warmth of the bed to comfort her.

When a passing guest laughs obnoxiously, startling her, Nicole realizes she's fallen asleep again. After a few disorientating seconds she feels her bladder protesting. Her room isn't as bright as last time. The light has shifted outside. It's softened with the approaching evening. Panicked, she wonders how long she slept for this time. Her phone tells her it's now 7.10 p.m. "Shit."

She has four more missed calls but ignores them as she gets out of bed and heads to the bathroom, feeling guilty for sleeping so long. She knows that if she delays for one more minute she'll never get up. Not today anyway.

After a halfhearted shower she switches the TV on for company while she dresses. The local news channel is showing footage of her father answering questions at yesterday's press conference. An anchor tells viewers what Jennifer Manvers asked him about: the sexual assault allegation.

"Could it be that Henderson's longstanding sheriff has been hiding a disturbing past of his own?" asks the suited male anchor with the chiseled jaw and thick head of slicked-back hair. Nicole's frozen to the spot as he continues. "Many are speculating that instead of protecting his citizens, Sheriff Ron Chambers could himself be a predator, and that the discovery of Lori Peterson's body during the time his own daughter is missing might not be the coincidence it seems. We'll have more on that at eight o'clock."

Nicole perches on the bed. This is bad. This is exactly what her father was trying to avoid. She considers whether her own safety is at risk more now than ever. Because now everything is out in the open for the press to digest, her father could become desperate. She'll have to be careful from now on. She'll need to avoid being alone with either of her parents. She pulls on jeans and a T-shirt, then shoots a quick message to Lucas as he was one of her missed calls.

I just need some time. We'll talk soon.

She leaves her room and heads downtown for something to eat as she can't ignore her hunger pangs. After a Subway sandwich and coffee, she feels less groggy and more alert. The horrible taste in her mouth disappears. She passes a newsstand, where the main headline on the local paper screams: *Oates County Sheriff Accused of Sexually Assaulting a Minor.*

"Oh God." Although this is bad, part of her can't help but wonder whether the girl who accused him all those years ago, now a woman, will come forward to give her side of the story. That could provide Nicole with some much-needed answers.

As it's nearby, she walks toward the sheriff's office intending to call Kurt from outside and see if he's around. She wants an update on what she missed while she slept. Before she gets there a car pulls over to the sidewalk and stops. "Where have you been?" Kurt asks. His face is serious and full of concern.

"Why? What's happened?" She approaches his window.

"Nothing, but when I couldn't get ahold of you, I assumed you'd done something stupid. I saw the way your dad looked at you when that reporter brought up the allegations against him." He glances around to check no one is listening, but there are few pedestrians around. "I was about to head to your hotel to check on you. Are you okay?"

"Sure." She takes a deep breath. "I just needed to catch up on some sleep, that's all. Can I get in?"

He nods and once she's in the passenger seat he drives away from the sheriff's office. He finds a quiet corner in a liquor store parking lot and switches the engine off. They watch some kids on skateboards practicing tricks outside the store. "Where's Lucas?" he asks.

"He left after the stupid fight between you two at the hotel. Thanks for that, by the way," she says sarcastically. "You may have ended my marriage."

He touches her hand gently. "I'm sorry. He pissed me off. I never liked the fact he got away with cheating on you, but I didn't mean to hurt you. I probably shouldn't have said anything."

"I guess it was for the best," she says. "Because if he's still inclined to cheat, I won't be staying with him."

Kurt looks up sharply. "Really?"

She nods. "I'm not staying with someone who doesn't want to be with me, and what clearer indication is there than screwing other women?" She lowers her eyes and rubs her wedding ring. She always thought Lucas would be the father of her children. "I don't know. I need time to process what he did." She scoffs. "Although now I'm stuck all alone in a hotel I can't afford with nothing to do but go out of my mind."

"So come stay with me."

She frowns. There's no way she wants to be in the same house as Brian Butler. Every word she said there would get back to her father. "Thanks, but I don't think that's a good idea. Your dad needs his privacy. I'd feel awkward."

Kurt nods thoughtfully. "Well, the offer's there. You wouldn't have to see my dad. He sleeps downstairs these days." He looks at her. "I'm worried about you. This is a lot to deal with. I know because I'm feeling it too, and that's just the part about Lori being found. It's worse for you with your sister missing and this tension between you and your folks."

It's touching that he cares. "Thanks. I feel like I'm going out of my mind, so I'm glad it's not just me who sees how screwed up things are." She sighs. "If only it were possible to go back to that time and stay with Lori all night. I wouldn't let her out of my sight. I would take her to my house to stop whatever happened to her from happening."

He leans forward, resting his forearms on the steering wheel. "If only. God knows I'd like my childhood back."

She looks at him as he rubs his face.

"I feel like it came to an abrupt end when Lori vanished," he says. "I didn't get a chance to become who I was meant to be. Neither did you. Everything changed when I found out she was gone. And then they found that patch of blood in the grass near the playground..." He swallows. "I know it's a shitty thing to say, but it was unfair for all of us, not just for Lori."

She rubs his warm back, unsure how to respond even though she understands exactly how he feels.

"I want to be back in school," he continues. "Carefree and hanging out with you in my spare time."

"And the others, right?" she asks. "Lori and Lucas."

He looks at her, his eyes red-rimmed. He quickly looks away again. "Why doesn't anyone tell us we only get one try? One chance at being carefree and happy."

She smiles sadly. "Think we'd listen if they did? Not at that age."

He sits back. "I still don't get it. How *she* was targeted. Someone must've been waiting for her to be alone, because she was always with one of us. I wish I'd been with her. I could've..." He doesn't finish the thought.

"Kurt? You and Lucas had football practice. You couldn't be with her twenty-four-seven. None of us could. That's not our fault. The only person responsible for what happened is her killer."

He doesn't respond.

She frowns. "You guys *did* have football practice, right?"

Hesitantly, he nods. They sit in silence while they watch the last of the news vans drive by.

THIRTY

The evening sky is subtly darkening, but the air is warm as it gently blows through the car windows. Nicole's feeling sleepy again. It's as if her mind is trying to block out everything that's going on and just wants her to shut down instead. She feels guilty for sitting here with Kurt instead of doing something practical like searching for Aimee or handing out the missing person posters. But still, she doesn't move. She doesn't know where to begin fixing everything. She wants someone else to do it for her because it seems such an impossible task.

Eventually Kurt breaks the silence. "Your dad's pissed. He's still convinced it was you who told the journalist about the allegations against him, even though she denied it."

"He spoke to her?"

"Right. He called the newspaper's editor to complain. It didn't go down well. People are saying it just makes him look even more guilty." Kurt doesn't ask whether it was her who told Jennifer. Maybe he knows she wouldn't stoop that low. "I searched the police database," he says. "Even though I could get into trouble. No one has ever filed a complaint against him."

She raises her eyebrows. "You did that?"

He nods. "I had to know. And I doubt I'm the only deputy checking. So what's he going to do, fire us all?" He takes a deep breath. "Just because no complaint was filed on the system doesn't mean an allegation wasn't made. He's in charge, remember. The report might never have made it onto the computer."

She's disappointed. "So that means there's no record of who accused him?"

"Right. But now it's all over the news, you better believe it won't go away anytime soon. If the girl who accused him back then wants to see him pay for what he did, she might feel able to come forward again now that she's older. Maybe she'll feel ready to expose him."

Nicole's overcome with guilt that the poor woman will have to relive her ordeal, whether she chooses to do that privately or publicly. "If no one comes forward, there's a possibility that the allegations were false, right? I hope they were. I really don't want to be right about him, because that could mean he's responsible for Aimee's disappearance and I don't know how I'd ever get over that."

He tries to offer reassurance. "Well, it wouldn't be the first time someone's falsely accused a cop of a crime. Maybe Ron once arrested someone in the girl's family and they decided they wanted revenge. The girl could've been a pawn."

Nicole would prefer that explanation. "Has Tommy been found yet?"

"No," says Kurt. "It's just a matter of time though. When someone absconds unexpectedly, they always end up coming home for clothes and money. He'll try to sneak back temporarily; I have no doubt about that. You can't get far in this country without money. Not as a man anyway. No one picks up male hitchhikers or gives men a job if they don't have references. He'll come home. In the meantime, your dad's waiting for a judge to sign a warrant so he can search Tommy's apartment and try to get access to his cell phone records."

Nicole fixes her eyes on one of the teenage skaters. The thought of someone's apartment being searched for signs of her sister makes everything more real. What if Aimee's clothes are found in there? Or a bloodied murder weapon? A chill runs through her. Theresa must be going out of her mind with worry. Her only remaining child could be a killer. Despite what Kurt says, Tommy might never come back. He might realize his situation is hopeless and decide there's no way out but suicide. Especially if Aimee is dead.

A car enters the parking lot behind them and slowly approaches. When it pulls up alongside Kurt's, they watch Nicole's mother get out. Nicole's surprised to see her. She reluctantly rolls her window down farther and braces herself for an earful.

Her mother doesn't appear angry though. She leans down and acknowledges Kurt through the window before saying to Nicole, "I need to talk to you. I've tried calling you all day. Would you come home with me?"

Dread fills Nicole's stomach. "Why? What do you want to talk about?"

"I can't get into that here. No offense, Kurt, but this is family business."

He nods. "Not a problem."

Nicole gets out of the car. That's when she notices her father approaching them. He's parked farther away. "What's going on?" She has a bad feeling about this. As if she's about to be arrested.

Kurt gets out of the car and looks like he's going to walk away. "I'll give you all some space."

"No!" says Nicole. "Please don't go."

Ron stops next to his wife and to Kurt he says, "You should be looking for Tommy Peterson. You're not fifteen anymore,

Deputy, and the citizens of Henderson aren't paying you to hang out with my daughter, so get back to work."

"Dad, I want him here. Please, just tell me what's going on."

Kurt rests his hands on his hips. He appears uncomfortable but to his credit he stays put.

"Fine. If you insist." Ron looks around impatiently. When he's sure no one is paying them any attention he turns to Nicole and says, "These accusations you keep making about me have to stop. This attitude you have toward your mother and me is misplaced. I think it's time we had an honest conversation in the privacy of our home and not out here where reporters could catch us."

Nicole's afraid. She doesn't trust them. "Can't we talk in your office? It's right around the corner." She's tempted to add *where there will be witnesses*.

"I'd rather not," says Ron. "You never know who's listening and this is a family matter." He looks around. "In fact, where's Lucas? He should probably be here for this, not Deputy Butler."

She's beginning to feel trapped, like they're about to stage some kind of intervention. "He left town. We fell out."

Her parents share a look, as if they expected it. They're probably assuming Nicole has pushed Lucas away.

"Look, we have some answers to your questions," says Debbie. "And we don't want to talk about it here. Kurt can come if you feel you need a friend with you."

Ron doesn't look too happy about that. "Deputy Butler should be helping the others with the search. I need as many people out there as possible."

"I want him with me," says Nicole. If Lucas were here, she wouldn't need Kurt, but there's no way she's going home alone with them. Her heart rate spikes. This isn't normal. She shouldn't be afraid of her parents. She gets the urge to run away, which feels stupid, but her fear is real. At least if Kurt's with her, they can't do anything. They can't hurt her. Not physically anyway.

"Come on," says Kurt, motioning to the car. "It'll be fine. I'll take you."

She looks at her parents. Instead of anger on their faces, she sees pity. And, somehow, that feels so much worse.

THIRTY-ONE

Everything is bathed in orange as the sun dips low beyond the horizon. The fields and farmland around here are so flat that nothing blocks Kurt's view of it. Farms, haystacks and outbuildings become a blur as he follows Ron and Debbie's vehicles on the short journey to their home. Nicole is silent next to him, absently twisting her wedding ring so much it's making her finger red. She had tried calling Lucas but he didn't pick up. Kurt hopes she doesn't forgive him and attempt to stay in that marriage. He's willing to bet that because Lucas cheated on her in high school, he's done it again since. It angers him just to think of the asshole getting away with it.

His radio chatter increases with possible sightings of Tommy Peterson, so he turns the volume down since he can't help with the search right now. He glances at Nicole. "Are you okay? They're not going to hurt you, you know. It sounded like they just want to talk."

She's visibly trembling. "I don't know what they want. Why they suddenly want to talk to me now. They've been brushing me off ever since I got here, so why the turnaround?"

He can't understand her fear. Sure, Ron's intimidating and

Debbie doesn't show any affection for her daughter, but Nicole's being paranoid if she thinks they're going to hurt her. Unless he's totally misread the situation. He considers then whether coming with her was a bad idea. If she seriously believes Ron killed Lori, and that he would kill his youngest daughter to cover that up, then maybe there's a possibility he'd silence one of his deputies too. Especially one he isn't that keen on to begin with.

Kurt shakes the thought away. It's not possible. Ron would never do that to the son of his closest friend. "They can probably see you're struggling and want to step in before things get any worse," he says. "Try to give them a chance. Maybe it's time to bury the hatchet."

She turns away and watches the landscape go by. "No one ever believes me," she says. "It's exhausting."

He concentrates on the back of Ron's cruiser. He can see the sheriff's eyes on him in the rearview mirror. It's unsettling. Ron has a way of making Kurt feel like he knows something about him and he's just waiting for him to confess. He's heard people say that's how they feel in the presence of any law enforcement agent, but Kurt's only ever felt that way around Ron. "All we can do is see what they have to say and take it from there. If they're hiding something, or trying to gaslight us, I'll know."

Nicole scoffs. "You're so naïve."

Something about the way she says it makes the hairs on the back of his neck stand on end. When they reach the house, Kurt pulls up behind Ron's vehicle. Debbie is first into the house, closely followed by her husband. Neither of them waits for Kurt and Nicole. He's starting to feel a little on edge himself. He's never felt welcome here and today's no exception.

They get out of the car and Nicole reluctantly climbs the porch steps. Kurt follows her into the cool farmhouse. Debbie's in the kitchen, fixing drinks. "Go on into the living room," she says. "I'll just be a minute."

Kurt gives Nicole's hand a squeeze as she brushes past him to turn back toward the living room. Her hand is clammy with sweat. Ron switches the dim table lamps on before taking a seat in an armchair. Nicole opts for the couch. The seat nearest the door. She tucks her hands under her thighs and keeps her eyes lowered. She's clearly anxious. Kurt stands behind the couch, not wanting to sit unless invited. And, sure enough, the invite never comes.

"Did you hear the radio?" says Ron, looking at him.

"No, I turned it down. Have we found Tommy?"

"Not yet. Deputy Moore is following a sighting." Ron doesn't add any details in front of Nicole. Deputy Moore is a dedicated cop as well as a badass. If anyone can safely apprehend Tommy, she can.

"Tommy would never hurt Aimee," says Nicole, without looking up.

"He's no longer the sweet little kid you knew, Nicole," says her father. "He's changed a lot these past years."

Debbie enters the room with a tray of cups: two coffees and two sodas. No one reaches for one when she places the tray on the large coffee table in the center of the room. Debbie takes a seat on the couch, at the opposite end to Nicole. She looks at her husband and nods.

After a few seconds of silence, Ron says, "You look terrible, Nicole. Tell me what's going on with you."

Nicole looks up at last. "I just want my sister found. Then I'll leave town and forget I ever had a family." Her voice hitches at the end and Kurt assumes she's crying. He can't see from behind her. He leans forward and rubs her shoulder.

Debbie says, "You seem to think we don't want Aimee found. Why are you talking to newspaper journalists about us?

Have you seen the atrocious headlines? Can't you see you've made things so much worse?"

"No, I can't!" yells Nicole, coming to life. "I can't understand why you wouldn't talk to every journalist out there! It makes me think you've done something to her."

"Oh, for God's sake," says Debbie. She runs a hand through her hair in exasperation. "Why on earth would we hurt our daughter and grandchild? It doesn't make any sense!"

Nicole jumps up with tears streaming down her face. She's reached the end of her tether. "Because Dad killed Lori and you helped him to cover it up! Aimee must've found out and you silenced her."

The accusation hangs in the air while Nicole waits for them to react. Kurt can feel the tension in the room. He looks at both Ron and Debbie, but they don't react. Which is not what he would expect from two people who've just been accused of murder. He gets a horrible feeling in the pit of his stomach.

They know something.

Could Nicole be right? He watches them closely. His body goes on high alert and his right hand twitches for his service weapon. Because if what she said is true, and they're not even going to deny it, there's no way in hell that Ron Chambers will let him and Nicole walk out of here tonight. Not now Kurt's a witness to the accusation. He realizes it will be up to him to try to arrest the sheriff and get Nicole out of here alive.

Nicole's not done. "You killed Lori and you blamed it on Jim Marsh. But really it was you who put Lori's body in that silo, wasn't it?" She wipes the tears that stream down her face. "Aimee must have found out about it and threatened to tell someone. That's why you killed her too, isn't it? Tell me I'm wrong, Dad. *Please* tell me I'm wrong!"

Debbie lowers her head into her hands. She couldn't look more guilty if she tried. It makes Kurt nervous. After a deep breath she turns to her husband. "We have no choice," she says. "We have to tell her."

Kurt touches the butt of his weapon, convinced he'll have to use it any minute. He keeps his eyes on Ron. Especially when Ron's hands go to his holster. The sheriff unclips a small cigar case. They all watch in anticipation as he pulls out a cigar and lights it. He takes the first puff casually, as if being accused of two murders isn't something that bothers him. "Think she can handle it?"

"Handle what?" says Nicole, sounding unsure of herself now. She's still standing. "Are you finally going to admit it?" Her voice betrays her uncertainty. She's pushed them to this place but she doesn't want it confirmed. And who can blame her? Even Kurt is wishing he hadn't come here.

"Nicole, sit down." Ron stands. Like an eclipse, his tall figure blocks out the orange glow that streams into the window behind him. He looks at Kurt. "We're about to have a private family discussion, so I'd like you to leave."

Nicole turns to Kurt with fear in her eyes. "No, please. Don't leave me alone here with them." She walks around the couch to stand next to him.

Kurt licks his lips. "With all due respect, Sheriff, I'm not going anywhere without your daughter."

Ron's eyes bore into him. It's evident that it pains the man to have someone outside the family witnessing this episode. Ron has always protected his privacy, and at some point you have to question why that is. What he's hiding? Eventually the sheriff relents. "Then what I'm about to say is confidential. If you ever repeat a word of it outside these four walls, you can consider yourself fired. I don't care who your father is, I won't be rein-stating you under any circumstances."

Refusing to be intimidated, Kurt's eyes don't leave Ron's. "I hear you loud and clear."

"Good," says Ron. "And you should know that unemployment will be the least of your problems."

"Why are you being so mean to him?" says Nicole. "Just tell us what's going on."

"Fine." Ron and his wife stand in front of the couch. All four of them face off. Finally Ron says, "I didn't kill your friend, Nicole. I've never hurt a woman in my life, physically, mentally or... sexually."

Debbie shakes her head as if disgusted by the very thought.

"But I did move your friend's body."

Kurt stares at his boss, breathless. Next to him, Nicole gasps.

"I hid Lori so that she couldn't easily be found. And for that, I won't apologize."

Nicole leans against Kurt's side and clings on to his shirt. Kurt can barely stand upright himself. "Why would you do that?" he says, incredulous.

Nicole's body rocks with sobs. Her world has just imploded. Her worst fears have been realized. Kurt doesn't know how she's going to cope with this. Whether she can. Because if her father hid Lori's body, he must have been the one to kill her. Kurt's jaw is clenched so tight it hurts. Anger runs through him. Lori was his girlfriend. He cared about her. His world shattered when she vanished. And this son of a bitch is admitting to knowing where she was all along. He's on the verge of jumping over this couch to punch Ron Chambers.

"Nicole, listen to your father carefully," says Debbie. "He's telling you the truth."

When she regains some composure Nicole looks at them both, her lip quivering as she says, "I don't understand. Why did you hide her? And in that terrible place! You literally couldn't have dumped her anywhere worse."

Ron's hand trembles slightly as he takes a drag on his cigar. After exhaling the smoke, he says, "I was protecting her killer."

"*What?*" says Nicole. "That doesn't make any sense. Why would you do that?"

Kurt's hand still hovers over his weapon as Ron and Debbie exchange a look. There's a long agonizing silence before Ron manages to get out the words he clearly doesn't want to say. "Because it was you, Nicole."

Kurt's heart skips a beat as he struggles to understand.

Ron doesn't blink as he adds, "All this time I was protecting *you*."

THIRTY-TWO

Nicole's ears are ringing. Someone has seated her on the couch. Kurt's rubbing her hand. He's sitting too close. She needs space. Air. Room to breathe. She can't catch her breath. Her lungs conspire against her, only letting in a tiny amount of oxygen at a time. Her head spins with her father's words.

It was you, Nicole... I was protecting you.

She can't understand why he would say something like that. Perhaps it's retaliation because she accused *him*. This must be a selfish last-ditch attempt to shut her up. Or to gaslight her into believing she would harm her best friend. She loved Lori. They spent every single day together. Sure, they argued, but Lori was still alive when she left her that evening. Then confusion creeps in. Because she can't understand why her parents would be so cruel to her. And that night... she can't remember all of it.

Through her tears she says, "Do you hate me so much that you would let me take the fall for this? Just to save yourselves."

Her mother switches places with Kurt and takes Nicole's cold clammy hands in her warm ones. "You're in shock right now," she says. "You've forgotten most of what happened that summer. That's okay, it's probably a side effect of trauma, and the drugs you were on afterward made you groggy." She squeezes Nicole's hands. "Until now we thought you were unable to admit it, but when you kept insisting that we had something to do with it we realized you genuinely don't remember what you did. And once you'd gone to the press, we knew we had to remind you. I wish we'd done it sooner, to stop you from spreading those vicious lies about your father."

"We didn't want to remind you," says Ron, his expression grave. "This isn't easy for us, Nicole. We take no pleasure from it."

Nicole looks up at him but he won't maintain eye contact. He can barely look at her. "You told me to come back here in the first place," she says. "Why do that if I'm the cause of all your problems? It doesn't make any sense."

"It was a mistake," says Debbie. "We thought Aimee might come home if she knew you were here. But we didn't realize how confused you still were. We should've spoken to Lucas first. I'm sorry." She shakes her head. "I wish I'd spoken to him."

They always loved Lucas. He was the son they never had, and when Nicole and Lucas left town together, she felt her parents were more upset at losing him than her.

"Now we've told you, it will all start coming back to you over time," says Debbie. "In pieces, probably. We're here for you, Nicole. We're here to help you remember and to help you cope with it all over again. Just promise me you won't do anything stupid, no matter how afraid or guilty you feel. And that you'll stop accusing your father of sexual assault and murder."

Nicole shakes her head, incredulous that her mother has fallen for her father's lies. He's admitted moving Lori's body, so how can she believe Nicole killed her? Panic threatens to overwhelm her.

"Okay, I've got to say something," says Kurt. He's standing by the door like he wants to flee. Nicole wouldn't blame him if he did. If her legs weren't numb, she'd flee with him. "You both need to back up and explain what the hell you're talking about," he says. "Because I don't believe for one second that Nicole killed Lori."

"This is none of your damn business," says Ron. "So don't demand anything from me, boy." His tone is filled with anger.

Kurt steps forward, shoulders back. "Don't call me boy. I'm not going to stand by and witness you accuse your daughter of murder when I know she had nothing to do with it."

"Really." says Ron. "Care to explain how you know she didn't? Were you there that night? Did you see it happen?" He steps forward. "Was it you? I can see it now: your little girl-friend got nervous when you got too handsy with her, so you took what you wanted and then needed to silence her. Is that how it happened?"

Nicole watches as Kurt lunges forward and punches her father hard in the jaw. Ron's cigar falls to the floor. She and her mom gasp.

Kurt takes a step back, as if he's suddenly come to his senses.

"Wait until your father finds out what you just did," says Ron. "He'll be even more ashamed of you than he already is." His face is flushed red.

"Dad, stop!" yells Nicole. "Stop hurting everyone!"

Kurt turns away from them all and hovers by the door, his back to them.

Nicole doesn't know what he'll do next. She doesn't know why her father would say that to Kurt. She turns to her mother. "Why do you believe I killed her?" She has hiccups from the stress she's under. Each sentence comes out broken. "Is this why you hate me?"

Debbie pulls her in for a long embrace and it's so nice that there's a second where Nicole thinks maybe she *could* take the blame for this if it means her parents will love her again. When she pulls away, Debbie goes back to clutching her hand. "Tell her everything, Ron. Kurt too. After all, this involves his father."

Kurt spins around to look at Ron. "What's she talking about?"

Ron collects his cigar from the floor and goes to the corner of the room. He opens the drinks cabinet and fixes himself a neat bourbon. After ditching the cigar, he downs the drink. With his back to them, he takes a deep breath. "I wasn't technically on duty that night but I'd been shooting the shit with Brian at the office when he got a call-out at around midnight. So, knowing Debbie and the girls would already be asleep, I decided to ride with him. We found ourselves at a property just three miles from the park with the playground where the four of you liked to hang out and get high in secret."

Nicole lowers her eyes. She had no idea her parents knew she sometimes went there to smoke or drink with the others. She resists the urge to look at Kurt. He's the one who always brought the pot and rolled the joints.

"We attended a domestic," he continues. "A couple who'd had too much to drink. Seemed simple, yet it went on forever. They were at each other's throats and we could barely separate them long enough to cool them down. We eventually managed to get the guy to leave for the night and sleep in his car outside his buddy's house, giving them both time to sober up. It was almost one a.m. by the time we drove by the park. Brian saw something reflecting in the moonlight. I thought it was a pile of sweaters left behind by a bunch of kids, or maybe someone sleeping rough, but it bothered him, so we pulled over. After retrieving my flashlight from the trunk, we walked over to where it was."

Nicole slams her hands over her ears. She doesn't want to hear what he's going to say. She doesn't want to picture her friend that way. Her mom gently removes her hands. "You need to hear this."

Kurt remains deadly still.

"We came across Lori. She was lying on her back." He pours another drink and downs it. "It was obvious that she was already dead."

Snot and tears run down Nicole's face. Her mom retrieves a tissue from her pocket and wipes it away the best she can. Nicole stares at her father's back. "Why didn't you take her to the hospital? Call her mom? Tell anyone what had happened?"

"Brian wanted to. He almost radioed it in. Except, I found the rock that was used to hit her. It was bloodied and stuck to it were strands of her—" He stops himself from going further.

"But I don't understand why you're saying *I* did it," Nicole says. "Do you need me to take the blame for this? Is that what it'll take for you to bring Aimee back? Please don't hurt her, Dad. Aimee's done nothing wrong. Wherever she is, whatever you've done, please tell me there's still time to bring her home alive? I'll confess to this if you just bring my sister home." She's helpless against the tears that stream down her face.

Debbie gets up and walks away, sniffing back her own tears. Kurt approaches and rests a hand on Nicole's shoulder. "You're not confessing to anything," he says. "I won't let you."

She looks up at him. "I just want my sister back."

Her father finally turns to look at her. His face is etched with anguish and it hurts to see him this way. "Nicole. I know it was you, alright? I..." Struggling to find the right words, he doesn't finish his thought.

Debbie looks at her. "I think you should go lie down. You're so upset, and I'm worried about you. We can pick this up again in the morning. It's been a long day and your dad needs to get back to work to try to find Tommy."

Nicole doesn't want to pick this up again, ever, but she's confused and emotionally drained. She wants to go to sleep so she can wake up and find out this was all a bad dream. Everything. From Lori's murder to Lucas cheating on her, and her parents trying to blame her for something she didn't do.

Kurt steps forward. "We're not getting anywhere, so we should go for now. Come stay with me. I don't think you should stay here. It's not good for you."

Ron bristles. "This is her home."

Spinning around, Kurt yells, "I don't care. She needs a break from you people. You're destroying her with this stuff. Can't you see that?"

They stare each other down until Ron says, "Deputy? If you get the urge to tell anyone that I moved Lori's Peterson's body, just remember that it will be Nicole who suffers the most."

"Your dad too," says Debbie. "Because, like Ron, he never told anyone."

Kurt stiffens, his face a ball of anguish. "Are you saying my dad helped you move her body?" He slowly shakes his head. "I don't believe for a second he'd do that. He wouldn't do that to me, let alone to Lori's parents."

"No, he didn't," says Ron. "He refused to help. But when we had reason to believe Nicole had killed her, he agreed not to tell anyone what I did. It didn't sit easy with him, I know that, but he did what any good friend would do. He helped me to protect my daughter."

Nicole stares at Kurt. He must be relieved to hear that his father isn't as corrupt as hers. Brian would still be in trouble though, if all this comes out. Assuming he lives long enough. With trembling legs, she stands. She needs to get out of here as fast as possible as she doesn't have the energy to keep fighting for answers. Not right now. She needs time away from them in case she starts believing what they've accused her of.

Her father leaves the room ahead of them, without any final

parting shot. Her mother turns away as Kurt takes Nicole's hand. "Let's collect your things from the hotel."

Dazed, Nicole follows him out of the living room. She glances back to look at her mother in case she wants to tell her this is all a sick joke. But Debbie is already pouring herself a drink.

THIRTY-THREE

When they arrive at Kurt's childhood home, Nicole doesn't want to get out of the car. The sun has set, leaving the house shrouded in darkness. The porch light is on but the house isn't lit from within, and with none of the usual signs of life, such as a flickering TV or movement behind the windows, it doesn't look welcoming at all. She finds herself wondering whether Brian has passed away inside while Kurt's been distracted, which keeps her glued to her seat.

She can't go inside if he's dead. It might be selfish but she doesn't feel able to cope with anything else tonight. Death has followed her since she was fifteen and now, she just wants to run from it.

"Come on," says Kurt, opening her door from the outside. "You don't have to talk to my dad. He's more or less confined to his bed now, so you won't even see him."

She looks up at his face, masked with shadows. It hasn't escaped her notice that she's spent more time with Kurt over the last few days than with her husband. She'll need to tell Lucas what's happened. What her parents accused her of. But not tonight. She doesn't have the energy and she can't shake this incessant headache. For Kurt, she forces herself out of the car and follows him to the house. "Are you sure your dad won't mind me being here? He won't want his privacy? You should check with him before I go in."

Kurt turns his key in the lock. "I'm sure he won't care. And it's not like there's anything he can do about it even if he does, right?"

Inside, there is just one light on, at the end of the long hallway. That must be Brian's makeshift bedroom. Kurt switches on some lamps. The soft yellow glow illuminates the quiet home, making it instantly less frightening. "Go on upstairs," he says. "You can have my room, second door on the right. There's fresh bedding in the closet. I'll just check on my dad before I come up. You want coffee? I have decaf."

"No, I want vodka or tequila. Got any?"

He smiles. "I'm sure I can find something." He disappears along the hallway.

Having checked out of the hotel, Nicole has her suitcase with her, haphazardly stuffed with the belongings she assumed she would only need for a couple of days away from home. She climbs the stairs, suitcase in one hand. The upstairs is dark but she finds the correct room and flicks the light switch on. Signs of Kurt are everywhere: police uniforms hanging over the closet door, a row of sneakers at the foot of the bed, free weights scattered on the floor. A large TV sits on the dresser. She switches it on to give Kurt and his father some privacy. A cookery show comes on. She makes sure the volume isn't too loud before abandoning her suitcase and collapsing onto the bed.

Her body feels numb. A lot like after Lori vanished. She doesn't know how to process what happened tonight. It was so bizarre and upsetting. If Kurt hadn't been with her, she might be left wondering whether she had dreamed it all. Her father genuinely appeared to believe she killed Lori, but she's not buying it. If he's capable of hiding a teenager's body when he's in a position of trust, he's shown himself capable of lying about anything. She swallows back a sob. How could he have done that?

He let Lori's family go through fourteen years of hell when he knew all along where she was. How did he sleep at night? Memories of him sitting in the darkened living room with just the glow from his cigar come back to her. When she would wake up needing a glass of water, she would have to pass the living room. He spent a lot of late nights just sitting in the dark. Now she knows why. Her father was alone with his thoughts. With his horrifying memories. He would have been remembering what he'd done: climbing the ladder on the silo with Lori's lifeless body flung over his shoulder. Was she heavy? Lori didn't weigh much, but Nicole knows from the animal shelter where she works that dead weight adds pounds. Her father dropped Lori into the weather-beaten silo instead of doing his job. If Lori had been found inside there any sooner, Jim Marsh could have gone to prison for life.

It occurs to Nicole that she doesn't know her parents at all. They would even care for Tommy when the Petersons couldn't cope. And still they said nothing. They kept their terrible secret.

She wipes away a tear. If they can be that deceitful, and then blame it all on *her*, it shows they're capable of harming Aimee. Just the thought of it makes her tremble. She doesn't know where she's meant to go from here. What she can do. No one at the sheriff's office is going to help her, so she'll need to tell Jennifer Manvers everything. Her father should be locked up for what he's done. Someone needs to investigate what really happened that night.

But the flip side of that needs consideration. It would undoubtably result in her parents telling the world that they believe *she* killed Lori. What if people believe them? Lucas might leave her. Lori's parents would hate her. She could go to prison for murder. Her heart thuds in her chest as she realizes it will be her word against her parents'. And no one in town except Kurt would take her side. She feels sick. She just wants to end this once and for all, but it's not a fight she feels able to take on.

Familiar feelings of fear, dread and a complete lack of control threaten to overwhelm her. Her mind pushes her to consider other ways out. More final options. It has a way of making them seem reasonable in times of trauma. Her hands tremble harder. It would be a relief to not have to deal with any of this. To not have to think about going through another day feeling this way. She swallows, afraid of where her mind is going, because it doesn't seem unreasonable right now.

Raised voices reach her from downstairs. She sits up and presses mute on the remote control. She tries to listen. Kurt's pissed. His dad must be unhappy about her staying. Her own dad probably called Brian to give him the heads-up.

Wanting to distract herself from harmful thoughts, she gets up to go downstairs and face Brian Butler. He must believe her father's lies and she wants to know why. He was there when they found Lori. He might be able to fill in the missing pieces for her. She follows their voices to the back of the house. Kurt and his father are in the middle of a heated discussion when she rounds the corner and sees Brian.

She almost gasps. He's no longer the man he used to be. Once a broad guy with muscles that strained against his uniform thanks to his love of boxing, he's now a bag of bones. His mouth is caving inward as the muscle and fat wastes away from his cheeks. His skin is pale and heavily lined. His head bald. Nicole's no expert but it doesn't look like he has long left. And that makes her heart ache for Kurt.

Any resentment she had for her father's closest friend drains out of her. "I'm sorry," she says. "I just came to say thank you for letting me stay the night, but I don't want to cause problems between you two. I can return to the hotel, it's not a problem."

"You're the problem," says Brian, his expression resentful. "You have been all along. Can't you see that? Can't you see how many lives you've ruined? If my son wasn't in love with you, he'd see it too. He'd run a mile. I'd make sure of it."

Nicole's eyes fill up but she blinks back the tears. "I don't want to fight with you. I'm sorry. I'll go." She swings around and runs along the hallway to the front door but Kurt follows and manages to stop her before she can get out of the house.

"Nicole, stop." He grabs her hand and spins her around. "Don't listen to him. He's lashing out at everyone right now, afraid of what's happening to him. You can't take it personally. At least stay the night. We can figure something else out tomorrow."

She gulps back a sob. Everyone thinks she's trouble, but she's not. She's just trying to find her sister. "I'm so sorry about your dad. I wish he could get better. I don't want to stress him out."

"It's fine. Just because he's ill doesn't mean he should get away with being a dick."

Knowing she doesn't have the energy to go anywhere else tonight, she lets Kurt lead her upstairs. In his room she slumps back on the bed and closes her eyes. Kurt busies himself around her, tidying up. Eventually, he gently lays a blanket over her. "I was going to sleep on the couch but I can stay awhile if you'd like?"

She opens her eyes. The TV is off, and the small lamp on the nightstand is on instead of the big light. Kurt's changed out of his uniform, into jeans. His chest is bare, exposing his tattoos. He slips on a T-shirt as he sits next to her on the bed. Brian said Kurt's in love with her but that's not true. Kurt's just confused right now. Recent events leave them both tethered to a time in history that they can never change, no matter how much they want to. He needs a friend as much as she does. And neither of them wants to be alone. "Stay."

He lies beside her and they both stare at the ceiling. Her headache is finally beginning to subside, but she doesn't feel like herself. Every movement has a dreamlike quality. It almost feels like when she would smoke one of Kurt's joints. She's half expecting to wake up in her own bed at home with Lucas beside her. The last time she had been this fuzzy headed was after Lori disappeared.

"I wonder if your dad will fire me," says Kurt. "I don't even know if it's worth going to work tomorrow."

"He can't fire you. You know something about him that's so bad it would get him fired and then vilified in the press. His beloved community would finally see him for the person he really is. He needs you—both of us—to keep that secret."

"True." He smiles sadly. "I guess I need to figure out whether I like being a cop more than I want to see him get what he deserves."

She looks at him. "If you tell anyone, I'll be in the firing line too. We need to find out why he thinks he can blame me for Lori's death. He might have faked some evidence or something."

Kurt's quiet for a long time. Eventually he asks, "Why did you pull out of school after Lori vanished?"

She swallows. "I didn't. My parents put me in the hospital."

He turns onto his shoulder and looks at her. "What do you mean?"

She closes her eyes against the disjointed memories of that time. "I guess I had some kind of breakdown. I couldn't cope without Lori, or with the thought of what must've happened to her. Because of the allegations against my dad, I was convinced right away that he'd killed her. That night, he came home hours after her disappearance even though he wasn't on duty. It raised my suspicions once we knew for sure that Lori had been attacked."

"Now we know where he was," says Kurt. "What he was doing."

"Do we though? He said he moved her body but he wouldn't admit to killing her."

Kurt looks thoughtful. "No, and he never will. People like him never do. He doesn't want to lose the control he has over this town. The power that comes with his position."

He could be right. Nicole tries to warm her freezing hands by rubbing them together. "Eventually I outright accused him, and do you know what he did? What they both did?"

He shakes his head.

"They told me I was ill. That I was having a break from reality and they were worried I was going to hurt myself."

He looks disgusted. "Were they trying to silence you?"

She looks into his eyes. He was present at their home tonight, which means he's finally witnessed what they can be like. He's finally starting to believe her. "They must've been." She tries to get her head around what's happened tonight. "The only other reason they would accuse me of killing Lori is if they genuinely believed I killed her." She shudders at the thought. Something is eating away at her and she doesn't want to acknowledge it. "Kurt? What if they're right? What if I did kill Lori?"

He takes her cold hands in his. It's more comforting than she could've expected. "You don't remember that night?" he asks.

She looks away as a tear slides down the side of her face onto the pillow. "I'm so confused. Everything is so hazy from that time. Not just that night but my hospital stay afterward. I don't even know what meds I was on. I just took whatever the nurses gave me. I had no choice. My parents were in charge of my care. I had no say and no control."

She only remembers those months through flashbacks, but she won't let them in. She forces them away as soon as they rear up.

Kurt turns her face to his and fixes his eyes on hers. He leans in and kisses her.

She freezes. It feels wrong to pull away from him again. He's helping her. He's the only person she can trust right now. But when he moves closer, she turns her face away. "No. We can't. I'm sorry."

He hesitates. "I'm just trying to comfort you."

Nicole sits up. "Kurt, I've told you before that we can't do this. I'm married."

He gets off the bed. "Your husband is a cheating sack of shit who's probably screwing another woman right this minute and you're worried about hurting *his* feelings?"

She's never seen him like this before and it worries her. She considers whether her actions have unintentionally led him to believe she has feelings for him. She doesn't think so. "I'm in the middle of an emotional crisis. I need you to be my friend. I don't need you hitting on me."

He turns away from her and runs a hand though his hair as he calms down. Eventually he turns back around but he won't look at her. "Sure. I'm sorry. I'll sleep on the couch."

She watches him leave. When he's gone, she feels even more confused. What he did was wrong and inappropriate. So why does *she* feel guilty?

THIRTY-FOUR

After an unsettled night, Nicole gets up early and waits in Kurt's room for him to wake. She's more alert than yesterday, but she'd kill for some coffee. Not that she's planning on going downstairs to find the kitchen. She doesn't want to wake anybody, especially not Brian. He may have been hard on her but she can't wish him any ill will. Not when he's so close to death.

Quenching her thirst will have to wait. Kurt will need some clean clothes before heading to work, so he'll have to come upstairs sooner or later. She's dreading seeing him after what happened, but that's the least of her worries. She wants to get out of town and go home to Lucas, and in order to do that she needs to know what happened to Aimee. Now that there's some momentum with news coverage thanks to the recent press conference, she's hopeful new leads might have come in. And the only willing contact she has inside the sheriff's office is Kurt.

Her phone buzzes with a text message from her mother.

Please put my mind at rest. You won't tell anyone what your dad said last night, will you?

Nicole rolls her eyes. They're only concerned about them-selves. They don't want anyone knowing her father moved Lori's body. She's not surprised. It's practically an admission of guilt. Her phone buzzes again.

Let's focus on finding your sister. Everything else comes second to that.

She sits with her phone in her hands, unsure how to respond. It's easier to communicate by text than face to face, so she can see why her mother reached out this way. But she can picture her father watching the phone over Debbie's shoulder. He's probably telling her what to say. Eventually, she replies.

Why does Dad think I did it?

Minutes go by with no response. Nicole gets up and approaches the window, peering outside. It's another perfect summer's morning. The neighbors' kids are already heading out on their bikes and she wonders what fresh adventures await them. She's jealous that they're so carefree. Maybe they need warning about the dangers that await them. How life can turn on a dime and those you trust the most can turn out to be the worst people you'll ever meet. Far worse than any stranger.

"Jeez, I'm messed up," she mutters with a sigh. "They're just kids. Let them have their fun."

Her phone vibrates on the bed. She goes to it. Her mother has replied.

There was evidence at the scene that proved you're the one who hurt her.

Nicole's heart skips a beat. They must have planted something to make her look guilty. That's the only explanation. *Isn't it?*

But we know you didn't mean to kill her.

We know you loved her.

You must've lashed out in anger. You admitted you'd argued, right?

Nicole's eyes fill with tears. This is too much. They're accusing her of murder one minute, then declaring she's not a bad person the next. That she didn't mean it. They're messing with her mind. And these are her *parents*. The people who are meant to love and protect her. She sniffs back tears and hardens her heart as she replies.

Prove it. Tell me what he found.

She throws her phone on the bed and slumps back against the pillows. It's true that she had argued with Lori that evening. That she had left Lori alone in the park while she ran home alone. Her memory is hazy. She remembers she had been drinking, and they had smoked a couple of Kurt's joints. They were stronger than usual. The pot had made her feel strange. Out of it. That's probably what caused the argument and made them paranoid. She vaguely remembers what the argument was about though. Lucas. The next thing she remembers after running home was the following morning, when her mom told her that her dad had been working all night, even though he wasn't scheduled to.

An hour after that, Theresa had called their home looking for Lori. She'd said Lori's bed hadn't been slept in and her cell

phone was on her nightstand. Nicole remembers Lori intentionally leaving it there before they went to the park that evening.
Lori had explained she wasn't expecting to hear from Kurt that
night and the only other person who would contact her was
Nicole, so she didn't need it.

Nicole tries to concentrate on the sequence of events, but
everything else comes to her in short blasts. News reports about
blood being found in the park. Kurt's distraught face when he
arrived at her house to ask if it was true. It was the first time
she'd ever seen him cry. Or seen any teenage boy cry. It was
unsettling. Until then she believed boys didn't cry. Lucas
arrived later. He looked like he'd seen a ghost and was subdued.
Unlike the rest of them, he hadn't asked any questions. It was as
if he couldn't believe it could happen to someone they knew.

She remembers trashing her room that day, and screaming
at her parents, constantly accusing them of hiding something.
Then, disjointed memories of weeks and weeks in the hospital.
Inedible hospital food. A psychotic girl in the bed next to her,
always screaming at the nurses, stopping Nicole from getting
any peace. She remembers constantly feeling either drowsy or
nauseous, never well or alert. She remembers her mother's
strained face as she sat next to the bed during visiting hours.
And doctors asking her over and over again whether she wanted
to harm herself.

That reminds her of something. She had told her mother
she wanted to die. She cringes as she recalls telling anyone who
would listen how she would do it if they let her out. She had a
plan. She groans as she recalls what it was but quickly pushes
the memory away. It had taken her a long time to realize she
should be saying the opposite to people, so that she could actually get out of the hospital and make good on her promise.

She doesn't remember being discharged but, once home,
Lucas was with her every day. Her parents let him sleep in her
room with her. Although she was only fifteen and Lucas a year

older, they were allowed to share a bed. Nothing happened between them. Like Lori before she disappeared, Nicole was still a virgin. And Lucas never tried anything with her while she was suffering. But the fact her parents let them share a bed at that age shows how worried they were for her mental health. They must have been desperate. They must have believed Lucas could stop her from harming herself if he was with her as much as possible. Because she didn't want to be around them on her own.

It was clear from their frightened expressions during that time that they let him take care of her because they didn't know how to. Not after she accused her father of killing Lori. Lucas had stayed with her through that terrible time, after seeing her at her worst. It would have been a difficult time for him. A haunting experience for someone so young. It's probably why Sindy always treated her with barely concealed resentment. He had spent more time with Nicole during those months than with his mother.

Because of Lucas's care and devotion back then, it would be tempting to give him a pass for cheating on her, especially if it was during those months when he was under a lot of pressure. But he shouldn't have stayed with her if it was out of a sense of duty. He should only be with her if he loves her. She'd rather he ask for a divorce than stay while cheating on her. Maybe he doesn't think she could handle it.

The silence is broken with more text messages. She reaches for her phone.

> *We can't trust that you won't tell a reporter what it is.*
> *We're trying to protect you, Nicole. You have to believe us.*

She doesn't know what to believe. Because if she's completely honest with herself, her memory isn't to be trusted.

Fear grips her. She's always believed she left Lori in that park alive.

But what if she didn't?

THIRTY-FIVE
SUMMER 2008

Lori clutches her wallet and cell phone tightly after retrieving them from Lucas's house. She glances over her shoulder as she walks. No one is there, but she feels eyes on her.

Lucas's home is near to where the sex workers hang out during the evening. A nearby halfway house attracts drug dealers and pimps. Sheriff Chambers is always warning Lori and Nicole to stay away from there, and to run away from any cars that might roll up beside them as they walk. He's told them anything could happen here, and he was right. Lori never liked being here alone, and after what just happened she's determined to never return. It's tempting to call her mother for a ride but she could really do without the inevitable lecture that would follow. Besides, her mother will never let her out of her sight if she learns what just happened.

It's quiet for a summer's day. A day that warrants a relaxing walk in the sunshine. But Lori walks much faster than usual, and by the time she reaches Nicole's street she's forgotten to stop by the library first to get a new book to read. She just wants to be somewhere safe and familiar. Her hands tremble so much she drops her phone. "Shit."

She quickly scoops it off the ground. The screen is unbroken but she doesn't hang around to see if it still works.

Continuing her journey, she wonders whether being with Nicole is a good idea. Lori has a secret so damaging that she can never tell anyone, and that doesn't work with best friends. Nicole can read her like a book. She'll know something's happened.

Too late, she realizes she's at Nicole's house. She drags her feet up the driveway and is startled by Debbie leaving for work. Lori wishes she had arrived a minute or so later to have avoided her, because she can't look Nicole's mother in the eye.

"Hi, Lori," says Debbie. She's dressed in scrubs and headed out to her car. "Nicole's on the porch out back with Aimee and Tommy. Your mom dropped him by on her way to fetch groceries. Help yourself to anything from the fridge."

"Okay. Thanks, Mrs. Chambers." Debbie gets into her car and Lori's relieved when she notices the sheriff's cruiser isn't here.

Debbie rolls the window down and looks at her before reversing out of the drive. "Everything okay, honey? You look a little spooked."

"Uh-huh." She nods.

"Well, alright. You kids be good." Debbie's car slowly creeps away from the house.

Lori climbs the porch steps and lets herself into the house. She walks through the cool, silent interior to the kitchen. From the fridge she grabs a bottle of water and holds it to her head to try to cool down. She takes a deep breath in an attempt to calm her nerves. This afternoon hasn't gone as she planned and she isn't sure how to process it.

Without warning, four-year-old Aimee bursts into the kitchen from the backyard, chasing a ball. She jumps when she spots Lori.

"Hi!" says Lori brightly, masking her anxiety. "Where's your sister?"

Aimee picks up her ball and grins before running out of the house. It makes Lori smile. She's so damn cute, just like Tommy. She follows her outside where Nicole is reading in the shade on the top step of the porch. Nicole looks up at her. "You took your time! Where are your books?"

"I couldn't be bothered to go back to the library in the end."

Nicole frowns. "But you walked right by it to get here."

Lori doesn't reply. Instead, she places her water next to Nicole and offers to play catch with the kids. She needs to distract herself and, of course, the kids agree. Tommy has a Band-Aid over one knee. She gently touches it as she leans down to hug him. "What did you do?"

Tommy says, "Don't touch it! I fell off my bike. Mommy said I was going too fast but I wasn't."

"Sure," she says playfully. "I believe you." She throws the large air-filled ball to Aimee first.

"I kissed it better," says Aimee while enthusiastically scissoring her arms and closing her eyes in an attempt to catch the ball. She fails.

"Eww." Lori screws her face up to make them laugh. "I hope you kissed it *over* the Band-Aid."

The kids giggle before taking turns to drop the ball. Aimee is wearing a cute peach-colored sundress, with bare feet. Her curls are sun-kissed. Lori slips her own shoes off and feels comforted by the warmth of the grass beneath her. It would be easy to believe nothing terrifying happened less than an hour ago, but the sensation is short-lived.

"Lori?" says Aimee. "Are you my best friend or Nicole's best friend?"

Lori smiles. "We're all best friends."

"No!" says Tommy. "I'm Aimee's bestest friend." He looks at Aimee. "Okay?"

Aimee nods emphatically. "Okay. You can sleep in my room tonight."

Lori and Nicole share a look to suggest they could melt from a cuteness overload. But Lori's hands are still trembling, so she quickly looks away before Nicole picks up on her unease.

THIRTY-SIX

SUMMER 2022

Nicole needs to call Lucas. She needs to tell him her parents think she's a killer. With the house still silent, she doesn't want to wake anyone by talking too loudly, so she tiptoes downstairs with her suitcase in one hand. A creak on the old wooden stairs makes her wince. She stops, waiting to hear whether anyone stirs. They don't, so she continues past the living room. She can see Kurt asleep on the couch. His expression is peaceful, his hair messy.

Once outside, she dumps her suitcase by the side of the house before walking around to the backyard for privacy, making sure she's far enough away from Brian's window before she places the call. The drapes are still closed. Lucas answers on the fourth ring. "Hey."

Her shoulders loosen a little at hearing her husband's voice. "Hi. Did I wake you?"

"No, I've just showered. I was going to head into work today seeing as you're still in Henderson and you clearly don't need me."

She kicks at a weed in the middle of the sun-scorched lawn. "Actually, I need you more than ever right now."

"Why?" His voice becomes full of concern. "Have they found Aimee?"

"No. But the media are all over that now, so hopefully it's just a matter of time before someone comes forward with a sighting or something. I'm going to stay a little longer. I want to be here when they find her. I've messaged my boss to let her know."

"Of course, stay as long as you need to. Do you want me to come back? Have you fallen out with your parents?"

She takes a deep breath. "You remember when I was in the hospital, right?"

"Of course. I'll never forget that time."

"Did my parents tell you why I was admitted?"

He doesn't respond right away. "You'd had some kind of breakdown because of Lori's disappearance. They said you wanted to hurt yourself."

Nicole nods, even though he can't see her. "Did they tell you anything else?"

He sighs down the line. It makes her edgy. It feels as if he's just realized something. "I take it they've finally told you?" he says.

The way he says it blindsides her. *He knows.* He's known all along. Which begs the question: why is he with her if her parents believe she killed Lori?

"Nicole?"

"Sorry. I..." She doesn't know how to react. Lowering her voice, she says, "They told me they have evidence that I killed Lori, and that my father hid her body to protect me."

"Wait. *What?*"

"Oh. You didn't know?"

"That's insane!" says Lucas. "All they told me back then was that they had reason to believe you might've been involved in whatever happened to Lori. But they never told me Ron hid her body! As far as I knew, Ron and his team didn't know where she was."

With closed eyes, she says, "They weren't honest with you." She tries to explain everything that happened at their house last night, and how the press is also looking into the allegations against her father. When she's done, Lucas is silent. She watches a bird dig for worms in the soil near her feet.

Eventually Lucas says, "I'm coming back. You shouldn't go through this alone."

She was hoping he would say that. Nervously she asks, "Do you think I killed Lori? I mean, surely you can't if you stayed with me even after my parents told you they thought I was involved somehow?"

"Come on, Nicole, of course I don't." His answer is immediate. "The fact that you argued right before she disappeared means nothing. You pair were always arguing over something, right? I don't care how high or drunk you were, neither of you would hurt each other." He sighs shakily. "If Ron's admitted to moving her body, he could be lying about everything else to do with that night."

Her heart sinks. "I know." There's a very real possibility that her father could spend the rest of his life in prison if anyone else finds out. Nicole wants Lori's killer to pay for what they did, but she can't imagine her father behind bars. It doesn't bear thinking about.

"I never believed your parents when they pointed the finger at you. I just couldn't tell them that back then. I was young and your dad's intimidating, so I just shut my mouth and took care of you."

She feels better knowing he's on her side. He knows her better than anyone. "How come you never told me what they said?"

"Because I've seen you hit rock bottom once already and I

never want to see you there again. Listen, I'm going to pack a bag and drive back to Henderson. You're at the hotel, right?"

"No, I'm staying at Kurt's house." As soon as she says it, she realizes it was a mistake, but she has to be honest.

"What the hell are you doing there?"

"We can't exactly afford the hotel, Lucas. And I was upset. Kurt's been here for me."

Lucas is silent for a minute and Nicole can picture him rolling his eyes in annoyance. "I'll be there midafternoon," he says. "Don't leave your stuff at Kurt's place. We'll stay at my mom's house. I'm sure she'd love the company."

He's right, so she agrees. "Sure. Call me when you get here." Hesitantly, she adds, "I love you."

"I love you too," he says, before adding, "We can figure our shit out, can't we? There's no one else, Nicole. Only you."

She blinks back tears as she says, "I'm sure we can."

THIRTY-SEVEN

Kurt wakes to the sound of his phone ringing. It's disorientating, especially as he wakes on the couch instead of in his bed. He also got quietly wasted after Nicole pushed him away for the second time. His tongue is furry from the liquor, and his head is pounding from the pills. He'd give anything for another couple of hours' sleep, but the cell phone's ringtone is shrill, piercing his brain as it increases in volume the longer it goes unanswered. Eventually he locates the phone on the floor, but it's bound to have woken his father.

The caller ID tells him it's Julie from dispatch. "Hey." His headache pounds harder as he stands.

"You're needed ASAP. Sheriff Chambers has organized another search for his daughter after some new information came in. He wants everyone to report in."

Considering Kurt punched the guy not that long ago, he hesitates. "Did he specifically ask for me?"

"No. What do you want, a written invitation?" Julie has a slight attitude problem, but the team lets it go considering how high-pressured her job is. She once calmly talked a five-year-old girl through resuscitating a two-week-old baby. Once the EMT arrived at the address, Julie ended the call and broke down alone in the evidence locker. She allowed herself two minutes of emotion before returning to her desk and answering the next emergency. The team assumes her prickly personality is her way of keeping emotion at bay.

Kurt hasn't heard anything to suggest Ron doesn't want him there, so he decides he needs to carry on as if he doesn't know a damaging secret about the guy. "Is Tommy in custody yet?"

"That's a negative."

He's surprised Tommy has managed to elude them for this long. "I'll be right in."

"Don't come here. I'll message you the location of the search."

"Understood." He ends the call. Pain shoots through his neck as he turns too fast. Sleeping on the uncomfortable couch isn't good for him. Needing a fresh uniform, he quietly heads upstairs in the hope his father slept through that. He expects to find Nicole in his bed, but the room is empty. Her suitcase is gone. She must have crept out. He gets changed before heading to the bathroom, where he looks at himself in the mirror. "Congratulations. You screwed up. Again."

He brushes his teeth and splashes cold water over his face. Once he's ready for work, service weapon holstered, he goes to check on his dad. The back room is in darkness, so he opens the drapes, letting in the morning sunshine. His father stirs behind him.

"Hey, Dad. Want some breakfast? Coffee?"

"No," says Brian, attempting to sit up. When his arms fail him, Kurt plumps his cushions and gently pulls him into a seated position. If he's losing his arm strength, he might not be able to hobble to the downstairs bathroom for much longer. He'll need a commode or a bedpan.

"Water then?"

Brian nods. The water by the bedside is old, so Kurt

changes it in the kitchen. He hovers a little longer than necessary because of the growing sense of unease he feels whenever he's around his father. Brian's appetite shrinks more every day. His energy levels are rapidly diminishing. Watching his father die a slow, painful death is taking its toll on Kurt. He looks up at the ceiling in an attempt to hold back the tears that threaten to fall.

The temptation to skip town is overwhelming. He's been considering it for a while now. He could leave all this behind: his father's inevitable death, Lori's murder and the disappearance of Aimee Chambers. He could go somewhere new where no one knows him and a fresh start would be possible. Someplace where he hasn't made any mistakes and has no history. No childhood friends dragging him backward. And someplace where he wouldn't need to be responsible for burying his father. Let the sheriff take care of that task. It would be apt considering the pair are so devoted to each other that they would lie to the parents of a dead teenager.

Kurt shakes his head. In a way he hopes his father passes soon. It would relieve both their suffering, and it would mean certain things could remain hidden. With his thoughts turning dark, Kurt realizes he can't care for his father on his own any longer. It's time to get some help. He grabs the water and heads back to the makeshift bedroom.

Passing the glass to his father, he says, "I'm going to call the nursing service we used last time and arrange for someone to come check on you regularly again. They can prepare your meals, change your sheets and be around for emergencies."

His father doesn't respond.

"I know you've always said you don't want strangers in your house, and you don't want to be in the hospital, but I can't be here twenty-four-seven. Besides, they'll bring the good drugs. And I get the feeling you could do with some of those, right?"

Brian reluctantly nods. "The pain is getting worse."

Kurt sits next to his father and takes one of his hands. "Why didn't you tell me sooner?"

"Because I hate being this way. Just put an end to me now, would you? I don't want to die like this."

This isn't the first time they've had this discussion and Kurt knows it won't be the last. "I'll call them this morning. The spare key will be under the brown plant pot by the front door so they can let themselves in. Be nice this time, okay?"

Brian squeezes his hand hard. "Is she still here?"

He means Nicole. "No, she left. You didn't exactly provide the warmest of welcomes."

"Stay away from her, son. You don't know what I know."

With a deep sigh, Kurt stands and looks at his father. "Ron told me what happened. I know everything. And trust me, I wish I didn't."

Trepidation flutters across Brian's face. "He told you?"

"He and Debbie were trying to stop Nicole from talking to the press. She wanted me there with her. So I know that you and Ron found Lori's body and never reported it."

Brian lowers his eyes. He looks disappointed in himself. Ashamed even. "I would've done if it were up to me, but he wanted to protect his daughter. Ron Chambers is practically my brother. I couldn't go against his decision. Later, after witnessing the pain it was causing you and Lori's family by not knowing what happened to her, where she was, I realized I should have reported it. But it was too late by then. I couldn't tell anyone without exposing what Ron had done. He would've been fired for tampering with evidence. And Nicole would've gone to prison for murder."

Kurt should be angry with his father for keeping this secret so long, and for misleading everyone, especially his own son. But it's pointless being angry now. It won't change anything. He squeezes his father's hand. "You don't have to explain anything. The whole situation was screwed up, and the decision was ultimately Ron's to make. He went about it all wrong. You both did, but you know that already. And, for the record, I refuse to believe Nicole had anything to do with Lori's murder, and nothing you say will convince me otherwise."

Before his father can reply, Kurt leaves the room. Over his shoulder he shouts, "See you later, Dad. Be nice to the nurses."

A sense of relief always washes over him when he leaves the house, quickly followed by guilt. He's relieved he gets a reprieve from his father's suffering, and then immediately feels like an asshole for it. He slips the spare key under the large plant pot on the porch.

"Hey."

He spins around. Nicole is standing on the driveway with her suitcase on the ground at her feet. Her hair is disheveled, but she looks better than she did yesterday. Less exhausted. "How long have you been hiding out here?" he asks.

"Not long. I'm sorry about last night. If I put out the wrong signals..."

He waves a dismissive hand. "Not at all. I don't know what I was thinking." He sighs. "Everything's such a mess. I just wish we could get a time out on the madness, you know? Just one day where nothing insane happens."

She smiles ruefully. "Wouldn't that be nice? Are you heading straight to work?"

"Right. Your dad's organized another search party for Aimee."

She steps forward. "Has someone come forward with information?"

"I don't know. All I've been told is to report in ASAP." He checks his phone, where a message from dispatch is waiting to be read. "They want me at the east entrance to the Franklin Woods."

Nicole picks up her suitcase. "I'm coming with you. I'll store this in your trunk for now. That okay with you?"

He knows there's no point in saying no to her. Nerves build in his stomach. "Have you spoken to Lucas since he left town?"

"Yes. He's coming back today. He already knew my parents believed I had something to do with Lori's disappearance. They told him while he was caring for me that summer."

"And he never told you?" That seems strange to Kurt.

"He didn't want to make me even more upset."

Kurt wonders why Ron Chambers would confide in Lucas Rivers of all people. Lucas was just a teenager at the time, and not exactly trustworthy. He could have gone to the press with that news. It must have been tempting given how much coverage there was. Lori's parents even offered a small reward for information. Maybe Lucas was looking out for his girlfriend, or maybe he knows more than he's letting on. Kurt hopes not, for Nicole's sake.

He nods to his cruiser. "Get in."

THIRTY-EIGHT

The narrow access road to the Franklin Woods is completely blocked with cruisers. To Nicole it looks as if the whole of the sheriff's office is here to help with the search. The woods appear dense with a thicket of trees and overgrown brush. It would be a good place to hide a body, especially as the narrow dirt track seems to disappear inside, providing easy access for a vehicle. Minimal effort would be required for a killer to dump their victim from the trunk without ever being seen. The thought sends goosebumps up her arms and she says a silent prayer in the hope that's not what happened to Aimee.

"That's Beau Michaels," says Kurt, nodding to a wiry older guy making his way over to the dirt track. "He's our best search-and-rescue volunteer."

That explains the high-visibility vest and his all-weather attire. The volunteer has a gorgeous bloodhound with him. The dog looks to be old, with a graying muzzle. Despite his age, he's straining at his leash raring to go. Nicole suddenly realizes this is a trained cadaver dog. Her stomach flutters with nerves. Today could be the day she gets the answers she's been looking for. But this isn't where she had hoped to find them.

Beau and his dog disappear into the woods. It looks like the majority of the search party is long gone, leaving just one deputy behind to turn away any dog walkers or potential onlookers. The male deputy approaches Kurt as they get out of the car. "Took your time, didn't you?"

Kurt bristles. "I had to take care of my dad, asshole." Then, to Nicole, he says, "This is Deputy Hayes." Kurt looks exhausted. When Nicole first arrived in town, he seemed different, lighthearted and put together. Now he looks unkempt and irritable, like he's done pretending. "How come we're searching this area?" he asks. "Did we get a lead?"

Deputy Hayes shrugs. "Don't ask me. I'm just here to look pretty." He spits on the ground at their feet. "For all I know launching a full-scale search is the sheriff's attempt at distracting the press from those false allegations made against him." He looks at Nicole. "I hear they originated from you." His eyes assess her, hovering for a second at her sneakered feet. "I don't think your dad would want you here after what you did," he says. "Besides, you shouldn't go in there. You never know what you might find."

Nicole gives him a blank stare. "Try stopping me." She heads toward the woods. Kurt joins her. The sound of a car skidding to a stop nearby makes her glance over her shoulder.

"Nicole!" Jennifer Manvers gets out of her car and comes running over. "I need to talk to you. Just for a second." She looks at Kurt. "In private."

Nicole stops as she braces herself for more bad news. Kurt takes a few steps away, edging closer to the woods. "What is it?" she asks.

"I've been looking into Lori's disappearance." Sympathy fills Jennifer's eyes. "Why didn't you tell me you were hospitalized afterward?"

"How do you know that?" Nicole's a little annoyed that Jennifer's digging into her past now, but she knows it was bound to come out eventually. It's not like her parents kept that a secret. They made sure they told everyone she was unwell but never specified what was wrong with her. No one really knew.

"It doesn't matter," says Jennifer. "I wanted to give you the heads-up because I have to put it in the article I'm writing. I'm covering what happened back then in a bid to try to find more information about who killed Lori. I'm sorry. I'm not trying to make things harder for you."

Nicole swallows, her mouth suddenly dry. "What good will it do to tell people I had an emotional breakdown? I mean, I'd just lost my best friend. How was I supposed to react?"

Jennifer rubs Nicole's arm. "I have to be honest with you, Nicole. I think you know more than you're telling me." She pauses. "In fact, I think you know what happened to your friend." When Nicole freezes, instead of denying it, Jennifer says, "Who are you protecting? Is it someone close to you?"

It would be tempting to tell this woman about her father moving Lori's body. But if she does, Nicole knows it will gain a whole new level of traction. Her father could be immediately arrested. Then who would oversee finding Aimee? Would this search, and the investigation, get overshadowed by the head-lines about her father? It's a strong possibility.

As she doesn't reply, Jennifer says, "Jim Marsh didn't kill your friend."

Nicole looks at her. "How do you know for sure?"

"Because I spoke to his kids. Brad Marsh found some old diaries his mother kept. They confirm Jim was out of town at an agricultural show at the time Lori died. Edna was home alone. Brad said she always wore earplugs in bed to help her sleep. She wouldn't have heard someone crawling around their land that night."

Kurt approaches. "We need to join the search," he says. He takes Nicole's arm and gently motions for her to follow him. She does.

"At least call me later so you can clarify anything I might've got wrong," says Jennifer. "I can let you see the first draft." When Nicole doesn't reply she shouts, "You need to tell me what happened the night your friend died. This is your chance to put things right."

Deputy Hayes approaches Jennifer. "You can't follow them in there. No press or media are allowed near the search."

The sound of approaching vehicles fills the air. Probably news vans arriving to film the search, each vying to be the first news station to capture the gruesome images of whatever gets found here today. In her mind Nicole sees a stretcher covered with a white sheet being carried out of this exact spot in a couple of hours, while cameras zoom in. She wonders how these reporters would like it if it were *their* loved one the police were currently searching for.

Before entering the woods, she hears Jennifer ask Deputy Hayes for more details about what the sheriff's office is doing here and whether they're here because remains have already been found.

Nicole wonders how long it will be before Jennifer puts two and two together and realizes Ron Chambers makes a good suspect for Aimee's disappearance, as well as Lori's murder.

THIRTY-NINE

Together Nicole and Kurt walk for almost ten minutes in silence, neither of them knowing what to say about Jennifer's next potentially damaging article. It feels like they'll never be able to move on from their pasts. Nicole's desperate to see her husband. She needs him here. She's been too dependent on Kurt these last few days and it's not fair on him. How can he help her when he's suffering so much himself?

It's pleasantly cool under the tree canopy. Small hidden animals scurry through the brush, and birds call to each other as Nicole and Kurt pass their nests. Under different circumstances it would be an enjoyable walk. It doesn't take long before her cheap sneakers start rubbing her feet though. They're not designed for hikes.

When the sound of running water reaches them, it's followed by two loud barks. Nicole grinds to a halt and looks at Kurt. "Does that mean the dog's found something?"

Kurt doesn't stop. "There's only one way to find out."

She realizes then that he appears nervous. His expression is grim and he's not making any eye contact. He isn't offering her any reassurance. Maybe he's dreading what they're about to stumble across, or maybe he's reached his breaking point.

The gently flowing stream appears. It sits under a break in the canopy, and the clear water reflects shards of sunlight onto the surrounding trees. Ron Chambers and his search team stand in the brightest spot. It's a lot warmer here than under the trees. Ron's talking to Beau. The bloodhound is lying at Beau's feet chewing on a tennis ball. When Ron notices Nicole he asks, "What are you doing here?"

Nicole sees the bruise on his jaw where Kurt hit him last night. Pity washes over her. It would have been humiliating for her father to turn up to work like this. Others would have noticed. She tries not to let her eyes rest there too long and replies with her own question. "Have you found something?"

Her father moves away from Beau and takes her arm, leading her away. She goes with him a few steps until he stops and turns to her. His expression uncharacteristically softens, and he looks momentarily lost for words. It blindsides her, as she's not used to seeing his softer side. His change of character is so alarming that she realizes she would take the guarded Ron Chambers over this one if it meant he wasn't about to give her the news she's been dreading. Tears prickle her eyes as the realization hits her.

They must have found Aimee.

"Please, no," she says, shaking her head. "Don't say it."

Ron rests a hand on her shoulder before squeezing it. She can see his chest battling to stay in control of his emotions as tears stream down her own face. Standing closer to him than she's been in years, his uniform smells of her father from childhood. She misses that version of him. The one who was gentle and loving, right up until the night Lori vanished. What she wouldn't give to get him back permanently. To erase everything that's happened between then and now. The feeling is so powerful that she's hit with a moment of grief. For the man who disappeared.

After a minute or so, he drops his hand and takes a deep breath. "The dog can smell something. Now, that doesn't mean it's your sister." His voice hitches, so he clears his throat. "We had a call early this morning from a guy who was out walking his dog before work. His name's Charlie; he's a good guy. A hard worker. I know him from—"

"Dad, please," she begs. "Get to the point."

He nods. "His dog found a bone."

She closes her eyes tight.

"The damn creature managed to get it all the way back to the car before Charlie even noticed he had it in his mouth, so he couldn't say exactly where the dog picked it up from, despite going back to look. That's why we brought Beau and Duke in. That dog's got the best nose in the business. Officially, he retired two years ago but is always willing to come back for jobs like this. In fact—"

"Please stop talking about the damn dog." She rubs her eyes. He's rambling. It must be nerves. "Is it a human bone?"

A slow nod. "Beau thinks so, but he could be wrong. He's no expert. I've called the coroner. He's on his way."

"Has Duke found anything?"

Her father turns to survey the scene. Kurt and another deputy are securing the area with yellow tape. Nicole can't lower her eyes to the ground. She doesn't want to see what the cadaver dog found. She doesn't want to see her sister's bones.

Eventually Ron says, "We'll need to dig. To see what Duke can smell. There's a good chance that whatever's buried down there was an animal."

It feels like he's clutching at straws. "Come on, Dad. Who would bury an animal out in the woods?"

They stand in silence for a while, as everyone gets busy

around them. A strange sense of calm envelops her. Her mind starts considering practicalities. "Aimee's only been missing for, what, thirteen days? Do you know how much decomposition would have to take place before her bones would be exposed?"

Her father winces at the question. "It's been a hot summer... I don't know. Gerry's the expert. Once he arrives, we'll know more." He shakes his head as he wrestles with whether or not to say something else.

"What is it?" she presses.

He pulls a handkerchief from his pocket and rubs the sweat from his neck. "About nine years ago there was a missing pregnant woman who was driving through Henderson on her way north when she suddenly vanished. Hayley Barbet. Did you hear about her?"

The name isn't familiar. Nicole didn't keep up to date with the news from home once she'd left town. "No."

"It was an awful case. Her car turned up before she did. It was burned out. Empty inside. It took eleven months to find her body." He rubs his eyes with the cloth.

She rests her hand on his warm arm. It feels natural, despite their strained relationship. "Did you find her?"

He nods, before taking a minute to collect himself. "I'll never forget seeing that tiny baby's bones curled up inside her mother's."

Nicole covers her face with her hands. The image is too much to bear. She hadn't even thought about what it would look like. How, if it is Aimee down there, the baby will never leave Aimee's body naturally. Someone from the coroner's office will be given the devastating task of collecting its bones, separate to its mother's, and then piecing them back together again for the burial. They should be buried together.

"I'm sorry, Nicky," says Ron. "I shouldn't have told you that. I had nightmares for weeks afterward."

Nicole takes a deep breath. This is too much. She wants to

get out of here. Out of Henderson. She wishes her mother had never made that call. If she hadn't, Nicole would be at work now, entering paperwork onto the computer and checking on the animals during her break. She'd always thought she had a raw deal in life, because of Lori, but she'd had no idea it could get even worse. In an effort to distract herself from the image of the baby's bones she asks, "Have you found any clothes in the area? Or her purse?"

"We're about to continue the search, for belongings," says Ron. "In fact, I need to ask you to leave so that you don't contaminate the area. Because if that is Aimee down there, I want the scene to be clean in order to find DNA from the bastard who put her there. You better believe someone is going to pay for this."

Nicole studies her father's face. He's aged in the last few minutes. The lines on his forehead and under his eyes are more pronounced. He's genuinely distressed. His eyes are haunted. An overwhelming certainty hits her.

He didn't do this.

He had nothing to do with Aimee's disappearance.

She's convinced that if the bone that was discovered came from Aimee's remains, and she's been buried here after being brutally murdered, her father had nothing to do with it. The thought makes her dizzy with relief. "We need to tell Mom about this."

"No. Not yet," he says. "She's at work and I don't want to worry her unnecessarily."

"But she might see it on TV. Reporters are showing up here already."

Ron rubs the graying stubble on his jaw. "She'll be too busy to pay any attention to the TV. I want to speak to Gerry first. He'll know immediately whether the bone is human or animal."

Raised voices behind them make them turn. Kurt is pushing everyone back from something on the ground, about two feet away from the spot Duke picked out. The vegetation is disturbed. "Careful," he says. "Get a marker over here." He looks up at Nicole before fixing his eyes on Ron. "We have large skull fragments here, Sheriff."

Nicole's knees go weak.

FORTY

Kurt drops Nicole at her parents' place after promising to keep her updated. She'll be eagerly awaiting the coroner's impressions, as well as Lucas's appearance. She was surprisingly calm considering what's going on. To Kurt it feels like she's already accepted the inevitable.

When they left the woods there were far more news vans than either of them expected. The allegations against the sheriff have reached far and wide, bringing more attention to Aimee's disappearance. The whole situation makes Kurt nervous. It's times like this he wishes he wasn't a cop. That he had no responsibility and didn't have to be involved with what's happening.

His radio buzzes to life and Sheriff Chambers orders him over to Tommy Peterson's apartment. "We have a go on the search warrant and you're the nearest unit," says Ron. There's been no mention of what passed between them at the sheriff's house, despite the bruise on Ron's jaw being evident. "Hayes will join you shortly. I want you to turn that place upside down for something that tells me what he did to my daughter."

Kurt inwardly sighs. The sheriff is pinning all his hopes on Tommy being responsible for this. "Copy that."

"His neighbor is willing to give you the spare key."

Kurt speeds to Tommy's apartment, hoping to beat Hayes over there. Tommy lives above an old record store. It hasn't been in business for two years now and the shutters are covered in graffiti. A woman pushing a baby stroller glances at him as he gets out of his vehicle. He wonders if she's seen the news coverage from the woods.

At the stairwell to the apartments, he climbs the steps and is greeted with two doors at the top. The one on the left opens and a young woman appears. He doesn't know her. She's wearing glasses and has a paintbrush in one hand, a key in the other. "Here's Tommy's spare key."

He takes it from her. "Thanks. Have you seen him lately?"

"Not since he evaded the sheriff, no," she replies.

"Heard any noises coming from his apartment?"

She shakes her head. "Nothing. I don't think he's coming back. It's a shame. He was a good neighbor. I liked him. And I'm hoping I wasn't a terrible judge of character because who am I meant to trust then, right?" She sighs. "Not whoever moves in after him, that's for sure."

He nods to the key. "Thanks for this. We'll keep it for now."

She closes her door as Kurt slips the key into Tommy's lock. He steps inside and closes the door behind him. He doesn't want to be taken by surprise. A look around the apartment tells him Tommy's neat. There are few dirty dishes waiting to be washed. No clothes absently thrown over the couch. The apartment is recently vacuumed.

He checks the only bedroom and the bathroom in case anyone's hiding. They're both clear. He slips on some latex gloves and begins his search in the bedroom, seeing as that's where most people keep the things they want to hide. The nightstand has two drawers. Inside the top drawer is a flashlight, cell phone chargers, a watch and a couple of unused condoms. The bottom drawer contains underwear. Kurt rummages around regardless and finds nothing of interest.

He jumps when his radio sparks into life with Sheriff Chambers asking if he's managed to access the property yet. "I'm inside. It's clear. I'm just beginning the search," Kurt replies.

"Has Hayes arrived yet?"

"Negative."

The line goes dead. Ron offers no updates from his end. The space underneath Tommy's bed reveals no secrets, but Kurt lifts the mattress just in case. Nothing there. He moves to the double closet next. Hangers are filled with clothes and grease-stained coveralls. It doesn't look as though anything's missing, which means Tommy hasn't slipped home in the dead of night to collect any belongings. It's just a matter of time though. Even if he has a buddy who's letting him hide, that can only last so long. He can't hide forever, and it's unlikely he'll leave town for good. Kurt doesn't think Tommy would do that to his parents.

Kurt and Lucas both found Tommy annoying when he was a kid. He wanted to follow Lori everywhere and she frequently brought him with her to whatever they were doing. It meant they couldn't go very far and had to hide their cigarettes and alcohol. You can't trust kids not to tell everyone what you're up to. They have loose lips. It was better when Nicole brought Aimee along too, as Aimee would keep Tommy occupied and distracted. She was a cute kid. A mini Nicole in many ways, except that as she got older, she turned out different, personality-wise. She isn't studious or self-conscious like Nicole was. She's more of a free spirit.

The bottom of the closet isn't hiding anything, just sneakers and clean blankets for the bed. There's a gap of about two inches underneath the closet. Kurt runs his hand under there.

His fingers find something. "What are you hiding, Tommy?" he mutters.

Kurt lies flat on his stomach to reach for the object. It's some kind of book. When he pulls it out, he feels the blood drain out of his face as he reads the cover.

The Journal of Aimee Chambers.

The room suddenly feels airless. Kurt had no idea Aimee kept a journal. Her parents hadn't said. And the fact Tommy Peterson has it hidden under his closet can only be bad news.

FORTY-ONE

From the Journal of Aimee Chambers

October 12, 2021—Age 17

I'm seeing someone. I can't tell anyone about him because he doesn't want people to know. It could cause all kinds of problems that I don't even want to think about right now. And obviously I don't want Tommy to know. He'd spoil it. He'd probably tell my parents and they would freak out. They already treat me like a child. Nicole would be pissed about it. But she can go to hell for all I care.

This relationship feels different to any I've had previously. It's intense. He's older than me. He treats me well. And he buys me little gifts. He makes me feel like I'm worth loving. He doesn't even compare to boys my age. I can't get enough of him. I'm literally obsessed!

It feels amazing to have something positive in my life. So, of course, I'm worried about screwing it up.

June 28, 2022—Age 18

I literally cringe when I look back at earlier entries. I thought I was in a relationship. Turns out he was just using me like every other guy I've ever dated. When you're my age, it feels like everyone wants something from you: guys want sex, your parents want good grades, your friends want your time. Everyone's using you for something.

He's never wanted to believe the baby is his which is so insulting I could cry. On top of all that I'm getting random text messages from an anonymous person that are scaring the shit out of me. I can't deal with this right now. My baby gets stressed when I get stressed. I can tell. I need to stay calm for him or her. But it's so hard when I'm dealing with this kind of crap.

The texts I got yesterday said:
  Lori Peterson deserves justice.
  Your sister got away with murder.

And this morning:
  Your father's been protecting your sister.
  I'm going to the press.

I've told Dad and he's going to try to trace the number but he said it's probably a burner phone. Why would someone go to the effort of buying a second phone just to send crazy messages? Dad looked as panicked as I was by them, but it was more than that. He looked afraid. I haven't seen him like that for years, not since Lori disappeared. It made me wonder whether this person is telling the truth. I tried asking him if it's true but he said we'll talk later. He didn't deny it!!

Instead, he made it sound like there's a lot I don't know. WTAF? As if Nicole would hurt Lori. That's not true. Someone is spreading lies. Maybe they don't want dad to get reelected. It's either that or Mom and Dad are hiding some-

thing from me. Maybe I don't know them at all. Or maybe everything I thought I knew about Nicole is wrong.

This town is full of secrets and lies. And now I'm just as bad as them because my doomed "relationship" has to be kept secret. I can't tell anyone who my baby's father is, which means people are speculating. Stacey told me that people are saying I had an affair with our English teacher. As if! He's like forty years old or something.

I hate myself for being like the rest of this town. Maybe it's time to tell everyone who I've been seeing. To get it over with and deal with the repercussions. Oh God. Just the thought of it brings me out in a cold sweat. I'm scared of how he'd react. He's already threatened me, but he did it in a way that suggested he was only joking. It didn't feel like a joke though.

That's why I'm writing this. If I should disappear, you should all know what happened to me. It sounds so dramatic when I write it down! I'll see how things go once the baby's born. You never know. He might come to his senses and be the father our baby needs. And for some reason, I think I still love him.

FORTY-TWO

Kurt notices that last entry was written just over a week before Aimee vanished from her home. His leg painfully cramps from his position on the floor, so he stands up to help the blood flow. Before he can read the next entry he's startled by a loud knock at the door. "It's Hayes. You in there, Butler?"

Deputy Hayes keeps banging, annoying the hell out of Kurt, who quickly exits the bedroom and opens the door to the apartment. "Keep it down. Why are you being a dick? Tommy could return any minute."

"What, are you crazy?" Hayes mocks him. "He won't set foot anywhere near this place once he sees our cruisers outside." He spots the journal in Kurt's hand. "What's that you've found?"

Kurt kicks himself for not hiding it from this asshole. He doesn't want Hayes peering into Aimee's private life, so he keeps a hold of it. "Says it's Aimee's journal, but there's always a possibility it's been faked."

Hayes raises his eyebrows. "Shit. Looks like the sheriff was right. Tommy is involved. Why else would that be here?"

That's what Kurt wants to know. "I'll bag it. You keep

searching. I've finished the bedroom." He leaves Hayes behind while he heads downstairs to fetch an evidence bag from the trunk of his car. He desperately wants to keep reading, so he slips into the driver's seat. Before he even has time to open the journal, dispatch radios through to tell him there's been a potential sighting of Tommy. Kurt's jaw clenches when he learns Tommy is in the vicinity of the sheriff's neighborhood. Where Nicole is.

"He's heading eastbound and driving a red Dodge Ram but the caller didn't get the license plate," says Julie. "You're the closest unit to that area, Deputy Butler. Can I mark you as being en route?"

Kurt drops the journal on the passenger seat. "Copy that. Heading there now." Determined to make sure Tommy doesn't get anywhere near Nicole, Kurt lights up the cruiser and starts the engine.

FORTY-THREE

All Nicole can think about as she lies on the bed in Aimee's room is the image her father gave her of the bones of a baby inside that of its mother. Nicole doesn't think she would be able to get over that if that is what's happened to her sister. And why would she want to? She doesn't want to live in a world where something so horrifying could happen to anyone, let alone to her little sister.

She moves her phone to wake it, even though it's remained silent since Kurt brought her here. The screen lights up, but it's empty of notifications. Her thoughts turn to her mother, who is currently oblivious to the horror unfolding in those woods. Nicole doesn't want to be responsible for breaking the news, so she listens to her father for once and doesn't message her.

She takes a deep breath as she tries to think positive. "Don't assume the worst," she whispers. "It might not be Aimee."

A knock at the door makes her heart hammer against her chest. She's frozen to the bed. That could be Kurt with news. Bad news.

The knock is louder the second time, so she's forced off the bed. Maybe it's Lucas. She had tried calling him to explain where he could find her when he arrives in town, but he must have been driving as he didn't answer, so she texted him instead. The thought that it could be her husband makes her walk quickly to the front door of her parents' home. Her legs are shaky, as if she hasn't eaten for a while. It occurs to her then that she skipped breakfast.

When the door swings open, she's face to face with Tommy Peterson. He looks disheveled. His black hair needs washing and his eyes keep darting over his shoulder. "Can I come in?"

She instinctively moves aside, but not before glancing at his hands to see if he's carrying a weapon. He doesn't appear to be. He's hidden the car he was driving, a red Dodge, behind the barn out of view. If he attempts to harm her, no one would know until they found her body. For a split second she considers shutting him in the house while she makes a run for it. He could probably easily outrun her though.

Closing the door behind him but leaving it unlocked she asks, "Where have you been? Are you okay?"

"Can I get a drink? Something to eat?" he says. "I know your parents aren't here right now. I'll leave as soon as I've eaten. I couldn't go to my mom's house. It's too obvious."

He must be famished to risk coming here. What if she had Lucas or Kurt with her? Maybe he's been watching the property. "Of course. Follow me."

She leads him to the kitchen and pours coffee before making some toast. She gets cheese, milk and butter out of the fridge. He drinks and eats ravenously between talking. "Sorry about this. I didn't know who else I could trust. I'm not here to hurt anyone."

"I know that," she says. "I don't believe you'd hurt anyone. Including Aimee." She sits across from him at the kitchen table. "But do you know where she is? We're running out of time to get her home before the baby's born."

He shakes his head and after swallowing a mouthful of

toast, he says, "I honestly don't know where she's at right now. You have to believe me."

Her heart sinks. Part of her was hoping Tommy *was* involved, because at least then Aimee would still be alive. He's probably the most trustworthy person her sister knows in this town. "They've found bones in the Franklin Woods," she says. "Skull fragments."

He drops the slice of toast he was holding, his appetite vanishing. "Jesus Christ." His whole demeanor changes from that of someone on the run to someone who has just lost all his fight. His shoulders slump. "It can't be her. She hasn't been missing long enough to be reduced to just bones already, surely?" His eyes become red-rimmed. It's clear he hasn't hurt her sister.

"I hope not," she says. "But if that's not her, then who is it? And where is she?"

"That's why I came here," he says. "Not just for this." He motions to the food. "I have to tell you something. You're going to be pissed at me, but you have to believe me. I was just trying to help."

She frowns, not liking the sound of this. "What do you mean?"

They hear sirens in the distance and both look up at the window.

"Shit." Tommy jumps up. "How did they know I was here?" He glances at her phone, which is by her hand on the table. "Did you message someone?"

"What? No. Tommy, I wouldn't do that." She stands too. "Just tell me what you were going to say. There's no point running, they're too close."

Tommy goes to the back door. The sirens grow louder by the second. He turns back to face her, looking defeated. "They're going to try to pin this on me. I didn't do this, Nicole. You have to believe me. I love your sister no matter who she's dating. I helped her get away, that's all. Whatever happened to her afterward, that was nothing to do with me."

Nicole's mouth drops open. "You helped her run away?"

He nods. "I paid for a motel room over in Dartmoor."

Dartmoor doesn't fall under their father's jurisdiction and Nicole wonders if that's why Aimee went there. She knew she would have a different police department to help her. One where her father wasn't in charge. But Nicole's reminded of the look on her father's face when they were in the woods and he was telling her about the discovery. *Did he fake that?*

"I visited her at the motel every morning and evening before and after work. And then one night she was gone." Tommy looks incredulous, as if he can't believe it himself. "Just gone. I don't know where she went. She left behind her clothes but not her cell phone and purse. She was booked into the motel under a fake name and none of the staff knew where she'd gone. They wouldn't let me check their surveillance footage."

Nicole has so many questions but their time is limited. "Why did she run away from home in the first place? Did something happen to cause it?"

He glances out of the window. "Your parents, they..." He trails off as the sirens fall silent. A car skids to a halt outside and they listen to footsteps running over gravel, toward the house. Tommy's eyes widen. "You have to tell your dad I didn't do this!" he pleads. "Don't let him frame me, Nicole. Especially if that's her in the woods." He turns to leave.

Nicole's stunned. Everything's happening so fast. "No, don't run, please! You could be my only hope of finding her." Desperate to get as much information from him as possible before the cops enter, she asks, "When did you last see her? At the motel, I mean."

The front door bursts open and someone runs into the house. Kurt appears at the kitchen door, his weapon outstretched. "Get on the ground now!" he yells.

Nicole steps away as Tommy opens the door. He's about to make the biggest mistake of his life. "Kurt, don't shoot!" she yells. Then to Tommy she says, "Tommy, stop! When did you last see Aimee? Who was she dating?"

Tommy hesitates in the doorway for a split second and the bang of a gunshot echoes around the room. Nicole's ears ring painfully. She covers them with her hands in case Kurt shoots again.

Someone else enters the house behind Kurt. A female deputy. "Shots fired! Shots fired!" yells the woman into her radio. The deputy glances at Kurt, who looks like he's about to fire again, so the woman says, "Stand down! He's unarmed and wounded. He's not going anywhere."

Kurt lowers his weapon.

Nicole watches in horror as Tommy slides against the wall, slowly sinking to the floor. She goes to him.

"Get back, Nicole!" shouts Kurt. "He could be armed."

"Suspect is hit," says the female into her radio. "Dispatch EMS."

Nicole ignores Kurt and kneels next to Tommy. "He needs an ambulance!" she screams. Tommy's shoulder has taken a direct hit. Blood runs down his T-shirt. Tommy groans as she rests his head in her lap. "It's okay, Tommy. You're going to be okay. Can you speak?"

Suddenly she gets dragged backward by someone and falls onto her ass on the floor. She's been forced away from Tommy. They genuinely believe he's a threat to her and she can't understand it.

"He's not who you think he is," says Kurt. "I found something at his apartment, Nicole. Something of Aimee's. Stay away from him."

Nicole can only watch in horror as Lori's little brother loses consciousness.

FORTY-FOUR

Tommy is whisked away in an ambulance. A paramedic managed to regulate his breathing but the mess left behind in the kitchen suggests it's going to be touch and go for him. Nicole thinks of how Theresa and Antony will take the news. She has to tell them before they see it on TV.

Forcing herself to move, her left foot slips in Tommy's blood. She blinks back tears as she collapses into a chair at the kitchen table. Using some paper towel, she wipes the blood from under her sneaker. It's disgusting. Someone needs to clean the floor but she doesn't know if it's considered a crime scene. No one told her anything. Kurt rushed out behind the EMTs. He must be following them to the hospital to watch Tommy.

She drops the soiled paper towel onto the floor and opens her phone. She dials the only landline number, other than her parents', that is forever etched into her memory: Lori's house.

Theresa answers it within three rings. "Hello?"

Nicole tries to keep her gaze off of the floor. "Mrs. Peterson, it's Nicole."

There's a slight hesitation before Theresa says, "What's

happened? They've found him, haven't they? I can hear it in your voice."

Nicole takes a deep breath. "Tommy came here. I gave him something to eat. But the police turned up." The words catch in her throat. She doesn't want to explain he was shot.

"Nicole?" Theresa's voice hardens. "Is he alive?"

"He's in an ambulance. They're on their way to the hospital."

Theresa gasps. "No. I can't lose another one."

With tears streaming down her face Nicole tries to offer some reassurance but it feels hollow given how bad Tommy looked when they strapped him to a gurney. "He was shot once in the shoulder. He was still breathing when they left. I wanted you to know so you can be with him."

Theresa's reply is immediate. "Thank you. For taking him in and for letting me know where he is." She hangs up.

Nicole considers what to do with the news Tommy gave her. Even though Aimee is no longer there, she needs to find the motel her sister was staying in, but she has no clue how to go about it. She's reluctant to tell her father yet, and Kurt's busy. It occurs to her that maybe Stacey knows more than she initially let on, considering she's close to both Aimee and Tommy. Nicole scrolls through her phone contacts to locate the number of Aimee's best friend and hits call. But Stacey doesn't pick up so Nicole texts her.

Please answer. It's about Tommy.

Within a minute, Stacey calls her back. "Sorry, I hate talking on the phone," she says by way of an explanation. "It makes me anxious."

"I won't keep you long," says Nicole. "Tommy turned up at my parents' house."

"Oh my God, is he okay?"

"No. He was shot by an officer while trying to escape again. He's still alive, but barely."

Stacey's stunned for a second. "Aimee's going to be devastated."

"Are you going to tell her?" demands Nicole.

"What?" The girl laughs nervously. "How can I? I don't know where she is."

"Are you sure about that?" says Nicole. "Because I'm not so old that I don't remember what it was like to be young and to have a friend I loved so much that I would tell her everything. And I mean *everything*. So I find it difficult to believe she didn't confide in you about running away."

Stacey gasps. "How do you know she ran away?"

Nicole leans her head back. Finally, she's getting somewhere. "Tommy told me he helped her get away, to a motel, but I don't know why she wanted to leave." When she's met with silence Nicole asks, "Can you tell me what you know? Please. I can't state strongly enough how important it is that we get my sister and the baby home."

Stacey begins weeping down the line. "If you remember what it's like to be our age, then you'll remember how best friends also keep each other's secrets."

"Of course. But this is about her safety. Nothing else matters. She's not going to be mad at you for telling me. She could die if you don't! *Please*. I want to know why she left in the first place as I honestly believe that will help me find her."

After a minute's hesitation Stacey opens up. "I knew Tommy was helping her to disappear for a while but neither of them told me where she was. Which motel she was at. She and I were still texting each other after she left—"

Nicole interjects. "Using her usual number?"

"No, she bought a cheap phone to use so her dad couldn't trace her."

Nicole's heart rate quickens. Her sister did not want to be

found. She must have been badly spooked. Threatened maybe. She realizes she can't tell her father what she knows yet. Just in case he's the one Aimee was trying to flee. "Give me the number you were texting. Maybe I can get someone to check where it currently is and when it was last used."

"But that's just it: she stopped replying once she went missing from the motel. I even tried calling her but the burner phone was disconnected. There was no ringtone or voicemail."

Nicole doesn't know what to say. She's enveloped by the biggest feeling of dread yet. The phone could have been smashed up by whoever took Aimee from the motel. "Did you hear about the bones found in the Franklin Woods?"

"Yeah. I can't even let my mind go there right now."

"Send me the number you were using. I'll see what I can do." Nicole will ask Kurt to do whatever the police do in these situations. There might be a way he can do it without her father finding out. "Tommy told me that Aimee wanted to leave because of something to do with my parents. Do you know what he means?"

Stacey takes a deep breath. "They told her something upsetting." A pause. "It was about you."

"What?" Suddenly it all makes sense. "Oh God. They told her I killed Lori Peterson, didn't they?"

"Right. She was devastated."

Nicole wipes tears from her eyes. "Did she believe them?"

"She didn't want to. And now I've met you I don't believe them. I figure you wouldn't still be around after she was found in that silo, because there could be evidence in there with her."

Aimee had gone missing before Lori's remains were found. "That's why she messaged me on Facebook."

"Right," says Stacey. "She wanted to tell you what they were saying about you."

"But why did they tell her I'd do something like that? It was bound to upset her, whether or not it was true." Nicole can understand why Aimee felt the need to leave town. She must have been so confused and upset.

"Because she told them she wanted to reunite with you. She always missed you. She would check your social media but she couldn't learn anything about you there because you never posted anything. She was frustrated."

Nicole's heart sings at the thought of her sister wanting to reunite. That's what *she* always wanted. It's bittersweet to know that it might never happen now.

"She even talked about approaching Lucas," says Stacey.

Nicole frowns. "Lucas? Why?"

"She knew he came home to visit his mom occasionally. She was building up the courage to see if he'd pass on a message to you, to see whether you were even interested in getting back in touch. She wasn't sure how you felt about her because you stayed away for so long. She thought you might not care about her."

"I do care," Nicole whispers.

"How could she know that with zero communication? Anyway, your folks could tell she was thinking of contacting you, maybe she asked too many questions or something, and that's when they told her that crap about you being responsible for hurting Lori. It's like they were trying to keep her away from you."

Nicole tries not to dwell on why that is. "Who's the father of her baby? You must know."

"I don't. Seriously, she never told me," says Stacey. "She was infatuated with the guy and tried to protect him so they could keep seeing each other. Then he changed toward her when she got pregnant."

Alarm bells ring for Nicole. "How so?"

"He was annoyed she'd gotten pregnant. He kept on seeing her, but she said he wasn't as loving anymore. I think she became afraid of him the further along the pregnancy she got, but she wouldn't tell me much. She was ashamed and embarrassed. I think she had assumed they would get married someday."

"Did she consider an abortion?"

Stacey sighs. "I think she left it too late to make any decisions. She was in denial at first."

It sounds like Aimee needed a big sister to talk to. Guilt weighs heavily on Nicole. She should have come home sooner. She left it too long. A knock at the front door makes her jump. "I have to go."

"Okay," says Stacey. "I don't know anything else anyway. I promise."

"Thanks for talking to me. And don't feel bad about telling me all this. I'm sure Aimee won't be mad at you."

Stacey ends the call without replying. Nicole gets up from her seat and sidesteps the blood on the floor. She doesn't know what new horror awaits her at the front door.

When she swings it open, Lucas is standing there.

FORTY-FIVE

Once Lucas learns what's happened, and he's seen the pool of Tommy's blood on the kitchen floor, he insists that they go to his mom's place right away. Nicole leaves a voice message for Kurt, asking him to call her urgently so that she can tell him about the motel and how Aimee voluntarily left Henderson before going missing for real.

Sindy is surprised to see them as they pull onto her land just after lunchtime. She greets them at the door with her hands on her hips. "What the hell's happening?" The sun breaks out from behind a white cloud, making her shield her eyes from the brightness. "The chick on the news is saying all sorts of crap."

Nicole approaches her as Lucas retrieves her suitcase from the trunk of his car. "To tell you the truth, Sindy, I don't even know where to start."

"Oh, sweetie." Her mother-in-law's eyes soften. "Come on inside. You look like you could do with a drink."

Nicole and Lucas follow her inside. Sindy goes to the kitchen but tells them to take a seat in the living room. Nicole sits on the worn couch, with Lucas beside her. She's glad to have somewhere else to go. She couldn't have stayed at her parents' house any longer.

Lucas slips a comforting arm around her shoulders and kisses her forehead. "I'm sorry I wasn't here. I shouldn't have left."

"It's fine," she says. The cheating issue has been forgotten for now. She needs her husband.

The TV is on, meaning Nicole can't avoid the live coverage from the Franklin Woods. They both watch as Gerry Smith gets into his car and makes a call. He's parked next to an unidentified van. It's black, with no windows in the back, clearly designed for discreetly transporting cadavers.

"The search for a recently graduated high school senior intensified today," says a blonde reporter on screen. "Aimee Chambers has been missing for just under two weeks, ever since she seemingly vanished from her home. The same home she shared with her father, Ron Chambers. Henderson's long-standing sheriff has recently been on the receiving end of some disturbing allegations, first made around 2008. They center around possible sexual offences against a minor."

"I'm turning this off," says Lucas.

"No," says Nicole. "I want to see how much they know."

The reporter continues. "Now, 2008 was the same year Lori Peterson vanished, after which, the sheriff's eldest daughter was hospitalized with possible mental health issues. Nicole Rivers is reportedly back in Henderson after a twelve-year hiatus to help find her missing younger sister." The camera zooms in over the shoulder of the blonde, attracted by something going on in the access road to the woods. "Sadly, it seems that crime has followed this family and, with today's discovery in the Franklin Woods, the question on viewer's lips will surely be: is it all of their own making?"

The blonde presses her earpiece as if receiving information from a producer at the station. She looks back to camera as she says, "I've just been notified that Tommy Peterson, a person of interest in the disappearance of Aimee Chambers, has now been located. Unconfirmed reports suggest he's been involved in an altercation with deputies from the sheriff's office and is currently in surgery at the local hospital."

"Wow," says Sindy as she enters the room. "That's a lot of information to digest." She sways a little and it's clear she's been on the sauce all morning. Maybe it's her day off work. In her hands are three whiskey glasses, each with generous shots of amber liquid. She clutches the bottle to her body using her elbow.

"Mom, it's only just past midday," says Lucas. "We don't need whiskey; we need coffee."

Nicole takes a glass before Sindy turns away. "Speak for yourself." She downs it. It burns her throat, but she doesn't care.

"That's my girl," says Sindy, impressed. She follows suit before placing the bottle and her now empty glass on the coffee table, leaving just the third glass in her hand. "It's been a while since I've had a drinking buddy. Wayne was good for that, if nothing else."

"Don't start badmouthing Dad again," says Lucas. "We've got enough problems without reliving history for the millionth time."

Once Sindy's seated in her favorite armchair, she turns the TV down a little. "I hope Tommy makes it. He's a good kid, and I wouldn't want to see his folks put through any more trauma."

Nicole considers telling her what Tommy revealed, that he helped Aimee to run away, but she doesn't have the energy. Everyone will find out eventually, once Tommy's interviewed. If he survives, that is. "Kurt said he'd found something of Aimee's at Tommy's place," says Nicole. "He told me Tommy isn't who I think he is."

"Is anyone?" says Sindy. "Hell, it's probably just a shirt of hers or something. They were friends. She would've spent time at his place." Her eyes narrow. "Who performed the search?"

Nicole frowns. "I don't know. Kurt didn't say. Why?"

"Maybe your dad planted whatever it was."

"Mom. Stop." Lucas removes his arm from Nicole's shoulders. "You could say that about anyone he's ever arrested, but it doesn't make it true."

"Why are you always defending him?" Sindy scowls. "Are you on his side or something?"

Nicole looks at Lucas. That's a good question. Lucas never likes discussing her suspicions that her father was involved in Lori's murder. And even now, when the pair of them know Ron's admitted to moving Lori's body, Lucas still doesn't like Sindy badmouthing him. "Why *do* you do that?" she asks.

He shrugs. "I'm just trying to be the voice of reason in a room filled with conspiracy theories."

Nicole's mouth drops open. "Are you kidding me? You think I'm spouting conspiracy theories?"

"No, that's not what I mean." He leans back and away from her. "I'm sick to death of all this. It never ends. The fact is, if Lori hadn't been careless enough to stay out alone that night, none of this would've happened. We could have all lived normal lives. I'm sorry, I know it's harsh, but it's how I feel."

He must be truly sick of it if he'd blame Lori for getting killed. Nicole's disappointed by his reaction, but the TV distracts her when her father approaches the cameras. "Turn it up."

Ron looks directly into the camera as he says, "I know you're all waiting for an update, so here's what I have so far. We've found remains, and the coroner has confirmed that they *are* human."

Lucas leans closer to Nicole and rubs her back. She feels like her heart might explode.

"It's currently unclear whether they're male or female until the remains are recovered in their entirety. What's also unclear is how long this body has been in its current position. However, from an initial inspection the coroner believes the decomposition may be too advanced to be that of my missing daughter, given the short time she's been missing." His throat visibly seizes. He swallows, before adding, "We'll know more in due course. For now, we're still working under the assumption that Aimee is alive and being kept against her will. If anyone has any information that could help us bring her home, you are again urged to contact my office immediately."

Nicole covers her face with her hands as sobs of relief tear through her body.

"That's good news," says Sindy. "I'm happy for you. Maybe she can still be found alive."

Lucas remains silent as he strokes Nicole's hair. She feels him twirl her curls around his fingers. A few minutes pass.

Eventually, Sindy says, "What happened the night your friend went missing, Nicole?"

She looks up, wiping her face with her hands. "What?"

Sindy pours herself another whiskey and holds the bottle out to see if either of them want one. They both decline. She downs her drink and stares at the empty glass. "Let's be real for a minute. After all, we're all family here. I've heard rumblings that you and your friend had a falling-out right before she was killed. Is that true?"

"Mom, I'm begging you," says Lucas, his eyes fixed on his mother's. "Drop it."

"Is that what you want?" Sindy directs her question at Nicole. "You want me to drop it? Or have you got something you want to get off your chest at long last? Because you know, it could ease your burden to talk about it. And whatever you say won't leave these four walls. I can promise you that. You two are all the family I have."

Nicole slumps back against the couch. Lucas takes her hand. "You don't need to talk about it."

"I think it would do her some good," says Sindy. "Besides, I've always wondered what could be so bad that a girl would leave her best friend all alone and vulnerable in the dark like she did."

Nicole's ambushed by guilt and flashbacks. She's unsure how to respond. But she knows one thing: her mother-in-law is right. She did leave Lori alone and vulnerable that night. Which means, no matter what else happened, she had a hand in Lori's death.

FORTY-SIX

SUMMER 2008

The sun has set. Lori sits beside her friend in the semidarkness of the park. They are softly illuminated by the orange glow of a streetlight that stands on the edge of the children's playground. Lori's eyes are tired and she has a faint headache forming. She hadn't wanted to leave Nicole's house earlier. It felt safe there, but they had to get Tommy home for dinner. Nicole's mom had called about a last-minute change to her schedule. She had to work an extra shift at the hospital, meaning she wouldn't be home in time to prepare dinner for everyone. Once they took Tommy home, Aimee asked to stay with him, which freed Lori and Nicole to do whatever they wanted for the evening.

They told Lori's mom they were going to see a movie. They lied. With Lucas and Kurt at football practice, Nicole suggested they go to the park and smoke a couple of joints that Kurt gave them earlier. Lori left her phone at home so she didn't have to carry anything, and by the time they reached the playground, it was starting to empty for the evening. There's no one else here now besides them and an old man sitting on a bench. His dog is sniffing the area, but neither of them pay Lori and Nicole any attention. Lori briefly wonders if he could be a flasher or a sex pest, but he soon leaves.

With it being dark, she thinks it's time they should head home themselves, but Lori can't force herself to get up off the warm grass. "Were you planning on seeing Lucas after football practice?" she asks. "Because he's probably home by now."

"No." Nicole takes a puff on her joint. "He said it would go on too late and he'll be tired after. Why? Were you supposed to see Kurt?"

Lori shakes her head. She wants to see him. She wants to tell both Kurt and Nicole what happened earlier, after she left the library. But their fathers are both cops and she knows they would feel compelled to tell their dads what happened. Lori had made a promise. To keep it secret. She had no choice. So she remains silent and inhales the marijuana. It makes her cough hard. She's already decided this will be the last time she'll smoke one of these. She's never enjoyed it, but tonight she felt as if she needed something to calm her nerves. It's already having an effect, numbing her feelings about what happened earlier.

Nicole finishes her joint and as she stubs it out on the grass she starts giggling. With that and the large glass of wine she'd stolen from her mom's stash earlier, she's getting wasted. It doesn't take much. They skipped dinner too, and Lori's stomach is growling in protest. But she can't think about food right now. "Did your dad ask where I was going when he gave you a ride home from the library earlier?"

"Yeah," says Nicole. "He wondered why you didn't come with me. He said he thought you and I came as a pair." She rolls her eyes. "So I told him you were going back to Lucas's house."

Lori thinks of how Sheriff Chambers invited her to dinner at their place. The way he complimented her on her tan. Pushing the thought aside she asks, "Do you love Lucas?"

"Of course," says Nicole, looking at her. "He's perfect for me." Her smile fades a little. "Don't you love Kurt?"

Lori considers it carefully before answering. Kurt's nice and all, but she doesn't think this is what love feels like. It's difficult to put her feelings into words, but she wouldn't feel too bad if they broke up one day. It would be a relief in some ways. Maybe because she knows it has to happen sooner or later. Deep down she knows she's not Kurt's type. Nicole is, but she's taken. And Kurt's too nice to break up with Lori while all four of them hang out. It would make things awkward. "I don't know. How do you know you love Lucas?"

Nicole grins. "Because I think about him all the time. And I trust him."

"You do?"

"Of course." Nicole rests her head against her friend's shoulder. "He'd never cheat on me."

Lori looks away. "How can you be so sure?"

"Because look at me!" Nicole giggles. "Why would he cheat on someone who looks this good?"

Despite her reservations, Lori smiles faintly. Nicole isn't usually this confident. It's the marijuana talking. "Do you think you'll marry him one day?"

"Probably."

Lori scoffs. "Most high school romances end when school ends. You know that, right?"

"Ouch." Nicole looks at her, with slightly dilated eyes. "That's not a very nice thing to say."

"Well, it's the truth."

"Lori, why are you being a bitch about it? And what's with all the questions?"

"No reason."

"No, seriously," says Nicole with her eyes fixed on Lori. "What's wrong? You've been acting weird all afternoon."

"No I haven't," says Lori defensively.

"You have. You couldn't wait to ditch Tommy and Aimee. What's wrong with you?" When Lori doesn't reply she says, "Is it Lucas? Has he upset you?"

Turning to face her, Lori says, "Why do you think that?"

All lightheartedness vanishes from Nicole's face. She appears hurt. "You're still annoyed that you think Kurt has the hots for me, right? So you're taking it out on Lucas and me. Our relationship."

Lori rolls her eyes. "Not this again." This is what they argued about yesterday, after Kurt flirted with Nicole. "I'm not sabotaging your stupid relationship with your stupid boyfriend," she says. "Even though I know you can do better than a stupid jock."

Nicole surprises her by standing. "I want to go home."

Lori gets up too fast. Her head swims as she stands. "No, don't. I don't want to leave yet."

With a sharp look Nicole says, "Well maybe not everything is about what you want. Did you ever consider that?"

Lori frowns. "Why are you being mean?"

Nicole faces her. "Me? You're the one calling my boyfriend stupid! What's with you tonight? You were fine when I left you at the library. Then you were acting weird after." She seems to consider something. "Was Lucas still at the house?" Her eyes narrow. "Are you into him? Did you two do something?"

Lori's headache is getting worse. It happens every time she smokes. She rubs her eyes. "I thought you said you trusted him? If you really did, you wouldn't ask me that."

"Oh my God, you're not even going to deny it!" yells Nicole. She's getting herself worked up.

"Please don't scream at me, my head hurts."

"Tell me what happened earlier," demands Nicole.

Lori can't do that. She'll never be able to tell anyone what happened. There would be too many repercussions. The park starts spinning, like the first time she ever got drunk. She bends forward as she feels like vomiting. She places her hands on her knees to hold herself steady. "I can't." She retches. "Nicole, I feel weird."

But Nicole doesn't care. "I can't believe you. I can't believe you've been accusing me of cheating with Kurt when you've been cheating with my boyfriend all along!"

"I haven't been." She's crying now. "Please, just sit down with me. I'm scared."

"Stop faking it!" yells Nicole.

Lori glances at her, struggling to focus on Nicole's face. She's crying too, and she's too wasted and upset to listen to her. "I can't tell you what happened earlier. I'm sorry. It's too... bad. I wish I'd gone with you, to your house instead."

Nicole's eyes widen. "You had sex with him."

Lori kneels on the ground, trying to shake her head, but doing that makes the park spin more. "I just need to sit down for a minute."

"Even I haven't had sex with him," says Nicole. She's over-reacting. If she wasn't high, she would be giving Lori a chance to explain. "That's the ultimate betrayal, Lori! I'll never speak to you again."

"Nicole, please! Listen to me."

"Go to hell." Nicole takes off.

All Lori can do is watch her friend leave while she tries not to vomit. They shouldn't separate this late at night. Lori doesn't have her phone. Someone could grab Nicole on her way home. She could be abducted or raped. They should stick together. "Come back!" she sobs. "Please, Nicole. Wait for me!"

But the darkness envelops her best friend, leaving Lori disoriented and alone.

FORTY-SEVEN

SUMMER 2022

By midafternoon Nicole wants to get out of Sindy's house for some alone time. She leaves Lucas behind with his mother, having declined to talk about that night. She has no doubt her mother-in-law has the best of intentions by trying to help figure out what happened to Lori, but forcing her to relive the worst time in her life won't help anybody.

Nicole drives aimlessly for a while, with the windows down. The warm afternoon breeze feels good on her face. For the first time since she arrived in town the sky is filled with white clouds that occasionally obscure the sun. Before too long she finds herself outside the Marshes' farm. With the car idling on the edge of the long driveway, she stares at the scene ahead of her. There appears to be just one officer guarding the property. He sits in his cruiser looking down at something, probably his phone, paying her no attention.

Nicole's eyes are drawn to the silo. She didn't kill Lori. She knows she wouldn't have done that, no matter how high or upset she was. Someone else bashed Lori's head with a rock and then either left her for dead, if her father's telling the truth, or carried her up that ladder afterward, and dumped her into the silo. In which case it was her father. If Chief Deputy Butler can lie for her father about one thing, he's not above lying about the rest of it. He could know Ron killed her. He might even have witnessed it. Maybe they were in it together. She closes her eyes against the thought.

Her phone rings. She scrambles to retrieve it from her purse on the passenger seat. It's Kurt. "Hey," she says. "Did you hear it might not be Aimee in the woods?"

"Yeah," he says. "Which begs the question: who is it?"

She's ashamed to admit she doesn't care who it is as long as it's not her sister. "Hopefully just some really old guy who had a heart attack while fishing alone." She glances at the cruiser. No movement. The driver doesn't care that she's here. Maybe he thinks she's a reporter. "How's Tommy doing?"

"He's in surgery. I've been told to wait for him to come out." Kurt sighs heavily. "God, I hate hospitals."

She feels for him. He'll be thinking about his father's condition. "I really hope Tommy makes it."

"You do? Even though he probably harmed your sister?" Kurt sounds weary. Like he doesn't care anymore.

"Of course I do. Kurt, he told me some things before you showed up. I know where Aimee went now."

Kurt doesn't respond right away. "What did he say? Did he admit to being the baby's father?"

"No. He told me he helped her to hide. He paid for a motel room for her in Dartmoor."

"A motel room? What was she running from?"

"My parents had recently told her I killed Lori and she didn't know whether to believe them. On top of that I think she was afraid of whoever she was dating because I found out from her best friend, Stacey, that the guy had changed toward her. He wasn't happy that she got pregnant. So it can't be Tommy. He'd probably be overjoyed if she was having their baby."

Kurt scoffs. "Oh please. Come on, Nicole. That sounds to

me like a cover story. Tommy claims he was saving her because he wants to be seen as some kind of hero instead of a killer. And, trust me, it wouldn't be the first time a killer has been in love with his victim." He takes a deep breath. "You need to be more careful because he'll take advantage of you. Just because we knew the guy as a kid doesn't mean he's still sweet and innocent. People change."

Annoyed by his attitude she says, "The only way we'll know if he's telling the truth is if we visit the motel and see her room, speak to the front desk. You could ask for the surveillance footage."

"What's the motel called?"

"That's the problem, I don't know. You shot him before I could get any more information out of him."

"He was about to run again." He sounds irritated. "I had no choice."

"I know. He shouldn't have run, I get it," she says. "But he thinks he's being framed, so can you blame him?" She doesn't wait for a response. "Back at the house you said you found something in his apartment. What was it?"

"I can't tell you that."

Sensing Kurt's patience is running thin, she doesn't push it. "Fine. I have a way we can find out which motel she was staying at."

"How?"

"While she was there, Aimee was in touch with Stacey for a while, via text. Stacey's sent me the number of the phone Aimee was using. Aimee was so afraid of someone that she bought a burner phone. I mean, can you even believe that?"

"So you think I can find the location of the motel by getting the service provider to ping her phone?" he says.

"Right."

"I can't do anything until I'm released from watching

Tommy," says Kurt. "Besides, your dad would have to approve that. Are you okay with him knowing all this?"

Nicole swallows. "Can't you do it without telling him?"

"No. I can't." His tone hardens. "I've done enough. No offense, Nicole, but I'm tired of all this. I'm tired of getting between you and your parents. I'm tired of your entire family."

"Kurt!" She's shocked by the outburst. "Why are you being like this?"

"I have enough on my plate right now. I can't help you anymore. Ask your husband to take over if he's such a great guy. I'm sorry." He ends the call.

Nicole stares in disbelief at her phone. "What the hell just happened?" Kurt's refusal to help means she's on her own with following leads. She won't be able to find the motel Aimee was staying at. Maybe it wouldn't help anyway, considering she's no longer there. It's unlikely the staff would hand over surveillance footage to Nicole. At this point all she can do is pray Tommy recovers well enough to tell her where he last saw her sister.

She wonders whether Tommy knows who Aimee was seeing. It was clearly someone who wasn't happy at the prospect of being a father. Aimee might have still been in touch with this guy after she ran away to the motel. Maybe he showed up one night and decided to put an end to her pregnancy, along with her life. What better way to silence someone? Especially if he was already married and had something to lose.

She takes a deep breath. The only other explanation is that her parents found Aimee. Maybe they tried to get her to go home with them and she declined. Things could have gotten heated. "But then, why ask me to come home?" she mutters.

Maybe so they could blame Aimee's murder on her. Just like they have Lori's. This could all be one big setup. To get Nicole imprisoned for life and out of their hair for good.

Nicole's heart rate spikes. "They wouldn't," she says aloud. "Would they?"

FORTY-EIGHT

Kurt sits on an uncomfortable blue chair in the hospital's waiting area on the third floor, between the nurse's station and a bunch of vending machines. It's quieter now visiting hours are over until later. The patients are getting dinner delivered to their beds. It smells like beef, which is an improvement on the underlying medicinal smell. Both aromas remind him to call his father. He waits patiently for him to pick up.

"What do you want?" says Brian, sounding annoyed.

"I'm just checking you've been fed. Did the nurses come?"

"Sure, they came. With their fake smiles and stupid jokes." He coughs. "They think I can't see right through them."

"They're just doing their job, Dad, like you did when you were a cop," says Kurt patiently. "You can't tell me you never had to put on a front in the interests of a victim, right?"

"I'm not a victim. I'm dying. I know it and they know it, so I'd rather they just cut the crap and do their jobs without the forced sense of humor."

"Sure, I get it." Kurt rubs his temples. "Do you need anything? You've had your meds and you've been helped to the bathroom, right?"

"Stop fussing," says Brian. "I can take care of myself. When are you coming home?"

"I'm at the hospital waiting for Tommy Peterson to come out of surgery. I could be here all night." His father doesn't respond, which means he's disappointed. "Do you need anything?"

Brian says, "I'll message Ron and tell him to switch you with Hayes. Let that asshole work all night for a change."

"Why? You need me to be home?"

"I don't need anything. Just don't stay there all night."

Kurt smiles sadly as the call ends. His father isn't very good at putting on a brave face. He must feel better when Kurt's nearby. It's not surprising. He's the most vulnerable he's ever been in his life, and rotting away on his own in their empty house can't be pleasant.

A male nurse approaches. "Your guy's been taken to recovery. He'll be there while we monitor him. If he does well, which he appears to be doing so far, we'll move him to a bed up here."

Kurt nods. "Understood. Thanks." He checks the time. Almost five o'clock. He could be here all night unless his father does message the sheriff. He goes to a machine that dispenses bad coffee and slides in a couple of dollars. As his coffee cup fills, he spots Ron getting off the elevator.

"Any update?" asks Ron as he approaches. He looks around the waiting area, anywhere but at Kurt.

Kurt tries to keep his eyes off the bruise on the sheriff's jaw. "He's in recovery. They'll let me know when he's out, but he's doing fine right now."

Ron nods.

"I'm glad to hear it wasn't Aimee in the woods," says Kurt. "I bet you're relieved."

"I'll be relieved when my daughter's home safe." Ron eyeballs him. "What did you find at Tommy's apartment?"

"Nothing. I got called away to apprehend Tommy, so I left Hayes in charge."

"Hayes said you found something that could be a journal."

The vending machine is beeping for Kurt to take the coffee out of the dispenser, so he does. "Oh right. Sure. I left it with Hayes. I don't know if it *is* a journal. I didn't get the chance to read it. Could be a book of poetry for all I know. Maybe Tommy's into that shit."

"Hayes told me you took it with you."

Kurt shakes his head. "No. I left it with him when I got the call from dispatch."

Ron's cell phone buzzes at his hip. He breaks eye contact to read a message. "It seems your dad wants you home tonight. He having a bad day or something?"

"I think every day's a bad day now." Kurt sips his coffee and grimaces. It's only lukewarm. "I should probably try to spend as much time with him as possible over the coming days."

"He's that bad?" Ron's expression becomes pained. "I should visit him more. It's just, with Aimee missing..."

"He gets it," says Kurt. "Trust me. But it would help if I could take some time off. He hates the nurses that come. He wants to do everything himself."

Ron smiles sadly. "I bet he does." He stands straight. "I'll get Hayes or Moore to take over here. Stay with Tommy until someone arrives. Then go be with your dad. I'll notify dispatch you're only to be called in emergencies."

Kurt should be surprised at the sheriff's kindness, but he knows it's only because Ron is thinking of Brian. Not how this is affecting him. "Thanks. I appreciate it."

"I'd appreciate the heads-up when you think he's close. I'd like to be there."

Kurt unexpectedly has to swallow back the urge to sob. He nods while staring into his coffee.

Ron walks away, leaving him alone again. Kurt finds a seat

in the corner of the room, away from prying eyes. He takes a minute to compose himself. He can't think about his father's looming death. Not right now. He'll deal with it when the time comes.

Instead, he pulls Aimee's journal from his back pocket and opens it where he left off.

FORTY-NINE

From the Journal of Aimee Chambers

June 30, 2022—Age 18

Mom dropped a bombshell tonight, and I don't know how to feel about it. My whole life feels like a lie and I have no one to talk to. I'm not supposed to tell anyone, not even Tommy. Then, straight after that, Dad told me something so bad about Nicole that I don't even want to consider it being true. It's devastating. There's so much wrong with my life right now and I have no idea how to cope with it all. I don't even know if I believe him. Mom said it was true. She sat there as if it was the most natural thing in the world. I can't even write it down in case anyone sees this.

I'm so confused and upset by what they told me that I've sent Nicole a message on FB. I did it without thinking, before I could change my mind. Now I keep obsessively checking my phone for a reply. She hasn't even read it yet. I told her to call me ASAP because I need to see her. I need to tell her what

Mom and Dad are accusing her of. I have no idea how she'll take it, but this must be why she left town.

And now I'm scared, because if she does reply, it's going to open a whole new can of worms. She'll learn the truth about what I've been doing. I'll have to tell her I'm pregnant, and she'll want to know who by. Obviously I won't tell her right away. Not until we can meet in person and I can judge how she would react.

It would be easier to just forget I ever sent her a message, forget what Mom and Dad told me and just skip town. Have my baby alone. Maybe let Tommy take care of us. I know he'd do that. He's too good to me. And he wants to beat up the guy who got me pregnant, because I broke down and told him who it was. I told him I felt threatened. That I'm worried the baby's father will kill me or something. You see it all the time on the news. I'm a walking cliché. Tommy said he'd take me some-place safe. I'm tempted to let him.

I don't know. This is all too much.

FIFTY

Kurt frowns as he reads. Because that's not how it was. "I didn't threaten her," he mumbles. "Not seriously. It was a joke." It doesn't surprise him that Aimee was being dramatic, given her age, but these accusations are damning. He glances around to make sure no one's paying him any attention. There's only one nurse at the desk but she's on the phone. An elderly couple have entered and are taking their time choosing seats. The old man nods at Kurt, who nods back. Eventually they sit well away from him.

Kurt turns his attention back to the journal and flips to the next page to see what else Aimee has written. But it's empty. That was the last entry. She must have left town shortly after, having given Tommy her journal so her parents didn't find it during their search of her room.

Kurt's shoulders are tense as he thinks of Tommy's role in all this. The guy's an asshole. Sure, he's not the drug dealer Kurt has made him out to be, but he *is* a loser. He's so infatuated with Aimee that he's become her lapdog. He was hiding her, and keeping her secrets. Probably in the hope that one day Aimee will sleep with him. Kurt scoffs. That will never happen.

Until reading that last entry he hadn't known for sure that Tommy knew about him. About who got her pregnant. He suspected she might have told him, but because Tommy had been good at keeping it to himself, Kurt thought there was a chance she hadn't. Tommy could have easily spilled his guts to Ron when the sheriff turned up to question him, and he must have been mightily tempted. But his loyalty to Aimee meant he didn't. Maybe now Tommy's been shot he's more likely to break his silence. Especially as he could go down for Aimee's murder otherwise.

Which means Tommy's a liability.

"Kurt!" Theresa Peterson comes running over to him from the elevator. "What's going on? Where's Tommy?"

Kurt discreetly slips the journal away. "You're not allowed up here, Theresa. I'm sorry. Sheriff's orders."

The anguish on her face ages her. "But my son's been shot! Someone shot him!"

Kurt doesn't volunteer that it was he who shot Tommy. "He's doing okay and is recovering from surgery, but you shouldn't be here. I'm going to have to ask you to leave."

"Why? I don't understand!" Tears roll down her face. The older couple are staring at her.

Kurt gently pulls her aside. "Your son is a suspect in Aimee's disappearance," he says quietly. "We need to interview him before you can see him."

"But, Kurt," she pleads. "I'm his *mother*! And he's all I have. You have to let me see him."

The pain in her eyes is so great that Kurt has to break eye contact. "I'm sorry, I can't. But I'll call you as soon as he wakes up. I'll keep you updated on his situation."

She shakes her head in disbelief. "This is disgusting. You've known Tommy since he was a little boy. You know he's not capable of hurting Aimee Chambers of all people. I expected more from you, Kurt. Your father would've let me in. Brian was always fair and empathetic. You need to be more like him." She turns and slowly shuffles back to the elevator.

Her words sting. But Kurt can't think about her feelings right now. He collapses back into his seat and considers how she'll cope if Tommy doesn't pull through. She was a mess after Lori vanished. Losing two kids might be too much for her to bear.

A few minutes after Theresa leaves, the nurse reappears clutching a wad of paperwork to his chest. He looks as tired as Kurt feels. "You can see him for a few minutes now if you want. He's been taken to room 227." He turns and points. "Right at the end of the hallway, last door on the left."

"Will do, thanks." Kurt stands, feeling for the journal in his back pocket. It's safe.

FIFTY-ONE

Nicole arranges to meet Jennifer Manvers at the newspaper's office. She checks her phone as she waits in the reception area. Awaiting her attention is a text message from her mother.

Are you okay? Thank God it's not Aimee.

Nicole replies.

You need a cleanup team at the house.
Tommy was shot in your kitchen.

Debbie's response is brief.

Understood.

"Hey. How are you?" Jennifer approaches. Her long red hair is swept up in a ponytail and she looks intrigued. She doesn't know why Nicole's here.

"Hi," says Nicole. "Thanks for meeting with me."

"No problem. Want to do this here or at my desk?"

Nicole's hands are shaking. "In private would be good. You have meeting rooms, right?"

Jennifer quickly picks up on her nerves. "Sure. I'll lead the way." Nicole follows her to the office. "Most people have left for the day," says Jennifer. "But some are still at the woods, waiting for another update from your dad. The remains will probably be taken away soon and my editor wants a photograph to go on tomorrow's front page."

Nicole doesn't respond, but she has a feeling what she's about to say will bump the body-in-the-woods story off the front page.

"Here we are," says Jennifer, opening a door to a small, tidy room which has one window overlooking the downtown stores. "Coffee? Water?"

Nicole's too warm for coffee. Her body knows what she's about to do and it's conspiring against her, increasing her nerves and making her sweat. "Water would be great. Thanks."

The journalist leaves for a minute. Nicole takes a seat facing the window as she checks her phone. A message from Lucas asks where she is. He wants her to have dinner at Sindy's place with them.

Eat without me. Be back as soon as I can. Love you.

She knows he'll be disappointed. He wants her to make more of an effort with his mother. And she will. Later.

Jennifer returns and places a plastic cup of water on the table in front of Nicole. A legal pad is clutched under her arm. A pen behind her ear. She closes the door before sitting opposite Nicole and placing the items on the table. "So, what can I do for you?"

Nicole sips the water, managing to spill some down her T-shirt.

Concerned, Jennifer says, "Your hands are shaking. Is everything okay?"

She takes a deep breath. "I have a lot to get off my chest. I've had enough of protecting the wrong people."

The pen is removed from behind Jennifer's ear. The legal pad is brought front and center. "What do you mean?"

"It's time everyone knows what I know," says Nicole. "I want it all out there. Because I want my sister to come home, and I think I'm the only person in this town with Aimee's best interests at heart. So I'm going to stop protecting... certain people." She pauses. "Specifically, my parents."

Jennifer's taken aback for a second. "You want it on record, right? I can write about whatever you tell me?"

Without second-guessing herself, Nicole nods. Her phone buzzes on the table.

Why do I get the feeling you're doing something you shouldn't be?

It's Lucas. He's worried. She doesn't reply. There's no point. No one can stop her from what she's about to do.

FIFTY-TWO

"You can quote me," says Nicole, finding an inner strength. "And once I'm done you can ask me anything you want to know."

Jennifer tries to hide her excitement but doesn't quite manage it. Her eyes are awash with intrigue and she suddenly stands. "Let me get a recorder and my laptop. I don't want to make any mistakes."

While she's gone Nicole gets a call from a number she doesn't recognize. She frowns, wondering who it is. When she declines the call, it's quickly followed up with a text.

It's Dad. Call me.

She wonders what he wants. Maybe the coroner has a better idea about who the remains in the woods could belong to. Or maybe one of his deputies spotted her coming here and gave her dad the heads-up. Then she thinks of Lucas's messages. It's possible he's told her father she's gone AWOL.

She looks out of the glass partition and sees Jennifer talking to her editor. The editor looks Nicole's way. It makes her wonder whether she's doing the right thing. What if they make the article more about her than Lori's real killer? She looks away when Jennifer heads back to the meeting room.

"Okay," says Jennifer, closing the door behind her. She opens her laptop and hits record on her cell phone before taking her seat. "Where do you want to start?"

Nicole takes a deep breath. If she doesn't take a risk and get everything out in the open, Aimee may never be found. "I guess I want to start with confirming I don't know who told Lori about the sexual assault allegations against my dad. I don't know if they were Lori's allegations. If he was assaulting her, she never told me that was the case."

Jennifer nods, her fingers skating over the keyboard of her laptop as she makes notes. "Do you know any specifics?"

Nicole thinks back to the original conversation. It was during the walk home from school one afternoon. Lori had seemed embarrassed to bring it up. She'd admitted she was only telling Nicole because she didn't want her to hear about it from anyone else. "No. All she said was that she'd heard a fourteen-year-old girl had been inappropriately touched by my dad. I asked her if she was joking, but her expression was deadly serious. She had tears in her eyes. I don't know whether they were tears for me, with it being my dad we were talking about, or whether the tears were for herself."

"Do you know if it was limited to inappropriate touching?"

Nicole shakes her head. "I asked if she meant rape, but Lori said she wasn't sure. You have to understand that we weren't experienced in sex at all. We were only fifteen and pretty naïve back then, both still virgins." Well, Nicole was. If her suspicions about Lucas and Lori were true, which is what caused their argument that night in the park, perhaps Lori wasn't. Nicole doesn't let her mind go there. Lucas had promised his indiscretion was a one-off, and only with Mia, the cheerleader.

"Forgive me for asking," says Jennifer, softening her tone, "but were you ever sexually abused by your father?"

"Not at all. Which is why I don't know if the allegations are true. But once Lori vanished, I started believing they might be."

"You did?"

"I was confused and upset. And..." Here goes. "I started to believe that my father killed Lori."

Jennifer stops typing. She leans back in her seat. "Whoa. I wasn't expecting you to say that. What made you think it was him?"

It's too late to stop now. Nicole has to go all the way. "Because even though he wasn't scheduled to work that night, he was out with Chief Deputy Butler. And he didn't return until the early hours, giving him time to kill her."

"That's interesting, because he never confirmed where he was that night. Not satisfactorily anyway. He just said he was working."

"I know," says Nicole. "And now I know why."

Leaning forward, Jennifer says, "Go on."

Nicole's hands are sweating and she's acutely aware she's about to betray both her parents. But they've pushed her to this point with their stupid secrets and accusations. She's also aware she could be giving her father the opportunity to go public with his claim about her. But Nicole knows she didn't kill Lori. Not directly. So she has nothing to hide. But her father does. And ultimately, she just wants Aimee found, which her dad seems incapable of doing. With a deep breath she says, "Last night my father told me that he was the one who dumped Lori's body in Jim Marsh's silo."

The air changes in the small meeting room. Jennifer doesn't say a word. She just blinks. It's then that Nicole knows there's no coming back from this. Her relationship with her parents is now officially dead.

FIFTY-THREE

Kurt enters Tommy's hospital room, careful to close the door behind him. The nurse who was administering pain meds has given him the all-clear to talk to the patient, as long as he's careful not to upset him. Apparently, things could still take a turn for the worse if his blood pressure rises.

Approaching the bed, Kurt surveys the scene. Tommy's surrounded by machines doing their best to help monitor his condition. His skin is pallid, probably from losing so much blood. His bullet wound is covered with bandages. Half his chest has been shaved. His shoulder is going to hurt for a long time. It may even affect the use of his right arm. Kurt feels a pang of guilt. He remembers back in the day trying to help Lori's little brother figure out how to use a skateboard without smashing his face on the sidewalk. He was only five at the time, and the kid had no balance whatsoever. He was skinny and too needy for attention. Physically, he's changed as he's become an adult. He's broad and muscular, and not unattractive.

Tommy's eyes flicker open. He removes the oxygen mask from his face as his vision clears. When he realizes it's Kurt in front of him, his eyes widen. "What are you doing here?" he croaks. "Come to finish the job?"

Kurt takes a step closer to the bed. "Calm down. I'm not meant to upset you. It'll mess up your heart rate or something."

"Then leave." Tommy coughs and then winces from the pain it causes his shoulder. "Shit!" He takes a deep breath. "You need to tell the sheriff what you did to Aimee."

Next to the bed, the heart rate monitor fastens its pace.

"How much did she tell you?" asks Kurt.

"Get out of here, man. I'm not messing with you. I'll tell him myself if you don't stay away from me." The fear in his eyes indicates what he's thinking. He's convinced Kurt's here to finish him off.

"How much did she tell you?" Kurt presses.

Tommy swallows before licking his lips. He's probably thirsty for the water on his nightstand. Kurt doesn't offer to help him take a sip. "Enough to know you groomed her."

"What?" Kurt rolls his eyes. "How do you figure?"

"Because you started small and built up over time. You showered her with attention, then added gifts and dates. Dates at places where no one would spot you together. You wanted her to keep your sordid affair a secret because you don't have the balls to be honest about what you've done."

"I'm not ashamed," says Kurt. "It was consensual. She wanted to be with me."

"But you were more interested in her sister."

Kurt clenches his jaw.

"Aimee told me how you'd talk about Nicole all the time. You kept comparing the two of them." Tommy shakes his head. "Why didn't you just go after Nicole if you were that obsessed?"

Kurt scoffs. "Says the guy who's obsessed with Aimee even though she wants nothing to do with you. Not physically anyway." It occurs to him then that he's not so different to Tommy. It's a depressing thought. And Tommy's right, he was wrong to date Nicole's little sister. The age gap is only eleven years, but if there was nothing wrong with it, why keep it a secret?

Tommy's expression is pained. It obviously hurts to know the woman you want doesn't want you. Especially when everyone can see it but you. "What did you do to her?" Tommy asks.

"I was about to ask you the same," says Kurt. "You're the one who took her to a motel and kept her location a secret. As a law enforcement officer, I've got to tell you that sounds like abduction to me."

Shaking his head, Tommy says, "No, that's not how it was. She asked for my help. She wanted to get away from you after you threatened her."

"Come on! I didn't threaten her. I told her she was being dramatic, that's all."

"So why did you make sure she could see you were resting your hand on your weapon at the time? Why insist she keeps quiet about who got her pregnant? You knew what you were doing."

"Oh yeah, what's that?" says Kurt, trying to keep his cool.

"You were threatening her life. You put the fear of God into an eighteen-year-old girl who was carrying your baby."

Kurt tries to remember the exact moment. Aimee had been crying her eyes out, as usual. She wanted him to commit to her by telling her parents he was the father of their grandchild. But he couldn't do it. He knew what the consequences would be. He would've been fired on the spot. Besides, he didn't love Aimee. He was lonely when she came on to him. His father had recently been diagnosed with cancer and Kurt had no one to talk to about it. He needed to distract himself and have some fun. She took it too seriously. "Maybe it appeared that way to her because she's so damn sensitive, but I wasn't threatening her. I just wanted our relationship to be over. And I didn't want to be a father. She made the decision to keep the baby without consulting me."

"So you killed her?" Tommy spits.

"For all I know it could've been anyone's baby." Kurt's eyes narrow. "Maybe you raped her when you got sick of her telling you no."

Tommy leans forward in anger. "You piece of shit."

Kurt's cell phone rings. It's his dad. He walks to the corner of the room as he answers. "Dad? Everything okay?"

"Get home. I need you." His father pants as if he's exerted himself.

"On my way." Kurt ends the call but stays where he is while he figures out how to silence Tommy. Eventually, he turns to face him. The fear in Tommy's eyes is unmissable. Kurt takes a step forward.

FIFTY-FOUR

"Are you kidding me?" says Jennifer. She sits stunned at Nicole's revelation. "Let me get this straight. You're saying that Sheriff Ron Chambers killed Lori Peterson?"

"No, I'm saying he confessed to dumping her body in the silo and then covering up her location. He pretended he had no clue where she was and went on to lie to Lori's entire family. Then, when her body was found by the scrap guy who bought the silos, my father went on pretending he had no idea how she got there."

Full of nervous energy, Jennifer stands. "But that suggests he was responsible for killing her, right?"

Nicole knows that. Which is why she's been so reluctant to tell anyone. "Right. But he denies killing her."

"So why hide the body?"

This is the part that could ruin Nicole's life. She hesitates for a second. "He said he was protecting me."

"From what? Your friend?"

"No. He's convinced that *I* killed Lori."

Jennifer's mouth drops open even farther. She shakes her head as she tries to figure out what's going on. After a minute or two she appears to come to a conclusion. "So he's gaslighting you?"

Nicole exhales with relief. Jennifer has seen right through her father and she couldn't be more grateful. "He almost had me believing it too."

"I bet he did. Narcissists, or psychos, whatever you want to label them, are good at what they do. And I bet he used your time in hospital, when you were presumably on strong meds, as a way to convince you that you didn't remember it. Am I right?"

Nicole nods. Tears build in her eyes. "I didn't hurt Lori. We fell out but I didn't hurt her."

Jennifer walks around the table and leans down to hug her. It feels good to have someone see things the way she does. Someone who immediately saw her father for what he is. Jennifer pulls away. "I've got to expose him," she says. "I mean, he's the *sheriff*! What else has he been getting away with all this time? Did he kill whoever that is in the Franklin Woods?" Then, as realization hits her, Jennifer gasps. "Oh my God. He could be a serial killer. Aimee could be another of his victims."

Nicole's body trembles at the thought of it. Goosebumps cover her arms. Whether he killed only Lori, or the others too, her father *is* a killer, and her instincts were right all along. When Jennifer returns to her seat, Nicole says, "My mom knew he hid the body and she's happy to let him frame me."

"Wow. Nice parents." Jennifer shakes her head. "Wait. How could they frame you for this?"

This is the part that worries Nicole the most. "They said I left some evidence behind at the scene."

Jennifer raises her eyebrows. "What evidence?"

"That's just it. They won't tell me. They didn't want me to know so I couldn't tell anyone."

"Which means they probably don't have anything. They're just putting the fear of God into you."

Nicole hopes so.

"Was anyone else around when they told you this?"

"Deputy Kurt Butler, but I want him left out of this."

Jennifer leans back. With disgust on her face she says, "And Butler didn't do anything about it? He didn't report him?"

"No," confirms Nicole. "But you have to understand: he would've lost his job. My father made that clear. He also said there would be more repercussions if it ever got out. Please don't print Kurt's name in your article. His father's dying. He's under a lot of pressure and he was friends with Lori too. He was devastated at Jim Marsh's farm the day Lori was found." She remembers the grim look on his face. "He's struggling to cope and I don't want to push him over the edge."

The journalist takes a minute to consider it. "Fine. For now, he's off the hook. Until the shit hits the fan at least. And I can't protect him from any retaliation your father makes."

"I know." Nicole lowers her eyes. There's only one way this can go for Kurt. If her father's arrested, she and Kurt will have to testify.

Jennifer appears sympathetic. "Hey. Just remember why you're doing this. You want your sister found."

She nods. "I have news about what happened to Aimee too. Kind of." Nicole sips her water as Jennifer checks her phone is still recording. Then she explains how Tommy took her sister to a motel, and why. "She was either afraid of my parents finding her or afraid of the baby's father finding her."

"Or both."

"Right. I'm considering phoning every motel in Dartmoor to see if I can find which one she was at."

Jennifer shakes her head. "There's no point. They won't be allowed to tell you anything, and besides, it's unlikely she used her real name."

Nicole's heart sinks. She feels useless.

"So Tommy doesn't know why she disappeared from the motel?" asks Jennifer.

"No. She hasn't contacted him since."

"How credible is this Tommy guy? Could his story be an attempt at saving his own skin? Because it could be that Aimee was afraid of *him* and fled the motel when she saw her chance to finally get away from him."

That's similar to what Kurt said. "I don't know him well enough to know for sure," says Nicole. "But my gut tells me he was trying to help Aimee, and now he's in the hospital for his trouble." She feels slightly better for coming here. For speaking to someone with no vested interest, and no connection to her father.

Jennifer looks over her notes. Eventually she glances at Nicole. "This is pretty sensational stuff. It's going to cause a furor when it comes out, and my editor will have the final say on what makes it into the article." She glances at the clock above the door. "But before I even show it to another person, I just need to check something." She takes a deep breath. "You understand that, at the bare minimum, when this gets out it will end your father's career, if not see him incarcerated for a long time, right?"

Nicole swallows. The enormity of what she's done makes her want to take it all back. But that wouldn't be fair to Aimee. So she nods, despite her fear. "I understand."

FIFTY-FIVE

With a heavy heart, Kurt switches off the car's engine. He's outside his father's home. The sun is disappearing, causing shadows around the property. His uniform is damp under the arms, and he's craving a cool shower. The phone call from his father had worried him, so he'd left the hospital as soon as he was done with Tommy and before anyone arrived to take over from him, but that's okay. Tommy was in no state to go anywhere. And now it's just a matter of time before Kurt's found out. The revelations will come thick and fast and the best thing he can do is take off his uniform for good and wait.

Maybe his father will pass before everything comes to light. Maybe Kurt could help him along so that he doesn't have to know what kind of person his son really is.

Kurt pops a pill before getting out of the car and wearily climbing the porch steps. Inside, the house is dark, with just one light switched on in the back room. Kurt unhooks his belt and weapon, leaving them behind. He unbuttons the collar of his shirt and takes a deep breath before entering his father's room.

The bed is empty, the sheets a tangled mess. "Dad?"

"Down here," comes a croak from the opposite side of the

room.

Kurt rushes around the bed to find his father on the floor, face down. It looks like he didn't even have the strength to push himself onto his back. "What the hell happened?" asks Kurt. He kneels next to his father and gently pushes him into a more comfortable position so he can assess any injuries. His father weighs next to nothing. With no muscle to grab, he's just bones.

Brian pants from the exertion, despite not helping. "I fell." His words are soft and barely audible. "Leaning for a drink... Damn nurse put it too far away."

Kurt blinks back tears at what his father's become. He's more like a child than a former law enforcement officer. Kurt collapses into a seated position on the floor and hugs his father to him as he leans his back against the wall. "I'm sorry. I should've been here." He swallows back emotion. "I'm quitting my job. I'll stay with you until the end."

Brian relaxes into his embrace, unable to fight it. "The hell you will."

Kurt sniffs back an unexpected laugh. "Hey, you don't get to tell me what to do anymore. I only became a cop in the first place because of you."

His father clutches his hand. "Live for yourself. Not for anyone else." His body rocks with coughs.

"Stop talking, Dad. Save your energy." Kurt passes him a bottle of water and helps him swallow some before resting the bottle on the floor.

"I'm serious," says Brian with some effort. "It's your life. Do what you want. Fill this house with kids—or don't. You can fill it with boyfriends for all I care."

Kurt freezes.

"Just live your life. Before it's too late."

Does he know? Kurt thinks maybe he was right when he said you can never really fool your parents. His father's always seen right through him.

"Son? I just want you to get off the pills you're taking and try to be happy. If that's with a guy, then do it. Live in this house with someone who'll make you feel good about yourself. Your mother made me happy, and once she died you made me happy." His father pants with the exertion of talking so much.

"Shush, Dad." Kurt's face burns with shame. His dad knows about the pills too. The ones he takes to help him face another day. He managed to give up marijuana years ago but recently replaced it with something stronger.

"What, you think I'm such a dinosaur I can't handle my son being attracted to men?" says Brian. "Let me tell you something: it's no one's business but yours. And I'd take seeing you with another man over seeing you with Nicole Rivers any day."

Kurt remains perfectly still. He doesn't want to admit to anything. He's too chickenshit.

"Nicole's bad news." More coughing. "She killed Lori."

"No. She didn't, Dad. You're wrong about that. Let's change the subject. You want some dinner? I can make you mac and cheese from scratch?"

Brian squeezes Kurt's wrist. "I have the proof. It's time she was exposed."

His father seems so convinced that Nicole was involved that Kurt is forced to ask, "What proof? Where is it?"

Brian points to his mahogany bureau. Kurt's eyes follow his finger but he hesitates to get up. He doesn't want to see what's inside there. He doesn't want it to be true. Lori didn't deserve to die, especially not over some stupid argument with her best friend. If she had lived, Kurt's life would be completely different right now. So would Nicole's and Aimee's. Lucas springs to mind. His life didn't change much at all. Sure, he cared for Nicole when she reached her breaking point, but he never really let Lori's death affect him. Maybe that's why Kurt resents the guy. Or maybe it's because he got to marry Nicole even after cheating on her.

"Go look," says Brian.

Reluctantly, Kurt maneuvers out from under his father. "Let's get you back in bed. Hold my neck." Brian does as he's told and it's as easy as Kurt expected to pick him up and gently place him back on the bed. Brian winces as he tries to get comfortable, so Kurt shoves some extra pillows behind his head. "All good?"

He nods.

Kurt turns his attention to the bureau. He finds various unopened letters in the top compartment. One is addressed to him, one to Ron. Others state the contents on the envelope: Brian Butler's last will and testament, insurance policies, a list of bank accounts. Kurt stops rifling through them as he's overwhelmed with grief. These were meant to be found after his father's death.

"Got it?"

Kurt sniffs. "Give me a chance, would you?" He forces himself to open each drawer in turn and, in the bottom drawer, near the back, he finds a brown padded envelope with *Confidential* stamped on the front. He pulls it out and holds it up so his father can see it. "This it?"

Brian nods. His eyelids are growing heavy. He'll be asleep before long.

Kurt opens the envelope and finds a piece of paper. He recognizes it as the form the sheriff's office used to use for handwritten witness statements. His father has written down what happened the night Lori vanished. It's signed and dated at the bottom. The date given is a week after she vanished. Maybe he didn't trust the sheriff to tell the truth if anyone found out what they did. Perhaps they weren't as close as Kurt was led to believe.

"Read it," croaks Brian. "Then tell everyone."

Kurt goes to his father's side and sits on the bed next to him. He takes one of his father's hands in his as he begins reading.

FIFTY-SIX

~~VICTIM~~/WITNESS STATEMENT
Oates County Sheriff's Office

I, CHIEF DEPUTY BRIAN BUTLER, **do hereby make the following statement about the incident witnessed on:** JULY 28, 2008 **at:** 12.50 a.m. **I understand that it is an ethical violation to make a sworn statement that contains false information and that I could be reprimanded by the Oates County Sheriff's Office for doing so. I declare the following information is the truth to the best of my knowledge.**

During the early hours of the aforementioned date, Sheriff Ron Chambers and I came across the body of fifteen-year-old Lori Peterson near to the children's playground on Sycamore Avenue. She was positioned on her back, wearing a white top with a denim skirt, and sneakers on her feet. Her skirt was above her waist, but there were no obvious signs of sexual assault and she was still wearing her underwear.

At first it was unclear whether she was still breathing. Upon closer inspection it became clear she was deceased. Instead of phoning for backup and securing the scene, we made decisions that were not just wrong, but unlawful.

I wanted to notify dispatch of the discovery but Sheriff Chambers stopped me. He had been inspecting the body and found something in the victim's hand. At the same time I had spotted a rock nearby. I shined my flashlight on it and saw it had what looked like blood on one corner, along with some long hairs. They were long and black and matted together with the blood. Visually, the hair matched the victim's. I checked the back of the victim's head, finding a large laceration. She had clearly experienced a good amount of blood loss. Therefore we surmised the rock was used to strike the victim, likely rendering her incapacitated.

I asked the sheriff for the second time whether I should now notify dispatch, but he again told me not to. He instructed me to bag the rock as evidence, which I did.

He then showed me what he had taken from the victim's grasp. It was a gold necklace, the chain broken apart as if grabbed during the incident. "This is my daughter's necklace," he said.

It suddenly became clear to me that the sheriff had come to the conclusion that his daughter was the perpetrator of the attack. He bagged the necklace while considering his next actions. Eventually he told me we had to hide both the body and the evidence.

I would not agree to either.

A heated discussion followed and I'm sorry to report that with a heavy heart, I eventually agreed not to disclose to anyone that we had discovered Lori Peterson's body. Sheriff Chambers said he would take care of the rest. We moved her body out of view. I then drove us to the sheriff's office so he could retrieve his vehicle. He asked me to take the necklace and hide it. He was to take the rock and hide that. I asked why he didn't send the rock to the crime lab for DNA testing in case his suspicions were incorrect, at which point he told me it contained not just the hair of the victim, but also some hairs that looked like his daughter's. She has distinctive curly brown hair and he didn't want his daughter's DNA showing up on any lab results linked to evidence from the scene. So to my knowledge, he never got the rock tested.

Against my better judgment I took the necklace. I'm ashamed to say I was stunned into submittal. I was shocked that the sheriff, a lifelong friend of mine, would be capable of misleading the victim's family. I believed he would change his mind about moving the body, or, shortly afterward, he would come clean. Now, a week after the incident, I still believe he will come to his senses shortly.

At the parking lot of the sheriff's office, I took the necklace from him and watched him get into his vehicle. Despite my trying to persuade him otherwise, he was determined to return to the crime scene and dispose of the body. Once he left, my involvement ended, aside from keeping silent about what had happened.

I write this unwitnessed statement in my own hand, in the hope I never need to use it. You should find the necklace with it. I have no knowledge of where the victim was dumped and what happened to the rock used to kill her. The sheriff and I have not spoken of that night since.

If Lori's parents should happen to read this at any point, I want to offer my sincere apologies for my part in your pain.

Signed: Chief Deputy Brian Butler

Date: August 4, 2008

Time: 11.45 p.m.
Witnessed:
Date:
Time:

FIFTY-SEVEN

When Nicole leaves the newspaper building, she feels like a weight has been lifted from her shoulders. Finally taking the potentially catastrophic step of sharing what she knows with someone else, especially a journalist, means everything can now be done to find Lori's real killer, and to find out once and for all whether Aimee's disappearance is linked to Lori's death.

But the effort has taken it out of her. She's hungry and in desperate need of caffeine, so she calls in at the nearby diner. Outside, it's just a regular brick building that sits between a coffee shop and a thrift store. Inside, it's decorated in vibrant colors, red leather booths and blue floor tiles, with white tables, giving it that all-American feel.

Unfortunately, with the nostalgic décor comes the clichéd old-timers sitting at the counter. All four old guys turn to watch as she enters, and she immediately regrets setting foot in here. It'll be full of her father's friends. An older waitress ignores her as she passes with a tray of food in her hand. There is no friendly welcome or invitation to take a seat.

Nicole's too hungry to let them intimidate her, so she slides into an empty booth and looks at the menu. It has all the typical options you'd expect from a place like this and her stomach rumbles at the thought of food. Especially when she sees the dessert section. The air is filled with the aroma of salty fries and greasy beef. It makes her mouth water.

Minutes pass with no service. Rather than make a big deal out of it she checks her phone and shoots Lucas a text.

Just grabbing some dinner. Back soon.

"Hi. What can I get you?" says a pretty waitress in her twenties.

Nicole smiles. "Can I get the chicken burger with fries and a Diet Coke."

"Sure thing." The waitress leaves.

Nicole stares out of the window onto the street but she's distracted by news coverage. A small TV above the counter shows a reporter outside the hospital where Tommy was taken.

"No one is being allowed in to see the suspect, not even his parents. Something his mother says is inhumane."

Theresa appears on screen. Her face is heavily lined and any makeup she wore today has been dissolved by tears. "I can't understand why I can't see my son. They can leave an officer in there with me if they want, I don't care. It's as if they're hiding something!"

"What exactly do you think the sheriff's office is hiding, Mrs. Peterson?" asks the reporter.

"I'm convinced they know what happened to my daughter back in 2008, and that's why they're blaming Tommy for whatever's happened to the sheriff's daughter. I think they tried to kill him today."

The reporter appears stunned for a second. "Why would law enforcement try to frame or kill someone?"

Theresa's eyes are wild as she says, "Because maybe Tommy knows something that can damage them. Or maybe they're trying to distract everyone from the fact that my daughter wasn't found for *fourteen* years! Something sinister is going on with them. Just ask the sheriff's other daughter, Nicole Rivers. She knows! I'm certain of it."

Nicole gasps as she turns away from the screen. She can feel all eyes on her, but no one dares to say anything, which surprises her. She wishes she'd gone to Sindy's place to be with Lucas. She shouldn't have come here.

The young waitress returns, oblivious to the change of atmosphere. She slides Nicole's food and drink in front of her. She's added a complimentary side of cheesy corn, and Nicole's stomach rumbles with hunger. But she can't stay now. She pulls out some cash and drops it on the table. "I have to go, sorry." She only takes her drink with her, and that's because her mouth is like sandpaper. A long slug of Diet Coke instantly refreshes her.

"I can wrap your food to go if you like?" The waitress's words fade as Nicole walks away.

She doesn't get all the way out the door before a police cruiser comes to a dramatic halt outside. Assuming it's Kurt, she gets a shock when she sees both of her parents getting out. She backs into the diner, where there are witnesses. They can't hurt her in here. Unless they have that much power over the locals that no one would do a thing about witnessing it. Her chest fills with dread at the thought.

Her parents step into the diner. Debbie looks exhausted. Ron eyes the diners and staff with an air of authority. Eventually he looks at the middle-aged guy behind the counter, possibly the owner, and says, "Sorry to bother you, Bob, but I'd like a minute alone with my daughter."

The owner doesn't hesitate to follow the command. "You heard him, people. Diner's temporarily closed. Take your food to the benches outside if you're still eating. Your first drink is on me when you next return."

There are some rumbles of discontent from younger diners,

who probably don't have a clue what's happening, but the old-timers up and leave. With growing alarm, Nicole realizes she's about to be left alone with her parents. "I'm leaving." She makes for the door.

Her mother steps forward and stops her. "Just give us five minutes. Please?"

When all the diners have left and the staff has been ushered out back to the kitchen, her father turns to her. "Is it true?" he asks. "Someone just told me they spotted you leaving the newspaper office. Have you been spreading more lies about me?"

Nicole backs away as her heart races. "You need to leave me alone."

Her mother says, "Nicole, come home. We need to talk about this."

"No. I can't trust you two. I know you told Aimee that I killed Lori. I know you tried to turn her against me."

Debbie's eyes widen. "That's not what we were trying to do. She turned eighteen and we had to make her aware of... certain things. Once we told her one thing, we thought it best to tell her everything in case you ever turned up out of the blue and tried to turn her against *us*."

Nicole shakes her head. She's so confused. "You're talking in riddles. What else did you tell her? It can't have been as bad as making her believe her sister was a killer."

Her mother and father share a look that sends shivers down Nicole's spine. "It probably was for Aimee," says Debbie. Her eyes turn red and watery. "I should've told you both years ago. I was just so ashamed that I... I couldn't do it. It was easier to pretend."

"What are you talking about?" Nicole's gaze flickers to the front window. She's hoping the small crowd outside—diners trying to finish their food—elicits attention from someone. Maybe Jennifer will walk by and glance in. But then, what could Jennifer do about this situation? It's not like calling the cops would help.

Nicole has her cell phone in her hand. She could try to secretly call Kurt. Maybe he would come running.

"Do you want to tell her or shall I?" says Ron to his wife.

Debbie closes her eyes briefly, as if coming to terms with something. Then she slowly approaches Nicole and takes her hand. It's warm but not comforting. "I did something stupid when you were younger." She pauses. "I'm not proud of it, which is why I don't talk—"

"Just tell me!" yells Nicole. "I'm so sick of all these secrets and games. Just tell me what you did and why it affects me. And then I want to know what evidence you think links me to Lori's murder, because I don't believe you have a damn thing! You're just emotionally blackmailing me." Her throat closes against a sob.

"Nicole, I can assure you that I do have evidence," says her father. His expression is deadly serious. "And it's damning. So I really hope you haven't told the press about me moving Lori's body, because I'll be forced to defend myself."

Nicole's knees buckle. She pulls away from her mother's grasp and slumps backward onto a seat. There it is. He's openly threatened her. She wishes there were witnesses. Lucas might not believe her otherwise.

Debbie crouches down in front of her. "I understand this is traumatic for you. We were trying to protect you from everything but you wouldn't believe us."

Nicole fixes her eyes on her mother's. With her voice low, she says, "What did you do that was so bad you had to tell Aimee?"

Debbie clears her throat self-consciously and forces the words out. "I had an affair and got pregnant. I cheated on your father. Your dad is not Aimee's biological father."

Nicole's entire body goes cold. She looks at her dad. He

won't make eye contact. She can't imagine him staying with her mother after that. He would have been humiliated. He would have wanted to kill whoever had the nerve to touch his wife behind his back. Turning her gaze back to her mother, she asks, "Who did you cheat with?"

Debbie lowers her eyes as she tries to compose herself. Nicole thinks she isn't going to answer her. A thousand thoughts go through her mind as she sits in stunned silence. She becomes aware of the male reporter on the small TV.

"The coroner has confirmed there was an identifiable object alongside the remains found in the Franklin Woods," he says. "And because of that the body has been identified as belonging to Wayne Rivers, a local man who was married to Sindy Rivers. A longtime resident who worked with Wayne has told us the couple split in 2004 after Wayne admitted to an extramarital affair. It was believed at the time that he had left Henderson to start a new life elsewhere after his wife demanded a divorce."

Nicole looks up at the TV as a creeping sensation of dread and realization tears through her body. A photograph of Wayne comes on screen. She can see the resemblance to Lucas. He has the same chiseled jaw. The same brown hair and matching eyes. He was a handsome man and she now understands where Lucas gets his athletic stature from. But none of that matters. He was found dead. Buried in the woods.

Nicole's knees are trembling so bad she can't keep her legs still. Her hands are frozen.

Debbie takes them in hers, forcing Nicole to look at her. But she doesn't offer any words of comfort. It's like she doesn't want to admit it out loud. It doesn't matter anyway. It's become abundantly clear who her mother cheated with. And that, once Nicole's father found out about the affair, Wayne Rivers was brutally murdered.

FIFTY-EIGHT

Nicole drives to Sindy's house in a state of panic. Relieved that her parents let her brush past them and leave the diner, she ignores the speed limits on the dusty roads and tries to think about how she can possibly begin to explain to her husband and mother-in-law that *her parents* killed Wayne. Lucas grew up without a father because of them. Sindy was left without a husband. That's undoubtedly what contributed to the woman's alcoholism. She continues to get worse every year because of her loneliness.

As her mind races, Nicole takes a corner too sharp and almost rolls the car before regaining control. The roads are mercifully quiet. Most people will be at home eating dinner with their families, while her life and that of everyone she knows falls apart.

She skids to a halt outside Sindy's house as a terrible thought hits her. Lucas could leave her over this. Before getting out of the car she stares up at the house. The glow of the TV flickers in the living-room window as the daylight vanishes. Lucas and Sindy must be watching the news. Which means they'll know that it was Wayne in those woods.

If Ron wasn't involved in Wayne's murder, he would be here right now doing the decent thing: delivering the death notification. Making sure Lucas and Sindy understood what had happened. Offering them help, support and a vow to find who did this to their loved one.

Instead, he went to find Nicole. To try to silence her. He couldn't look more guilty if he tried.

Reluctantly, she gets out of the car. When she slams the door shut, Sindy stands to peer out of the window at her. Her face is in shadow. If the woman didn't hate Nicole before this, she has reason to now. The front door opens as she approaches. Lucas stands there. His face is wet, his expression one of disbelief. "Have you heard?" he asks.

"I just saw the news." She steps forward and embraces him. "I'm so sorry."

Lucas sobs in her arms and she's helpless against her own tears. She feels so bad for him. He always believed his father left him behind voluntarily and now he knows that's not true. That they could have had a relationship if it wasn't for his killer. He's losing his father all over again.

Sindy comes to the door and ushers them inside. She steers Lucas to the living room and doesn't say a word to Nicole. It makes Nicole edgy. Has the woman already put two and two together?

The news coverage is on a loop. Wayne's face pops up again as Lucas stares at it. "I don't get it," he says, wiping his face with his sleeve. "Why would someone kill him?"

Sindy lights a cigarette with shaky hands. "I'm glad you're here for this, Lucas. I couldn't bear it alone." She takes a long drag on it and doesn't exhale for some time. Nicole realizes it's a joint. Sindy suddenly turns to her. "Where's your father? How come we're hearing about this on the news?"

Nicole stutters, "I-I-I'm not sure. He should've come here straight away. Maybe he—"

"Don't you dare defend him!" yells Sindy. "This ain't right. We should *not* be subjected to finding this out on TV at the same time as the rest of the damn town."

"Listen, I agree with you," says Nicole. "He's an asshole for that."

"He's an asshole full stop. I always hated the guy."

Knowing she has to break some more bad news, Nicole's afraid of how the woman will react. How Lucas will react. She sits next to him and rubs his back. Maybe if she tells Lucas first, by himself, he could break it to his mother. He could keep her calm. "Come for a walk with me," she says to him. "Let's go clear our heads."

He shakes his head. "No. I want to watch this." He nods to the TV. "And I want to be here when your dad finally shows up."

Nicole's stomach lurches with dread. She doesn't think her father will show up at all, which can only be a good thing considering what she has to tell them.

Sindy glances at her. "What's the matter with you?"

"Nothing," she says.

Sindy's eyes narrow. "You know something, don't you? You want to tell Lucas before me."

Lucas turns to Nicole, confused. "Is that right?"

Nicole looks up at the ceiling, not knowing how to do this.

Her husband touches her hand. "What is it? Just tell us. It can't be any worse than my dad being found buried in the woods after God knows how long!"

She looks into his warm brown eyes and feels tears streaming down her cheeks. She has no option. She has to tell him. He has a right to know. After telling Jennifer everything she knew about Lori and Aimee, she knew she had done the right thing. She knew she didn't want to keep anyone else's secrets anymore, so she stands and looks at Sindy. "Wayne was having an affair before he went missing, right?"

Sindy's expression turns to disgust. "Sure. That's why I kicked him out. He told me he was going to leave town and I'd never see him again."

Nicole nods. "Do you know who the other woman was?"

Lucas looks at his mom for her reaction.

"No idea," says Sindy. "Asshole was too chickenshit to tell me."

"Who was it?" Lucas asks Nicole.

She takes a deep breath. "Please don't shoot the messenger. I literally found out in the last half hour and I'm as disgusted as you are." Her voice is trembling. She doesn't like the way Sindy's eyeballing her.

Sindy stands, hands on hips. "Tell me who it was and why it matters this late in the game."

Nicole swallows. "I'm really sorry, Sindy. But he was cheating on you with my mom."

FIFTY-NINE

Sindy slowly collapses backward, into her armchair. "No way. It's not possible. Debbie was my friend."

Nicole remembers Sindy and her mom being close when she was still very young. As a child, she never thought to question why they stopped hanging out. Now, however, it's clear that her mother must have wanted to keep her distance once she started the affair with Sindy's husband.

"Who told you that?" asks Lucas. "Because I don't believe it."

"Wait a minute," says Sindy. "Wayne told me about the affair right around the time Debbie was pregnant with Aimee." Her face is drawn. "Are you telling me that Aimee is Wayne's child?"

Nicole nods and then looks at Lucas. "You and Aimee are half-siblings."

The blood drains out of Lucas's face as he comes to the wrong conclusion. "Does that mean you and I are related?"

"Don't be stupid," says Sindy. "You and Nicole don't share parents."

Lucas is visibly relieved. "For a minute there..."

Nicole sits next to him again. "This whole situation is so screwed up. I'm sorry." One thing remains unspoken and she's surprised neither of them have thought of it yet. She considers not mentioning it, but she knows it will occur to them sooner or later. Right now they're in shock and not thinking straight.

"I need a drink." Sindy passes them to go to the kitchen. They hear the fridge door open and the clink of a glass bottle.

Nicole whispers to Lucas, "Please come for a walk. I need to tell you something else."

"Stop whispering!" says Sindy returning with a liquor bottle and one glass. "Show me some goddamn respect in my own home. Whatever you have to say, you can say in front of me."

A piercing headache is forming behind Nicole's right eye. She wishes she was anywhere else but here.

"It's okay," says Lucas. "Just tell us."

With a growing sense of dread Nicole focuses on her husband as she speaks. "Did you ever tell your mom about what my dad told me?"

He understands what she means right away. "Of course not. You told me not to."

"More secrets, Nicole?" says Sindy. "I should've known considering your parents are masters of deception."

"Look, I'm sorry," says Nicole. "But I had to be careful because it's sensitive information that could get my dad locked up."

Sindy raises her eyebrows. "Then I think the whole town has a right to know."

Nicole nods. "I agree. That's why I told a journalist everything today. There's going to be a damning article in tomorrow's paper."

"You told that journalist about your dad?" says Lucas, incredulous. "What were you thinking?"

"I'm thinking I want to get my sister back alive!" she says exasperated. "You don't understand what it's like being caught in the crossfire. So far, I've tried hard to keep everyone happy while just sitting by in the hope that someone magically finds Aimee. But that hasn't worked, Lucas! So I've had enough. I think Jennifer can help me get to the bottom of exposing my father for who he really is."

"So tell us," says Sindy. "Who is he and why does that affect me and my son?"

With a deep breath, Nicole says, "My father found Lori's body on the night she died. He moved her to the silo and kept it a secret."

Sindy licks her lips before shaking her head. "Well. There it is. Now we know." She downs a shot of Jack Daniel's.

"But he swears he didn't kill Lori, right?" says Lucas.

Sindy scoffs. "Oh, well that's okay then." She thinks about it. "Someone should tell Theresa and Antony before it hits the morning papers."

Nicole nods. "I'm planning to drop by first thing tomorrow." She tries to steady her nerves by rubbing her shaking hands together. "If it turns out my dad killed Lori, I don't think it's too far-fetched to believe he's capable of hurting others too. So, when my mom confessed she'd been having an affair behind my father's back, and then I found out it was Wayne's body in the woods..." She eyes them both, waiting to see who will catch on first.

"Holy crap," says Sindy, her face clouding over. "You think your dad killed Wayne?"

"*What?*" Lucas jumps up. "You've got to be kidding me?"

Nicole lowers her eyes. It's all out on the table now. Everyone knows as much as she does about Lori's murder, Aimee's disappearance and the possible motive behind Wayne's demise.

"I trusted your dad!" yells Lucas aggressively. "I did him a massive favor by taking care of you after Lori's death! And the whole time the guy was responsible for killing my dad?"

She doesn't dare look at him. This isn't a side of him she sees often, but his feelings are understandable.

"Lucas? You were only eleven when your dad confessed to cheating on me," says Sindy. "Ron Chambers didn't owe you anything back then. It was before Nicole's breakdown. But I hope to God he felt guilt and shame as he watched you nurse his precious daughter back to good health."

Nicole's taken aback by the venom in her voice. It feels as though some of it's directed at *her,* despite none of this being her fault. "I can only apologize again," she says. "I didn't have anything to do with any of this."

Sindy stands. "Right now, Nicole, I don't even want you in my house."

Nicole doesn't know what to do. She looks at Lucas. "But I—"

Lucas has his head in his hands, like a broken man. But even though he's feeling betrayed by Nicole's parents, he still sticks up for her. "She's my wife," he says to his mother. "And she's staying. I think it's best we sleep on this before doing anything stupid, because right now I could easily do Ron Chambers some serious harm."

"So you should," says Sindy. "He deserves it."

Nicole tenses. She doesn't want her husband getting into any trouble and, despite everything that's happened, she can't stand by and watch her father get physically harmed. Justice is best served by the legal system.

"Tomorrow's newspaper article will rattle people," says Lucas. "We need to see how it plays out—what happens to the sheriff and whether he's replaced. Then we can seek justice for Dad. Until then, there's to be no retaliation. You hear me, Mom?"

Sindy grinds her teeth like she's itching to take a baying mob to the sheriff's house. But she loves her son. He's all she has. So she reluctantly nods before filling half her glass with whiskey.

Nicole's relieved that her mother-in-law will shortly be too wasted to do anything tonight.

"Fine," says Sindy. "Let's use tonight to plan his downfall. Because I won't let him get away with any of this."

The way she says it sends goosebumps up Nicole's arms. That's her father Sindy's talking about.

Lucas takes Nicole's hand and leads her upstairs.

SIXTY

After a long night of broken sleep, Nicole slowly wakes to sunlight streaming into the room. It feels early, and a glance at the digital clock on the nightstand confirms it's only a little after 6 a.m. Turning over to check on Lucas, she finds his side of the bed empty. He's gone. Last night he was pacing the room in between outbursts of grief and anger. He must have managed even less sleep than her. She had tried to comfort him, but he was inconsolable.

She sits up and grabs her phone. A waiting message tells her Lucas has gone out to clear his head. She wishes he'd woken her as she doesn't want him to go through this alone. It would be nice to get away from this house too. She's clearly not wanted here, and with Lucas being gone she's worried about facing Sindy's wrath alone. The woman had obviously been drinking late into the night as they listened to her banging around in the kitchen, emptying whatever bottles she could find into her glass. She had been cursing her late husband, telling him none of this would have happened if he had "kept it in his pants."

Nicole had questioned how Sindy could afford all the liquor she drinks, because her job at the convenience store can't

pay much. Lucas had wearily replied that she must steal it.
She's draining what little profit her poor boss makes, despite the
goodwill he's shown her over the years.

Now, the house is deadly silent, like the calm before a
storm. Jennifer's article will hit the newsstands shortly. Nicole's
stomach flips with dread at the thought. She needs to be
prepared for whatever the day will throw at her.

She gets out of the bed and quickly dresses before tying
back her unruly hair. Ideally, she'd shower, but Sindy's shower
isn't worth the effort as the water pressure is so low it's like
standing under a light rain shower. Nicole needs high pressure
to effectively wash her thick hair.

A glance out of the window shows Lucas's car is still here,
which means he's on foot and probably didn't go far. She looks
around for the keys to her rental car and finds them in her
purse. When her phone buzzes she expects it to be Lucas saying
he's on his way home. Instead, it's a text message from Kurt.

Can we meet? I need to tell you something. It's urgent.

She wonders what he could possibly tell her that she doesn't
already know. She's tempted to say no, especially after how he
treated her yesterday. He'd said he didn't want anything to do
with her and her family. It makes her wonder what's changed.

Sure. I'll drive to your place.

Nicole creeps down the stairs and at the bottom she listens
for any signs of life from Sindy. She hears heavy snoring coming
from the living room. The woman is out for the count. Relief
washes over her and she quietly opens the front door before
heading to the car.

On the way to Kurt's place, she stops at a drive-through for
two coffees. She drinks hers on the journey, and when she

arrives, Kurt is waiting for her on the porch. He's dressed casually, not in uniform. It must be his day off. She leaves her purse and phone behind as she gets out of the car and offers him the spare coffee. He takes it without comment and leads her around to the back of the house. Something about his demeanor makes her uneasy. "Is everything okay?"

Kurt chooses a patio chair outside Brian's window. The window is open, and Nicole's conscious Brian will hear whatever they discuss. She takes a seat opposite Kurt, with the glass table between them.

Kurt's face screws up and it doesn't take long for his chest to rock with sobs. "My dad died."

Nicole's floored for a second. She goes to him, wrapping her arms around him. "I'm so sorry," she says into his hair. "I'm so sorry, Kurt." They stay that way while the grief pours out of him. Nicole tries to hold back her own tears. She may have resented Brian Butler for being her father's closest ally, but she can still have empathy for Kurt during his tragic loss.

Eventually Kurt breaks free and wipes his face. She returns to her seat and waits for him to drink his coffee and compose himself. She doesn't speak. He probably doesn't want to hear platitudes at a time like this. He just wants company.

Kurt breaks the silence. "I slept beside him last night. He was in a lot of pain. Moaning on and off. I gave him a few more pain meds than he was probably allowed, but it was better than doing what he wanted me to do." He pauses. "He kept pointing to his service weapon." A tear escapes his eye. It's quickly wiped away.

Nicole can't imagine how hard it was for him to watch his father in pain. Especially when Brian was asking for his help to end it.

"To tell you the truth, I almost shot the both of us."

"Kurt, no!" She leans forward and grabs his hand. "I'm so glad you didn't. You're overwhelmed right now, but that feeling will pass with time. Please don't do anything stupid." She leans back in her seat. "I wish you'd called me. I would've come sit with you."

His bottom lip quivers as he tries to speak. Eventually he says, "He was still breathing when I fell asleep. I could feel his chest rise and fall. I held his hand." He wipes his eyes again. "When I woke up, I knew immediately. Even without looking at him. He was so still." The pain is etched on his face.

"What can I do?" she says. "Call the funeral director? Make arrangements?"

He shakes his head. "I've taken care of that. It's not why I wanted to see you." He pauses before looking her in the eye. "Everyone makes mistakes, right?"

"Of course," she says. "Me more than anyone." She attempts a laugh but she doesn't like the look in Kurt's eyes.

"And you know I'd never intentionally hurt anyone. Especially not you?"

Her instinct tells her to flee, which is ridiculous, so she stays put. "I'd hope not."

He takes a long, deep breath, and for a second Nicole thinks he's never going to tell her why she's really here. Eventually he looks her directly in the eye and says, "I'm the person Aimee was dating. I'm the father of her baby."

She hears the words but she doesn't believe them. A dog starts barking a few houses away and that's all she can focus on for the time being. He can't be serious. Because she's been in town for six days already while he's watched her go to hell and back during her search for her sister. He's one of her closest friends. He wouldn't harm Aimee.

"I need you to know that my relationship with Aimee was consensual."

Nicole jumps out of her seat. "Why are you saying these things? You're out of your mind." She wonders if grief is making him admit to things he hasn't done.

He stands and approaches her but she backs off. "I should have told you the minute you arrived," he says. "I was fearful of getting fired, and I knew you'd want nothing to do with me. I thought that if I could remind you of the reasons why we were friends, you'd be more forgiving." He runs a hand through his hair. "I messed up. I know that now. I've messed up my whole life. Ever since Lori vanished..."

"No!" she yells. "Don't you dare blame what happened to Lori for this."

"But it all stems from that!" he says desperately. "Lori's disappearance was shocking. It shocked me physically as well as mentally. She was my girlfriend. I spent so much time with her and then she was just gone. You all were. I didn't know how to deal with it. You went into the hospital and had people around to help you process it: doctors, Lucas, your parents. I didn't get any help. My dad just told me to move on whenever I mentioned it. I became a cop to stop it from happening again, to someone else. Maybe even to try to find Lori... But I can't even be a good cop with your dad in charge."

She struggles to feel any sympathy for him because he lied to her and he hasn't yet told her where Aimee is. "There was no online guy, right?" she says. "You're not struggling with your sexuality. You were just throwing me off track. Making sure I didn't see you as a potential predator."

He wearily shakes his head. "I didn't lie about that. I am struggling, with everything. I'm not a predator, Nicole. I'm your friend. I made a mistake by not telling you about me and Aimee. I'm sorry. I didn't physically hurt anyone, remember that."

"And after the baby was born," she says in disbelief, "what were you going to do then? Pay alimony? Marry her?"

"Honestly, I don't know."

He looks so despondent that she can almost see him shooting himself in the head with his father's service weapon. It unnerves her. As she comes to terms with the news that Kurt isn't who she thought he was, a more worrying thought occurs to her. "What did you do to my sister?"

"Nothing. You have to believe me." His gaze is imploring.

"So where is she?"

"I don't know. I only know what Tommy told you, about the motel in Dartmoor. Plus, he told me in the hospital that she had it in her head that I would hurt her because I didn't want to help raise the baby."

"You must have made her believe that."

"Maybe," he says. "But not intentionally. I'm not a killer, Nicole. Our relationship was mutual but she had stronger feelings for me than I did for her. I should never have slept with her; I know that now. I was looking for comfort in all the wrong places. But you have to believe me when I tell you that I did *not* hurt her."

Nicole starts backing away, intending to get to her car before he can do anything to her.

"Don't look at me like that," he says. "Please. Tommy knew I was the baby's father but he kept it quiet, for Aimee."

She eyes him suspiciously. "You didn't hurt him, did you?"

"Of course not! He's Lori's little brother. When I left the hospital, he was going into another surgery. He got stressed at me being in his room. His bandage started leaking blood, so I called for a nurse before leaving to check on my dad." He swallows. "I'm being honest when I tell you I don't know where Aimee is now. Someone else did this, Nicole. And... There's something else you need to know."

She stops backing away. He appears earnest, but then he's fooled her all this time so she's obviously not good at spotting when he's lying. "To be honest, Kurt, I've had enough revelations to last a lifetime."

He pulls out a brown envelope from his jeans pocket. "Your dad said he had evidence that you killed Lori, right?"

Hesitantly, she nods.

"I asked my dad about it last night. He told me to read this."
He hands her a written statement.

She frowns as she reads it. Blood roars in her ears as the
paper shakes in her hands. It's Brian Butler's account of what
happened that night. The evidence points to Nicole being
Lori's killer. Finally, she looks up at Kurt. "What necklace?"

He pulls it out of the envelope and holds it up.

She gasps. She hasn't seen this necklace in years. It was a
gift from her parents for her fourteenth birthday.

"I've seen you wear this necklace," says Kurt. He looks as
though he believes what he's read. He thinks she could've been
the one to hurt Lori.

She tries to think back to when she last saw it, but it's been
so long. Taking it from him, she studies the small pendant, an
open book. The gold chain is snapped. Her mouth drops open
as a memory comes to her. "Oh my God."

Kurt drops the envelope on the glass table and places his
hands on his hips. "How did your necklace get into Lori's hand
that night?"

Nicole bends forward, and it takes everything in her not to
vomit all over her shoes. Shooting pains tear through her chest.
"It *is* my necklace," she whispers. "But it was already snapped
before that night."

Eventually she straightens up and looks Kurt in the eye,
unable to believe what she's about to say. "I didn't have it when
Lori vanished. Because Lucas had offered to fix it for me." She
screws her eyes closed. "I'd already given it to him."

SIXTY-ONE

Kurt's fists are clenched. "Lucas killed Lori?" He's staring at Nicole but she doesn't answer. Even though he's grown to dislike Lucas, he doesn't take any pleasure in seeing Nicole this way. "The asshole planted your necklace so that you'd be locked up instead of him. He let you go on believing your father was involved somehow, when Ron was just trying to protect you by hiding the evidence. Do you see now that your husband isn't good for you?"

Nicole turns away from him, sobbing.

"Where is he right now?" he demands. "At his mom's place?"

"He wouldn't do that to me," she cries. "He's been so good to me."

"Nicole?" Kurt presses. "Where is he?"

"I don't know." She wipes her face with her hands, her back to him. "He left before I woke. Said he'd gone out for some air."

"He's on the run." Kurt's mind whirls with possibilities. "Maybe he's the one who has Aimee." As he considers it, he realizes it's not as outlandish as it seems. "Think about it: Lucas comes to town regularly to visit his mom, so he had ample opportunity. He would've bumped into Aimee at some point, maybe got talking one day. Maybe he learned Aimee was trying to clear your name and he felt she had to be silenced."

Nicole doesn't turn but her mind must be spinning. His sure is. He's desperate to find a link between Lucas and Aimee now that he knows the guy killed Lori. Kurt places the necklace and witness statement back in the envelope and slides it into his back pocket. "We need to go to your dad with this."

She spins around, her face red from crying. "We can't."

"Why? Lucas needs to be arrested immediately."

"Because there's a damning article coming out about my dad this morning, so he won't be sheriff by the end of the day, and he certainly won't want to ever see my face again. And on top of that he'll kill you when he finds out you're the one who got Aimee pregnant. It'll distract him from finding her."

Kurt hesitates. He doesn't know what to do. "Do you believe me when I tell you I haven't hurt Aimee?"

Her stare is mistrustful. "Kurt, I can never believe another word that comes out of your mouth."

Her words hit him like a train. The only person he ever wanted to impress now hates him. All he can do is try to make things right. "Send me the cell number Stacey was using to contact Aimee while she was in the motel."

"Why would I do that? I could be leading you right to her."

He steps forward and gently but urgently takes hold of her upper arms. "Listen to me. I swear on Lori's memory that I have *not* harmed your sister. The worst thing I did was tell her to keep our relationship a secret and make her feel afraid. It's bad, I know that and I'm not excusing it, but murder is on a different level, Nicole. I'm not capable of that."

She locks eyes with him, and he senses she wants to believe him.

"There's still a chance we could find her alive," he says. "If I can locate the motel she was staying at, I can search the room, speak to the staff. I'll take my badge. They'll talk to me. Maybe they have video footage of her leaving. We'll know then whether she left alone or was forced into someone's vehicle."

There's so much doubt in Nicole's eyes he could cry. Quietly she says, "I can't trust you, I can't trust my husband and I can't trust my parents." She shakes her head in quiet disbelief. "I just want to find Aimee. I want my niece or nephew to be safe."

Kurt swallows. That baby is his. He or she is now the only family he has and he'll do whatever it takes to make amends. Whether or not he and Aimee should have been in a relationship comes second to the safety of that baby. He feels like he's finally seeing straight. That his life finally has meaning. He just has to pray it's not short-lived. "Text me the number. I'll track down the service provider and ask for records to show which cell tower it last pinged from. But I'm serious, Nicole. It's time to ask your dad for help. He has more authority than me. And he could still have the rock that struck Lori's head. He could order DNA testing that could put Lucas behind bars."

When she doesn't answer, he adds, "Don't you want to clear your own name? Your parents think you killed Lori. This is your chance to show them you didn't." He knows it's a double-edged sword for her because by clearing herself she'll be condemning her husband.

Nicole appears to make a decision. She wipes her face. "I'll speak to my parents. If I go there now, they might not have seen the paper yet. But, Kurt?"

"What?"

"They can't know you're the baby's father. Not until we've found Aimee. Otherwise you won't be allowed anywhere near the investigation and I need you. Aimee and the baby need you. You understand?"

He swallows the lump in his throat. "I'll find them. I promise."

SIXTY-TWO

Nicole stands on the porch of her childhood home, afraid to knock on the door. The house that should be her safe haven right up until her parents pass away of old age is instead filled with terrible memories and deep-seated resentment.

Images of the kitchen spring to mind. That would have been cleaned up by now. Her father would have organized for a crime scene cleaner to attend to it, she has no doubt of that. He wouldn't have wanted Debbie to see all that blood in her house.

The door swings open before she knocks, making her jump. She comes face to face with her father. He's in uniform, ready to go to work. He's completely oblivious about how bad this day will end. Nicole's nerves take over. She goes lightheaded.

"What are you doing here?" Ron asks. "What's wrong?" He reaches for her when she goes dizzy. Leading her into the house with his arm around her waist, he calls for Debbie. "There's something wrong with Nicole."

Once seated on the couch, her mom tells her to put her head between her knees. "You need to get some blood into that crazy head of yours."

"Sorry," says Nicole as she starts to feel better.

Debbie disappears before returning with a cup of coffee. "I've added two sugars. That should help."

Nicole sips it and watches as her father stands opposite her. Her mother hovers nearby. The coffee tastes sickly sweet and doesn't stop her hands from shaking. She looks at her father's face. He's genuinely concerned for her. Could it be real? Could his version of events be true? If so, she might have ruined his career for nothing. A glance around the room shows no sign of a newspaper. The TV is off. Most of the town will only just be waking. "I need you to know that I believe you," she says.

Ron glances at Debbie before replying. "About what?"

"I know you found my necklace with Lori's body."

His face clouds over. "You remember leaving it behind?"

Tears spring to her eyes. He still thinks she killed Lori. Sure, the evidence is damning, but he should know she isn't capable of that. He should have put more faith in her from the minute he found it. He could have questioned her. She would have told him she'd given it to Lucas to fix. Lucas could've been arrested right away and she wouldn't have spent twelve years living with a killer. "Brian died overnight," she says. "Kurt just told me."

Ron stares at her for a few seconds before turning away and slumping into his armchair. Debbie goes to him. "I'm sorry, honey." She rubs his back. "We knew it was coming, but it doesn't make it any easier."

Despite everything that's happened, Nicole's heart aches for her father. "I'm sorry, Dad. Kurt was with him when he passed. He wasn't alone."

Ron clears his throat and looks at her. "Brian told his son about the necklace then?"

She nods. "Brian protected you right up until his death." They fall silent. This is difficult for Ron. The end of an era. He no longer has a loyal ally who will have his back. He's probably thinking about how different things will be from now on. Maybe he's considering retiring.

Nicole knows that choice won't be his to make. "I owe you an apology," she says. "You were trying to do the right thing when you hid the evidence. You tried to protect our family. But it was at the expense of Lori's family. Her parents—" She chokes back a sob. "They didn't deserve to live all these years without knowing where Lori was. Without having a grave to visit."

Surprisingly, Ron nods. "I didn't appreciate back then just how much they would suffer. How long it would take someone to find Lori's body. I've always regretted what I did. It was a spur-of-the-moment decision that turned out to be the wrong one. I should've taken time to think about it, to have been more logical and detached." His voice is thick with emotion. "And it was all for nothing really. I was terrified I'd lose you to a prison sentence, but you left town eventually anyway. For your mother and me the outcome was no different than if you'd done time for the murder. We lost you, Nicky. You exited our lives and never looked back." He sighs heavily. "I should have let it play out how it was supposed to. At least then we could've visited you in prison. Maintained some kind of relationship."

Nicole watches her mother cry. They think she's admitting to being there when Lori died. "You're misunderstanding me. I didn't kill Lori."

They exchange a weary look, evidently sick of the back and forth, just like she is.

"I'm serious," she says. "My necklace broke the week before Lori vanished. I'd given it to someone to fix. I wasn't even in possession of it. It was planted there to make me look guilty."

Debbie gasps as Ron slowly leans forward. He seems thrown. His expression turns to bewilderment. "That can't be true."

She can understand his reluctance to believe her after everything that's happened. What must also be racing through his mind is how he's inadvertently protected the real killer all these years. "I'm going to tell you who I gave it to," she says, "but I don't want you to blow up and tear out of here because there's something else you should know first.

Debbie walks over to the window, her hand to her chest. "My heart can't take any more stress."

Ron stands. "Spit it out then."

Nicole takes a deep breath and stands. "I went to Jennifer Manvers yesterday, before I knew the evidence you had was my necklace. Before I knew for sure that you didn't kill Lori." The next sentence sticks in her throat because she knows he's going to explode. "I'm really sorry, Dad, but I... I told her you admitted to moving Lori's body."

Ron's face flushes. Nobody says anything for a good minute. Despite the early hour, Debbie fixes herself a drink. Ron sits back down and pulls out a cigar.

"But I called her on my way here," she continues. "I told her it was all a big mistake and she needed to pull the story. She said it was too late. It had already gone to print and will be on the stands by now. She said the only way to control the damage was for you to issue a statement or hold a press conference immediately, to clarify why you moved Lori's body. I told her that might not be possible right away. That things are moving fast and we need to concentrate on locating the real killer, while also finding Aimee." Jennifer had been sympathetic, but she had also been pissed. Journalists value accuracy. Her reputation is on the line.

"Well," says Ron, before taking a long puff of his cigar. "That's my career in tatters."

"I'm so sorry," says Nicole, knowing her apology is meaningless to them. "I believed all along that you killed Lori. And then with Aimee vanishing too... I just wanted someone to find Aimee. I shouldn't have done it. I obviously know that now."

Ron exhales smoke. "I'll go to prison for this."

Debbie downs her drink and turns to Nicole. "I can't believe you'd do that to us."

The hurt in her mother's eyes is evident. "I'm sorry," Nicole says. "If you had been open with me from the beginning, told me about the necklace, I could've put you straight before all this got out of control."

Ron nods. "Ultimately, she's right, Debbie. Every decision I took was wrong from the get-go. I'm responsible for this mess, not her." He's eerily calm.

"That's not what I meant, Dad." She takes a step closer. "Yes, the headlines are going to have everyone talking, and you're going to face some difficult questions, but I think I know who killed Lori, and that can only help you. We can clear your name *and* mine if you arrest the killer. You still have the rock used to kill her, don't you?"

He nods. "In my safe. But it has strands of your hair on it."

She had seen that in Brian's statement. Lucas was taking no chances when he framed her. Leaving her necklace and her hair at the scene shows how much he wanted her to take the blame. She can't even begin to understand why. Only Lucas knows his reasoning.

"It wouldn't be difficult to get strands of anyone's hair," says Debbie. "Especially not long hair."

Nicole agrees. Lucas could have easily taken some of hers from her hairbrush, or just from having his arm around her. Her hair seems to get everywhere.

Ron stubs his cigar out before standing. "Who did you give the necklace to for fixing?"

Nicole tries to maintain her composure. She's afraid she might have it wrong about Lucas and she doesn't want to falsely accuse someone else. She's struggling to believe he could be that cruel. That someone who has shown her so much love and patience over the years could have wanted her to serve a life sentence. But there's no denying she gave him her necklace. At the bare minimum he needs to be questioned. "Lucas."

Debbie's eyes widen at the same time as Ron looks like he

could explode. "I trusted that boy. I let him sleep in our house and take care of you."

Nicole lowers her eyes. "I know. And I married him."

Debbie comes over and silently hugs her. Somehow, it's more comforting than a hug from anyone else could ever be.

"Where is he right this second?" spits Ron.

"He was staying at Sindy's place but he left before I woke up. Kurt thinks he's gone on the run."

Ron unlocks his gun cabinet and passes his wife a small handgun. Nicole knows she's fully trained in how to use it. "Stay inside and lock the doors," he says. "And use that if you need to. I'd imagine he's long gone so he shouldn't turn up here, but you never know. I'll brief the team and send someone over to watch the place."

In a split second her father disappears out of the house. Nicole hears the front door slam shut behind him. His car engine revs loudly out front. Red and blue lights flash in the window, lighting up the furniture.

Lucas won't be prepared for what's about to hit him.

SIXTY-THREE

Nicole stands at the living-room window with her mother by her side. They're keeping watch for Lucas while hiding from the article and any backlash it causes. So far all is quiet on the road at the end of their long driveway, but it won't be long before reporters turn up in the hope of getting a statement from the sheriff. The gun sits quietly on the coffee table, fully loaded, safety off.

While they stare out of the window and wait for Ron to apprehend Lucas, Nicole takes the opportunity to explain everything Tommy told her about Aimee going to stay in a motel. It answers some of her mother's questions about Aimee's disappearance, such as how she left the house willingly with no signs of forced entry or a disturbance, but it's added a new layer of guilt for her. "I knew we shouldn't have told her anything," says Debbie. "Your dad insisted she was old enough to deal with the fact he wasn't her biological father."

"Maybe she could've handled it if you hadn't also announced her sister was a killer at the same time."

Debbie lowers her eyes. "Parenting basically involves making one difficult decision after the next in the hope that one of them is the right one for your kids. Some days it feels like fewer than half of them are, despite your best intentions. Maybe one day you'll be able to put yourself in our position."

For the first time in a while Nicole thinks about what it will be like to be a mother. It's instantly followed by the realization that Lucas won't be the father of her children. She holds back tears, not wanting to go there right now. "Kurt's tracing the cell phone Aimee was using in order to find the motel she was booked into. But maybe Tommy will tell us before then. We should call the hospital to see if he's awake."

Debbie doesn't look convinced. "I checked in on him last night, after I finished my shift. He'd needed a second surgery and the doctor was concerned he might not pull through. I'm waiting for a co-worker to let me know when he's awake."

Nicole's heart is heavy at the thought Tommy might not make it. How much death can they take? And all because of Lucas. It occurs to her then that Lucas wouldn't have been responsible for his father's murder. He can't have been—he was only eleven at the time Wayne disappeared. Could that mean her parents still had something to do with that? The thought eats away at her for a while until her mom asks her what she's thinking. "I guess I'm wondering why you cheated on dad," she says. "And how he found out about it."

Debbie sips her coffee and looks thoughtful. "I always wanted a big family. So after you were born, I expected to get pregnant again right away, but it never happened. I couldn't understand it. I'd gotten pregnant so easily the first time around. I tried not to worry about it and concentrated on you instead. But that yearning never went away, so eventually I gave in and went for all the tests, not really wanting to know the outcome. I was surprised when the results showed the problem didn't lie with me." She rubs her temples. "I asked your father to go for tests and that's when he admitted he'd had a vasectomy without telling me."

Shocked, Nicole says, "What? Why would he do that?" In her eyes, that's grounds for divorce.

Debbie shrugs. "He couldn't really tell me. He muttered something about assuming I'd be happy with just one child, which was baloney. I got the feeling he found parenting too stressful. When you were a baby, he was terrified something would happen to you. Every time you napped, he would check on you constantly to make sure you were still breathing."

"I imagine that's how all parents feel, so that doesn't make getting a vasectomy okay. You must've felt betrayed?"

"I did," admits Debbie. "I couldn't trust him anymore. Our relationship suffered and I thought about leaving him, but I didn't want to take you away from him. You two were so close when you were younger. You always wanted to sit next to him on the couch, instead of next to me. You'd want to hold his hand when crossing the road, not mine. You'd hold mine if he wasn't there of course, but you were a classic daddy's girl in every sense."

Nicole remembers that. Her father was her hero, which made it all the more difficult when he emotionally pulled away from her after Lori's death. It made her breakdown harder to cope with. He wasn't there telling her she'd get through it. He wasn't promising to be by her side. And now she knows why. He thought he'd raised a killer.

"So when Wayne Rivers started flirting with me, I felt special. After all, he was attractive." Debbie looks at her. "Lucas is the spitting image of him, you know."

Nicole's stomach lurches with dread.

"I knew it was wrong and I broke it off after a couple of intense months. And then a month or so after Wayne and I stopped seeing each other, I found out I was pregnant with Aimee." She chews her bottom lip. "I almost took you and left town because I dreaded telling your father so much. I couldn't hide my pregnancy from him, and he'd know the baby wasn't his because of the vasectomy. In the end it all got too much and I just blurted it out."

"How did he react?" Nicole listens carefully to her mother's response.

"He was devastated. He thought it meant I wanted to leave him for Wayne, but I didn't. Wayne wasn't marriage material; Sindy had complained about that over the years and she was right." She sips her coffee. "Your dad surprised me. He said he'd raise the baby. He even said he would allow Wayne to visit if he wanted to be in his child's life. But Wayne skipped town—or so we thought. Now I know he never had a chance to do the right thing. He was probably already dead by the time Aimee was born."

Nicole has a new respect for her father. He loved her mother so much he agreed to raise another man's child.

"Sindy hadn't a clue about the affair of course," says Debbie. "She probably would have shot me if she'd ever found out."

"Well she knows now."

Alarmed, Debbie says, "You told her?"

Nicole nods. "Sorry. I thought dad might have had something to do with Wayne's death."

Debbie shakes her head in disappointment. "It won't be long before she bangs on my door then. That's not good. She's volatile these days. I better call her and apologize. I was a terrible friend to her."

"I think she'd appreciate that, but she was wasted last night. Be prepared for an earful." Nicole glances at her phone. She hasn't tried calling Lucas and he hasn't messaged to see where she is. She would rather let her father take care of him as she couldn't face it if he tries to tell her he loves her. Or if he admits to having harmed Aimee as well as Lori. "What do you think happened to Wayne?"

Her mother exhales. "Wayne was the kind of guy who had a lot of enemies. Clearly, he slept around, but he also borrowed money he couldn't afford to pay back and made promises he had no intention of keeping. I think it all caught up with him in the end."

"You don't think dad could've hurt him?"

Debbie sighs. "Nicole, not again. Why do you always blame your father? Do you really think he'd risk his job for someone like Wayne Rivers?"

"Maybe not, but you must have both noticed Wayne disappeared."

"We did, but Sindy threw him out after he told her about the affair, so we all just assumed he'd split. Your dad said he had thoughts on Wayne's disappearance, but he never shared them with me. We tried to steer clear of the topic. And when Wayne didn't show up to see his daughter, Ron raised Aimee as his own." She pauses. "She's still your sister. You may have different fathers, but she's just like you in many ways."

Nicole smiles sadly. "Hopefully I'll get to see that for myself."

Movement on the driveway makes her look out the window.

"Oh no," says Debbie. She leaves the room just as Theresa Peterson runs up the driveway and starts banging on the door. Nicole goes to the hallway and watches Theresa and Antony burst into the house. Theresa's holding a copy of today's paper and she throws it in Debbie's face. "Is this true?" she yells. "Your husband hid our daughter's body?"

Antony is clenching his fists. With a quiet intensity he says, "If the sheriff killed our daughter, I'll sue you both for every penny. I'll ruin you."

Nicole feels the aguish coming from them.

Calmly, Debbie says, "Come through to the living room. I'll explain everything."

"Just answer the question!" screams Theresa.

Debbie takes a step back. "No, my husband did not kill Lori. But he did make mistakes."

"Mistakes!" says Antony. "That's what you call dumping her body into a silo and letting us suffer for years?"

"And now our son's in the hospital on life support," adds Theresa. "And we're not even allowed to see him because he's being treated like some kind of monster!" She sobs. "Is Ron going to kill Tommy too?" She lowers her face into her hands. "Why, Debbie? What did we do to deserve this?"

Nicole can only watch as her mother tries to take control of the situation. She finds herself glancing back toward the kitchen to double-check Tommy's blood has been cleaned up. It has. The kitchen looks spotless from here.

Debbie grabs her car keys from the sideboard in the hallway and says, "Come with me. I can get you in to see him, and I'll answer all your questions on the way."

"Mom?" says Nicole trying to hide her concern. "Is that a good idea?"

"It'll be fine. Lock the door behind me, and remember what Dad left us?" Her mother gives her a look that conveys Nicole shouldn't say it out loud.

The gun. Still on the coffee table. Nicole nods.

"Good," says Debbie. "If you need to, use it."

Nicole watches them pile out of the house. She locks the door behind them, feeling vulnerable and afraid. She'd like to think she'll feel better once Lucas is in custody, but that will be the start of a whole new bunch of problems.

SIXTY-FOUR

Kurt enlisted the help of another deputy, Anna Moore, in narrowing down the cell provider Aimee used for her burner phone. Deputy Moore called the company and busted their balls until they agreed to expedite the retrieval of Aimee's last known whereabouts based on the last time she used the phone. The customer service agent she spoke to only agreed because Moore made it clear that an unborn baby's life was at risk and she would hold them personally responsible if they delayed sending her the information. She was impressive to watch and it made Kurt feel like the sheriff's office could thrive with the right people in charge. And that's something he would stick around for, if he has the choice.

Until the information arrives, all Kurt knows about the motel Aimee was staying in is that it was in the nearby town of Dartmoor. So he leaves Deputy Moore behind to keep chasing it while he races to Dartmoor to save time when it eventually comes through. The police radio chatter has made for interesting company on the journey.

He's learned that Nicole has told her father about Lucas. There's an APB out for the guy. Lucas is to be apprehended at all costs, with deputies being mindful he could be armed and dangerous. Kurt has never known Lucas to show any interest in firearms, so he would be surprised if his old high school friend was found with anything other than a knife on his person. This whole situation seems out of character for Lucas. Sure, he cheated on Nicole back then, before Lori disappeared, but he would never have guessed Lucas was capable of killing anyone.

Kurt gets caught in rush hour traffic. People are trying to get to work this bright morning, completely oblivious to his mission. His frustration grows as he sits at yet another red light before finally moving again. After a thirty-minute drive that feels like an hour, he finally crosses into Dartmoor. The town is larger than Henderson and attracts more crime, but the stores are a little more up-market. The residents have more disposable income on account of the nearby university being a major employer in the area.

The car radio crackles to life. "This is dispatch to unit twelve. Copy."

"This is Butler. Go ahead."

"Deputy Moore has asked me to tell you she's received the cell tower data and surmised the subject was staying at one of two motels that are located nearby." Julie reels off the names and addresses of both.

Kurt knows the location of only one of them without looking it up—The Bluemont Motel—so he races there first, siren wailing. "Copy that. On my way."

Traffic moves aside for him, which means he makes it to the motel in under four minutes. Skidding to a halt outside the front office, he looks around for any sign of Lucas. He shouldn't be here if he's on the run but he wouldn't be the first perp to make a bad decision under pressure. The motel building is painted white with blue doors on the guest rooms. The parking lot is well-maintained and surrounded with landscaped trees and shrubs. Tommy obviously didn't want Aimee staying some-where trashy or unsafe.

Kurt gets out of the car and heads straight to the office. Inside is warm, with a fan blowing directly at the clerk behind the desk. She's young, maybe twenty-four, and more interested in her phone than her customers. Her name badge identifies her as Candice. "Help you?" she asks, disinterested.

Flashing his badge he says, "I'm a deputy with the Oates County Sheriff's Office in Henderson. I'm looking for this girl." He pulls out his phone and shows the photo from Aimee's missing person poster. "She's heavily pregnant and I have reason to believe she may have stayed with you recently."

Another clerk joins her, this one a heavyset older woman named Flo. She removes her glasses and leans in to his phone. "Sure, that's Sally. She was here. I gave her some clothes for the baby." She smiles. "My grandson grew out of them so fast."

Kurt's adrenaline kicks in. Aimee was smart not to use her real name, but it's made it more difficult to help her. "Where is she now?"

"She left one night," says Flo. "Missed her final payment and left my baby clothes behind in her room as if they were garbage. You try to help people and that's the thanks you get."

"And the baby?" he presses.

The two clerks look at each other before the older woman says, "She was still pregnant as far as I know. After she left, the baby's father was devastated. She didn't tell him where she was going. He got all flustered and demanded to see our surveillance footage, but the boss, Irvine, said we can't show anyone without a badge. He said that for all we know this guy might be abusing her, so we didn't know what to believe."

"He definitely wasn't an abuser," says the younger girl. "I can spot them a mile off."

They must be talking about Tommy. They've assumed he's

the baby's father. He pulls up a photo of him from a news website. "This him?"

They both lean in for a look before nodding. He pulls his phone away before they finish reading the headline above his photo. "Did you watch the footage of that night yourselves, to see where she went?" he asks.

"I did after he asked about it," says Candice. "But nothing interesting happened."

He grips the counter as he says, "Tell me exactly what you saw."

With a weary sigh, suggesting she has better things to do, the young woman says, "A vehicle pulled into the lot and after a minute or two someone got out and went to her door. They were inside for a couple of minutes before Sally left with them. We haven't seen her since."

Kurt needs to know who that person was. "I need you to pull your footage from the night she disappeared. I want to watch it right now."

Flo hesitates. "I should probably give Irv a call to get permission."

"Ma'am? It's not a request," says Kurt. "That baby's life is currently in your hands and we cannot delay a second longer." He tries to keep his voice steady but he's painfully aware he's talking about his own child, and he doesn't want these women to know that.

The women appear surprised by his forcefulness. Flo turns away from him as she says, "Alright. Alright. Follow me."

In the back room she slowly fiddles with the old PC, making Kurt's blood pressure rise as he waits. Every second lost is a second they could have got to Aimee and the baby sooner. "Candice?" Flo yells over his shoulder. "What night was it again?"

Candice yells back and the older woman selects the correct file from a dizzying selection. Irvine obviously likes to keep evidence in case he's ever swindled or robbed. That's a good thing. So many people destroy surveillance footage far too soon. "Okay," she says. "Here we go." The footage comes to life on screen as she speeds through to the early hours.

Kurt watches car headlights pass quickly on the freeway beyond the parking lot. Finally, one of them enters the lot, the headlights temporarily dazzling the camera. "Hit play," he says. He fixes his eyes on the screen and waits while the driver sits in their vehicle. He can't identify the make or model of the car, and he doesn't think anyone would be able to read the license plate from this angle, so all hope rests on being able to identify the person when they exit the vehicle.

The car door opens. When the person steps out, Kurt leans in to the grainy footage. They're wearing a baseball cap and the camera is angled above them, giving no clue to their facial features. "Shit," he mutters. They appear to be of medium height and build, but they're wearing a winter coat despite the recent high temperatures. After knocking on Aimee's door, they enter the room, seemingly without trouble or hesitation on Aimee's part. Which means she knew her abductor.

Kurt waits patiently until the door opens again. Aimee walks out first. She's clearly visible. And she's clearly still pregnant. Kurt's heart races. He just wants to yell into the screen that she needs to get away from whoever's about to follow her out.

After a few seconds, the perpetrator appears. They have one hand in their pocket while the other closes the door behind them. That could be a gun in the pocket, aimed directly at Aimee's back. But they've made a fatal mistake. This time, their baseball cap is pushed upward, not covering their eyes. They glance in the direction of the camera.

Kurt gasps when he recognizes the face. "Wait, *what?*"

SIXTY-FIVE

Nicole has the TV on while she waits for information at her parents' house. The morning news has erupted thanks to Jennifer's article. Everyone has an opinion on the sheriff hiding Lori's body and most of them are bad. That's not to say everyone has automatically condemned him as Lori's killer; he still has some faithful friends, but the majority of reaction is shock mixed with anger.

In the last five minutes Jennifer has messaged to say she's getting constant phone calls from other press asking for Nicole's phone number. There are even offers of payment for Nicole to tell her story on camera. Nicole had firmly stated that Jennifer does not have her permission to give her number to anyone. Realistically though, it's just a matter of time before news vans turn up at the sheriff's office and maybe even here at the house. She bitterly regrets going to Jennifer with her concerns. She thought she was doing the right thing for her sister.

Nicole switches the TV off. The guilt is too much. She doesn't know if her father can ever recover from such negative press coverage, even if he explains everything.

As is becoming habit, she checks her phone, but she has no

new messages and Aimee still hasn't read Nicole's Facebook message. Her thoughts turn to her mother-in-law and how she'll react to finding out it was Lucas who killed Lori. Sindy deserves to know before she sees that on TV, especially after what happened yesterday with Wayne's remains. Ron hadn't gone to her before it was announced, and she deserves better than that. The media don't yet know Lucas is a killer on the run; they're focused on the sheriff's scandal instead, but it's just a matter of time before Lucas is apprehended, and when he is, there will undoubtedly be witnesses. That news will spread like wildfire.

Nicole selects Sindy's number on her phone and listens to it ring. Sindy's probably still sleeping off her hangover, so maybe now's not the right time to call her, but at least she can say she tried.

A bang at the back door makes Nicole jump so hard she drops her phone on the floor. "Shit." She spins around and looks toward the kitchen. Someone's out there. What if it's Lucas? She needs to see who it is.

As she passes the coffee table she glances at the gun. She doesn't want to touch it, but she should take it with her, just in case. The deadly weapon feels alien in her hand. Her father had always wanted her to learn how to shoot, but it wasn't something she had any interest in. She always assumed it can't be that difficult. You just point and shoot. As long as the safety's off, it should work.

A second loud and urgent bang at the door makes her slip the gun into the waistband of her jeans. She pulls her T-shirt over it so it's concealed. She doesn't know if she'd ever be able to bring herself to shoot someone, but she wants the option at least. If necessary.

"Anybody in there?" Sindy's voice.

Relief washes over her. She enters the kitchen. The aroma of bleach hangs in the air. The cleanup operation was excellent as there is no visible hint of what happened to Tommy in here.

At the door, Nicole's mother-in-law waits to be let in. A quick check of the perimeter shows no one is hiding out there, so Nicole unlocks the door. Once Sindy's inside, she locks the door behind her.

"Where's Lucas?" asks Sindy. Her words are slurred. The delicate skin around her eyes is haggard, as if she's severely dehydrated. She hasn't even brushed her hair yet.

"I don't know. He was gone when I woke up." With nerves in her stomach Nicole says, "Take a seat—I have something I need to tell you."

The sound of her cell phone ringing in the other room interrupts her thoughts. She should have brought it with her, not left it where it fell. She ignores it.

"Why do you look nervous?" asks Sindy.

"I'm not nervous. How about I fix us some coffee and maybe some breakfast?" Nicole approaches the coffee machine. "Then there's something important we need to discuss."

Sindy doesn't reply. She turns her back to Nicole and slumps over the sink as if she might vomit. Or maybe she's using it to hold herself up. She's wearing the same clothes as yesterday: dirty blue jeans and a faded gray T-shirt with yellow sweat stains around the armpits.

Nicole is struck with sadness for the woman. Not only has she had to deal with the agonizing news that her estranged husband was murdered, but now she's about to learn her son is a killer. Nicole wishes more than anything that she didn't have to be the one to break it to her. Her chest constricts as she anticipates how to say it, and how Sindy will receive it. Perhaps now isn't the right time. Maybe she should wait until Sindy sobers up. But she might not sober up today, and it's bound to be all over the news by lunchtime.

Sindy goes to the fridge. "I don't want coffee. I want a *real* drink with my daughter-in-law." She rips the door open so hard the contents shake. "I bet your parents don't drink, do they, Nicole? Being pillars of society and all that."

The shrill tone of the landline interrupts them. It could be the same person who tried calling her cell. Someone is desperate to get ahold of Nicole. "Sorry, I need to get that." The landline has an extension on the kitchen wall. She lifts the handset. "Hello?" Her eyes stay fixed on Sindy, who's found a six-pack of beer in the fridge. She pulls it out and places it on the kitchen table.

"It's me," says Lucas.

Nicole's heart flutters with nerves at the sound of her husband's voice. Will he want her to meet him somewhere? Does he know her father's looking for him? She closes her eyes, wishing things were different. Wishing she didn't know what he did. She tries to keep her voice neutral. "Where are you?"

"I'm at the sheriff's office," he says, bewildered. "I don't understand what's happening. Nicole, your dad's arrested me for Lori's murder!"

Nicole doesn't react. She doesn't want Sindy to know it's Lucas on the line. She wants a chance to explain everything to her first because it's unlikely Sindy will believe he's guilty. She'll try to defend him. She might lash out. Nicole needs to get the woman to sober up. "I don't understand," she says, keeping her voice steady.

"Neither do I!" shouts Lucas. "Your dad said something about one of your necklaces? He implied Lori was holding it, as if she'd managed to grab it while being attacked. For some reason he's saying that it's proof that *I* was at the crime scene!"

Nicole can't bring herself to respond.

"You still there?" he asks.

"Uh-huh." She's trying to hold back tears as she realizes this might be the last conversation she ever has with her husband.

"I didn't hurt her, Nicole. You have to believe me! You have to tell your dad I wouldn't do something like that." He sounds so convincing that it would be easy to believe him. To stay married to her childhood sweetheart and have children together.

"I gave it to you though," she says. "It could only have been there if you were there."

"I remember you gave it to me to fix," he says. "But I'd left it on my nightstand. I didn't have a chance to fix it yet. It went missing, so I assumed you'd taken it back while you were over one day. Then Lori vanished and I just forgot about it." He sighs heavily as if afraid. "Nicole, someone must've taken it from my room and planted it on Lori."

Nicole struggles to breathe as the implication hits her like a ton of bricks. Her palms turn sweaty and the handset almost slips from her grip. She watches as her mother-in-law pulls open a drawer near the sink and takes out a large steak knife.

With her legs trembling, Nicole's mind processes what this means. The other person who had twenty-four-hour access to Lucas's bedroom back then was the woman standing in front of her with a knife.

Sindy motions for her to end the call.

"I'll come down there," says Nicole to placate Lucas. "We can figure this out."

Sindy calmly takes the handset from her and places it back on the cradle before pulling the wire from the wall. "Who was it?"

"My dad," says Nicole, thinking fast. "The newspaper article is out and all over the news. He's been detained for questioning over Lori's murder."

Sindy's eyes light up. "Is that so? Maybe if he'd done the right thing when he found your necklace in Lori's grasp he wouldn't be in this position."

Nicole feels the blood drain from her limbs as she realizes she's locked herself in the house with a killer. She's so afraid for her life that she doesn't understand how she's still able to stand. A single tear rolls down her cheek. "Lori didn't deserve to die."

Sindy takes her hand. "I regret her death. She was a nice kid. But she was collateral damage."

Violently pulling her hand free, Nicole covers her ears. "No!" she yells. "She wasn't collateral damage. She was my *best friend*!"

SIXTY-SIX

SUMMER 2008

Lori sits as still as possible, completely alone on the warm grass in the park. Eventually, the park stops spinning around her. The incessant swirling of the streetlight grinds to a halt until it's still again. Relief washes over her and she vows never to smoke any more pot.

She needs to get up and go home as there's no way she'd catch up to Nicole now. She's long gone. Angry and upset, Nicole will probably never speak to her again. Best that Lori gets herself safe until the morning, when she can try apologizing to her friend.

Lori knows her mom will be mad at her for staying out this late. She'll probably be grounded for at least a month. She sighs heavily at the thought and smells marijuana on her breath. She'll need to try to get up to her bedroom undetected in order to allow time to brush her teeth before the inevitable inter-rogation.

As she slowly stands, she hears a car engine off to the left. The vehicle parks but she can't make it out in the dark. The headlights go out just as goosebumps tear through her. Someone is approaching. She can see a figure but not the face. She looks around for somewhere to hide but she doesn't have time. They've already seen her.

Lucas's mom stops a few feet away from Lori, who takes a step backward. "Hi, Mrs. Rivers," she says, trying to hide the fear in her voice. This is the last person she wants to see right now.

"Hey, sweetie. What are you doing out here all alone? Where's your friend?"

"Nicole just left. I should be heading home now too." She takes a few steps away from her.

"Not just yet," says Sindy. She doesn't advance but her demeanor is menacing all the same. It probably wouldn't be if Lori hadn't witnessed something terrifying at the woman's house earlier. "We need to have a little talk first." Sindy motions for Lori to follow to a spot away from the streetlight.

Lori glances over her shoulder first, looking for help. The road is still, the air silent. It's too late for passersby. She should have left immediately after Nicole stormed away. The rational part of her brain reminds her that this is Lucas's mom. She's not going to hurt her. But what happened earlier proved that Sindy Rivers *is* capable of hurting people, so why not Lori?

"Are you coming or not?" says Sindy ahead of her. "I'll give you a ride home myself after. You shouldn't be out here alone in the dark. It's not safe for a cute girl like you. Not with all the weirdos in this town. Like Sheriff Chambers."

Lori follows her voice.

"You remember what I told you about the sheriff, don't you?" Sindy stops near the overgrown brush, where the park meets the back of the Franklin Woods.

"I remember." Sindy was the one who told Lori about the fourteen-year-old girl who made allegations against Nicole's dad. Lori had felt compelled to tell her friend in case someone else got to her first. Or in case it was on the news one day. Lori had kept her distance from Sheriff Chambers after that, but she never really believed Sindy. Not a hundred percent. It felt as though Sindy might have had a grudge against the sheriff and could have made it up. Sheriff Chambers was always nice to Lori without being creepy. Although once she'd heard the allegations she read more into their interactions, like in the library. She would find herself second-guessing whether he was just being a friend's dad, or whether he was grooming her. They'd been taught about grooming in school earlier this year but she found the concept confusing.

Sindy lights a cigarette and then faces Lori. "I scared you back at the house earlier today, didn't I?"

Lori doesn't want to think about it. She had only returned to Lucas's house to collect her things, but they weren't in the yard where she left them. The back door was ajar, like always, but Lucas's car was gone. He'd already left for football practice. Lori had been in two minds about whether to go in and see if he'd left them somewhere obvious for her, like on the kitchen table, because she didn't want to leave without them, but also, she didn't want to be around Sindy on her own. Everyone knows the woman is an alcoholic and Lori doesn't know how to talk to her without other people around.

She had decided to poke her head around the door and peered into the kitchen. Sure enough, her belongings were on the table, so Lori thought nothing about creeping in to retrieve them. It was while she was in the kitchen that she heard Sindy talking to herself, like she always does.

Except, Lori learned that she wasn't talking to herself. She was having a whole conversation with someone else. Someone who used to exist.

"You look like you're gonna pee your pants," says Sindy now. "What's the matter with you, honey? I don't bite." She takes a drag of her cigarette, the orange glow lighting up in the dark. "Those things I said while you were sneaking around in my house—"

"I wasn't sneaking around. I just came to collect my things, that's all."

Sindy raises a hand to shush her. "You were listening to me without my knowledge. However you want to look at it, that's sneaking around. But that's alright. As long as you never repeat what I said."

"I've already promised I won't. I didn't even hear anything, honest!" But Lori heard everything. Sindy had been watching old footage of her wedding video while drinking liquor, and that's probably what brought on her resentment. Lori heard her telling her husband, Wayne, that he was an asshole for cheating on her years ago. That she can't understand why he gave up a relationship with his son and his wife just so he could get his rocks off with some whore. Sindy even named the supposed whore. Nicole's mom. And Lori knows Aimee isn't the sheriff's daughter, she's Wayne's. She had listened as Sindy declared to a ghost that she would kill him all over again given the chance. The woman had even joked that she still had the same cast-iron skillet she used the first time.

That had been too much for Lori. But in her attempt at a hasty departure she had knocked a table, making an ornament rattle. Sindy quickly caught up with her and made her promise she would never tell anyone, which she did. But now the woman appears to be here to silence her for good. Lori has trouble standing. She wants to run away.

"The problem I have," says Sindy, "is that you're best friends with the sheriff's daughter. You might be tempted to tell her that her sister has a different daddy, or that her mother's a whore."

"I would never do that!" cries Lori.

"Fine," says the older woman, stubbing out her cigarette on the grass. She places the stub in her pocket. "I'll take your word for it."

Lori frowns. She's confused. "So I can go?"

"Sure. I'll give you a ride. My car's over there."

Lori doesn't move. Frozen to the spot, she's convinced this is some kind of trick.

"After you," says Sindy.

Lori would prefer to walk home, sensing that's the safer option, but as Sindy follows her every step she has no choice but to head toward the car. She gets no farther than five steps when a massive jolt to her head makes her scream out in pain. She collapses forward, onto the ground. Dazed, she feels grass in her mouth. Her vision is blurred, so she closes her eyes.

Sindy rolls her onto her back and stuffs something into her hand. But Lori's losing all feeling in her limbs. The pain in her head starts increasing. Her heartbeat throbs in her ears. All she can do is lie there and wait for help to come.

SIXTY-SEVEN

SUMMER 2022

The room feels airless. Nicole, seated at the kitchen table, doesn't want to look at her mother-in-law. Her head spins as she struggles to make sense of Sindy's confession. The despicable woman's emotionless description of Lori's final moments alive is devastating. If only Nicole had gone back to Lucas's house with Lori. They wouldn't have stuck around to listen to Sindy. They would have been in and out unnoticed. And Lori would still be alive today.

Nicole absently wipes the tears from her puffy eyes. "There's something seriously wrong with you," she whispers in a shaky voice.

"What did you just say?" Sindy leans across the table.

Nicole looks into her soulless eyes. "You were already a killer years before Lori," she says. "You killed your own husband." Yesterday, when Nicole, Lucas and Sindy were watching the news about Wayne's body being identified, Sindy had appeared to be devastated. She even blamed Ron. It was all an act. A convincing one too.

Remorseless, the woman laughs. "And I'd do it again tomorrow given the chance."

Nicole's legs tremble so hard she feels the table moving. Her whole body is on high alert for whatever Sindy has planned for her. She knows there will be no getting out of here without a fight. Sindy has nothing left to lose. Not even Lucas. Once he finds out she killed his father and Lori, he'll disown her.

The cold metal from the gun against Nicole's skin suddenly feels heavy. Obvious even. She resists the urge to glance down and check if Sindy can see it through her T-shirt. She doesn't know if she's capable of shooting her mother-in-law dead in order to save herself. She doesn't want to find out. She remains as still as possible so as not to spook the woman into action. "Did you really kill Wayne just because he cheated on you?" she asks, trying to buy time for someone from the sheriff's office to arrive. Her father said he'd send someone to watch the house.

"He *humiliated* me," spits Sindy.

"Why not just divorce him? Were you after the life insurance money or something?"

Sindy scoffs. "Don't be stupid. That would've been too obvious. Besides, you can't claim that unless you have a body. And I made sure his body was hidden."

"We used to wonder who you were always cursing under your breath. You acted like he was still alive."

"That's because he is to me. I see him all the time," says Sindy, her face contorted with anger. "He won't leave me alone. A shrink would say it's a sign of guilt, but to tell you the truth I don't know if I feel guilty about it. Like I said, he humiliated me. And his actions meant my son grew up without a father."

Nicole could point out that was the result of Sindy's actions but she doesn't want to anger the woman. She's reminded of what her mother said: Sindy's volatile. And she's just confessed to murder in front of the sheriff's daughter. Nicole's heart is beating out of her chest. She needs air. She needs to get out of this kitchen and away from this killer. A glance at the back door confirms it's too far away to unlock and open before Sindy has time to stab her repeatedly in the back. Her situation feels hope-less, so she keeps talking for now. If Sindy lunges at her, Nicole knows she'll have to pull the gun. The thought alone makes her feel dizzy.

"Lori would have kept her word," she says, struggling to hold back more tears. "She came straight to my house after she overheard your confession and she never told me a thing. She had the opportunity to tell everyone, but she didn't. You killed her for nothing."

Her cell phone rings again in the living room but neither of them move. Instead, Sindy says, "She wasn't killed for nothing. If your dad had done the right thing, you would've gone to prison and your folks would've been in a world of pain for the rest of their lives. That was my intention. Instead, your dad showed how corrupt he was by hiding the evidence."

"Evidence you planted!" says Nicole incredulously.

"As payback for your mother screwing my husband!" yells Sindy, pointing the knife at her. "Wayne told me everything before I lashed out at him. I knew it was your mother he was screwing and I had to watch your parents pretend the baby was Ron's!" She gets angrier by the minute. "Can't you see now? Your parents are hypocrites! They're pretending to be good people while cheating behind their friend's back and lying to everyone they come into contact with."

Nicole slowly wipes her face with her hands. "So why didn't you tell someone he hid the evidence when your stupid plan didn't work? That he moved Lori's body?"

Sindy takes a long sip from one of Ron's beers before responding. "For one, I didn't know what he'd done with her body, so I had no proof. And for two, he had suspicions about what I'd done to Wayne. I know he did. He was constantly sniffing around the moment he realized Wayne was gone, back when your mom was pregnant with Aimee."

"That was four years before Lori died."

"It doesn't matter. He didn't believe me when I said Wayne left town. He told me he could easily get a search warrant of my property if he wanted to. So I pointed out I could tell the whole town his newborn daughter wasn't his and his wife was a cheating whore. He didn't like that, so he backed off. He didn't want to be publicly humiliated and have his wife's name tarnished."

So he let Sindy get away with suspected murder. Nicole shakes her head. Her father has made so many mistakes. He should have taken his family and left town to protect them when he realized someone like Sindy Rivers had something on him. This town is toxic. But instead he stayed. He couldn't bring himself to give up his role as sheriff. And so Lori was killed in an idiotic attempt at revenge. "My mom's not a whore," she whispers, trying to remain composed.

"Whatever." Sindy scoffs. "It angered me, watching him over the years after Lori's death. He was portraying himself as this pillar of society when instead he was putting her parents through years of pain. He should've done the right thing and told everyone what he'd done with Lori's body." She shakes her head. "You can imagine how annoyed I was when Lucas decided to marry *you* of all people. I thought your relationship would fizzle out long before that could happen. But I couldn't stop him proposing as he'd never visit me again if I kicked off about it."

Nicole's heard enough. "Lucas will never talk to you again once he finds out what you did to our friend."

"You're probably right." Sindy stares at her with bitter resentment in her eyes. "Take some advice from your old mother-in-law, Nicole. Don't have kids. It's not worth it. You're basically raising them to leave you at eighteen and go live with someone else. Someone you probably won't even like. Then, over time, they forget about you. I'm graced with two visits a year if I'm lucky." She shakes her head in disgust. "It wasn't worth the time and energy I put into him. Grandkids might change my mind but not if I won't ever see them because neither of you can be bothered to come visit me." The knife twirls in her steady hands as she talks.

"I'm left with nothing. I'm all alone in that house staring at old school photos. Photos of my adorable son frozen in time. The boy I raised. Now, the man who visits me is a stranger, always on his best behavior so as not to upset me and pretending he doesn't see my faults. My drinking." She snorts. "I'd rather he was honest with me. That our relationship was real, not maintained out of a sense of duty."

Nicole has no sympathy for the woman anymore. Not after what she's done. "Maybe if you were ever a proper mother to him, he'd want to visit you more often."

Sindy glares at her. "Don't kid yourself, girlie. It'll happen to you one day. No matter how much effort you put into your kids."

Nicole thinks of Aimee's baby. She had momentarily forgotten about her sister during these appalling revelations. A terrible thought occurs to her. Her mouth goes dry as she stares at the woman in front of her. "Oh God. You took Aimee, didn't you?"

SIXTY-EIGHT

For the first time, shame burns across Sindy's face. Nicole clutches the table, terrified of what she's going to say. When Sindy remains silent, Nicole slowly rises, her legs shaky underneath her. She pulls out the gun from her waistband, aiming it at her mother-in-law's chest.

Sindy barely flinches at seeing it. "Go ahead and shoot me. You're right, my son won't want anything to do with me now. I have nothing left to live for."

The gun shakes in Nicole's hand. The temptation to squeeze the trigger is overwhelming. "Tell me where she is."

"Her baby is Wayne's grandchild, my step-grandchild. I wanted to raise it. To have someone to live for. I wanted to fill the house with laughter again. But someplace else where no one knew me. Where no one would ask questions about a woman my age raising a baby alone." She wipes a tear from her face. The only tear she's shed during this whole sorry affair. And it's for herself. "I started texting your sister before she vanished. To make her aware that your father was hiding something. She never replied. Then she went missing and I just knew Tommy would be involved somehow. So I followed Tommy one night.

He took me right to her without even spotting me on his tail. I watched the motel for a while, then came back when I knew Tommy had left. Aimee let me right in. She was a nice girl. She had Wayne's eyes, but your mom's curly hair. Like you."

Nicole feels like she's about to fall apart because Sindy's suggesting all hope is lost. She's reminded of the missing woman her father told her about when they were in the woods. The mother found with her baby's bones inside hers. Is that Aimee's fate? Will she and her child be together forever in some undisclosed part of the woods? Nicole can't bear the thought. She can barely take a breath as she says, "Tell me where my sister is or I'll shoot you in the stomach and let you bleed out slowly and painfully."

Sindy silently stands. Nicole can tell she's realized this is the end of the road for her. The end of all the hurt and pain she's caused, and that which she's suffered herself. Her eyes are fixed on the weapon. She must believe Nicole will shoot, because she says, "I've been keeping her in the building behind the convenience store. Waiting for her to give birth." She licks her lips. "I couldn't bring myself to go there the last few days. She wasn't doing too well and I don't want to find a dead baby." Her voice is flat and completely devoid of emotion.

Nicole feels like she might collapse onto the floor. All hope is lost.

The faint sound of sirens in the distance has them both glance up at the window. Sindy uses the distraction to grab the gun from Nicole. She's fast. They struggle, with Nicole trying her hardest to keep hold of it, knowing full well her life is on the line if Sindy manages to overpower her.

Sindy's strong. She bashes Nicole's hands against the wall, sending pain shooting up Nicole's wrists. Scared the gun will go off and kill one of them, Nicole drops it, intending to kick it out of the way. But when it falls to the floor, Sindy ducks and grabs it.

The woman stands with a blank expression on her face and the weapon in one hand. Her eyes are glazed. It's frightening to witness. She looks as though she's made a decision and she doesn't care about the consequences. Nicole backs away slowly until Sindy stares at her and raises the weapon. "Please don't," says Nicole. "Haven't you done enough damage already? Think of Lucas."

"Your parents ruined my life. Why shouldn't I ruin theirs?"

Nicole turns and flees through the house and up the stairs. If she can get to the bathroom, she can lock herself inside. But Sindy's behind her already. Her hand finds Nicole's ankle and the woman pulls Nicole backward. She painfully falls onto her back on the sharp wooden steps. Sindy hits her across the forehead with the butt of the gun, making Nicole see stars. Her blood is roaring in her ears as she desperately tries to scramble away. She starts kicking out and manages to find Sindy's face with her foot.

"You bitch!" Sindy clutches her face with her spare hand.

Nicole knows she's fighting for her life, so she runs up the stairs toward the bathroom. A gunshot goes off behind her and the loud echo makes her stop in her tracks. She covers her ears and waits to feel the impact. It misses. She hears Sindy scramble up the stairs behind her and turns. The woman has a sick grin on her face, as if she's enjoying the hunt.

Nicole is transfixed by her expression. Is that the last thing Lori saw before she died? Is that what Aimee saw too? The thought angers Nicole so much that she holds her ground. Instead of running away she rushes forward and pushes the woman with all her force. Sindy falls backward down the stairs, twice hitting the wall with her head on her way down.

Panting from exertion, Nicole stands near the top step and looks down at her mother-in-law. She's sprawled at the bottom of the stairs, eyes closed. The gun is still in her limp hand. Nicole has to get out of the house but the only way out is past

Sindy. She hesitates. The sirens are getting louder, but if anyone forces the front door open, they'll be an easy target for Sindy, who can shoot them dead before they even know she's there. Nicole's father could be the first to arrive. She swallows. She has to do something.

Nicole holds her breath as she slowly descends the steps. Each one creaks when pressed with her weight, notifying Sindy how close she is. As she hovers on a step above Sindy, she plans to jump over the railing and run out of the house through the back door. But Sindy lunges forward and grabs her leg, yelling, "You're not going anywhere!"

Nicole can't get out of the woman's grip. All she can do is watch as Sindy tries to lift her arm to shoot her. But Sindy's arm must be broken. It doesn't move from the floor and Sindy screams in pain. The woman is sweating and her face is bloodless. Not to be defeated, she lets go of Nicole's leg and reaches for the gun with her good hand.

Nicole screams in fear as she jumps over the railing and tries to flee along the hallway. She hears another gunshot behind her and a framed glass painting smashes on the wall next to her ear. Glass shrapnel painfully hits Nicole's face.

"It's too late to save Aimee by now," pants Sindy behind her.

Nicole stops dead in her tracks. She slowly turns around.

"You're too late. You let your little sister die." Sindy pulls something out of her pocket and drops it onto the floor—a broken cell phone with no battery attached. Presumably Aimee's burner phone.

Nicole blinks back tears. She refuses to give up on her sister. She ignores the blood running down her face and runs as fast as she can out of the back door and toward the sirens.

At the front of the house a news van is just entering the driveway, following two cruisers. Behind her, a gunshot goes off. Nicole braces herself for a bullet to hit her. She holds her breath for what feels like hours. Nothing happens. She slowly turns back to look at the house. Sindy isn't in view. It becomes clear she wasn't shooting at Nicole this time.

Nicole's consumed with dread. She closes her eyes as she realizes what's happened. The only thought she has is of Lucas, and about how he'll take the news of his mother's suicide on top of everything else.

Footsteps approach and she turns to find Kurt and Deputy Hayes running up to her, their weapons drawn. "It was Sindy!" says Kurt. "Sindy took Aimee from the motel."

"I know," she tells them. "She's in the house."

Kurt's eyes widen.

"I think she just shot herself."

SIXTY-NINE

The yellow and green landscape flashes by in a blur as Nicole stares out of the cruiser's window. Kurt says her father has people searching both Sindy's property and that of her place of work in case Sindy was lying about Aimee's location in order to cause them even more pain. A team of volunteers is also searching the Franklin Woods in case Sindy used the same location for Aimee's grave.

Aimee's grave.

Words Nicole never wanted to hear.

"Deputy Hayes has been told to remain at the house and secure the scene," says Kurt.

Nicole doesn't think she can ever set foot in her childhood home again. Her parents will need to move. The house has become a symbol of tragedy, just like the Marshes' farm. Maybe like the whole town.

"Tommy's doing okay." Kurt glances at her. "His folks are with him and he's managed a few words. I think he's out of the woods."

She's glad, but she can't raise a smile.

They listen to the dispatcher issue a notice. "All units be

aware Deputy Moore has reported sounds coming from the outbuilding belonging to Talbot's Convenience Store. All spare units make your way there. EMS are on their way."

Nicole's stomach grows heavy with dread. She looks at Kurt.

With his eyes red, he grips her hand in his spare one. "I'm not one to pray, but I'll make an exception for this." He steps on the gas and skips three red lights in his haste to get to the convenience store. When they arrive, a female deputy is cordoning off the area. The cruiser skids to a halt outside the tape and they both tear out of the car. Nicole follows him around the side of the store through the parking lot and spots her father trying to force open the door to the outbuilding. It's heavily padlocked and all chains have been cut, but it's still not opening.

Nicole runs up to him. "They told you Sindy said Aimee's in here, right?"

Ron stops what he's doing and pulls her in for a hug. "Are you hurt?" He releases her. "Nicky, your face. You need to get to the hospital."

She waves the suggestion away. "I'm fine. Dad, Sindy said she thinks Aimee could be dead by now. She stopped checking on her a while ago."

Her father rubs the back of his neck as he tries to compose himself. "Someone heard banging from inside after we started forcing the door. She's got to still be alive."

Nicole can't help herself. She asks, "What if the baby's dead?" Her voice breaks. She clears her throat before adding, "I don't think you should be the first one inside."

Ron turns away from her and starts going at the door even harder than he was doing. Nicole steps back and lets the other deputies join in. All she can do is watch as they try to pry open the door with crowbars. Kurt stands quietly next to her as the midmorning sun beats down on them.

"Nicole!"

She turns to the voice. Lucas comes running over and hugs her. She hugs him back but immediately breaks down in tears. "It's okay," he says. "Whatever they find, we'll deal with it."

She looks up at her husband and is immediately consumed with guilt. "I'm so sorry you were arrested. We thought—"

"It doesn't matter," he says, kissing her forehead. "We can discuss all that later. Your dad said Kurt found footage of my mom taking Aimee from a motel room. I don't want to believe it. I mean, I don't get it." He looks shellshocked. "What was she thinking?"

Nicole gently runs her hand over his cheek. "I'm sorry. She was also the one who put my necklace in Lori's hand. She killed her, Lucas, and she tried to frame me." Tears spring from her already sore eyes.

Lucas turns white. "Why would she do that?" Nicole hugs him tightly while giving him time to let it all sink in. Eventually he whispers into her ear, "Does this mean she killed my dad too?"

Nicole can only nod as she squeezes him tighter. When she pulls away she notices the blood has vanished from his face. "I can't explain right now, but you need to know that she came to the house earlier. She tried to kill me."

"*What?*" His eyes widen in alarm. "Where is she now?"

Nicole looks away. She can't bring herself to say the words.

Kurt steps forward to tell him instead. "I'm sorry, man. Your mom took the easy way out."

"What do you mean?" asks Lucas.

Kurt's expression is pained as he explains. "Deputy Hayes confirmed your mom shot herself at the sheriff's house. She would've died instantly."

Lucas doubles over as if in pain. His hands fly to his head. Eventually he lowers himself to the ground and sits on the concrete as he tries to make sense of everything. Kurt kneels next to him with a hand on his shoulder. As Nicole looks at them both, two of her closest friends from high school, she imagines Lori sitting next to them, an imaginary hand on Lucas's back. She has to close her eyes against the haunting image.

"We're in!" Ron pulls open the door to the outbuilding, intending to rush in. But all movement stops dead when a baby's cry reaches them from within.

Nicole gasps. That's her niece or nephew. It must be. Relief washes over her, but she can't quite bring herself to believe that anything good can come out of today.

Kurt slowly rises next to her. "Is that...?"

Nicole holds her breath as her father disappears inside the building, closely followed by some of his team. They're probably gone for only a matter of minutes but it feels agonizingly slow. While they're inside, Nicole, Lucas and Kurt stand in silence, imagining the worst. Maybe the baby survived and Aimee didn't. Maybe it wasn't a child they heard crying. Maybe they were too late. Nicole steps forward, unable to wait any longer. But Kurt grabs her arm. She looks at him questioningly.

"Don't go in there," he says without explanation.

The solemn look on his face makes her eyes fill with tears. She doesn't know how she'd cope if her sister is dead.

Finally the deputies emerge, silently. Her father follows them out, yelling, "We need a paramedic down here *immediately*! Aimee's unresponsive."

Nicole's joy at finding Aimee's location is cut devastatingly short at the realization that her sister may not have made it.

SEVENTY

Everyone is ushered out of the way as the EMTs enter the outbuilding to get to work. Deputies secure the scene, pushing all onlookers back to the road. Even Nicole's not allowed to see the baby, or her sister. Both of them are quickly placed into different ambulances and rushed to the hospital, with sirens wailing.

Kurt drives Nicole and Lucas straight there and, after an excruciating hourlong vigil in the waiting room, Nicole grows fearful that neither her sister nor the baby made it. Because no one is telling them anything.

Lucas squeezes her hand as he stands next to her. Kurt is seated nearby, lost in thought. She doesn't know how to feel about him. He lied to her about not knowing who the baby's father was, and he caused her sister unnecessary fear. It will take some time before she even considers trusting him again. But she hopes for his sake that the baby survives. He's already lost his father today. She doesn't think he could handle losing his child too.

She glances up at Lucas and smiles wearily. He's been by her side all the way. She's not going to let one indiscretion derail their marriage. Hopefully he will be able to forgive her for entertaining the idea that he could have harmed Lori. It won't be easy. They have a lot to figure out. But she intends to fight for her marriage.

When the elevator doors open, her father steps out and approaches them all. "Any news?" he asks.

Nicole shakes her head. "Mom's been allowed in with them. She said she'll come see us as soon as she can."

He nods as he runs a trembling hand through his hair. It's been a horrendous few weeks for him. Nicole can only hope he will be open to repairing their fractured relationship. She knows he was trying to do his best all along, but he made some terrible decisions, just like she did with going to the press about her concerns. "There was so much blood in that building," he says shakily. "I don't know if Aimee can survive that much blood loss."

Nicole takes a deep breath, trying to prepare herself for the worst.

"It was a goods storage area for the convenience store," he adds. "But she was sectioned off in the windowless bathroom at the far end. She had access to water and Sindy had left some food for her, but no pain meds or anything to help with the labor."

"How did no one hear her in there?" asks Lucas.

"She was contained at the rear of the building. It's almost wall to wall with crates of groceries. Practically soundproofed. Gil Talbot says Sindy always retrieved the stock. He never went in there himself." Her father sighs heavily. He pulls his sheriff's badge from his shirt and pockets it.

Nicole eyes him questioningly.

"I don't deserve to wear it," he says, looking away. "And I'm ready to face the consequences of my actions."

Tears fill her eyes. She goes over and hugs him. Neither of them speak.

Lucas gently prods her arm and she looks up to find her mother approaching them. Debbie's expression is difficult to read but it's clear she's been crying. When she reaches them she takes a deep breath. "Aimee's afraid. She asked where Sindy is, so I've told her what's happened."

Lucas shifts position next to Nicole. He must feel ashamed at his mother's behavior. Nicole squeezes his hand.

Kurt stands and approaches them.

"Is Aimee going to be okay?" asks Ron.

"Well, apparently she delivered the baby last night," says Debbie. "But she's not certain, it could've been during the early hours of this morning. Thank God it wasn't any sooner, because she lost a lot of blood. She has a bad infection, a fever and some damage as a result of the labor, but she's been put on a course of antibiotics and pain meds. The doctors are going to monitor her closely."

Nicole closes her eyes as she says a silent prayer.

"And the baby?" asks Kurt. No one else knows that he's the baby's father yet. Nicole waits to see if he'll tell them.

Debbie takes Ron's hand and through her tears she says, "Our grandchild appears to be perfectly healthy."

Kurt's face crumples with emotion and he breaks down. He collapses back into his seat as the relief overwhelms him.

When her parents appear puzzled by his reaction, Nicole feels she has to explain. "He's the baby's father."

Ron's face immediately flushes with anger. He takes a step toward Kurt. "I had a feeling it was you but I couldn't prove it."

Nicole stops him from advancing. "Dad, wait. He didn't force himself on Aimee. They were in a relationship that turned sour. He says he never hurt her." With a look, she urges him to let it go for now.

Ron turns away, clearly pissed. Lucas walks over and places a hand on Kurt's shoulder.

They hover in awkward silence for a few minutes until Debbie looks at Nicole. "Would you like to see your sister?"

Nicole swallows the lump in her throat and nods. "I've wanted that for years."

She follows her mother along the corridor and feels her dad take her right hand. Leaving Lucas and Kurt behind, they enter Aimee's room as a united family.

A female nurse moves away from the bed when she notices them. "Just a few minutes, okay?"

Debbie nods at her.

Aimee is lying in bed with the baby in her arms. Her face is too pale, the circles under her eyes are too dark and she's way too gaunt. But when she smiles at Nicole, all four of them break down. Just minutes together as a family washes away years of unnecessary estrangement and all the resentment that goes with it. For now, at least. None of that matters in this moment.

The baby in Aimee's arms, swaddled in a white blanket with a knitted yellow hat on its head, appears confused and starts whimpering.

Nicole focuses on Aimee first. "I've missed you so much."

"Me too," says Aimee. "I'm so glad you're here." She holds out her hand and Nicole goes to her. They hug, careful to mind the baby. Years of emotion spill out of them until their sobs reduce to awkward laughter.

Once Nicole pulls away, Aimee says, "Where's Tommy? I bet he was frantic with worry when he came back to the motel and I was gone."

Their parents share a look and appear to decide not to tell Aimee he was shot and that he's currently just a few doors away from her. Debbie says, "He's going to visit you both later."

Aimee smiles and looks down at her baby. "I can't believe I was so afraid of you." She rocks the infant against her chest. When she looks up at Nicole she asks, "Want to hold your niece?"

Nicole gasps. "A girl?" She carefully takes the baby from her sister and tries to stop her tears dripping onto the baby's face. Her niece feels warm and satisfyingly plump in her arms. "She's beautiful. What are you going to call her?"

Aimee doesn't hesitate. "Loretta Chambers. Lori for short. Because I don't want to forget our friend. She was so good to me when I was little, and I think Tommy would appreciate it. Theresa and Antony too."

Nicole's heart sings as she thinks of her wonderful best friend. Part of her wonders if Kurt will mind the name, but she doesn't think he will. She has a feeling he'll embrace his new responsibility and do this little girl proud. That's if Aimee lets him, and she's well within her rights not to after the way he treated her. Nicole will support whatever decision her sister makes in that regard. The baby comes first.

She feels her father's strong arm around her shoulders as they both stare down at the beautiful baby girl who is about to change all their lives for the better. "You're going to be so well cared for," she says.

"She'll need her auntie in her life," says Aimee. "I'd love it if you and Lucas moved closer to us so you can watch her grow up."

Nicole squeezes her sister's hand. "I wouldn't miss it for the world."

A LETTER FROM WENDY

Thank you for reading *The Night She Vanished*. This is my *eleventh* thriller, and I haven't yet lost any of my enthusiasm for conjuring up fictional towns, twisted crimes and complex characters!

You can receive updates about my books, as well as access to my exclusive FREE short stories, by signing up to my newsletter here, and by following me on social media.

www.bookouture.com/wendy-dranfield

When I began writing this book, I had no idea it would revolve around family estrangement and who you can trust when you can't trust your parents. This is a topic I have experience with, unfortunately, and halfway through writing the book I unexpectedly lost my mother in tragic circumstances. Within weeks, we also lost my husband's wonderful father much sooner than anticipated.

Writing came to an abrupt halt as I tried to deal with the grief and trauma that followed. Getting back into a writing routine seemed unthinkable, but I sat at my desk shortly after my mother's death and opened the manuscript in the hope of some reprieve from my grief. I quickly became absorbed in Nicole's world and it became a welcome distraction from everything that was going on in mine.

I think the characters in this book are all complicated, with secrets, resentments and unresolved trauma holding them back from moving forward with their lives. Not unlike a lot of people in real life, me included. I'm glad it ended on a positive note for Nicole, and that there is hope she can reunite with her family and finally move on from her past. It's tempting to believe estrangement can be fixed by just *letting it go*, whatever "it" is. But estrangement happens for a reason and that reason is usually far worse than just a disagreement about something, or someone holding on to a grudge. Plus, everyone concerned needs to want to move forward, not just you. I think Nicole and her family will be just fine in the long run as they clearly care about each other.

If you enjoyed this book, you might enjoy my other recent standalone crime thriller—*The Birthday Party*—also published by Bookouture. For me, I'm now itching to get back to writing my Detective Madison Harper series, as it will feel like being surrounded by old friends.

As always, thank you to my loyal readers for coming on this journey with me, and to new readers for giving one of my books a try.

Wendy

www.wendydranfield.co.uk

facebook.com/WendyDranfield1
twitter.com/WendyDranfield
instagram.com/wendy_dranfield

ACKNOWLEDGMENTS

Thank you to the advance readers and book bloggers who review my books with so much enthusiasm. I love reading your reviews and sharing your posts.

As always, thank you to everyone at Bookouture who worked on my latest book. Extra special thanks go to my editor, Jessie, for her patience and understanding after the loss of my mother.

Finally, special thanks always goes to the reader of all my first drafts, and the person who got me through this year; my wonderful husband.

Printed in Great Britain
by Amazon